MAGIC BITES

ACE BOOKS BY ILONA ANDREWS

The Kate Daniels Novels

MAGIC BITES
MAGIC BURNS
MAGIC STRIKES
MAGIC BLEEDS
MAGIC SLAYS
MAGIC RISES
MAGIC BREAKS
MAGIC SHIFTS
MAGIC BINDS
MAGIC TRIUMPHS

The World of Kate Daniels

GUNMETAL MAGIC

The Edge Novels

ON THE EDGE
BAYOU MOON
FATE'S EDGE
STEEL'S EDGE

NOVELLAS

MAGIC MOURNS
MAGIC DREAMS
MAGIC GIFTS
MAGIC STEALS

ALPHAS: ORIGINS

MAGIC
RISES

ILONA ANDREWS

ACE
New York

ACE
Published by Berkley
An imprint of Penguin Random House LLC
1745 Broadway, New York, NY 10019

ISBN: 9781937007584

First Edition: August 2013

Printed in the United States of America

Cover art by Juliana Kolesova
Cover design by Jason Gill

To our fathers, wherever they may be

ACKNOWLEDGMENTS

Before we dive into acknowledgments, please note that we've included a bonus short story of Saiman's rescue. It's toward the end of the book, but you may want to read it first.

* * *

We would like to thank Anne Sowards, our editor, for believing in us and always working on making the book better. We also would like to thank our agent, Nancy Yost, for all of her help and her friendship.

Many other people have worked on creating these books. Michelle Kasper, the production editor, and Jamie Snider, the assistant production editor, oversaw the process of turning a manuscript into a finished book. Judith Lagerman, the art director; Juliana Kolesva, the artist; and Jason Gill, the cover designer, created a stunning cover. Amy Schneider had the difficult job of copyediting our mess. Rebecca Brewer, Anne's editorial assistant, and Sarah E. Younger, of Nancy Yost Literary Agency, valiantly tried to deal with our requests. We are deeply grateful to all of you.

Special thanks to the beta readers who helped make this book better: Ericka Brooks, Ying Areerat, Hasna Saadani, Laura Hobbs, Michelle Kubecka, Wendy Baceski, Joyce Casement, William Stonier, and others.

And finally, thank you to you, dear readers, for believing in Kate Daniels and her twisted world.

CHAPTER 1

———◆———

I SPUN THE SPEAR. "ONE MORE ARGUMENT AND I'LL ground you."

Julie rolled her eyes with all the scorn a fourteen-year-old could muster and pushed her blond hair away from her face. "Kate, like when will I ever use this in real life?"

"You'll use it in the next five seconds to keep me from impaling you."

In my twenty-six years, I've held many jobs. Teaching wasn't one of them. Mostly I killed people in bloody and creative ways. But Julie was my ward and my responsibility, and practicing with a spear was good for her. It built muscle, reflexes, and balance, and she would need all three when we moved on to the sword.

Several decades ago magic returned to our world, crushing our technological civilization and whatever illusion of safety we had with it. Magic and technology still fought over us, playing with the planet like two kids tossing a ball to each other. When one functioned, the other didn't.

The cops did the best they could, but half of the time the phones didn't work and all available officers responded to important emergencies, like saving schoolchildren from a flock of ravenous harpies. Meanwhile, with resources scarce and life cheap, people did a fine job preying on each other. Smart citizens didn't go out at night. If the lowlifes didn't get you, the magic aberrations with giant teeth would.

Every person was responsible for his or her own safety, and we relied on magic, guns, and blades. Julie's magic was rare, and highly prized, but useless in combat. Seeing the colors of magic wouldn't help her to kill a vampire. My best friend, Andrea, was teaching her to handle guns. I couldn't hit an elephant with a gun at ten feet, although I could probably bludgeon it to death. Melee weapons, those I could teach.

I struck at Julie's midsection, moving slow like molasses. She rotated her spear like an oar and slapped mine, knocking it down.

"And?"

She gave me a completely blank look. Most of the time Julie took practice seriously, but on days like this some switch malfunctioned in her head, disconnecting her brain from her body. There was probably some way to snap her out of it, some right "mom" words I could say, but I had found Julie about a year ago on the street and the whole parent thing was still new to me. My mother died before I could form any memories of her, so I didn't have any experience to fall back on.

To make things worse, I'd used magic to save Julie's life. She couldn't refuse a direct order from me, although she didn't know it and I was determined to keep it that way. I'd slipped up a few times and learned that intonation had a lot to do with it. As long as I gave her instructions instead of barking commands at her, she had no problem ignoring me.

Around us the Pack woods teemed with life. The afternoon sun shone bright. Leaves rustled in the breeze. Squirrels dashed to and fro on the branches, completely undeterred by several hundred werecarnivores living next door. In the distance the faint sound of chainsaws rumbled—the narrow road leading to the Keep was in danger of becoming impassable and a team of shapeshifters had been dispatched this morning to cut down some of the trees.

A yellow butterfly floated up. Julie watched it.

I pulled my spear back, reversed it, and stabbed her in the left shoulder with the butt.

"Ow!"

I sighed. "Pay attention, please."

Julie made a face. "My arm hurts."

"Then you better block me, so I don't make something else hurt."

"This is child abuse."

"You're whining. We're doing oar block."

I spun the spear business end forward and stabbed at her again, in slow motion. Julie pinned my spear with hers and stayed there.

"Don't just sit there with your spear. You have an opening, might want to do something about it."

She raised her spear and made a halfhearted attempt to stab me in the chest. I gave her a second to recover, but she didn't move. That was it. I'd had it.

I turned the spear and swept her legs from under her. She fell on her back and I drove the spear into the ground a couple of inches from her neck. She blinked, pale blond hair fanned out wide from her head.

"What's your deal today?"

"Kevin asked Maddie to the Moon Dance."

Maddie, a werebear, was Julie's best friend. The Moon Dance was the Pack's way of letting the teenagers blow off steam—every other Friday evening, provided the magic was down, the shapeshifters hauled the speakers out and blasted dance music from the Keep's battlements. Being invited to the Moon Dance by a boy was understandably a big deal. It still didn't explain why two months of lessons and spear practice had vanished from my ward's head.

"So?"

"I'm supposed to help pick the outfit for tomorrow," Julie said, lying there like a slug.

"And this is more important than practice?"

"Yes!"

I pulled my spear out. "Fine. Go do your thing. You'll owe me an hour on Saturday." No force on the planet could make her concentrate when she got like this, so making her practice was a waste of time anyway.

The slug-child turned into a nimble gazelle and sprang to her feet. "Thank you!"

"Yeah, yeah."

We headed out of the woods. The world blinked for a second

and a tide of magic splashed us, drowning the woods. The chainsaws sputtered and died, followed by loud cursing.

The official name for the phenomenon was post-Shift resonance, but everyone referred to it as magic waves. They'd come out of nowhere and roll across the world, snuffing out electricity, killing internal combustion engines, strangling guns, and spitting out monsters. Then the magic would vanish, the electric lights came on, and firearms once again became deadly. Nobody could predict how strong a wave would be or how long it would last. It made for a chaotic life, but we persevered.

The trees parted, revealing a vast grassy field. In the middle of it the Keep rose like a gray man-made mountain, an example of what happened if several hundred deeply paranoid and superhumanly strong people got together and decided they needed a safe place to crash. From one angle, the Keep resembled a modern fortress, from another, a medieval castle. We approached from the north, which gave us a view of the main tower, and from here the place looked like a grim, foreboding high-rise, complete with a penthouse, where Curran and I made our lair.

It wasn't always this way. We hadn't started out by looking at each other and instantly deciding we were soul mates. When we met, he thought I was a reckless merc who defied authority because I felt like it, and I thought he was an arrogant bastard who had enough issues to fill the Keep from top to bottom. But now we were together. He was the Beast Lord and I was his Consort, which put me in a position of authority over fifteen hundred shapeshifters, the largest pack in the South. I didn't want the responsibility, and given the choice, I would run as far as I could away from it, but it was the price I had to pay to stay with Curran. I loved him and he was worth it. He was worth everything.

We circled the Keep and passed through the wide, open gates into the inner courtyard. A group of shapeshifters worked on one of the Pack's vehicles, a modified Jeep, its hood bloated and misshapen by the need to contain two engines, one for gasoline, another for enchanted water. They waved at us as we walked by. We waved back. The shapeshifters accepted me, partially because I fought for my position and gave them no choice, and partially because while Curran was fair, he also had a very low tolerance for bullshit. We didn't always agree on things, but if the appeal had been made to me directly, he wouldn't overrule me, and the Pack liked having the option of a second opinion.

The reinforced steel door stood wide open. Late May in Georgia was hot and the summer would get hotter. Trying to air-condition the Keep was a losing proposition, so every door and window was open in an effort to create a breeze. We went through into a narrow hallway and started up the enormous staircase that was the bane of my existence. I started hating it the first time I had to climb it, and a knee injury only made my hate stronger.

Second floor.

Third floor. Stupid stairs.

"Consort!"

The urgency in the voice made me turn. An older woman ran toward me through the third-floor hallway, her eyes open wide, her mouth slack. Meredith Cole. Maddie's mother.

"They're killing them!" She grabbed onto me. "They're going to kill my girls!"

Every shapeshifter in the hallway froze. Putting hands on an alpha without permission counted as assault.

Tony, one of Doolittle's assistants, rounded the corner, running down the hallway toward us. "Meredith! Wait!"

Doolittle was the Pack's medmage. Dread washed over me. There was only one reason the Pack's medic would ever kill a child.

"Kate? What's happening? Where is Maddie?" Julie's voice spiked into high pitch.

"Help me!" Meredith clenched my arm. My bones groaned. "Don't let them kill my babies."

Tony halted, not sure what to do next.

I kept my voice calm. "Show me."

"This way. Doolittle has them." Meredith let go of me and pointed down the hallway.

"What's going on?" Julie squeaked.

I marched down the hall. "We'll find out in a minute."

Tony caught on and fell in behind us as we passed by him. The hallway brought us to the medical ward.

"He's in the back," Tony said. "I'll show you."

He took the lead and we followed him through the hospital wing to a round room. Six long, narrow hallways led from the room, concrete gray tunnels. Tony picked the one straight ahead. A steel door with a telltale silver sheen waited at the end. We walked to it, the sound of our steps bouncing off the walls. Three bars, each as thick as my wrist, guarded the door, for now unlocked. My heart sank. I didn't want to see what was behind it.

Tony grabbed the thick metal bracket that served as the door's handle, strained, and pulled it open, revealing a gloom-shrouded room. I stepped through. To my right, Doolittle stood next to some chairs, a black man in his early fifties, with dark skin and silver-salted hair. He turned to look at me, and his usually kind eyes told me everything I needed to know: my worst fear was true and there was no hope.

To my left two Plexiglas prison cells sat side by side, drenched in blue feylantern light. Steel and silver bars wrapped around each cell. I could see no doors. The only access to the cells was through a vending machine–style drop in the front.

Inside the cells two monsters waited. Misshapen, grotesque, their bodies twisted into a horrible nightmare of semi-human parts, oversized claws, and patches of dense fur, they cowered in the corner, separated by the Plexiglas and bars, but huddling together all the same. Their faces, with oversized jaws and oddly distorted teeth, wouldn't just stop you in your tracks, they'd give you a lifetime of flashbacks.

The monster on the left raised its head. Two human blue eyes looked at us, brimming with terror and pain.

"Maddie!" Julie dropped by the bars. "Maddie!"

The other monster stirred. I recognized the shock of brown hair. Maddie and Margo. Julie's best friend and her twin sister were going loup.

Every shapeshifter had to face a choice: to keep his or her humanity by imposing order and strict discipline and practicing constant restraint or to surrender to the violent cravings generated by the presence of Lyc-V, the shapeshifter virus, and become an insane loup. Loups murdered, tortured, and reveled in the pain of others. They could no longer maintain a pure human or animal form. Once a shapeshifter went loup, there was no turning back. The Pack put them down.

During times of extreme stress, Lyc-V exploded in huge numbers within the shapeshifter's body. Adolescence, with its hormone fluctuations and emotional roller coasters, was the most stressful time a shapeshifter faced. A quarter of the children didn't survive it.

"Tell him," Meredith pleaded. "Tell him not to kill my children."

Doolittle looked at me.

The Pack had a complicated way of figuring out the probability of loupism based on the amount of virus in the blood. "What's the Lycos number?"

"Two thousand six hundred for Maddie and two thousand four hundred for Margo," he said.

Over a thousand was pretty much a guarantee of loupism.

"How long have they been like this?" I asked.

"Since two o'clock last night," Doolittle said.

It was over. It was over fourteen hours ago. We were just trying to put off the inevitable. Damn it.

Julie held on to the bars. My heart constricted into a painful hard ball. A few months ago, she had looked just like that, a mess of human and animal, her body ravaged by the virus. I still had nightmares where I stood over her while she growled at me, strapped into a hospital bed, and when I woke up, I'd walk down to her room in the middle of the night to reassure myself she was alive and well.

"Please, Consort. Please," Meredith whispered. "You made Julie get better."

She had no idea what she was asking. The price was too high. Even if I would agree to it—which I wouldn't—purging the virus from Julie required the magic of a full coven, the power of several pagan priests, and my near death. It was a onetime thing, and I couldn't replicate it.

"Julie recovered because of her magic," I lied, keeping my voice gentle.

"Please!"

"I'm so sorry." The words tasted like crushed glass in my mouth. There was nothing I could do.

"You can't!" Julie turned to me. "You can't kill them. You don't know. They might still come out of it."

No, they wouldn't. I knew it, but I glanced at Doolittle anyway. He shook his head. If the girls had any chance of a recovery, they would've shown the signs by now.

"They just need more time." Meredith grasped onto Julie's words like a drowning man grabbed at a straw. "Just more time."

"We will wait," I said.

"We would be only prolonging it," Doolittle said quietly.

"We will wait," I repeated. It was the least we could do for her. "Sit with me, Meredith."

We sat together in the neighboring chairs.

"How long?" Doolittle asked quietly.

I glanced at Meredith. She was staring at her daughters. Tears ran down her face.

"As long as it takes."

I CHECKED THE CLOCK ON THE WALL. WE HAD been in the room for over six hours. The girls showed no change. Occasionally one, then the other, would rage, pounding on the Plexiglas, snarling in mindless fury, and then they would drop to the floor, exhausted. Looking at them hurt.

Doolittle had left for a couple of hours, but now he was back, sitting off by himself near the other wall, his face ashen. He hadn't said a word.

A few minutes ago Jennifer Hinton, the alpha of clan Wolf, had come into the room. She stood, leaning against the wall, cradling her stomach and the baby inside with her hands. Her face had a haunted look, and the anxiety in her eyes verged on panic. Approximately ten percent of werewolves went loup at birth.

Meredith slipped off her chair. She sat on the floor by the Plexiglas and began to sing. Her voice shook.

"Hush, little baby, don't say a word . . ."

Oh God.

Jennifer clamped her hand over her mouth and fled out of the room.

"Momma's gonna buy you a mockingbird . . ."

Margo stirred and crawled to her mother, dragging one twisted leg behind her. Maddie followed. They huddled together, the three of them, pressed against the Plexiglas. Meredith kept singing, desperate. Her lullaby was woven from years of love and hope, and all of it was now dying. My eyes teared.

Julie rose and slipped out of the room.

I listened to Meredith sing and wished I had more magic. Different magic. I wished I were more. From the time I could remember, my adoptive father, Voron, had honed me into a weapon. My earliest memory was of eating ice cream and holding my saber on my lap. I had learned dozens of martial arts styles; I fought in arenas and sand pits; I could walk into the wilderness and emerge months later, no worse for wear. I could control the undead, which I hid from everyone. I could mold my blood into a solid spike and use it as a weapon. I'd learned several power words, words in a language so primal, so potent, that they commanded the raw magic itself. One couldn't just know them; you had to make them yours or die. I fought against them and made them my own. At the height of a magic tsunami, I had used one to force a demonic army to kneel before me.

And none of it could help me now. All of my power, and I couldn't help two scared girls and their mother crying her heart out. I could only destroy, and kill, and crush. I wished I could make this go away, just wave my arms, pay whatever price I had to pay, and make everything be okay. I wanted so desperately to make everything okay.

Meredith had fallen silent.

Julie returned, carrying a Snickers bar. She unwrapped it with shaking fingers, broke the candy in half, and dropped each piece through the slits.

Maddie reached out. Her hand with four stubby nubs of fingers and a single four-inch claw speared the candy. She pulled it to her. Her jaws unhinged and she took one tiny bite of chocolate with crooked teeth. My heart was breaking.

Margo lunged at the glass, snarling and crying. The half-a-foot-thick Plexiglas didn't even shudder. She hurled herself against it again, and again, wailing. Each time her body hit the wall, Meredith's shoulders jerked.

The door opened. I saw the familiar muscular body and short blond hair. Curran.

He must've been out of the Keep, because instead of his regular sweatpants, he wore jeans. When you looked at him, you got an overwhelming impression of strength. His broad shoulders and powerful chest strained his T-shirt. Carved biceps bulged on his arms. His stomach was flat and hard. Everything about him spoke of sheer physical power, contained but ready to be released. He moved like a cat on the prowl, graceful, supple, and completely quiet, stalking the Keep's hallways, a lion in his stone lair. If I didn't know him and I saw him coming in a dark alley, I'd make myself scarce.

His physical presence was alarming, but his real power was in his eyes. The moment you looked into his gray irises, you knew he would tolerate no challenge to his authority, and if his eyes turned gold, you knew you were going to die. In a fit of cosmic irony, he had fallen in love with me. I challenged his authority on a weekly basis.

Curran didn't look at me. Usually when he entered the room, our stares would cross for that silent moment of connection, a quick check of *Hey, are you okay?* He wasn't looking at me and his face was grim. Something was seriously wrong. Something besides Maddie.

Curran walked past me to Doolittle and handed him a small plastic bag filled with olive-colored paste.

Doolittle opened the bag and sniffed the contents. His eyes widened. "Where . . ."

Curran shook his head.

"Is that the panacea?" Meredith spun toward him, eyes suddenly alive again.

The panacea was produced by European shapeshifters, who guarded it like gold. The Pack had been trying to reverse engineer it for years and had gotten nowhere. The herbal mixture reduced chances of loupism at birth by seventy-five percent and reversed midtransformation in one third of teenagers. There used to be a man in Atlanta who somehow managed to smuggle it in small batches, which he sold to the Pack at exorbitant prices, but a few weeks ago the shapeshifters had found him floating in a pond with his throat cut. Jim's security crew tracked the killers to the coast. They had sailed out of our jurisdiction. Now Curran held a bag of it. *What have you been up to, Your Furry Majesty?*

"There is only enough for a single dose," Doolittle said.

Damn it. "Can you get more?"

Curran shook his head.

"You must choose," Doolittle said.

"I can't." Meredith shrunk back.

"Don't make her pick." How the hell could you choose one child over the other?

"Split it," Curran said.

Doolittle shook his head. "My lord, we have a chance to save one of them . . ."

"I said split it." Curran growled. His eyes flashed gold. I was right. Something bad had happened, and it wasn't just Maddie and Margo.

Doolittle clamped his mouth shut.

Curran moved back and leaned against the wall, his arms crossed.

The paste was split into two equal portions. Tony mixed each into a pound of ground beef and dropped it into the cells. The children pounced on the meat, licking it off the floor. Seconds crawled by, towing minutes in their wake.

Margo jerked. The fur on her body melted. Her bones folded on themselves, shrank, realigned . . . She cried out, and a human girl, naked and bloody, fell to the floor.

Thank you. Thank you, whoever you are upstairs.

"Margo!" Meredith called. "Margo, honey, answer me. Answer me, baby."

"Mom?" Margo whispered.

"My baby!"

Maddie's body shuddered. Her limbs twisted. The distortion in her body shrank, but the signs of animal remained. My heart sank. It didn't work.

"She's down to two," Doolittle said.

The shift coefficient, the measure of how much a body had shifted from one form to the other. "What does that mean?"

"It's progress," he said. "If we had more of the panacea, I would be optimistic."

But we didn't. Tony hadn't just emptied the bag, he had cut it and rubbed the inside of the plastic on the meat and then scraped it clean with the back of the knife. Maddie was still going loup. We had to get more panacea. We had to save her.

"You can't kill her!" Julie's voice shot into high pitch. "You can't!"

"How long can you keep the child under?" Curran asked.

"How long is necessary?" Doolittle asked.

"Three months," Curran said.

Doolittle frowned. "You're asking me to induce a coma."

"Can you do it?"

"Yes," Doolittle said. "The alternative is termination."

Curran's voice was clipped. "Effective immediately, all loupism-related terminations of children are suspended. Sedate them instead." He turned and walked out.

I paused for half a second to tell Julie that it would be okay and chased after him.

The hallway was empty. The Beast Lord was gone.

CHAPTER 2

I CLIMBED THE STAIRS OF DOOM TO THE TOP FLOOR. I had wanted to chase Curran down, but Julie was still freaked-out and Meredith ping-ponged from hugging one daughter to crying over another. She didn't want us to induce a coma. She wanted more panacea and couldn't understand that there was none to be had. It took the three of us—Doolittle, Julie, and me—over two hours to convince her that Maddie needed to be sedated. By the time I finally left the medical ward, Curran was long gone. The guards at the entrance saw him walk out, but nobody knew where he went.

I reached the guard station at the entrance to our floor. Living in the Keep was like trying to find privacy in a glass bowl, and the two top floors of the main tower were my refuge. Nobody entered here unless the Beast Lord's personal guard vetted them, and they weren't charitable when approving visitors.

Sitting in a dark room watching a child suffer while her mother's soul died bit by bit was more than I could handle. I needed to do something. I had to vent or I would explode.

I nodded at the guards and went down the hallway to a long glass wall that separated our private gym. I took off my shoes and stepped inside. Weights waited for me, some free, some attached to machines. Several heavy punching bags hung from chains in the corner, next to a speed bag. Swords, axes, and spears rested in the hooks on the wall.

My adoptive father, Voron, died when I was fifteen, and afterward my guardian, Greg Feldman, took care of me. Greg had spent years accumulating a collection of weapons and artifacts, which he left to me. It was all gone now. My aunt paid us a visit and left a chunk of Atlanta a smoking ruin, including the apartment I had inherited from Greg. But I was rebuilding it slowly. I didn't have any prized weapons in my collection, except for Slayer, my saber, but all of my weapons were functional and well made.

I shrugged off the back sheath with Slayer in it, lowered it to the floor, and did push-ups for a couple of minutes to warm up, but my weight wasn't enough, so I switched to the bag, hammering punches and spinning kicks. The pressure, building in me for the past several hours, fueled me. The bag shuddered from the impact.

It wasn't fair that children went loup. It wasn't fair that there were no warning signs. It wasn't fair that I could do absolutely nothing about it. It wasn't fair that if Curran and I ever had children, I would be like Jennifer, stroking my stomach and terrified of the future. And if my children went loup, I'd have to kill them. The thought spurred me on, whipping me into a frenzy. I wouldn't be able to do it. If Curran and I had a baby, I couldn't kill him or her. I didn't have it in me. Even thinking about it was like the shock of jumping into an iced-over pond.

I worked the bag for the better part of an hour, switched to weights, then did the bag again, trying to drive myself to near exhaustion. If I got tired enough, I would stop thinking.

Exhaustion proved elusive. I'd spent the last few weeks recuperating, training, eating well, and making love whenever I felt like it. I had more stamina than the battery bunny from the old commercials. Eventually I lost myself to the simple physical exertion. When I finally came up for air, sweat slicked my body and my muscles ached.

I took a Cherkassy saber off the wall and went and picked up Slayer. The saber had cost me an arm and a leg many years ago, when I still worked for the Mercenary Guild. I had kept it at my old house, and it had survived my aunt's reign of terror.

I raised the two swords—the Cherkassy saber was heavier

and more curved, while Slayer was lighter and straighter—and began to chop, loosening the muscles. One sword a shiny wide circle in front of me, one behind me, reverse, picking up speed until a whirlwind of sharp steel surrounded me. Slayer sang, whistling as it sliced the air, the pale, opaque blade like the ray of a steel sun. I reversed the direction, switching to the defense, and worked for another five minutes or so; while walking, I turned and saw Barabas standing by the glass.

A weremongoose, Barabas was raised in the bouda clan. They loved him, but it soon became apparent that he didn't fit into the werehyena hierarchy, so Aunt B, the alpha of Clan Bouda, had offered his services to me. He and Jezebel, the other of Aunt B's misfits, acted as my nannies. Jezebel watched my back, and Barabas had the unenviable task of steering me through the Pack's politics and laws.

Slender and pale, Barabas was born with a chip on his shoulder, and he made everything into a statement, including his hair. It stood straight up on his head, forming spiky peaks of brilliant orange and pretending that it was on fire. Today, the hair was particularly aggressive. He looked electrocuted.

"Yes?"

Barabas opened the glass door and stepped into the gym, his eyes tracking the movement of my swords. "Don't take this the wrong way, but sometimes you scare me, Kate."

"Barabas, you grow two-inch claws and can bench-press a Shetland pony. And you find me scary?"

He nodded. "And I work with some very scary people. That should tell you something. How do you not cut yourself?"

"Practice." I'd been practicing since I was tall enough to keep my swords from snagging on the ground.

"It looks impressive."

"That's mostly the point. This is the style of bladework used when you're knocked off your horse and surrounded by enemies. It's designed to let you carve your way out of the crowd as quickly as possible. Most people will see you doing this and decide they should be somewhere else."

"I don't doubt it. What if it's one super swordsman guy that jumps in front of you?" Barabas asked.

I raised Slayer and drew a horizontal eight with the sword, rolling my wrist.

"Infinity symbol."

"Butterfly." I sped it up and added the second sword below. "One butterfly higher, one butterfly lower, switch arms, repeat as necessary. Throat, stomach, throat, stomach. Now he isn't sure what to guard, so either you kill him or he gets out of your way, and you keep walking until you're out of the crowd. Did you want something?"

"Curran is here."

I stopped.

"He came in about an hour ago, stood here for a while, watching you, and went upstairs. I think I heard the roof door. I thought that perhaps he would come down, but it's been a while, so I thought you might want to know."

I put the saber down, grabbed Slayer and the sheath, and went down the hallway to a short staircase. The first landing led to our private quarters, the second to the roof. The roof was our sanctuary, a place we went when we wanted to pretend we were alone.

I pushed the heavy metal door open and stepped outside. The roof stretched before me, a wide rectangle of stone, bordered by a three-foot wall. In the distance, at the horizon, the skeleton of Atlanta rose against the backdrop of moonlit sky. Haze shrouded the ruined buildings, turning them pale blue, almost translucent, and the husk of the once-vibrant city seemed little more than a mirage. The night was almost over. I hadn't realized so much time had passed.

Curran crouched in the center of the roof, on top of some cardboard. He was still wearing the same gray T-shirt and jeans. In front of him a black metal contraption lay on its side. It resembled half of a barrel with long metal bits protruding to the side. The long bits were probably legs. The other half of the barrel waited upside down to the left. An assortment of screws in small plastic bags lay scattered around, with an instruction manual nearby, its pages shifting in the breeze.

Curran looked at me. His eyes were the color of rain, solemn and grim. He looked like a man who was resigned to his fate but really didn't like it. Whatever he was thinking, he wasn't in a good place.

"Hey there, ass kicker."

"That's my line," he said.

I made my voice sound casual. "What are you building?"

"A smoker."

The fact that we already had a grill and a perfectly fine fire pit about ten feet behind him must've escaped his notice.

"Where did you get it?"

"Raphael's reclamation crew pulled a bunch of these out of the rubble of an old home improvement store. He sent me one as a gift."

Judging by the number of parts, this smoker was more complicated than a nuclear reactor. "Did you read the instructions?"

He shook his head.

"Why, were you afraid they'd take your man card away?"

"Are you going to help me or just make fun of me?"

"Can't I do both?"

I found the instructions, flipped to the right page, and passed him the washers and nuts for his screws. He threaded them onto the bolts and tightened them with his fingers. The bolts groaned a bit. If I ever wanted to take this thing apart, I'd need a large wrench to do it. And possibly a hammer to hit the wrench when it wouldn't move.

Curran lined up the hinges with the top of the smoker. They didn't look right.

"I think these hinges are backward."

He shook his head. "It will fit."

He forced the bolts through the hinge holes, tightened the screws, and tried to attach the top to the bottom. I watched him turn it around about six times. He threaded the bolts in, attached them, and stared at the mutilated smoker. The lid was upside down and backward.

Curran glared at it in disgust. "To hell with it."

"What's bugging you?"

He leaned against the wall. "Did I ever tell you about the time I went to Europe?"

"No."

I came over to stand next to him.

"When I was twenty-two years old, Mike Wilson, the alpha of Ice Fury, came to me with an invitation to the Iberian Summit."

Mike Wilson ran a pack in Alaska. It was the only pack in the United States that rivaled ours in size.

"Wilson's wife was European, Belgian, I think, and they used to cross the Atlantic every couple of years to visit her family. She's his ex-wife now. They had a falling out, so she took their daughter and went home to her parents."

Considering that home was across the Atlantic Ocean, she must've really wanted away from Wilson. "Mike didn't fight for his kid?"

"No. But ten years ago they were still together. They stopped in Atlanta on their way to the summit, and Wilson invited me to come with them to Spain. He made it sound like a deal for panacea was on the table, so I went."

"How did it go?"

"I expected it to go badly. Turns out I was overly optimistic." Curran crossed his arms on his chest, making his biceps bulge. "Things in Europe are different. The population density is higher, the magic traditions are wider spread, and many structures are old enough to stand through the magic waves. The shapeshifters are more numerous, and they started hammering out packs and claiming territory early on. There were nine different packs at the summit, nine sets of alphas, all of them strong, all of them ready to rip my throat out at any minute, and none of them honest. It was all big smiles to my face and claws at my back the moment I turned around."

"Sounds fun. Did you kill anyone?"

"No. But I really wanted to. A werejackal from one of the packs approached me to make a deal to sell panacea, and the next day we found his corpse outside with a rock the size of a car tire where his head used to be."

"Fun."

"Yeah. I brought ten people with me, some of the best fighters in the Pack. I thought all of them were solid and loyal. I went home with four. Two died in 'unfortunate accidents,' three were lured away by better money, and one got married. The Pack was still young. Losing every single one of them hurt, and there wasn't anything I could've done about it. It took months for the power vacuum to sort itself out."

Old frustration laced his voice. He must've spent weeks thinking it over, dissecting every moment looking for what he could've done differently. I wished I could reach through time and space and punch some people.

"We came in outnumbered and outgunned, and went home empty-handed. I said never again."

I waited. There had to be more.

"One of the alphas I met was Jarek Kral. Tough, vicious sonovabitch. He owns a chunk of the Eastern Carpathian

Mountains and has been steadily expanding. The man is obsessed with his legacy. He thinks he's some sort of a king. Most of his children died, either from going loup or from being his children. Only one daughter survived to adulthood, and he tried to give her to me."

"He what?"

Curran faced me. "When I got back to our ship, there was a seventeen-year-old girl named Desandra waiting for me with a note. The plan was that I would marry her, and he'd pay me each year, as long as I agreed to send one of my sons his way. Jarek preferred two, as an insurance against one of them dying, but would settle for one."

Charming. Fifteen minutes in a room with Curran would tell anyone with half a brain that he couldn't be bought and he would never sell his children.

"You didn't take him up on his generous offer, I take it?"

Curran shook his head. "I didn't even talk to her. We sent her back where she came from. Jarek married her off to another pack, the Volkodavi from Ukraine."

Wolf Killers, huh. Interesting name for a shapeshifter pack.

"Desandra lived with the Volkodavi for a few months, and then Jarek changed his mind, so she had to get a divorce. Later Jarek sold her off into another marriage, this time to a pack from Italy, Belve Ravennati."

"He's a kind and loving father." I hopped on the parapet. I could write a book on bad fathers, but Desandra would probably give me a run for my money.

A corner of Curran's mouth rose in contempt. "He isn't her father. He's her pimp. He got into some sort of dispute with the Belve Ravennati during the last Iberian Summit and they pissed him off, so he ordered Desandra to come back home again. Desandra had a fit. Her current husband and her ex-husband were both at the summit, so she slept with both of them. Now she's carrying twins, and the amniotic tests are showing DNA from both men."

"How does that work, exactly?"

"That's what I said." He grimaced. "I had to ask Doolittle. There is a term for it, hang on . . ." He pulled a piece of paper out of the pocket of his jeans and read it. "*Heteropaternal superfecundation.* Apparently, it means twins from different fathers. I've never heard of it, but Doolittle says it's a real thing and it happens with shapeshifters more often than with normal humans. From what he says, there are identical twins and then there are fraternal twins. Fraternal twins occur when two eggs inside a mother are fertilized at once. The super-whatever happens when they are fertilized by different fathers."

"I still fail to see how any of this epic mess is our problem."

Curran grimaced. "Jarek controls a large chunk of the Carpathians. He was trying to make marrying Desandra more attractive, so he set up Desandra's firstborn to inherit a profitable mountain pass. Apparently during the fight at the summit, Jarek told Desandra's current husband that if she got pregnant, he would rather kill her and not have any grandchildren before he would let Belve Ravennati get their hands on the pass."

Killing a woman to murder the child in her womb. Now that sounded eerily familiar. "Would he?"

Curran growled under his breath. "It's complicated. Jarek always had a big mouth, and he did kill one of his sons during a challenge. But the Jarek I remember was also hell-bent on making himself a dynasty. Now he's supposedly making public threats and considering killing his daughter, who is his only chance at getting that dynasty going. He's got no kids left— Desandra is it. Something else must be going on. But anyway, Desandra must've believed it, because when she realized she was pregnant, she freaked the hell out. She hid her pregnancy until the three packs were together again and then sprang it on them in public. Jarek tried to attack her right there and almost started a war, because the other two packs piled in to stop him."

"Sure. They want the pass." A dead Desandra couldn't give birth.

"Exactly. In the end, they found some sort of neutral guy who invited Desandra to his place away from everybody. She stayed there for most of her pregnancy, but she's due in two months and the three packs are coming there to witness the birth. Depending on which child is born first, either pack could claim the inheritance. The Carpathian Mountains are right between the Volkodavi and Belve Ravennati territories, so they both desperately want it. Neither of the two fathers trusts the other, and they trust Jarek even less. They want someone strong to guard her and her children and serve as an impartial witness to the birth until the inheritance is settled. The packs invited me to be that somebody."

The pieces clicked in my head. "They're paying you with the panacea." That was where he got it.

Curran nodded. "Ten drums. It would last us for ten months to a year."

We could save Maddie. We could save Jennifer's unborn baby. If I got pregnant with Curran's child . . . I pushed that thought firmly out of my mind. I couldn't bring any babies into this world. Not while my father was still in it. But if I did . . . "We have to go."

Curran looked like he bit into a rotten apple. "Yes, we do."

A year of no children going loup. Maddie's horrible half-animal face flashed before me. The way Meredith had looked at her, her eyes haunted, her face withdrawn with pain, gave me all of the motivation I needed. A few short months ago I had been in the exact same place she was, locked in the terrified haze where all you want to do is wake up and see your kid be okay. You want it so much, so desperately that you will do anything, anything at all for some magic cure, for the smallest chance. You want the nightmare to end, but it never does. How do you put a price on avoiding that?

Curran studied the pieces of the smoker. "The spiel is that since I'm far away, I'll be fair and neutral. None of their neighbors have volunteered for the job."

"They already have her in a neutral location," I thought out loud. "It doesn't make sense that they couldn't find someone strong enough close by to keep the three packs in line. This is like going to L.A. to hire a bodyguard for a job in Atlanta."

"Mm-hm. Their story doesn't quite add up. Desandra is still alive, which means one of two things: Jarek doesn't really want to kill her, which means they don't need me, or they've got her in a fortress where she is completely secure and he can't get to her, in which case, again, they don't need me."

"Did you ask them about it?"

"They're claiming that since all three packs will be in the place at the same time, only I am strong enough to keep them from turning the place into a slaughterhouse."

I liked this less and less. They could only give us a flimsy reason, but they wanted Curran specifically and dangled panacea in front of our noses. They knew he wouldn't turn it down. "It's a trap."

"Oh, I know it's a trap." Curran bared his teeth. "They've

baited it with something they know I can't refuse and let the Pack know about it. I met the envoys yesterday, just me and Jim alone. When I came back from the meeting, the rats and the jackals had already left messages asking if they could assist me in any way."

"Clever." The shapeshifters gossiped worse than old ladies at a church picnic. Right now rumors about the ten drums of panacea were spreading through the Pack like wildfire. If Curran balked at going, every parent with a child under twenty would storm the Keep and riot.

The Pack had very little contact with European shapeshifters. There were some tentative trade agreements, but the only thing Curran was really interested in was the panacea, and the European packs weren't willing to sell or share.

We looked at each other.

"Have you done something to attract their attention?" I asked. "Why us? Why now?"

He shook his head, his voice tinted with a growl. "I've done nothing and I don't know."

"What could they possibly want from us?"

"I don't know. I'll find out one way or another."

"What did Jim say?"

"He doesn't know either. He's looking into it."

Jim Shrapshire was as devious as you could get. As the Pack's chief of security, he hoarded information like gold. If he didn't know what was going on, either it didn't matter or it was really bad. My money was on really bad.

"When do we need to be there?"

"As soon as we can. She's staying in a small town on the coast of the Black Sea. If we take a ship from Savannah across the Atlantic, we're looking at about three weeks or more of travel, provided nothing happens."

We'd need to leave fast. The biggest hurdle would be finding a ship. Passages across the Atlantic didn't always work out. The Black Sea wasn't easy to cross either. The ancient Greeks called it Pontos Axenos, the Hostile Sea. In our day and age, Greek myths were lifesaving required reading, and I'd read enough of them to know that the Black Sea wasn't a fun place.

"Where on the Black Sea?"

"Georgia."

Colchis. Bodyguard detail in the land of the Golden Fleece, dragons, and witches, where the Argonauts had sailed and nearly died. "We should get the terms in writing."

"Kate, do you think I'd walk out of that meeting without a contract?" He picked up a stack of papers pinned to the roof by the box and passed it to me. I scanned it. The three clans collectively hired us to protect Desandra from all threats and act in her best interests until the birth of her children and for three days after.

"That 'acting in her best interest' is a really broad clause," I thought out loud.

"Mm-hm. I've wondered about that. Somebody must've insisted on putting that in."

"It almost sounds like she isn't in her right mind and they're worried she'll harm herself." I realized Curran was looking at me. "Yes?"

"The invitation is for the Beast Lord and the Consort. I understand if you choose not to go."

I just looked at him. Really? He meant everything to me. If I had to die so he could live, I would put my life on the line in an instant, and he would do the same for me. "I'm sorry, run that by me again?"

"We'll have to cross the ocean in the middle of hurricane season, go to a foreign country filled with hostile shapeshifters, and babysit a pregnant woman, while everyone plots and waits for an opportunity to stab us in the back."

I shrugged. "Well, it sounds bad if you put it that way . . ."

"Kate," he growled.

"Yes?"

"I'm trying to tell you that you don't have to go. I have to, but you can stay if you want."

Ha-ha. "I thought we were a team."

"We are."

"You're sending some confusing signals."

Curran growled deep in his throat.

"That's impressive but not really informative, Your Furriness."

"This is going to suck," Curran said. "It will suck much less if you come with me. You want me to level, here it is: I need you. I need you because I love you. Three months without you will be hell. But even if we weren't together, I would still need you. You're a good fighter, you've worked as a bodyguard, and you know magic. We may not have many magic users, but we don't know if those packs do, and if they hit us with magic, we have no way to counter." He spread his arms. "But I love you and I don't want you to be hurt. I'm not going to ask you to come with me. That would be like stepping in front of a moving train and saying, 'Hey, honey, come stand next to me.'"

I hopped off the wall and stood next to him. "Anytime."

He just looked at me.

"I've never killed a train before. It might be fun to try."

"Are you sure?"

"One time I was dying in a cage inside a palace that was flying over a magic jungle. And some idiot went in there, chased the palace down, fought his way through hundreds of rakshasas, and rescued me."

"I remember," he said.

"That's when I realized you loved me," I said. "I was in the cage and I heard you roar."

He chuckled. The tension in his shoulders eased. He hugged me and I kissed him. He tasted like Curran—male, healthy, and mine—and I would know that taste anywhere.

"I'm coming with you, Your Foolishness. You can't get rid of me."

"Thank you."

Besides, it would be good to get out of Atlanta. And away from Hugh d'Ambray—my father's warlord.

My family background is complicated. If my real father discovered I was still breathing, he would move heaven and earth to choke the life out of my body. For twenty-six years I had managed to hide in plain sight. But then my path had crossed with Hugh d'Ambray's, and a couple of months ago he'd figured out who I probably was. I didn't think he was one hundred percent sure, but he had to have strong suspicions. Sooner or later, Hugh d'Ambray would come knocking at my door, and I wasn't ready. My body had healed and I was learning how to mold my blood into weapons and armor, which was one of my father's greatest powers, but I needed more practice.

The trip would buy me some time, and every day I'd grow stronger. *Good luck looking for me across the ocean, Hugh.*

Curran stepped closer. I leaned against him. Below us the

forest stretched into the distance, and beyond it to the right, the twisted ruins of Atlanta darkened the horizon.

The anxiety swelled in me and crested. The words came out on their own. "If we have children, how likely are they to go loup?"

"Less likely than most," Curran said. "I'm a First, and we don't go crazy as often."

Firsts were a different breed from other shapeshifters. They were stronger and faster and had greater control of changing shape. But they were still subject to Lyc-V and the horror of loupism. "Is it possible?"

"Yes."

I could feel the anxiety building inside me, like I was a windup toy being cranked up. "What are the chances?"

He sighed. "I don't know, Kate. Nobody in my family went loup as far as I know, but I was too young to ask about things like this. I just know it's less likely. We'll get the panacea, baby. I promise you that we will get it."

"I know."

"Do you want to have children?"

I tried to wrap my mind around the idea of having Curran's children. It wasn't even a thought; it was a distant hazy idea, and looking at it too closely seemed too complicated right now. I tried to imagine myself pregnant and couldn't. What if my father found me and killed my kids? What if they went loup?

Curran had the strangest look on his face. I realized I was hugging myself.

Hey, baby, do you want to have my children? Here, let me curl into a fetal ball in response. Ugh. I was a moron.

"Maybe. Eventually. When things settle down. Do you want to have children?"

He put his arm around me. "Sure. Later on. I'm in no rush."

Wind bathed us, fresh and carrying a promise of a new day. As we stood together, the sun crested the forest, a narrow golden sliver so bright, it was painful to see.

We would be together and we would get panacea for Maddie. That was all that mattered for now.

CHAPTER 3

WHEN CURRAN AND I GOT DOWN FROM THE ROOF in search of breakfast, Barabas ambushed us with stacks of paper.

"What is this?" I pondered the two-inch stack.

"This is everything you have to do before you can leave for the Black Sea." He pointed to the nearest conference room. A breakfast had been laid out. Plates with scrambled eggs, heaps of bacon, piles of sausage, and mountains of fried meat shared space with pitchers of coffee and towers of pancakes. The smell swirled around me. Suddenly I was ravenous.

"Does the whole Keep know we're leaving?" Curran asked.

"I'm sure a few people are still asleep, but everyone else does, yes." Barabas placed a stack on the table and held the chair out for me. "For you."

"I'm hungry and I don't have time for this."

Barabas's eyes held no mercy. "Make time, Alpha. You have two hands. You can eat and sign simultaneously."

Curran grinned.

"Enjoying my suffering?" I asked.

"I find it hilarious that you'll run into a gunfight with nothing but your sword, but paperwork makes you panic."

Barabas put a thicker stack in front of him. "This is yours, m'lord."

Curran swore.

The shapeshifters enjoyed high metabolisms, which helped them blast through nutrients and save up energy for changing shape. But that same metabolism made them gorge themselves. Watching Curran go through food was a frightening experience. He didn't rush or devour his food with his hands. He just ate a very large amount of it. I thought I'd get used to it with time, but when he went in for his third heaping plate, I blinked. He must've skipped dinner last night.

The door to the conference room opened and Jim strode in, like an impending storm. Six feet tall, with dark, smooth skin and a gaze that made you want to back away and look for the nearest exit, Jim served as the Pack's chief of security. He and I knew each other from way back, when we both worked for the Mercenary Guild and we occasionally teamed up. I had needed the money and Jim couldn't stomach working with anyone else.

Jim leaned on the table. "I'm going."

"No," Curran said. "I need you here. You have to run the Pack while we're gone."

"Make Mahon do it."

Mahon Delany, an alpha of Clan Heavy, served as the Pack's executioner. He'd raised Curran after Curran's family was murdered, and he was probably the most respected among the fourteen alphas of the Pack. He was not universally loved, however.

"The jackals would riot and you know it," Curran said. "You can hold the clans together. Mahon can't. He's old-fashioned and ham-fisted, and if I put him in charge, we'd come back to a civil war."

"And who's going to watch your ass while you're over there? It's not just about what they *are* doing, it's thinking about what they could do and how they could do it. Who'll do that for you?"

"Not you," Curran said. "I need you here."

Jim turned to me. "Kate?"

If he thought I was getting in the middle of that, he was crazy. "Oh, look at all this paperwork I have. Can't talk now, very busy."

Jim landed in the chair, looking like he wanted to strangle someone.

Barabas put another piece of paper in front of me. Oy.

"You should let Kate handle it," Jim said. "You've never done a large-scale bodyguard detail. She has more experience and she's decent at it."

I pointed a piece of bacon at him. "I'm not just decent. I'm damn good and you know it."

"We've talked it over," Curran said. "She guards Desandra, I snarl and run interference with the packs, and when she tells me to push, I push. We've got this, Jim."

"Or at least they think they do." Barabas took the paper I'd just signed and blew on the ink.

"Take Barabas," Jim said suddenly. "If you won't take me, take Barabas. He's devious, paranoid, and obsessive. He'll be perfect."

Curran looked at me. I looked at Barabas. He bared even, sharp teeth. "Well, after that recommendation, how can I say no?"

"Who do you want for support?" I asked.

"George," Barabas said.

George's real name was Georgetta and she threatened to murder people who dared to actually use it. She was Mahon's daughter, and she served as the Pack's clerk of court.

"She knows the laws," Barabas said. "And she's the exact opposite of high-strung."

"If you take George, Mahon will want to go," Jim said.

"That's not a bad thing," Curran said. "Mahon is a hell of a fighter, and it will get him out of your hair. Besides, he's a bear. The Carpathians will respect that."

"Since I'm going," Barabas said. "Jezebel will also want to go."

"No." Jezebel, my other bouda nanny, had a hell of a temper.

"May I ask why?"

"Did you have an argument with Ethan on Wednesday?"

Barabas drew himself back. Ethan was his guy and their relationship had started out great but now was going off the rails fast. "It wasn't an argument. It was a heated discussion."

"Do you know how I found out about it?"

"I'm sure you will tell me."

"I saw Jezebel marching off with a determined look on her face, and I had to spend the next half an hour explaining to her that breaking Ethan's legs would not help your relationship. She reacts with overwhelming force to any insult. We're going to a place where we'll be outnumbered, insulted, and constantly provoked. One wrong punch from her and we're done."

"Point taken," Barabas said. "I'll break it to her gently."

"How about Keira?" Jim said.

Curran raised his eyebrows. "Are you sure?"

"Yes."

"Who's Keira?" I asked.

"My sister," Jim said.

"You have a sister?" I knew that Jim had a family. I'd just never met or seen any of them.

"He has three," Curran said.

"How come I never met her?"

"You have," Jim said. "You just don't remember because I didn't tell you who she was."

"Oh, so your family is only on a need-to-know basis, huh?"

He gave me a hard stare. "That's right."

When a joke flies past a sulking werejaguar, does it make a sound? "Are you sure you want to send your sister off across the ocean with us? Since I don't even rank high enough to meet her and all that."

"Keira is an Army vet," Jim said. "She's good and she won't turn on you."

I tried to picture a female version of Jim and got Jim in a dress instead. The image was disturbing.

"Did you at least ask her?" Curran asked.

"I know she'll go."

"Well, then she's in unless she says no."

I'd signed six things and my stack wasn't getting any smaller. It was like the paperwork was breeding while I worked.

"Where are you going to get a ship?" Jim asked.

"We can use a commercial freighter and catch a ride," Curran said.

"Won't work," Jim said. "Crossing the Atlantic is a bitch. You can get there in three weeks or so, but you may have to get out in a hurry, with ten drums of the panacea, and there is no guarantee the freighter will come back for another trip in time. You'll need to hire a ship and crew, and they will have to sit in port for about a month waiting for you."

"Then let's hire one," Curran said. "Or buy one. I don't care."

"I don't know if we can. It's not just a question of money. It's getting an experienced captain and crew on short notice." Jim drummed his fingers on the table and rose. "I need to get on that."

A young man walked up and stopped in the doorway. He moved with complete silence, like a ghost. Still lean, but on the way to filling out, he had short brown hair and the kind of face that made you stop in your tracks. Not that long ago, people stopped and stared because he was beautiful. Now they stopped because they weren't sure what a man with a face like that would do next.

Back when he was pretty, Jim had used him for covert work. People had discounted Derek Gaunt as a boy toy, but he missed nothing. He didn't exactly have a happy childhood. It made him ruthless, hard, and disciplined, and he dedicated himself to the task completely.

Then bad things happened and Derek's face paid the price. His good bone structure was still there, but trauma had thickened his clean lines and stripped any remnants of softness from his features. His brown eyes had turned hard and distant, and when he decided to be unfriendly, they went completely flat. I'd seen that kind of stare from veteran pit fighters. It said you weren't a human being. You were an object to be removed.

The stare worried me. Derek was a friend. Even if the entire Pack turned on me, he would stay in my corner. But the humor, the spark that used to make Derek who he was, was growing dimmer and dimmer. If it disappeared, Derek would be in a bad place. I'd been there and it was hard to claw your way out of that hole.

Curran pretended not to see him. Derek didn't say anything. He simply stood.

"Yes," Curran said without turning.

Derek nodded and walked away without a word. Now we had five: Barabas, George, Mahon, Derek, and tentatively Keira. The contract had specified that the Carpathians expected us to bring no more than fifteen people. Curran and I settled on ten, excluding ourselves. It was a nice number and it showed that we weren't afraid.

Jim was sitting there with that slightly glazed-over look in his eyes that usually meant that three fourths of his brain was engaged somewhere else.

"You okay?" I asked him.

He looked at me. "Where the hell am I going to find a ship . . . ?"

A guard approached the door.

"Yes?" I asked.

"Aunt B is here to speak with the Consort."

Meeting with the alpha of Clan Bouda was like sticking your hand into a garbage disposal. The switch could be flicked on at any second.

Curran got up. "I've got to go."

"Coward," I told him.

He grinned at me. "Later, baby. Come on, Jim, you have to go, too."

They took off down the hallway.

I looked at Barabas. "There is only one exit. How do they plan to get by her?"

"They'll hide in the guard room until she comes through. Shall I show Aunt B in?" Barabas asked.

"There is no escape, is there?"

"No."

I sighed. "Okay. Let's get this over with."

THE ALPHA OF CLAN BOUDA WORE A CHEERY white sundress with an overlapping pattern of large red poppies. Her hair was rolled into a loose, carefree bun. A pair of sunglasses perched above her forehead. If you added a straw hat and a picnic basket, she would be all set.

Aunt B was in her early fifties, but the kind of fifties to which most women would aspire. Her skin was smooth, her makeup understated but expert, her figure generous but still athletic. Her lips smiled often, and her voice was all sweetness and cookies, but when she really looked at you, the hair on the back of your neck stood on end, because you realized that she was smart, ruthless, and dangerous as hell. She ruled the bouda clan, and anybody able to hold more than three dozen werehyenas in check should never be taken lightly. I'd seen her in action. Not many things gave me the creeps, but she managed. For now Aunt B was in my corner, but I had no delusions. Ours was a conditional kind of friendship: if I stopped being useful to her and hers, she'd forget my name.

Behind her, Andrea Nash, my best friend and the current beta female of Clan Bouda, walked into the room. Short, blond, and lethal, Andrea was engaged to Aunt B's son, Raphael. People really liked Andrea. She seemed nice and approachable. She also could shoot the dots off dominoes from great distances and turned into a monster with claws the size of my pinkies.

I smiled at Aunt B and pointed at the table. "Please, join me."

For shapeshifters, an offering of food held a certain significance. It could be a declaration of romantic interest, or it could be a confirmation of alpha status. Those who offered food declared themselves responsible for those who took it. Despite the fact that Aunt B had clued me in on the custom before I became the Consort, she had tried to feed me. Since I stood higher than Aunt B on the food chain, the tables had turned.

"Don't mind if I do." Aunt B seated herself on my right. Andrea took position behind her, as beta.

I glanced at her. "Really?"

Andrea sighed. "Oh fine, just don't tell anybody." She dropped into the chair next to me. I passed her a plate.

"What brings you up all these stairs?"

"I'm concerned for your well-being." Aunt B slid a piece of bacon into a pancake, folded it, and bit off a small piece. "And about the future of my clan, naturally."

Naturally. "Is it about the trip to the Black Sea?"

"Of course. Did Curran mention the Desandra incident?"

Here we go. "Yes."

"Did he also happen to mention that I was the one who had escorted that poor child back to her father?"

Oh boy. "No."

"How forgetful of him." Aunt B took another bite of the pancake. "Both my late husband and I had gone on that trip. His family was from the Iberian Peninsula. Half of our clan comes from Africa and the other half from Iberia, but I digress. Bottom line, I was there. I've met Jarek Kral, Desandra's father. He is a troglodyte."

I choked on my coffee.

"He is a ruthless, violent vandal without any shred of conscience."

Wow.

"He came from nothing, so he's obsessed with building his

'royal line.' He's so hung up on passing down his own meager genes, it's making him crazy, and he wasn't playing with a full deck to begin with. Every single one of his children, except for Desandra, has gone loup or gotten themselves killed, so he sells and bargains with her like she was some prized heifer, and she goes right along with it. Desandra is a doormat."

Okay. This was clearly the day for frank revelations from the bouda clan.

I added more coffee to my cup. Curran was right. If Jarek was all about his dynasty, he shouldn't have been eager to kill his only daughter to keep some mountain pass. The Carpathian shapeshifters were playing a complicated game, and I had a feeling they planned on scoring goals by punting our severed heads.

Aunt B looked at her cup. Barabas filled it with coffee.

"Thank you, dear. Kate, you must understand the way you will be perceived. Curran is the Beast Lord, an oddity among alphas. Most alphas lead packs consisting of one species, with an occasional odd shapeshifter or two, and most of them have to fend off challenges from rivals from inside and outside their territory. Curran rules a huge prosperous pack and his competition here in the States is minimal. His territory is secure."

"That's because nobody here is dumb enough to take him on," Andrea said.

"Precisely. But the Carpathian alphas don't fully understand what he's capable of, and to them Curran presents an opportunity. They will want to either kill him for the bragging rights—a dangerous proposition, and most of them aren't suicidal—or benefit from an alliance with him. The point is, to them he has value. You, on the other hand, have no value at all. They don't know you and they win nothing by making friends with you. To them you're Curran's passing amusement that has grown into an obsession. A hindrance that should be removed, because the easiest way to Curran is through a woman."

"Or panacea." I still wasn't sure where she was going with this.

"I have my doubts about their willingness to actually part with panacea." Aunt B made another pancake wrap. "But I'm sure that the moment you step off that boat, you'll be a target. Can we agree on that?"

"If they want to dance, I'll be happy to oblige."

Aunt B sighed. "I have no doubt in your martial abilities, dear. I think all of us here know that you can hold your own. I'm worried about finding you at the bottom of some mountain ravine with your skull cracked open as you stumbled off the path in a 'regrettable' accident. Or the roof of one of those charming European cottages collapsing on you, completely by chance. Or someone accidentally shooting you in the back from half a mile away. It would be terrible. Everyone would express their condolences, and then they'd send a compassionate beautiful young girl wrapped in a pretty ribbon with a bow to Curran's bedroom to console him."

I leaned forward. "Do you honestly think he would take that consolation prize?"

She leaned toward me. "I don't want to find out. I also know that Mahon is thinking of going, and when the old bear wants something, he usually gets his way."

How the hell did she find out? "Do you have spies in Clan Heavy?"

"I have spies everywhere."

I looked at Andrea, who was hoarding bacon on her plate.

"She had tea with Mahon's wife," Andrea said.

Aunt B looked at her. "You and I need to work on your air of mystery."

Andrea shrugged. "She's my best friend. I won't lie to her."

I raised my fist and she bumped it with hers.

Aunt B sighed. "Mahon missed out on the last trip. He blames himself for our abject failure. He got to stay home and run the Pack and he nearly broke everything Curran worked so hard to build. Remind me sometime, and I'll tell you about what he did to the jackals. Mahon isn't your friend. He'll support you, because Curran chose you, but in his eyes the lowliest shapeshifter is more acceptable as Curran's mate than you are. It's not personal. Mahon had a lot of tragedy in his life, and it made him closed-minded where nonshapeshifters are concerned. He will never stoop to harming you, but if something unfortunate happened to you, he would breathe a sigh of relief and hope that Curran finds himself a nice shapeshifter girl."

Mahon and I had reached an understanding. We weren't the best of friends, but I doubted he'd stab me in the back. It just wasn't who he was. "Is there a cookie at the end of this lecture?"

"You need a friend on that team," Aunt B said.

"Which is why I'm going with you." Andrea stuffed some bacon in her mouth and chewed.

"What about you being beastkin?" Andrea's father began his life as an animal who had gained an ability to transform into a human. It made her beastkin, and some shapeshifters believed that people like her should be killed on sight.

"They don't care," Aunt B said. "In some ways the Europeans are more reactionary, and in others they're not. There are a lot of shapeshifters in Carpathians, and beastkin are rare but not an oddity. Andrea will be fine."

"And Raphael will be joining us," Andrea said. "So you get twice the backup. Nobody will be killing you on our watch."

So that was what this was all about. I got a cookie after all. "Aww. I had no idea you cared. I'm touched."

"You should be." Andrea bit another bacon slice. "I'm willing to abandon the tender embrace of my future mother-in-law for your sake."

"About that," Aunt B said. "I'm coming, too."

Dear God, the cookie was poisoned.

Andrea's mouth hung open and I got a view of half-eaten bacon I wished I could unsee.

"I take it that's the first time you've heard about it?" I asked.

She nodded. "That's not what we agreed on! We agreed that Raphael and I would be coming with her."

Aunt B shrugged. "That's the prerogative of the alpha. We can change our minds."

Andrea gaped at her. "What about the clan?"

"Leigh and Tybalt can run it in our absence. They will survive by themselves for three months."

"Curran won't go for it," I told her. I wasn't sure *I* would go for it.

"He will, if you ask him, dear. What I say here must not leave this room." Aunt B put her fork down. "Any Consort who is agreeable to Mahon is bad for us. If the bear has his way, you, Kate, will never carry Curran's child. And you"—she turned to Andrea—"you will never sit on the Pack Council. You're beastkin. He won't kill you, but you can bet that he'll do everything in his power to push you out. Your children—my grandchildren—will grow up knowing what it's like to be one step lower than everyone."

In an instant the funny blonde vanished, and a cold killer with a thousand-yard stare sat in Andrea's place. "Let him try."

"No!" Red, bright like backlit rubies, sparked in Aunt B's eyes. "We don't wait for him to try. There aren't enough of us to be reactive. We think a step ahead of our opponents. We force them to respond. You'll watch her back, Raphael will watch Curran's, and I'll look after our collective interests. You will need panacea, my dear. Trust me. I'll make sure we'll get it."

Andrea raised her finger and opened her mouth.

"That is final, Andrea."

Andrea clamped her mouth shut.

"Talk to Curran about it. Talk among yourselves. I will be packing. Thank you for a lovely breakfast."

Aunt B rose and left.

We waited until the doors down the hall shut behind her.

"That woman drives me crazy," Andrea growled.

"Is she for real?"

"She's been a bit obsessed lately," Andrea said. "Ever since I became a beta and then Raphael proposed, all she's been talking about is how she'll retire and spend her years cuddling grandchildren. These are theoretical grandchildren. Raphael and I aren't in a hurry. She says she is tired."

"Does she seem tired to you?"

"She'll outlive me. I'll be an old woman, and she'll be still promising to retire. I know that look. She's coming on this trip, whether we like it or not."

I sighed.

Andrea shook her head. "The Black Sea, right? That's the place where the Golden Fleece was and Jason grew an army out of dragon teeth?"

"That's the one."

"Whatever happened to Jason afterward?"

"He married Medea, a witch-princess who was from Colchis."

"Did they live happily ever after?"

"He left her for another woman, so she killed their children, chopped them into stew, and fed it to him."

Andrea put a half-eaten sausage link on her plate and pushed it away. "Well, at least I'll be there to watch your back."

And it already made me breathe easier. "Thank you."

Andrea grimaced. "You're welcome. I've got to go tell Raphael that his dear mother is coming with. He'll just love this new development."

I WENT TO LOOK FOR CURRAN. KNOWING HIM, HE was probably holed up somewhere with Jim trying to finalize the list of shapeshifters we would be taking with us. I bet that "somewhere" was Jim's not-so-secret lair two floors below the top level of the Keep.

Jim genuinely loved his job, and he somehow always found people who loved it as much as he did. They took the whole spy thing to the next level. Somehow simply walking through their hallway to the break room didn't seem enough. I should've gotten a black cloak and slunk dramatically, flashing my knives.

I was about fifteen feet from the break room when I heard Mahon's voice and stopped. ". . . not questioning her ability. She's proud, undisciplined, and she doesn't take anything from anybody. We're going into a shit storm. They will attack her appearance, your relationship, and her human status, and I question how well she will hold up under the stress."

Mahon and I would never see eye to eye. That was the long and short of it. I had decided that I didn't want or need his approval, so I'd stopped trying.

"Kate will be fine," Curran said.

"It's a bad idea."

"I heard you the first time," Curran said. "Kate is coming with us. You worry too much."

I walked into the room. Curran, Jim, and Mahon stood around a small kitchen table. Curran and Jim both had mugs, which probably contained Jim's patented coffee: black as tar and just as viscous. A piece of paper lay on the table—the list of ten names. Curran and Jim had hashed out the list of who was coming, and I was about to change it.

"I was just going," Mahon rumbled, and walked out of the room.

"Coffee?" Jim asked.

"No, thank you." I knew exactly what his coffee tasted like. "Aunt B, Raphael, and Andrea would like to be included."

Curran raised his eyebrows. "Why?"

"Aunt B says she's worried about my well-being."

"She's mostly worried about getting her paws on panacea," Jim said.

"Yeah, she mentioned it." I looked at Curran. "The way I look at it, we're taking ten people. You get five and I get five. If I take Aunt B, Raphael, Andrea, Barabas, and Derek, that will take care of my half."

"Fair enough," Curran said. "I can count Derek as one of mine. It will give you an extra spot."

"No, it's cool. You should take the extra spot."

"I honestly don't mind," Curran said.

"I don't mind either. You're giving me Aunt B. I probably owe you a spot for that."

"Damn it," Jim said, his face disgusted. "You're like an old married couple who found twenty bucks in a parking lot. 'You take it.' 'No, you take it.' I can't stand it." He put the coffee down and shook his head.

"Fine," Curran said. "If you want Derek, he's yours. That fills the list."

"That means we're axing Paola from the list. The rats will be pissed," Jim said.

"I'll handle the rats," Curran said.

CHAPTER 4

━━━━◆━━━━

I STOOD ON THE GRASSY HILL. IN FRONT OF ME A
*garish sunset burned with violent intensity, the scarlet and
crimson clouds floating like bandages in the open wound of
the sanguine sky. Against the sunset, on the plain below, people were building a tower. Magic churned and roiled around
them as the roughly hewn stone blocks rose in the air, held up
by power and human will. Far in the distance, another tower
stretched to the sky.*

*I wanted to stop it. Every instinct I had screamed that this
was wrong. It was dangerous and wrong, and we would all suffer at the end of it. Something terrible would happen if it was
completed. I wanted to go down there and scatter the stones.*

I couldn't move.

*Cold sweat drenched me. I couldn't look away. I just watched
as the tower rose block by block, a monument to my father's
growing power and ambition. It kept going up, unstoppable, like
an ancient legion, like a tank crushing all that stood before it.*

*Someone moved to the right of me. I strained, trying to tear
myself from the scene, turned, and saw Julie. Wind stirred her
blond hair. She looked back at me, her eyes terrified. Tears
ran down her cheeks.*

"Julie!"

I sat upright in my bed. Darkness reigned, diluted but not conquered by moonlight coming through the open window. My face felt damp. I brushed my fingers at my hairline. They came away wet. Sweat. Great. I used to have nightmares about Roland and being found, but they stopped when Curran started holding me at night. They were never this vivid.

Maybe Roland was trying to find me. I had a vision of him sitting several states away, broadcasting screwed-up dreams like a TV tower. I needed to have my head examined, except anybody who actually tried would run away screaming.

The covers next to me were rumpled. Curran must've slipped out of our bed in the middle of the night. Well, that explained it. He was gone, and watching Maddie going loup had rattled me. It was stress. Eventually my dear dad would find me, but not today.

I had to check on Julie. I wouldn't be able to sleep if I didn't. I slipped out of bed, pulled my sweatpants on, and went out, down the stairs. Julie's door stood slightly ajar. Odd. I rapped my knuckles on a skull-and-crossbones DO NOT ENTER sign that took up most of the door. No answer.

Janice, a shapeshifter in her late thirties, stuck her blond head out of the guardroom to my right. "She took her blanket and a pillow and went downstairs."

"When?"

"About two hours ago."

That would be one o'clock in the morning. There was only one place Julie could've gone.

Five minutes later I walked into the dim room, moving quietly on my toes. The only illumination came from the glass coffin in front of me. In it, submerged in the green liquid of Doolittle's healing solution, floated Maddie. Several IV tubes ran from her arms to the metal stand with fluid bags. Julie sat next to her on the floor, slumped over on her blanket, her elbows propped on her knees, her face hidden in her hands.

Oh, Julie. I crossed the room and sat next to her. She gave no indication she heard me.

Maddie's bones protruded at odd angles, the flesh stretched over the distorted skeleton like half-melted rubber. Here and there patches of fur dappled her, melting back into human skin. The left side of her jaw bulged, the lips too short to hide the bone, and through the gap I could see her human teeth. Her right arm, almost completely human, seemed so thin, so fragile, little more than bone sheathed in skin.

When I sat there and watched her, my heart squeezed itself into a hard painful rock. It wasn't just Maddie. It was the haunted desperation in her mother and sister. It was the panic in Jennifer's face. It was the masked fear in Andrea, who had come to see Maddie last night. I'd watched my best friend as she crossed her arms on her chest trying to convince herself that this wasn't her future. She loved Raphael. She wanted children and a family, and both of Raphael's brothers went loup at puberty and had to be killed. When Aunt B said they would need panacea, she meant it.

It was the icy nagging dread inside me that said, *This could be your child.*

Maddie, the cute funny girl, whom we all knew and took for granted. We had to save her. I had to save her. If there was one thing I could accomplish, it would be giving her life back to her.

Julie straightened. Her eyes were red, the skin around them puffy. I wished I could do something.

"She isn't hurting."

"I know." Julie sniffed.

"I read to her. Her mom does too, and Doolittle's nurses. She isn't alone."

"It's not that."

"Then what is it?"

"I'm trying to understand why." Her voice broke. "Why?" She turned and looked at me, tear-filled eyes bright and brimming with hurt. "She was my best friend. I only have one. Why did it have to be her?"

The million-dollar question. "Would you rather it be Margo?"

"No." Julie shook her head. "No. She feels horrible, because she's okay and Maddie isn't. I hugged her and I told her that I was so glad that she made it."

"I'm proud of you."

"It's not Margo's fault that the medicine didn't work. I just don't want it to be Maddie. I want her to be okay. It's like this is the cost."

"The cost of what?"

"Of magic. Of being a shapeshifter. Like they're strong and fast and somebody has to pay the price for that. But why her?"

I wish I knew. I'd asked myself the exact same question when I found Voron dead, when I saw the ruin of Greg Feldman's body, and when Julie lay in a hospital bed, so sedated her heart was barely beating. I wanted so much to spare Julie from that. It killed me that I couldn't. I didn't know why some people had tragedy after tragedy thrown at them, as if life were testing them, and others lived blissfully, untouched by grief.

I told her the truth. "I don't know. I think it's because a child is the most precious thing we have. There is a price for everything, and it's never something you can afford to give up. It's always someone you love."

Julie stared at me. "Why?"

"I don't know. That's the way it always is."

Julie drew back. "I don't want it. If that's the way it's going to be, I don't want to have any babies."

Life had finally scarred Julie deep enough. Now my kid had decided not to have children, not because she didn't want to be a mother, but because she was too scared of the world into which she would be bringing her children. That was so screwed up. I wanted to stab something.

Julie was looking at me, waiting for something.

"Having children or not having them is your choice, Julie. Whether you do or don't, Curran and I will love you anyway. You don't ever have to worry that we'll stop."

"Good, because I don't want kids."

We fell silent.

"You're leaving," she said.

"Yes. Are you scared?"

Julie shrugged. "You're the alpha and you have to go."

"That's right."

"And if anybody will get the medicine, it's you. I understand." Her voice was tiny. "Don't die. Just don't die, okay?"

"I have no plans to die. I'm coming back with panacea and we're getting Maddie out of the healing tank."

"I heard Jim talking," Julie said quietly.

Oh boy.

"He said that it was a trap and you might not come back."

Thank you, Mr. Positive Peggy, we appreciate your vote of confidence. "Does the spy master know you're spying on him?"

"No. I'm very careful and he doesn't look up very often."

Eventually I'd have to figure out what that meant. "It *is* a trap. The people who laid it think that we're weak and stupid. I promise you that if they try to hurt us when we get there, they will deeply regret it. We'll sail away with panacea, and they will still be figuring out why they're sitting in a puddle of their own blood trying to hold on to their guts. You've seen me take on dangerous things before."

"You get hurt, Kate. A lot."

"But I survive and they don't." I hugged her with one arm. "Don't worry. We've got this."

"Okay," she said. "I just . . ."

She clenched her hands together, staring straight ahead.

"Yes?"

"I have bad dreams."

So do I. "What do you dream about?"

She turned to me, her eyes haunted. "Towers. I see them being built on the grass. They are terrible towers. I look at them and cry. And I see you, and you're looking at me, and you're calling me . . ."

Oh no. Cold claws pricked my spine.

Why would we have the same dream? It had to be magic. If my dream was the result of my magic or the result of Roland looking for me, it shouldn't affect Julie. He couldn't possibly know about Julie.

The ritual. That was the most likely explanation. When I healed Julie, I'd mixed my blood with hers. Some of my magic had tainted her. Now we shared dreams. If we were lucky, this was just a by-product of my magic stretching itself while I dreamed. If we were unlucky, then Roland was trying to find me by broadcasting visions into my head, and Julie was picking up the signal.

Damn it.

It must've shown on my face, because Julie focused on me. "It means something, doesn't it? What does it mean, Kate? I saw you. You were in my dream. Did you see me, too?"

I didn't want to have this conversation. Not here and not now. In fact, I didn't want to have it at all.

"Tell me, please! I have to know."

I wasn't planning on going to my funeral, but one never plans to die. If something happened to me, Julie would be left without answers. She had to know something at least. In her place, I would want to know.

"Kate, please . . ."

"Hush, please."

The need to hide had been hammered into me since I could understand words. The number of people knowing my secret had gone up from one to five in the past year, and thinking about it shot me right off the beaten path into an irrational place where I contemplated killing those who knew. I couldn't kill them—they were my friends and my chosen family—but breaking a lifetime of conditioning was a bitch.

If I didn't tell her and I died, she would make mistakes. Roland would find her and use her. She didn't realize it yet, but she was a weapon. Like me. I had created her, and I had a responsibility to keep her safe and to keep others safe from her.

"What I'm about to tell you can't be repeated. Don't write it in your diary, don't tell your best friend, don't react if you hear about it. Do you understand?"

"Yes."

"There are people who would kill you if they knew about you. I'm very serious, Julie. This is a life-and-death conversation."

"I understand," Julie said.

"You've learned in school about the theory of the First Shift?"

"Sure." Julie nodded. "Thousands of years ago magic and technology existed in a balance. Then people began working the magic, making it stronger and stronger, until the imbalance became too great and the technology flooded the world in waves, which was the First Shift. The magic civilizations collapsed. Now the same thing is happening, but we get magic waves instead of technological ones. Some people think that it's a cycle and it just keeps happening over and over."

Good. She knew the basics, so this would be easier. "You heard me talk about Voron."

"Your dad," Julie said.

"Voron wasn't my biological father. My father, my real father, walked the planet thousands of years ago, when the magic flowed full force. Back then he was a king, a conqueror, and a wizard. He was very powerful and he had some radical ideas about how a society should be structured, so he and some of his siblings built a huge army and rampaged back and forth across what's now known as Saudi Arabia, Turkey, Iran, and eastern Egypt. The world was a different place then geologically, and my dad, the

wizard-king, had a large fertile area in which to build his kingdom. His magic kept him alive for hundreds of years, and he
succeeded in creating an empire as advanced as our civilization.
And wherever he went, he built towers."

Julie blinked. "But . . ."

"Wait until I finish, please." The words stuck in my throat
and I had to strain to push them out. "When the First Shift
came, the technology began to overwhelm magic. The magical
cities crumbled. My father saw the writing on the wall and
decided it was time for a long nap. He sealed himself away, how
or where nobody knows, and fell asleep. A tiny trickle of magic
still remained in the world, and it was enough to keep him alive.
He slept until the Shift, our apocalypse, woke him up. He got
up, bright-eyed and bushy-tailed, and immediately started to
rebuild his empire. He can't stop, Julie. It's what gives his existence meaning. This time he started with the undead."

"The People," Julie said, understanding in her eyes.

"Exactly. My father chose to call himself Roland and
started gathering individuals with the ability to navigate vampires. He organized them into the People."

The People were a cross between a corporation and a
research institute. Professional and brutally efficient, they
maintained large stables of vampires and had a chapter in
every major city.

"Nobody ever talks about Roland," I told her. "Most people don't know he exists. And almost nobody, not even the
navigators, know that shortly after he awoke, Roland fell in
love. Her name was Kalina and she also had powerful magic.
She could make anyone love her. Kalina wanted a baby, so
Roland decided to give her one. I was that baby."

Julie opened her mouth. I raised my hand. If she interrupted me, I might not get through this.

"My father always had issues with his children. They
turned out powerful and smart, and as soon as they wised up,
they tried to nuke him. Roland changed his mind and decided
I'd be better off not being born. My mother knew that to save
me she had to run away. She needed a protector, and Roland's
warlord, Voron, seemed like a good choice. Voron was bound
to Roland by a blood ritual, and my mother had to use every
bit of her power to make Voron love her, so much so that she
made Voron slightly insane."

"So she basically used him," Julie said.

"You got it. Together they ran away. My mother gave birth to me, but Roland was closing in on them. She knew that Voron was better suited to keeping the baby alive and Roland would never stop chasing her, so she stayed behind to buy Voron time. Roland caught up with her and killed her. Voron ran with me and then spent every moment of his life training me so one day I could kill my own father."

Julie turned pale.

I waited for her to digest all of it.

"Do you want to kill him?"

That was a complicated question. "I will if I have to, but I won't go out looking for him. I have Curran and you. All I want to do right now is keep both of you safe. But if Roland ever finds me, he *will* confront me, Julie, and I'm not sure I would survive. Remember the picture of a man I showed you? Hugh d'Ambray?"

I'd given it to her a few weeks ago and told her that he was an enemy. At the time I wasn't ready for long explanations.

"Yes."

"Hugh is Voron's replacement. He's Roland's new warlord. Not many people know about the lost baby, but he does. He stumbled across me and now he's very interested."

Now came the hard part. "When you were turning loup, I couldn't heal you. Nobody could heal you. So I . . ." *Robbed you of your free will.* ". . . cleaned your blood with mine to burn off the Lyc-V. It was the only choice. Without it, I would've had to kill you."

Julie stared at me.

"We're bound now. Some of my magic is yours. My blood contaminated you. I dreamed tonight. I saw a plain, a sunset, and towers. And I saw you and called you."

"What does it mean?" Julie whispered. "Does that mean Roland is in our heads?"

"I don't know. I don't know if we're seeing the past or the future or if it's my father messing with our minds from several states away. Whatever the hell it is, it isn't good. You have to take precautions. Don't leave your blood where it can be found. If you bleed, burn the bandages. If you bleed a lot, set the scene on fire or dump bleach on it. Hide your magic as much as you can. I'm not planning on dying. I will come back and I will help you sort this out. But if something happens to us, Jim knows. You can trust him."

A door swung open behind us. Doolittle stepped into the room.

"Doolittle knows, too." I told her. "There are some books in my room. I'll make you a list of what you need to read . . ."

Maddie stirred. A bulge rolled across her chest, like a tennis ball sliding just under her skin.

"Involuntary movements," Doolittle said. "Nothing to worry about."

I realized my hand was holding Slayer's hilt and let go. If Maddie went loup and lunged out of that tank at Julie, I would cut her down with no hesitation. That thought made my insides churn.

Julie's eyes were huge on her face.

"It will be okay," I told her.

"I don't think it will," Julie said. "Nothing is okay. Nothing will be okay."

She stood up.

"Julie . . ."

I watched her walk out. The door clanged shut. That didn't go the way I'd wanted it to. I wanted a do-over, but in life you rarely get those.

Doolittle was looking at me. "It's good you told her."

It didn't feel good. It felt downright crappy. "I need a favor."

"If it is within my power," he said.

"Curran and I have both written our wills. If I don't come back, Meredith will take care of Julie. I've already spoken to her. But if I don't come back, at some point, Julie may come to you for answers. I'd like you to have my blood. Studying it might help." He'd already done some analysis on it once. He would be the best person to study it more.

Doolittle rubbed his face, hesitated—as if deciding—and finally said, "This trip is a foolish endeavor."

"There is a chance we will succeed."

"A very small chance. We can't trust these people. They don't intend to honor their promises."

"I'll force them to honor them, if I have to. I can't sit by Maddie and watch her die a little bit every day. It's not in me, Doc."

"It is not in me either," he said. "I'm afraid we're drawing it out. Delaying the inevitable only leads to more suffering. That's why death must be quick and painless."

"You told me once that we don't have a choice in what we are. We do have a choice in *who* we are. I'm the person who must get on that boat or I won't be able to ever look Maddie's mother in the eye. Will you please draw my blood?"

Doolittle sighed. "Of course I will."

"KATE?"

Curran's voice slipped through my dream. Mmmm...I smiled and opened my eyes, still half-asleep. Curran leaned over me. My handsome psycho. When I came back from speaking with Julie, I crawled into bed. I awoke a couple of hours later when he slid into bed next to me. He pulled me close, his body so warm against mine. We made love and I fell asleep on his chest.

"Kate?" Curran repeated. "Baby?"

I reached over and touched his cheek just to make sure he was really there. "You should stay in bed with me."

"I'd love to," he said. "But I just spoke with Barabas."

"Mm-hm." He really was ridiculously handsome in a gruff, kill-anything-that-moves way. Exactly how I liked it. "What did he say?"

"Saiman is waiting for us in a conference room. He says he owes you a favor and Barabas called him to invite him to the Keep on your behalf." Gold flared in Curran's eyes. "Would you care to explain this, because I'm all ears?"

Ten minutes later Curran and I marched down the hallway toward the conference room. When you live in a building with excellent acoustics populated by people with supernatural hearing, you learn to argue under your breath, which was precisely what we were doing.

A month ago I'd gotten a late-night call from the Mercenary Guild informing me that Saiman had been kidnapped. An information broker and a magic expert, Saiman was a shrewd businessman who had his fingers in all sorts of pies, from illegal gladiatorial combat to a shady import/export business. He charged exorbitant prices for his services, but because I amused him, he had offered me a discount in the past. I had consulted him a few times, but he kept trying to entice me into his bed to prove a philosophical point. I'd put up with it until he had the stupidity to parade our connection in front of Curran. The Beast Lord and I had been in a rough spot in our relationship, and Curran didn't take that exhibition well, which he expressed by turning a warehouse full of luxury cars Saiman had slipped past customs into crushed Coke cans. Since then, Saiman, who feared physical pain above all else, lived in mortal fear of Curran.

Saiman maintained a VIP account at the Mercenary Guild for times when he needed to use brute force, so when some thugs decided it would be a good idea to hold him for ransom, his accountant put the call in to the Guild, which in turn called me. I'd dealt with the kidnappers and rescued Saiman. In return he owed me a favor. Yesterday I'd called him and told him that I would like to collect.

I had successfully managed to hide the incident from Curran precisely because I knew he would go ballistic. Explaining all this now proved a little complicated.

"The clerk called and said Saiman was kidnapped. What the hell was I supposed to do, leave him there?"

"Let me think . . . Yes!"

"Well, I didn't."

"He doesn't care about you. If you died saving him, he wouldn't give a shit. Nobody even knew where you went."

"Jim knew where I went." Aaand I shouldn't have said that.

Curran stopped and stared at me.

"I took backup," I told him.

"Like who?"

"Grendel and Derek."

Curran's eyebrows came together. He realized that Derek knew and hadn't snitched. I shouldn't have said that either.

The best defense is a vigorous offense. "You're overreacting."

"You left in the middle of the night to rescue a man without any shred of conscience who cares nothing about your safety, who schemed and manipulated to seduce you, and when he found he couldn't, acted like a coward and put you in danger. How am I supposed to react?"

"Last time I checked, I was a big girl, all grown up and able to put on my shoes and swing my sword all by myself. You don't have to like it."

"Kate!"

"He owes us a favor. A big favor."

"I don't need any favors from him," Curran snarled.

"Yes, you do. Do you remember that warehouse of luxury cars you demolished?"

Curran just looked at me.

"How did those expensive foreign cars get into the country?"

The realization hit Curran like a ton of bricks. His scowl vanished. "He shipped them in." He started down the hallway, accelerating.

"Exactly." I matched his stride.

"And he avoided customs because they came in on his vessel. He owns a fleet."

"Bingo."

We turned the corner. A shapeshifter heading in our direction saw our faces and tried to abruptly reverse her course. Curran pointed at her. "Get Jim for me, please."

She broke into a jog.

"We don't even know if his ships go to the Mediterranean," Curran said.

"Yes, we do. During the Midnight Games he brought in a minotaur from Greece."

We reached the door and I opened it.

A beautiful Asian woman waited for us in the North Conference Room. She was on the cusp of thirty, of average height and flawless build, with a slender, delicately curved waist and long legs. A dark green sweater dress, complete with a draped cowl and a sash, hugged her figure, showcasing her beautiful dark hair.

A male shapeshifter was watching her the way one would watch a rabid dog cornered in an alley.

Curran didn't miss a bit. "Saiman, you look lovely. Thank you for dressing up."

The woman looked up and I saw the familiar air of disdain in her eyes.

"Did you come as a woman so Curran wouldn't hit you?"

The woman grimaced. Odd bulges slid over her face and arms, as if someone had struck billiard balls under her skin with a cue and they spun, rolling in all directions. I willed my stomach to keep still.

"No," the woman said, as her flesh crawled, stretching, twisting, and reshaping itself in a revolting riot. "I simply had a prior appointment."

Her hair shed, her breasts dissolved into a flat male chest, her hips narrowed, all moving simultaneously in a grotesque coordinated process. Acid burned my tongue. Shapeshifter change was an explosion, a quick burst of movement over in a couple of seconds. Saiman's change was a controlled methodical adjustment, and watching it never failed to make my stomach panic and attempt to empty itself by any means necessary. I closed my eyes for a long moment, opened them, and saw a slender bald man crossing his new arms. In his neutral form, Saiman was a blank canvas: neither ugly nor handsome, average height, average features, average skin color, sparse frame. The sweater dress made him look completely ridiculous. I had a sudden urge to laugh and clamped down on it.

"I've brought some currency." Saiman pointed at the suitcase next to him. "I believe the standard Guild fee for rescuing a kidnapped victim is ten percent of the ransom. Feel free to count it."

Of course. Money was Saiman's default response. Paying us off would be the easiest way to get rid of his debt.

Curran offered him a chair with a sweep of his hand. "We're not interested in money. Would you care for something to drink?"

"Is it poisoned?"

"It's Saturday," I said. "We only serve poison during the week."

"Yes, we're not complete savages." Curran sat. "Shawn, could you please bring some water for me and Kate, and a scotch for our guest?"

The male shapeshifter nodded and departed.

"Feeling better?"

Saiman didn't look at me. "I'm sorry, I'd love to answer that, but you see, if I attempt a conversation, your furry paramour will pummel me into bits."

Oh, you fussy baby.

"Not at all," Curran said. "I have no plans to pummel anyone this morning."

Shawn stepped into the room, bringing a platter with a pitcher of water, a decanter filled with amber-colored scotch, and three glasses. Curran took it from his hands and set it on the table. "Thank you."

Shawn left, and Curran poured water into two of the

glasses and scotch into the third. "There is no reason we can't all be civil."

His tone was light, his face relaxed and friendly. The Beast Lord was in rare form. We really needed the ship.

Saiman sipped the amber liquid and held it in his mouth for a long moment. "So. You refuse my money, you serve me thirty-year-old Highland Park scotch, and we've been in the same room for approximately five minutes, yet none of my bones are broken. This leads me to believe that your back is against the wall and you desperately need me for something. I'm dying to know what that is."

In his place I'd be careful with my choice of words.

"I have a business proposal for you," Curran said. "I'd like to hire one of your shipping vessels to transport the two of us and ten of my people. We will pay you a reasonable rate."

"My reasonable or yours?" Saiman studied his drink.

"Ours. In turn, you will no longer owe the Pack and we will make your life less inconvenient. For example, we'll stop blocking your real estate purchases."

"You've been blocking his purchases?" I looked at Curran.

"Not me personally."

"The Pack and its many proxies." Saiman drained his glass and poured himself more. "If I choose to move on a project, the Pack will inevitably bid against me, drive up the price, and then abandon the bid, leaving me holding the purse strings. It's been most inconvenient."

I bet.

"You've always struck me as a man who enjoys attention," Curran said.

"That was completely unfair." Saiman pointed his index finger at him while still holding the glass. "Let's cut to the chase. I know that a delegation of shapeshifters disembarked in Charleston, I know that Desandra Kral, formerly of the Obluda pack, is having twins, and I know that you have been invited to act as her bodyguard and mediator of the inheritance dispute and that you will be paid in panacea to do so."

Saiman in a nutshell. I had no idea how he knew all of this, but he did.

"You need a ship. This vessel will have to be oceanworthy, will need an experienced crew, and will require cabin space for at least fifteen people. What's the destination?"

"Gagra on the northern coast of the Republic of Georgia."

Saiman blinked. "You mean the Black Sea? Do you really want to go to the Black Sea?"

"Yes," Curran said.

I nodded. "We do."

Saying things like *We think this is a trap* and *We would rather cut off our left foot than go* would endanger our ship acquisition and our badass image.

Saiman poured himself more scotch. "I can't help but point out that the three packs involved could've found someone in the immediate vicinity to act as a neutral fourth party."

"Your opinion is noted," Curran said.

"Have you ever tried to reverse engineer the panacea?" I asked.

"Yes, as a matter of fact I have," Saiman said. "I can give you the exact list of ingredients and quantities. The secret isn't in the chemical composition; it's in the process of preparation, which I'm unable to replicate. To put it plainly, they cook it with magic and I don't know the specifics. I'm also reasonably certain that the panacea is manufactured by a single entity or organization and then distributed throughout Europe."

"Why?" I asked.

"It's a well-known secret that five years ago your partner offered three hundred thousand dollars and Pack protection to anyone willing to sell him the recipe and demonstrate its preparation. If the panacea were manufactured by each pack individually, someone would've been desperate enough to take him up on his offer."

Curran grimaced. "It's five hundred thousand now."

"Still no takers?" Saiman arched his eyebrow.

"No."

Saiman swirled the whiskey in his glass. "Suppose I provide a vessel. Crossing the Atlantic is a dangerous venture. Between the hurricanes, the pirates, and the sea monsters, there is a very real possibility that your ship will sink and not at all in a metaphorical sense. I've been in shipping for over a decade and I still lose two to four ships per year. If you were to meet your untimely demise, your thugs would blame me."

"Most likely," Curran said.

"If you die—through no fault of my own, of course—the probability of my survival drops rather drastically. I'm expected to risk my ship, my crew, and my finances for some tenuous promise of possible goodwill. I'm looking for the silver lining and not finding any."

"You risk your ship, crew, and money, while we will be risking our lives," Curran said. "And since we're on the subject, I guarantee that if another vessel from your fleet pulls up next to out ship in the middle of the night and its crew attempts to murder us and scuttle our vessel to hide the evidence, you won't survive."

Saiman leaned back and laughed.

"What do you want?" I asked him.

"Friend of the Pack status," Saiman said. "Granted prior to departure."

Friend of the Pack would make him an ally. It guaranteed that shapeshifters would stay out of his business and protect him if one of them observed Saiman in imminent danger. It would also grant him the ability to visit the shapeshifter offices without being immediately detained.

"No," Curran said. "I won't give you that much access."

"Not only that, but if you become Friend of the Pack and then sink your ship with us on board, the shapeshifters can't come after you," I said.

"Do you really think I would drown you, Kate?"

"In a heartbeat," I told him. "You still owe me, Saiman."

"And I'm trying to work with you, but you must meet me halfway."

"No," I said. "You won't be getting Friend of the Pack status until we return."

Saiman smiled. "Then we're at an impasse."

We looked at each other.

"What if I come with you?"

"What?" I must've misheard.

"I'll join you on your wonderful adventure, Kate. That way, if our vessel does sink, I cannot be blamed, because I was on board."

"Why would you be doing this?" Curran asked.

"I'm overdue for a trip to the Mediterranean. I have business interests there."

"No," I said.

The two men looked at me.

"It's not a bad idea," Curran said.

"Have you two gone crazy? This is a horrible idea. First, the two of you hate each other."

"I don't hate him." Saiman shrugged. "It's too strong a word."

"If I hated him, he'd be dead," Curran said.

They were nuts. "How long does it take to cross the Atlantic?"

Saiman frowned. "Depends on the magic waves, but generally between twelve and eighteen days."

I turned to Curran. "We'll be stuck together on a small boat for at least two weeks. What happens when on day two he gets bored?"

"It will be fine," Curran said. "We can handle it. If he gets out of hand, we'll tie him to the mast."

Saiman gave him a derisive look. "We will be taking the *Rush*. It runs on enchanted water, steam, and diesel. It doesn't have a mast strong enough to hold me."

Curran exhaled. "Then we'll lock you in a cellar."

"Brig," Saiman corrected.

"Whatever." Curran dismissed it with a wave of his hand.

"Draw up a formal contract," I said. Saiman was egotistical and sometimes cowardly, but he had a ridiculously strong work ethic. If we could lock him in with a contract, he wouldn't break it.

"Oh, we will," Curran assured me. "Let's talk numbers."

Fifteen minutes later a satisfied Saiman left, escorted by Shawn. He was carrying his suitcase and ours. He was happy, the Beast Lord was happy, so why was I so uneasy?

"You'll regret this," I told Curran.

"I know. We don't have a choice. We have to get the panacea." He leaned over and kissed me. "I love you. Thank you for the ship. Thank you for doing this with me."

A little thrill ran through me. "I love you, too."

Getting the panacea meant that each baby born to the Pack would have a forty percent better chance of survival. It meant Maddie could become herself again. To make this happen, Curran would swallow his pride. He'd make a deal with Saiman, he'd bargain with Carpathians who had humiliated him, he'd cross the Atlantic and half a continent. And I would back him up every step of the way. Curran was responsible for the welfare of the Pack, and so was I.

"We have to get the panacea," I agreed. That was all there was to it.

CHAPTER 5

THE CARAVAN OF PACK VEHICLES ROARED AND thundered down the road. The magic was up full force and enchanted water engines belched so much noise, all of the windows were closed. Curran drove. In the backseat Barabas and Derek sat next to each other.

We left Julie in the Keep. She wanted to come and then she didn't want to. We said our good-byes. She hugged me and cried, so desperate and sad that I almost cried with her. I sat with her for twenty minutes, until finally we couldn't delay any longer. She was still crying when I walked out. I hoped this wouldn't be my last memory of her.

Somehow I always managed to screw things up when it came to Julie.

The highway snaked its way through a flat salt marsh. Reeds and grasses swayed gently, giving us a glimpse of wet mud exposed as low tide sucked the water out of the marsh. A sign flashed by, a yellow diamond with a turtle on it, followed immediately by another sign, a triangle bordered in red. A turtle in the center of the triangle had a dark cone touching its mouth.

"What does that mean?" Barabas asked from the backseat.

"Magic turtle crossing."

"I got that one, but what about the second one?"

"Beware the magic turtles."

"Why?"

"They spit fire."

Curran chuckled to himself.

The road turned. We shot onto a wooden bridge, the boards thudding a little under the pressure of the tires. Another half-mile and we rolled through the massive iron gates of the port.

"Which dock did Saiman say?" Curran asked.

I checked the paper. "Berth two. Just below the bridge."

The ruin of the Eugene Talmadge Memorial Bridge swung into view as if on cue, its concrete supports sticking sadly out of the water, the steel cables hanging over them like a torn spider web. We passed the remnants of the bridge and Curran stopped before a pier. A large vessel waited on the water, its two black masts rising above the deck that had to be close to four hundred feet long. I knew next to nothing about ships, but even I could tell this was no merchant freighter. It looked more like a naval ship, and the enormous gun mounted on the deck in front of the bridge only made that fact more apparent.

Curran studied the ship. "That's a Coast Guard High Endurance Cutter."

"How do you know?"

"We bought a gun from a decommissioned vessel. That's what's mounted in the forward tower by the gates."

"Do you think Saiman bought a Coast Guard cutter? How much money . . ."

"Millions," Barabas said, his voice dry.

We stared at the cutter.

A man strode down the gangplank. Large, broad-shouldered, he wore a plain sweater and jeans. A short brown beard traced his jaw. He looked like he worked for a living.

We got out.

The man approached us. I checked his eyes and saw the familiar superiority. He was painfully aware that his world was populated with people of lesser intelligence, and his eyes told me he was regretfully resigned to slumming. Saiman.

"May I present the *Rush*?" Saiman said. "Once USCGC *Rush*, now just the *Rush*. Three hundred and seventy-eight feet long, forty-three feet high, displacement of three thousand two hundred and fifty tons. Two gas turbines, four enchanted water generators, maximum speed during magic twenty knots, during tech twenty-nine knots. Otobreda seventy-six-millimeter super-rapid artillery gun, three ballistas, and a number of other bells and whistles, which makes it the finest vessel in my fleet. My flagship."

"Spared no expense?" I said.

Saiman grinned, displaying even, white teeth. "I prefer to travel safely or not at all."

I STOOD ON THE DECK OF THE *RUSH*, SMELLING THE salty, ocean-saturated air, and watched our supplies being loaded. The sailors on the ship at the next pier watched also. They had a crane. We had Eduardo Ortego, who picked up five-hundred-pound containers and casually tossed them onto the deck, where Mahon and Curran caught them and lowered them into the cargo hold.

The human sailors were looking a little sick. I was glad Eduardo was coming with us. Mahon had chosen the massive werebuffalo as his backup and nobody objected.

Family members and various shapeshifters swarmed over the *Rush*. Jim marched about, muttering things under his breath. George was showing cabins to her mother. The wind tugged on the unruly halo of her long dark curls, which she unsuccessfully tried to tame with a rubber band. Mahon's wife, a plump, happy African American woman, followed her daughter with a proud smile on her face. George was built like her dad—taller, sturdier, broader in the shoulders than her mother—but her big smile was the same: bright and infectious. I wasn't the smiling type, but when either of them smiled at you, it was hard not to grin back.

The deck under my feet was moving. The moment I shifted my balance to compensate, the ship tried to make a break for it. Last time I'd taken a ship was almost three years ago. Clearly, this wasn't at all like riding a bicycle.

Andrea, on the other hand, seemed no worse for wear. She leaned on the rail on my right, smiling. Raphael stood next to her. Where Andrea was short and blond, Raphael was tall, lean, and dark, with a wave of nearly black hair falling to his shoulders. He was also smoking hot. Some men had that indescribable quality, a kind of masculine sensual air. They looked at you and you knew having sex with them would be a memorable experience. Raphael didn't just have the air; he was his own seductive tornado. He was also one of the deadliest knife fighters I've encountered. Raphael loved Andrea more than fish loved the sea. She loved him back and flashed her guns when single women strayed too close.

Barabas stood on the other side of me, looking like he would hurl any minute. "Does it always move this much?"

"It gets worse," Raphael told him.

"You'll get used to it," Andrea promised.

A woman came down the pier, heading for the ship. She walked with an easy, lazy grace that spoke of strength and perfect balance, despite the dangerously tall heels of her black leather boots. Shapeshifter walk. Always a dead giveaway.

Black jeans hugged her hips, and a rust-red blouse with a jean jacket over it showed off her curves. Her hair, worked into a mane of dark tight spirals, moved as she walked, underscoring her smooth stride. She turned and I saw her face. She was striking: a heart-shaped face, skin the color of coffee, with smart dark eyes and a full, sensual mouth.

Eduardo picked up the next container and saw the woman. His face fell. "Hi, Keira."

Ha! So that was what Jim's sister looked like.

Keira winked at Eduardo. "Hello, delicious."

All of the blood drained from Eduardo's face. The container whistled through the air, cleared the deck, and plunged into the water on the other side.

Keira laughed, a low contralto chuckle, and kept going.

"Oops," Eduardo called out.

"What the hell?" Curran growled.

"I'm sorry, that one was lighter."

"You threw it, you fish it out."

If that container was the one with my herbal supplies and weapons, I'd be really put out.

Keira walked up the plank. "Hey, Barabas." She offered me her hand. "Keira. Jim's sister."

"Kate. Jim's friend." I shook her hand. Good grip.

"Hi, Raphael. And you must be Andrea. From the Order, right?" Keira asked.

"Yes," Andrea said.

"Good to meet you."

"What's the deal with you and Eduardo?" Barabas asked.

Keira grinned. "It's a funny story. When Eduardo first came to the city, he decided our laws didn't apply to him and he failed to come and say hi. Jim sent me to fetch him. I might have hunted him a little. For fun."

"Hunted?" Barabas asked.

"Mm-hm." She smiled, a slow lazy parting of lips. "I also might have implied that I find buffalo scrumptious."

A Pack Jeep pulled up to the pier. The doors opened and the Jeep disgorged Doolittle and two of his assistants. The Pack medic surveyed the ship, nodded, plucked a bag from the back of the Jeep, and headed up the plank. The assistants followed him, carrying bags and cases.

Ummm. "What's going on?"

"No idea." Barabas pondered Doolittle. "Whatever it is, it's not my fault."

"Hello." Doolittle climbed aboard. "Please direct me toward the cabins."

"Why do you need the cabins? Are you coming with us?"

He drew himself to his full height. "Yes. Yes, I am."

"When was this decided?" Curran hadn't said anything about it to me. Nor had Doolittle mentioned it when I came to see him.

"It was decided this morning. The cabins, milady?"

Hmmm. Maybe Curran in his typical fashion didn't tell me. I pointed at the stairs. "Straight down."

"This way." Doolittle went down the stairs. The assistants followed.

Barabas leaned over the side and vomited into the wind.

"You do realize we're not even out to sea?" Saiman asked from behind us.

Barabas flipped him off without looking.

Saiman shook his head.

Something had occurred to me. "Saiman, how loud are those magic generators?" Riding in a car powered by enchanted water did a number on one's hearing. A generator was likely much bigger.

"The engine room is significantly larger than the space under a typical car hood," Saiman said. "The ship generators are suspended in water rather than enclosing it, as car motors do, and the engine room itself is soundproofed. You should hear a pleasant hum, nothing more. Otherwise, the sailors would go insane from the constant noise."

He went on.

Half an hour later, the last crate was loaded and secured. Doolittle's assistants left. The crew moved about the ship in a complex dance, getting ready to sail. Andrea and Raphael moved on. The last family members left the ship.

Barabas surveyed the crowd gathered on the pier. His upper lip trembled in the beginning of a sneer. "Fuck it."

He turned, barely avoiding Curran, and went down the stairs.

His Furriness leaned on the rail next to me. "What's his problem?"

I kept my voice low. "Ethan didn't come to say good-bye. A few days ago Ethan told Barabas that he wasn't sure they had a future together. That's why I had to talk Jezebel out of breaking Ethan's legs."

Curran shook his head. "I guess he's sure now."

"Yep."

The deckhands cast off the lines.

"He said four enchanted water generators, right?" I asked.

"Yes."

"The rule is, the bigger the magic engine, the longer it takes. Four giant generators, and the crew is what, two dozen people? I wonder how long it will take them to get us started." We could be sitting in port for another hour.

"Why do I smell Doolittle?" Curran asked.

"He went through here on the way to his cabin."

"Ah. Wait, what?"

"He said he's coming with us. I thought that was your idea."

"What?"

"He said it was decided."

"It is." Doolittle came up the ladder. "I decided it."

The deck around us was suddenly silent. Everyone looked at Curran. I decided to look at him too, so I wouldn't feel left out.

"Why?" Curran asked quietly.

"Do you know what goes into panacea?"

"I know when I smell it," Curran said.

"But you don't know if it's potent. You don't know if it will actually do what they say it will do. You don't know how to test it."

"What about the Pack?"

"Please. I'm leaving the Pack in the care of five medmages

based in a state-of-the-art facility. You will have only me."
Doolittle surveyed us. "I've brought half of the people here
back from the brink of death. Left to your own devices, you
lose what small drop of common sense you have and do things
like running through fire, breaking your bones, and taking on
creatures of much larger size. If you persist in this foolishness, I should be there to make sure at least some of you get
home alive."

Doolittle didn't quite bare his teeth, but if he had fur, it
would've stood on end.

Curran smiled. "We appreciate having you on board, Doctor."

Doolittle blinked. He had expected a bigger fight, and now
Curran had cut his feet from under him. "That's right," he
finally managed, then turned around and walked away.

Saiman walked onto the deck and stopped near the nose of
the ship. "Your attention, please!"

Everyone looked at him.

"We're about to sail. I ask you to please be silent so the
crew can begin."

Everyone shut up.

Saiman leaned back. A subtle change came over him. He
seemed to belong here on the deck of the ship. He opened his
mouth and sang out, in a rough but clear voice.

"Old Storm Along is dead and gone!"

The crew caught the melody and sang out in a chorus. *"Ay,
ay, ay, Mr. Storm Along!"*

"Old Storm Along is dead and gone!" Saiman called out,
louder.

"Ay, ay, ay, Mr. Storm Along!"

Something stirred beneath the ship like a slumbering giant
slowly waking up from a deep sleep.

"It's a sea shanty," Curran whispered to me.

Magic streamed from Saiman and the crew, melting
together, seeping into the steel bones of the ship, as if they
were at once bringing it to life with their voices and making it
theirs in the process.

When Stormy died, I dug his grave,
Ay, ay, ay, Mr. Storm Along!
I dug his grave with a silver spade,
Ay, ay, ay, Mr. Storm Along!

Something purred deep within the ship. Magic sparked deep below. The hair on the back of my neck rose. The song and magic braided together and pulled me in. I wanted to join in, even though I didn't know the words and my singing would scare off the fish in the ocean. The crew was singing full out now, Saiman's voice blending with the others, part of the strong powerful chorus, its rhythm like the beating of a heart.

I hove him up with an iron crane,
Ay, ay, ay, Mr. Storm Along!
And lowered him down with a golden chain,
Ay, ay, ay, Mr. Storm Along!

The enchanted water generators came on, expelling magic in a thrilling cascade. The *Rush* shuddered and pulled away from the pier.

Wind bathed us, pulling at my hair. Another tremor shook the ship. The *Rush* surged forward, into the ocean. The crew clapped. Saiman took a bow, grinning. I had no idea he had it in him.

"We're off," Curran said.

"Yes, we are." We would get there, we would fight, and we would return.

WE HIT OUR FIRST STORM ONE DAY OUT. THE ocean churned and boiled, its waters leaden gray and frothy with foam. Huge waves rolled, each as big as a house, and our large cutter bobbed up and down, tossed about like a paper boat. Water hammered at the hull, and the vessel careened until I thought it would overturn and the lot of us would drown, only to roll back the other way the next second.

Saiman tied himself outside. When I asked the crew to check on him, they assured me that the ship needed a forward lookout and this was his favorite thing to do. I made it to the bridge and caught a glimpse outside. The world looked like a nightmare, with wind and water locked together in a furious primal combat. Saiman stared into the wind with a big smile on his rain-splattered face, while the ocean pretended it was a moving mountain range. The waves would crest and drench the deck, and he would disappear from view behind the curtain of water.

While Saiman was getting his freak on outside, the rest of us huddled belowdecks. One by one we all gathered in the mess hall. It was either safety in numbers or misery loves company—either one would do. Eduardo and Barabas seemed to be having the worst time of the lot. Eduardo paled and prayed quietly, while Barabas hugged his bucket and looked green. Finally Barabas informed us that it was fitting that he would die here after being dumped and he was sorry he was taking us with him. Eduardo told him to shut up and offered to throw him into a lifeboat, and then Barabas demonstrated that weremongooses did go zero to sixty in less than a second and offered to amuse himself by playing with Eduardo's guts. They had to be told to go and sit in separate corners of the mess hall. I curled up next to Curran and fell asleep. If the ship decided to sink, there wasn't much I could do about it.

The magic drowned the technology soon after midnight. By morning the ocean had smoothed out and the ship had stopped trying to impersonate a drunken sailor at the end of his first night of liberty.

We got some breakfast and I escaped the mess hall and climbed onto the deck. The sea lay perfectly calm, like an infinite translucent crystal, polished to satin smoothness. The magic engines made almost no noise and the ship glided over the bottomless blue depths. The ocean and the sky seemed endless.

I surveyed the sea for a few long minutes and moved on to explore the deck. In the rear I found a large clear space marked by an *H*. A helipad. No helicopter in sight. I walked out onto the helipad. Such a nice clear space. I felt slightly off after sleeping on the floor. A little exertion would do me good. I stretched, turned, and kicked the air. And one more time. I launched a quick combination, jumped, and smashed my foot into an invisible opponent's chin.

"A knockout," Curran said behind me.

I jumped in the air about a foot and managed to land with some semblance of dignity. He had managed to sneak up on me again. Time to save face. "Nah. That wasn't a knockout. I just staggered him a bit."

"I wasn't talking about the kick, baby."

Oh. "Smooth, Your Furriness." I backed up and spread my arms. "Want to play?"

He pulled off his shoes.

Five minutes later, we were rolling around on the helipad as he tried to muscle his way out of my armlock, after slamming me onto the helipad.

"I finally realized the source of your mutual attraction," Saiman said, his voice dry.

I looked up. He was standing a few feet away.

"Do enlighten us." Curran tried to roll into me to break the lock. *Oh no you don't.*

"You both think violence is foreplay."

I laughed.

Derek came over, moving in that languid wolfish stride, took off his boots and socks, and dropped down into a one-armed push-up. He was still doing them fifteen minutes later, when Barabas and Keira emerged onto the helideck and began sparring. Barabas was shockingly fast, but Keira and Jim clearly shared a gene pool, because she just kept on coming.

Andrea and Raphael were next, and then Eduardo, George, and Mahon also found the helideck. Watching Eduardo and Mahon spar was like watching two rhinos trying to wrestle. They smashed against each other and then puffed and strained for ten minutes without moving an inch. Finally, red-faced, they broke apart and shook.

"Thank you," Eduardo said.

"Good match," Mahon said.

Raphael stripped off his shirt. He wore a black muscle shirt underneath that left his shoulders exposed. Andrea raised her eyebrows, clearly appreciating the view. Raphael walked out onto the helipad with a plain six-inch knife in his hand. It was the only weapon permitted during the Pack challenges, and during the marathon of shapeshifter attacks that earned me my place as the Pack's "Beast Lady," I had gotten very good use out of mine. Barabas joined Raphael. They clashed, lightning fast, and danced across the helipad. The core difference between a sword fighter and a knife fighter wasn't speed or strength. When a swordmaster took out his sword, the outcome wasn't always certain. He might have meant to injure his opponent or to disarm him. But when a knife fighter pulled out a knife, he meant to kill.

Aunt B walked out onto the helipad wearing loose yoga pants. "I'm just here to stretch. Kate, want to help?"

"Sure."

Thirty seconds later, as I was flying through the air, I decided that this wasn't the best idea.

"Watch yourself," Doolittle said. He sat on the side, holding a book.

"Are you going to join us, Doc?" Raphael asked.

"I'm sunbathing," Doolittle told him. "And enjoying my book. Don't bother me with your foolishness."

Barabas held up a folder. "As long as we're all here, I need to brief you on our situation."

"Maybe later?" Keira said. "I have plans."

"What plans?" Barabas peered at her.

"I was going to go and think deep thoughts, somewhere in the sun."

"With your eyes closed?" George asked.

"Possibly."

"Someone sit on her before she escapes." Barabas raised his folder. "It's my job to make sure we don't go into this venture blind. You're all here, so you will have to suffer through this whether you like it or not."

"But . . ." Keira began.

Curran glanced at her.

"Oh, fine." She stretched out on the deck. "I'm listening."

"You've all heard about Desandra and the twins by now," Barabas began. "However, this fight isn't really about the babies. It's about territory. The Carpathians form a mountain range in the shape of a backward C that runs through many different countries, including Poland, Slovakia, Hungary, Romania, Ukraine, and Serbia. These mountains constitute Europe's largest forested area and contain over a third of all European plant species."

Keira yawned.

Barabas rolled his eyes. "Here is the deal. It's shapeshifter paradise. Miles and miles of wooded mountains, lakes, rivers, and a good supply of fresh water and game. The terrain is harsh and the human population is light. You could dump a battalion of Army Rangers into the Carpathians, and they would wander around for years, shooting at shadows."

"Sounds good," Mahon boomed.

"It is. Prime country. So this guy, Jarek Kral, figured this out early on. He clawed his way to the top of a small wolf pack and spent the next twenty years murdering, bargaining, and scheming to get more land. Now he controls a big chunk in the northeast. He's a powerful sonovabitch, and he's got serious anger management issues. Holds grudges and never forgets an insult. There was this werebear who said something Jarek didn't like. Three years later Jarek sees him at a dinner, walks over, stabs him with a knife, rips the guy's heart out of his body, throws it on the ground, and stomps it into mush. And then goes back to finish his food. He's famous for it."

"Sounds like a lovely man," George said.

"Here, I've got a picture." Barabas passed a photograph to Eduardo on his left. "Jarek is a powerful guy, but he has a problem. In thirty years he managed eleven children. Seven went loup, two were killed with their mother when a rival pack ambushed them, one challenged Jarek and lost, and that leaves him with Desandra. Jarek is like our Mahon. He's all about dynasties and alliances. It's killing him that he doesn't have a son."

Mahon sighed. "Wait until you live as long as I have. And I have a son. I just wasn't his first father, that's all."

Curran grinned.

The photograph of Jarek finally made its way to me. A man in his late forties stared to the side with an expression of derision and disbelief on his face, as if he had just stepped on a worm and was flabbergasted that the creature had managed to get itself plastered to the bottom of his shoe. His brown wavy hair fell around his face, reaching to his broad shoulders, but did nothing to soften the impact of the face. Jarek's features were made with broad strokes: large eyes under bushy slanted eyebrows, large nose, wide mouth, firm chin and a square jaw. It was a powerful face, male and strong, but lacking refinement. He didn't look like a thug, but rather like a man without conscience, who killed because it was convenient.

Not the type of man I'd want to cross.

Curran looked over my shoulder. "Yes. That's him."

I leaned against him and passed the picture to Raphael.

"So back to Desandra," Barabas said. "Nobody wanted to ally themselves with Jarek, because he isn't exactly a man of his word. So he bargained with his daughter. By herself, Desandra is penniless. However, her first son will inherit Prislop Pass. It's a pass in northern Romania, on the edge of his territory, and it has a ley line running through it. If you're going from Russia, Ukraine, or Moldova to Hungary or Romania, you're going to take that pass. Which brings us to the other two packs."

He held up a picture. A family sat around the table. Three younger men, one elderly, and three women. "Volkodavi. A mixed pack, part Polish, part Ukrainian, part whatever. They're rubbing up against the Carpathians from the east, in Ukraine, and they control the eastern hills. Here is Radomil, Desandra's first husband."

Barabas handed the photograph to Eduardo, who passed it to George. George blinked and sat up straighter. "Whoa."

"I know, right?" Barabas grinned.

Andrea leaned over. "Let me see. Not my type." She leaned over to show Aunt B. Aunt B raised her eyebrows.

The picture went from hand to hand until I finally got it. Radomil was pretty. There was no other word for it. His hair, a rich golden blond, lay in waves on his head, framing a perfectly symmetrical face. A generous mouth stretched in a happy smile showing white teeth, a touch of stubble on the chin, high cheekbones, and glass-bottle-green eyes, framed in dense, dark blond eyelashes.

Curran looked over my shoulder and studied it with a perfectly neutral expression.

"Radomil's older brother and sister pretty much run the pack," Barabas said. "We don't know very much about them. Look here." He lifted another photo. Two parents and two grown sons, both handsome, dark-haired, hazel-eyed, with narrow faces, short haircuts, and clean-shaven square jaws.

"Gerardo and Ignazio Lovari, sons of Isabella and Cosimo Lovari. We're interested in Gerardo."

"No, dear," Aunt B said. "We're interested in Isabella. I've met her before. That woman rules Belve Ravennati. All of the Wild Beasts of Ravenna answer to her including her two sons. They're a very disciplined pack. Mostly lupine and very acquisition-minded."

"Try to remember their faces. All these people will be there," Barabas said. "And that brings us to our lovely destination. We're actually going to Abkhazia. It's a disputed territory on the border between Russia and Georgia, and it's directly across the Black Sea for everyone involved. Once every fifty or sixty years, Russia and Georgia have a war over it and it changes hands. The local pack is a werejackal pack, not large, but enough people to slaughter the lot of us. We don't know anything about it. But we do know several things." Barabas held up a finger. "One, the alpha couple will be the most likely target."

Everyone looked in our direction. Curran smiled.

"That's how I would do it," Mahon said. "Split the alphas and you split the pack. If you do it right, the pack will turn on itself."

Being a target didn't thrill me, but it wouldn't be the first time.

Barabas held up two fingers. "Two, they'll try to reduce our numbers."

"Buddy system," Curran said. "Nobody goes anywhere without someone with them. Pick your buddy and stick with them."

"Three." Barabas raised three fingers. "Trust no one. I don't know where they'll put us, but we'll have no privacy. Even if your rooms are empty, you can be sure that someone is listening to you breathe. Don't discuss anything important unless you're outside and you can see a mile around you."

"And four," Curran said. "We will be provoked on every turn. Collectively the three packs want us there. Individually, they don't. The only reason they want an arbitration is that none of the packs is strong enough to take the other two. If two clans fight, the third will destroy the victor."

"So even if you win, you lose," Andrea said.

Curran nodded. "To them, we are collateral damage. The packs have made plans, and some of them hinge on provoking us to violence. No matter what is said to you, do not let yourself be goaded into throwing the first punch. Our behavior must be beyond reproach."

"This is going to be so much fun," George murmured in a voice usually reserved for lamenting extra work piled on your desk on the last minute of Friday.

"You said it." Raphael grinned. "This will be the best vacation ever."

"Boudas." George wrinkled her nose.

AS LONG AS THE BIG TECH TURBINES PROPELLED the *Rush* forward, the ocean remained lifeless, but as soon as the noise disappeared, life gathered around the ship. Dolphins dashed in the water, launching themselves in the air. Often larger, rainbow-hued fishes joined them, spinning above the water as they leaped. Once an enormous, fish-shaped shadow, as long as the ship, slid quietly under us and went on its way. Glittering schools of fish zipped back and forth next to the vessel.

A week into the trip we saw a sea serpent as we were getting our use out of the helipad. The ocean was smooth as glass and suddenly a dragonlike head the size of a car rose above the water on a graceful neck. The silver scales sparkled in the sun. The serpent looked at us with turquoise eyes, as big as a tire, and dove underwater. Saiman said it was only a baby, or things would've been considerably more difficult.

On the morning of the seventeenth day, we passed through the Strait of Gibraltar. It was less impressive than expected. A green shore stretched on one side for a while and then receded into the blue. The lack of drama was thoroughly disappointing.

We pressed on. Three days later, I climbed onto the deck to a beautiful day. Crystalline blue water spread as far as the eye could see. Here and there faint outlines of cliffs, the hints of distant islands, interrupted the blue. Gauzy veils of feathered clouds crossed the sky like thin spears of frost across a winter window. The magic was up, and the *Rush* slid across the water, a nimble steel bird.

I sat down with my coffee. Wind stirred my hair. Saiman came to stand near me.

"I never figured you for a sailor," I said.

"I never did either. I was seventeen when I happened to get on a crab fishing boat for reasons completely unrelated to fishing. I smelled the wet salt in the wind, felt the deck move, and didn't leave for three years. I was truly happy there. I do prefer cold seas. I like ice. It's the call of the blood, I suppose. Aesir or Jotun, take your pick."

"Why did you leave?"

Saiman shook his head. "It's not something I wish to share. Suffice to say, there are times when I think I should've stayed."

He leaned forward, scanning the horizon, and for the first time since we left port, his face was grim.

"Problems?"

Saiman nodded at the endless water. "We've crossed into the Aegean."

"Are you worried senior citizens will start diving off the cliffs because our ship is flying the wrong sails?"

Barabas wandered out onto the deck and came to stand by us.

"I never understood the legend of Theseus," Saiman said. "Or rather, I understand his motivation for killing the minotaur in an effort to establish himself as a leader. I can't fathom the rationale behind Aegeus throwing himself into the sea."

"He thought his son failed to kill the minotaur and died," I said.

"So he decided to destabilize the country already paying tribute to a foreign power even further by killing himself and destroying the established royal dynasty?" Saiman shook his head. "I think it's clear what really occurred. Theseus led the invasion of Crete, destroyed their superweapon in the form of the minotaur, returned home, and made his bid for power by pushing his dear old father off a cliff. Everyone pretended it was a suicide, and Theseus went on to found Athens and unify Attica under its banner."

Barabas barked a short laugh. "He's probably right."

"I prefer the other version," I said.

Saiman shrugged. "Romanticism will be your undoing, Kate. To answer your question, I'm not worried about suicidal Greeks, but about their more violent countrymen. The Aegean is a haven for pirates."

Romanticism will be your undoing, blah blah. "Isn't that why you have that gun mounted on the front? Or is it for other reasons, because I would've thought that a man with your powers would be past the urge to compensate."

Barabas grinned.

"I had forgotten that talking to you is like trying to pet a cactus," Saiman said dryly. "Thank you for reminding me."

"Always happy to oblige."

"I'm compensating for nothing. Pirates come in two types. Most of them are opportunistic, situationally homicidal, and driven by profit. They kill as means to an end. They evaluate a vessel of this size and realize that a sea battle would be too costly and their chances of winning it are slim. Unfortunately, there is the second type: the rash, the stupid, and the insane. The *Rush* wouldn't prove a deterrent; on the contrary, they would view it as a great prize. Capturing it would at once give them a flagship of decent firepower and allow them to make a name for themselves. They can't be reasoned with—"

A small cutter swung around the western edge of the nearest island. Saiman looked at it. Another boat joined the first, then a third, a fourth . . .

Saiman gave out a long-suffering sigh. "Right. Please go and get your brute, Kate. We're about to get boarded."

"I'll go." Barabas jogged away.

Over a dozen cutters now sped toward us. With magic up, the giant gun was useless.

A bell rang: three rings, pause, three rings, pause. A woman barked, her voice deep, "General quarters! All hands to battle stations! General quarters!"

"Shouldn't you be on the bridge?" I asked.

"The ship must have only one captain," Saiman said. "Russell is perfectly competent to handle any emergency, and I don't want to undermine him with my presence."

The shapeshifters spilled out onto the deck, Curran in the lead. Andrea brandished a crossbow. Raphael strode next to her, carrying knives. The boats headed straight for us. The Beast Lord braked next to me. "Are you planning to ram them?"

"That would be futile. Their boats are more maneuverable. They would simply scatter."

A person dived into the ocean off the lead boat. That must've been a cue, because the pirates began dropping overboard like their boats were on fire.

"What the hell?" Eduardo muttered.

"As I said, we're about to be boarded," Saiman said with afflicted patience.

Above us on top of the brig, two sailors manned a polybolos, a siege engine that looked like a crossbow on steroids. An antipersonnel weapon, a polybolos fired large crossbow bolts with deadly accuracy, and just for fun, it was self-loading and repeating, like a machine gun.

Sleek shapes dashed through the water toward us.

"Do they have trained dolphins?" George asked.

"Not exactly," Saiman backed away, toward the center of the deck.

The dolphins shot toward the *Rush* all but flying beneath the waves.

I pulled Slayer out.

"Form a perimeter," Curran called. "Let them get on the deck, where it's nice and dry. Don't let them pull you into the water."

We made a ring in the center of the deck.

"This is utterly ridiculous," Aunt B said.

Keira stretched. "Fun, fun, fun . . ."

Something smashed into the side of the hull. A deformed gray hand clutched the top edge of the deck and a creature leaped over the railing and landed, dripping water. Nude except for a leather harness, it stood on short muscular legs, hunched over but upright, the sun glistening on its thick, shiny hide. Its body was all chest with a smooth, wide trunk of a waist. Broad shoulders supported two massive arms with surprisingly small hands. Its neck, disproportionately thick, with a hump on the back, anchored a head armed with long, narrow dolphin jaws filled with razor-sharp teeth. Two human eyes stared at us from the thickly fleshed face. A big bastard. At least four hundred pounds.

A weredolphin. Pinch me, somebody.

Greek legends spoke of some pirates who'd captured the god Dionysus. They were planning to rape him and sell him into slavery. Furious, he transformed them into dolphins. Apparently, their descendants were alive and well and still in the family business.

The pirate glared at us. Hell of a neck. Strikes to the throat were right out.

Other pirates leaped over the railing. One, two . . . seven . . . thirteen. A baker's dozen. Wait, fifteen. Eighteen . . . Twenty-one. The odds weren't in our favor.

"Maybe they just came over to borrow a cup of sugar," I said.

Andrea barked a short laugh. Curran put his hand on my shoulder. "That's a lot of sugar. Must be a big cake."

The lead weredolphin opened his jaws, displaying teeth designed to pierce struggling prey and not let go. English words spilled out, sotto voce, accented and mangled. "Give us your ship and your cargo and you can go."

"He lies," Saiman said. "I lost two vessels to them in the last six months. They will butcher us like cattle for the sake of the cargo."

"Do you speak Greek?" Curran asked.

Saiman shrugged. "Naturally."

"Ask him if he thought this through."

A melodious language spilled from Saiman.

The weredolphin stared at Saiman like he had grown a second head.

"Leave this ship," Curran said, his voice deepening. He was about to explode. "And you will survive. This is your only warning."

Saiman translated.

The dolphin drew back and pointed at Curran. "First, I kill you. Then I rape your woman."

Gold drowned Curran's eyes. I've seen people put their foot in their mouth. This was the first time I saw a fin jammed into one.

Curran's body exploded. The change was so fast, it was almost instantaneous. One second a man stood next to me, the next a monster towered over me, fully seven and a half feet tall. Gray fur covered his muscular limbs, dark ghostly stripes crisscrossing it like the marks of a whip. The colossal leonine mouth gaped open, flashing scimitar fangs, and a huge sound burst forth, dangerous, rough, grating, primal in its fury and sheer power, like a battle challenge delivered by a tornado. It hit you straight in the gut, bypassing logic and thought, into the bundle of nerves that made you freeze. I've heard it dozens of times and it still shook me.

The weredolphins had never heard it before, and so they did exactly what most people would do when faced with an enraged lion. They cringed, paralyzed.

I lunged forward, drawing as I struck. The head pirate saw me coming and raised his arm to ward off the strike. Slayer's blade cut through the flesh and bone of the narrow wrist like a knife through warm butter. The hand fell to the deck. The pirate clutched the stump of his arm and screamed, a high-pitched, ear-piercing shriek. I buried my sword in his gut and disemboweled him with a single rip.

The pirates swarmed me. Behind me the shapeshifters snarled, in a terrifying chorus: the deep roar of the father-and-daughter Kodiaks mixing with the howls of the wolves and the pissed-off snarl of a jaguar, laced with hyenas' psychotic cackle.

I carved the closest attacker's chest, then slashed the side of the second one open and dropped him with a cut to the neck. The smell of blood filled the air. Behind me Derek moved, breaking the necks and limbs of the bleeding pirates before they had a chance to recover.

I sliced a gaping mouth across a weredolphin's groin. He dropped, snapping his teeth at me, and through the gap in the bodies, I saw Curran pick one of the pirates off the deck and break his spine over his knee. He tossed the limp body aside. His giant lion mouth gaped. Next he bit someone's shoulder. Bones crunched, followed by a blood-chilling desperate scream.

To the left a large weredolphin charged forward, shoving shapeshifters out of the way. The crossbow bolt whined, cutting the air, and sprouted in his eye. The weredolphin spun and the seven-foot-tall striped nightmare that was Aunt B lunged at him, slicing his stomach open. She buried her hand deep in the wound and yanked out a handful of pale guts. I kept moving, carving my way through the gray, shiny bodies.

Teeth bit my arm, ripping into the muscle. I reversed my sword and stabbed Slayer deep into the weredolphin's neck. He gurgled. Blood poured from between his teeth, burning my wound as the magic in my blood reacted to the Lyc-V in his. I twisted the blade, ripping through his throat. The pirate went down. To my left, two weredolphins rammed Eduardo at full speed and dove off the deck.

Crap. In the water they had an edge. I reversed my course, trying to cut my way to the side.

Another pirate blocked my way. I thrust. He turned into my strike, and the blade pierced the thick hump of his neck. The dolphin screamed and smashed into me. The impact took me off my feet. I flew a bit and hit the cabin with my back with a solid thud. Ow.

The dolphin dived at me, too fast to avoid, too heavy to impale. I raised my left leg. The body hit me, the full weight landing on my leg. Crooked dolphin teeth snapped at my face. Heavy sonovabitch. I grunted, bending my knee more, and slid him right onto the point of my sword. Nice and easy.

He jerked, flailing on the blade, as if shocked with a live wire, his weight pinning my legs. I pulled my throwing knife out with my left hand and stabbed it into his side, turning his innards into mush. The dolphin convulsed. Teeth ripped at my clothes, scratching my side. I stabbed him again and again. Blood wet my hand, spraying on my face in a hot mist. The pirate screeched, the high-pitched desperate shriek turning into a gurgle, and sagged on top of me. The four-hundred-some pounds pinned me in place. I strained. The body didn't move. Damn it.

Suddenly the weight was gone. The dolphin hovered three feet above me and was tossed unceremoniously aside. A gray monster stained with blood crouched by me.

Curran.

"You're taking a nap? Come on, Kate, I need you for this fight. Stop lying around."

You sonovabitch. I rolled to my feet and grabbed my sword. "You must think you're funny."

A weredolphin threw himself at us from the right. Curran tripped him and grabbed his shoulder, pulling him back, and I sliced the pirate's throat and punctured his heart with two quick strikes.

"Just saying, you have to pull your own weight. A hot body and flirting will only get you so far."

Hot body and flirting, huh. When I'm done killing people . . . "Everything I do, I learned from you, boy toy."

Another pirate rushed us. I dropped, slicing the tendons behind his knee, while Curran headbutted him and ripped out his throat. The pirate fell.

"Boy toy?" Curran asked.

"Would you prefer *man candy*?"

The deck was suddenly empty. Blood painted the ship. Gray corpses lay here and there, torn and savaged by claws and teeth. A huge shaggy Kodiak bear prowled the deck, his muzzle dripping gore. The last pirate still on his feet was running toward Andrea and Raphael near the bow. Andrea raised her crossbow. She was still in human form. Raphael stood next to her, light on his feet, his knives dripping red. A trail of bodies led to them, bristling with crossbow bolts. The pirate rushed her. She sank two bolts into his throat. He gurgled, his momentum carrying him forward. Raphael let him get within ten feet and cut him down in a fury of precise strikes.

Past them a black panther the size of a pony slapped a

weredolphin with a huge paw. The shapeshifter's skull split, crushed like an egg under a hammer.

On the left a humanoid creature crawled onto the deck, lean, furry, with a round head and short round ears. Disproportionately long, sharp brown claws protruded from his oversized fingers. He strained and heaved another, much larger body onto the deck. It landed in a splash of water and a shaggy pile of brown fur, turned over, and vomited salt water from a half-human half-bison muzzle. Eduardo.

The reddish beast sank next to him, baring sharp white teeth. His bright red eyes, the color of a ripe strawberry, had a horizontal pupil, like that of a goat. They made him look demonic. I knew of only one shapeshifter with eyes like that—Barabas.

"Why don't you know how to swim?" His diction was almost perfect.

Eduardo unloaded more water on the deck. "Never needed to."

"We are crossing an ocean. It didn't occur to you to learn?"

"Look, I've tried. I walk into a pool, I thrash, and then I sink."

Ahead the flotilla of boats fled behind the island. Bodies littered the deck. I counted. Fourteen. None of them ours. We were bloody, hurt, but alive. The pirates weren't.

What a waste of life.

And I'd loved it. I loved every second of it: the blood, the rush, the heady satisfaction of striking and seeing the cut or thrust find its target . . . Voron had succeeded. I was raised and trained to be a killer, and nothing, not even happy peaceful weeks in the Keep with the man I loved, could change that. I'd come to terms with what I was a long time ago, but sometimes, like right now, looking over the deck strewn with corpses, I felt a quiet regret for the person I could've been.

Curran, naked and covered with blood, wrapped his now-human arm around me. "You okay?" he asked quietly.

I nodded. "You?"

He grinned and squeezed me to him. My bones groaned.

"Congratulations," I squeezed out. "I survived the fight, but your hug did me in."

He grinned and let me go. We'd both made it.

"We have a live one," Raphael called out.

We crossed the deck to where he crouched. A young man, maybe early twenties, with a mass of dark curls, laid on his back, his right leg twisted under at an odd angle, his face contorted by pain. Raphael held the point of his knife over the man's liver.

The man's gaze fastened on Saiman. He held up his hand and said something, his words tumbling out in a rush.

Saiman asked something. The man answered.

Saiman turned to Curran. "He has some information that would be of particular interest to you. He will tell you if you set him free, et cetera, et cetera."

"Fine," Curran said.

Saiman nodded at the man. The pirate said something halting and looked at me. Saiman looked at me as well.

"What?"

Saiman turned to Curran. "It appears that this is for your ears only. I believe it's in your best interest to have this conversation in private."

"Give us some space," Curran said.

People moved back.

"Do you want me to stay?" I asked.

He reached out and squeezed my hand. "No."

I moved back with the others. Saiman leaned over and whispered something to Curran. They spoke quietly. Saiman asked the man something. The man answered. Saiman relayed it back.

Curran turned, his face dark. All humor fled from his expression. He met my gaze and didn't say anything. Not good.

"How can you stand it?" Andrea murmured next to me. "I'd be right in there."

"I didn't tell him about rescuing Saiman," I murmured back. "If he needs to keep something private, I'm fine with it. When he's ready, he'll tell me."

"Lock this man up," Saiman called.

Two sailors came, picked up the pirate, and carried him off.

"Let's get this place cleaned up," Curran called.

People spread out. He came toward me.

"Bad news?" I asked.

"Nothing we can't handle."

I nodded to him and we went to help scrub the gore off the deck.

CHAPTER 6

WE ARRIVED IN THE PORT OF GAGRA AT DUSK.
First we saw the mountains, triangular low peaks sheathed in
vibrant emerald green, as if blanketed with dense moss. The
sunset behind us shifted to the right as the ship turned in to a
sheltered harbor. The deep, almost purple waters of the Black
Sea lightened to blue.

All twelve of us were there, on the deck. The shapeshifters
looked uneasy. Even George, who usually met everything
with a smile, seemed grim. She stood next to her father, hugging herself, as the wind stirred the dark spirals of her hair.

"Are you alright, cookie?" Mahon said.

"I have a bad feeling about this," she murmured. "That's all."

"Shall I hoist the flag?" Saiman asked.

"Yes," Curran said.

The gray-and-black striped flag of the Pack with a black
lion paw on it rose up the mast.

The shore grew closer. The mountains wove in and out of
the sea in gentle curves, soaking their roots in the water. The
beach was a narrow strip of pebbled ground. Stone piers
stretched into the waves, as if beckoning to us, and behind
them, buildings of white stone sat perched on the side of the

mountains, their colonnades facing the sea. They looked Greek to me, but most of what I knew about Greece came from books.

The water turned turquoise. The *Rush* slowed, then came to a stop.

"What are we waiting for?" I asked.

"A signal from the port," Saiman said. "I would suggest you gather your belongings."

We had already packed. Everything I intended to take with me was in a backpack, which Barabas promptly confiscated. Apparently as an alpha, I wasn't permitted to carry my own luggage.

Twenty minutes later a blue flare shot from the pier.

"We're clear to land," Saiman said. "Once you disembark, I will depart. I have business in Tuapse, Odessa, and Istanbul. I'll return within a week or so."

That suited me just fine. Saiman loved to amuse himself, and we'd have our hands full without trying to contain him.

Fifteen minutes later the crew was tying the *Rush* to the pier. I stood on the crowded deck, Curran next to me. George's anxiety infected me. I wanted off the ship. I wanted to see Desandra and get to work. Unfortunately if I started pacing back and forth like a caged tiger, I'd be immediately told by nine people that it wasn't proper.

"A welcoming committee," Raphael announced.

I turned. Fourteen people hurried toward us along the pier. Six pairs of men in dark coats, cinched at the waist. Most were dark-haired, tan, and lean. A few had short beards. Each carried a rifle over his shoulder and a dagger on his belt. They looked like a flock of dark ravens flying in two lines.

Two women walked in front of them. The first wore a dark blue blouse and jeans. She was about my age, dark-haired, her skin a light bronze, her hair put away into a braid. Her face was interesting, with large, bold features: big eyes, wide mouth, a sharply drawn nose. The girl next to her looked to be on the cusp of her twenties. Shorter, paler, with a slender waist, she wore a white dress. The wind tugged at the cascade of her chocolate-brown hair and her clothes, and the diaphanous fabric flared, making her appear ethereal and light. She all but floated above the rough concrete.

The girl waved. "Curran!"

She knew him.

Curran swore under his breath. "I'll be damned. They dragged her into this."

Apparently he knew her, too.

"Curran!" She waved again, standing on her toes, and hurried toward us.

"Lorelei?" Curran called out.

The girl smiled. Wow. The night just got a bit brighter.

The sailors lowered the gangplank and Curran started down the moment it clanged against the pier. Apparently he couldn't wait to meet her.

"Who is Lorelei?" I asked quietly.

"Lorelei Wilson," Mahon said. "Daughter of the Ice Fury's alpha."

Lorelei's father led the Alaskan pack, the biggest shapeshifter group in the United States. The one who had left with her mother when Wilson and his European wife divorced. Well, wasn't that just peachy.

"How do you tempt the Beast Lord?" Barabas murmured. "Simple. Offer him a shapeshifter princess."

Aunt B reached over and gently popped him on the back of his head.

"I hate her already," Andrea told me. "George hates her too, right, George?"

"I think she is adorable." George volunteered next to me. "We should give her milk and cookies, and if she promises to be quiet, she can sit at the big people's table."

"Show some respect," Mahon said. "She is the heir to Ice Fury."

George arched her eyebrows at him. "Really, Dad?"

On the pier, Curran reached the procession. The woman in blue bowed. Lorelei stepped forward, her arms raised for a hug, then stopped abruptly, as if catching herself, and also bowed. Curran said something. She smiled again.

I touched Slayer's hilt just to make sure it was there.

"Diplomatic, Kate," Barabas suggested quietly. "Diplomatic."

I leaned close to him. "Find out who invited her, what are her attachments, and if she has strings, who is pulling."

He nodded.

I went down the gangplank. The rough concrete was dry under my feet. I managed a slow, deliberate march and the pier seemed to last forever. Did it need to be this long? Were they going to park a carrier here?

I finally got within hearing range.

"You grew up," Curran was saying.

"It's been ten years." Lorelei's voice had a light trace of an accent. Not quite French, not quite Italian. "I just turned twenty-one."

I closed in on them. Lorelei had striking eyes, large and pale blue, framed in dense eyelashes. High cheekbones, softened by smooth skin and just a touch of roundness that came from being young; a narrow, petite nose, a full pink mouth. Her hair, a rich brown, fell down her shoulders in relaxed waves. She radiated youth, beauty, and health. She looked . . . fresh. I was only five years older than her, but standing next to her, I suddenly felt old.

Curran was looking at her. Not in the same way he looked at me, but he was looking. An odd feeling flared in me, hot and angry, prickling my throat from the inside with hot sharp needles, and I realized it was jealousy. I guess there was a first time for everything.

"Have you seen my father?" Lorelei asked. "How is he?"

"I saw him last year," Curran said. "He's the same as always: tough and ornery."

I came to stand next to him.

Lorelei raised her eyebrows. Her eyes widened, and a sheen of pale green rolled over her irises. "You must be the human Consort."

Yes, that's me, the human invalid. "My name is Kate."

"Kate," she repeated, as if tasting the word. "It is an honor to meet you."

Curran was smiling at her, that handsome hot smile that usually made my day better. Pushing Lorelei into the ocean wouldn't be diplomatic, even if I really wanted to do it. "Likewise."

"I've heard so much about you. But where are my manners? You must be hungry and tired."

The woman in blue stepped forward, moving with a shapeshifter's grace. Her eyes flashed green, catching the light from the ship. So these were the local werejackals Barabas had mentioned. Her eyes told me she'd been there and done that, and got a bloody T-shirt for her trouble.

The woman in blue bowed. "My name is Hibla. I'm here to be your guide." She indicated the men next to her. "We are Djigits of Gagra."

I had read up on Abkhazia. "Djigit" meant a skilled rider or a fierce warrior. The djigits looked back at me, the light of the evening sun catching their eyes. Yep, everyone was a shapeshifter except for me.

"We will escort you to your quarters when you are ready," Hibla said.

Curran waved at the ship. Our small pack began its descent down to the pier. A few moments and they stood behind us.

Lorelei bowed to Mahon. "Greetings to the Kodiak of Atlanta."

Mahon grinned into his beard. "What happened? Last time I saw you, you were this big." He held out his arm at his waist level.

Lorelei smiled. "I wasn't *that* short."

Mahon chuckled.

Aunt B was next, smiling so bright, I needed shades. Her voice was sweet enough to spread on toast. "So you are Mike Wilson's daughter. He must be so proud. What a beautiful girl you are."

"Thank you." Lorelei almost glowed.

Oh, you naive thing. When a bouda smiles at you, that's not a good sign. Especially that particular bouda.

"On behalf of Gagra, I'm here to extend the hospitality of my beautiful city to you," Hibla said. "Gagra welcomes you with all of its warmth, its lakes and waterfalls, its beaches and orchards. But be forewarned, if you come here with violent intentions, we will leave your corpses for the crows. We have no problem murdering every single one of you."

"Awesome speech," Keira told her. Jim's sister was smiling, and it didn't look friendly.

"Thank you. I worked hard on it. Please, follow me."

We trailed her down the pier and onto the road paved with stone. Hibla kept a brisk pace, reciting in a throaty, lightly accented voice. "Welcome to Abkhazia. The city of Gagra is the warmest place on the Black Sea. We have a wonderful microclimate with warm winters and pleasant summers. You will find the most exquisite landmarks here."

It was like she was reading an invisible travel guide.

Curran was looking at Lorelei as we walked.

"We grow a variety of fruit: peaches, persimmons, apricots, pomegranates, tangerines, lemons, and grapes. Our region is famous for its wines."

That's nice. Maybe I could find a wine bottle hard enough to hit Curran over the head and knock some sense into him.

"What pack do you serve?" Barabas asked.

"The Djigits of Gagra are not affiliated with any of our guests. Our allegiance is to the local pack and to the lord of the castle."

It was as if I had stepped into a different world. Across the ocean there were crumbling skyscrapers. Here there were castles and lords. Well, technically the Keep was kind of a castle and people did call Curran *lord*, but at home shapeshifters said it with simple efficiency, the way one would say *sir*. Here it was said with a solemn reverence.

"Is the lord of the castle a shapeshifter?" Curran asked.

"No, he's a human," Lorelei said.

"Lord Megobari is a friend," Hibla said. "Our economy was always driven by tourism. After the Shift, the region collapsed. We had been battered by natural disasters and war. Our city and our lives were in ruins. The Megobari family helped us. They built hospitals, they restored our roads, and they brought business to us. They don't ask anything in return except for our protection, which is freely and gladly given."

Okay. The Megobari family were clearly saints, and the local jackal pack would die to keep them breathing. Considering how the men glared at us, we had to make sure not to offend the host, because these djigit shapeshifters took their duties deadly seriously.

We all followed Hibla through the town. The feylanterns in Gagra glowed pale lavender, turning the solid stone of the buildings into a faint mirage. Magic flowed down the narrow, curving roads. Neat little streets, some cobbled, some still bearing crumbling pavement, ran along the side of the mountain, all sloping up, bordered by houses of all shapes and sizes. Persian, Greek, and modern architecture collided, like wakes from three different ships.

We passed a stately mansion that could've been built for a Moorish prince. It rose, flanked by palms, three stories of narrow arched windows, textured parapets, and stone wall carvings that looked as light and delicate as lace. At one point it must've been glowing white, but now it had shed its paint, and green walls showed through. A Greek building of Doric columns the color of sand followed, and immediately after, the ruins of a modern apartment building lay scattered over the mountain slope. The rest of the world seemed a thousand miles away. If we ever got tired of the Pack or living in anticipation of being found by Roland, we could find something like this, an isolated quiet corner of the world. Nobody would ever find us here.

Well, nobody but Lorelei.

"When you saw my father, did he mention me?"

"No," Curran told her. "It wasn't a social meeting. I'm sure he thinks of you often."

Another once-beautiful and now-gutted building. I counted the stories. Seven. Too tall. Magic hated tall modern buildings and attacked them with extreme prejudice. This building was definitely abandoned—the black holes of its empty windows showed a charred interior. When magic waves took down a structure, they gnawed it to dust first. This one showed no signs of post-Shift damage.

"What happened here?" I asked.

"War," Hibla said.

"Who did you fight with?" George asked.

"Ourselves. Abkhazia is on the border between Russia and Georgia. Fifty years ago they fought. Neighbors turned on their neighbors. Families split. Russia won. The city was cleansed." She spat the word as if it were studded with broken glass. "Everyone who was Georgian was killed or exiled." She nodded at another building with boarded-up windows. "The city was scarred forever. The magic has destroyed the other buildings, but the war ruins remain."

"Such a shame," Aunt B said. "Your city was beautiful."

"She will be beautiful again," Hibla said.

We kept climbing, higher and higher. The city road narrowed. Dense trees on both sides blocked the view, their branches braided together with vines. Tiny fireflies floated on the breeze. Abruptly the trees ended and we stepped out on a plaza. To the left, far below, endless sea lapped at the narrow ribbon of the shore. Straight ahead, mountains curved gently to the waves.

"The castle." Hibla pointed to the far right, behind us. I

turned. An enormous stone castle crowned the top of the mountain, its stone walls rising like the natural extension of the living rock. Wide rectangular towers soared under pale blue roofs. The long narrow flags flying on the thin spires from the huge building of the main keep caught the last rays of the setting sun and glowed as if they were on fire.

"How old is the castle?" Mahon asked.

"We celebrated its twenty-year anniversary last fall."

Wow. Post-Shift. The amount of labor this structure took had to be staggering. How the hell did they even get that much stone up the mountain?

"Please." Hibla invited us with a sweep of her hand. "Up this road."

We went up the mountain at a brisk pace. Any faster and I'd have had to start running. The path was steep and the light was dying fast. Ten minutes later I broke a sweat. The shape-shifters around me seemed fresh as daisies.

"It must be very tiring for the Consort," Lorelei said next to me.

That was a bit unexpected. Was she actually concerned?

"The road is steep and she doesn't have the benefit of night vision."

She was looking at Curran. No, she wasn't checking if I was okay. She was talking about me as if I weren't even there. The way one would say, *Is your little dog thirsty? Does she need a bowl of water?*

"Perhaps a mount could be brought . . . ?" Lorelei suggested.

Out of a corner of my eye I saw both Barabas and George freeze. *Yes, I know I've been insulted. Settle down.* "Thank you for your concern. I can manage."

"Please, it's no trouble at all. You could hurt yourself. I know that even something minor like a twisted ankle would present a big problem for a human . . ."

Do not punch the pack princess; do not punch the pack princess . . .

"We wouldn't want you to struggle to keep up."

Okay, she went too far. I gave her a nice big smile.

Curran's face snapped into a neutral expression. "We just got here, baby. It's too early for you to start killing people."

Lorelei's eyes widened. "I didn't mean any offense."

Yeah, you did.

"I'm so sorry. I was only concerned. Please forgive me."

And now anything I said with any hint of hostility would make me look like an ass. She'd outmaneuvered me. Fine. There was always the next time. "Don't worry about it."

We rounded the bend. The castle loomed in front of us, shockingly huge. You could pack at least two Keeps within its walls. Thick walls, too. Had to be more than a couple of feet deep.

Hibla raised her head and howled, a high-pitched ghostly jackal howl. The sound rolled past us, streaming to the sky. Other howls answered. Metal clanged and the massive gates swung open.

Hibla bowed. "My lord and lady. Welcome to Castle Megobari."

I took a deep breath and walked next to Curran into the castle.

I WAS RIGHT. THE WALLS WERE SIX FEET THICK. I counted six ballistas and four high-caliber antipersonnel guns on the walls, and that was just what I could see. This castle was built to withstand an assault from supernatural assailants. The Megobari family had some serious cash to throw around, and they'd used it to arm themselves to the teeth.

I elbowed Curran. "Their castle is bigger."

He winked at me. "Mine is taller. It's not the size of the castle. It's what you do with it."

No obvious guards manned the gate, but as we passed under the portcullis, I felt watched. I was a hundred percent sure that if I made a sudden movement, someone would send an arrow my way. The question was, would they bother with a warning shot? I didn't especially want to test that theory.

We crossed the inner courtyard and followed Hibla into the main building. After the city, I had half expected carvings and moldings, but the inside of the castle was as devoid of ornamentation as the outside. Brown stone, straight-as-an-arrow hallways, arched windows. No doors but some niches, positioned in such a way that if the castle was breached, a couple of fighters with ranged firepower could hold off a flood of attackers. Everything was functional, solid, and meticulously clean.

We passed a pair of shapeshifter men in the hallway, both

blond. They stared at us with obvious hostility. I stared back. Looking is free. Touching will cost you an arm or a leg. Your choice.

"Your rooms are on the third floor," Hibla said. "Dinner will be served at ten."

"Late for a human," I said. In the Keep we typically ate dinner around nine. Shapeshifters weren't early risers, since they tended to stay up half of the night.

"The Megobari family respects the customs of its guests," Hibla said.

"I will see all of you at dinner." Lorelei said, looking directly at Curran.

"Looking forward to it," Curran said.

I felt an urge to stab something and squished it. Lorelei retreated down the hallway.

"Where is Desandra?" Curran asked.

"She is in her quarters, on the third floor also," Hibla said.

Curran turned. "Hibla, we need to see Desandra. Now."

Andrea passed her bag to Raphael and came to stand by me. Derek came to stand by Curran.

"Very well." Hibla said something in a lilting language.

The daggered dozen split: eight went with the rest of the group, led by an older man, and four came with us. We climbed the same stairs, and then Hibla turned right, while the rest of the shapeshifters turned left. We followed her to a metal door, guarded by a man and a woman in the same dark djigit coats. They moved aside as Hibla unlocked the door.

The stench of rotten citrus washed over me. Not good.

We stepped into a huge room. It was the size of my entire first apartment with all the walls knocked out. The vast ceiling rose to fully thirty feet in height, and gloom obscured the massive wooden beams running high above. Clothes lay strewn all over the floor, some shredded, some stained, punctuated by crumpled papers, food-stained plates, and shards of broken glass. A large wooden bed piled high with pillows and clumped blankets stood against one wall. A pregnant woman sat on it, her long hair tangled and dangling down over her purple dress. She looked up. Her irises shone with orange shapeshifter fluorescence.

I looked at Andrea. She looked back at me. I saw the exact same thought on her face: this job was going to suck.

"Hello, Desandra," Curran said.

"Fuck you."

"That's nice," Curran said. "It smells like rotten food in here."

Desandra shrugged. "Why are you here?"

No trace of an accent. She spoke like she was born in the United States.

"We're here to take care of you."

"That's bullshit and you know it." She bared her teeth. "You'll make the deal with whatever clan pays you more and sell these little parasites in my stomach. So go, make your deals. Nothing will change for me. Nothing ever changes for me."

"Are you done?" Curran asked.

"You could've taken me away from all this," she snarled.

"You wouldn't last a week in Atlanta," he said.

She stabbed her finger in my direction. "And she's better? After all of your grandstanding, and oh, I'm the Beast Lord and nobody is good enough for me, you mated with a human? A human? You're just like them." She waved her arm at Hibla and the djigits. "You don't give a fuck about what happens to your human wife if she's challenged. Why don't you just leave?"

Muscles played on Curran's jaw. "Think what you want, but I'll stay here and I will protect you."

"Do you really think they'll give you panacea for it? Come on, even you're not that stupid."

Gold flashed in Curran's irises. I had to stomp on this fast before it spiraled out of control.

I put my hand on Curran's shoulder. "I think it would be best if you gave us a little space."

He glanced at me.

"And if you don't mind, I'd appreciate it if you sent Doolittle up here."

Curran shook his head and looked at Derek. "Close the room. Nobody comes in unless Kate says so."

"Yes, my lord," Derek said.

Curran strode out of the room.

"That's right!" Desandra called out. "Walk away!"

Derek parked himself in the doorway.

I surveyed the bedroom. I'd seen this kind of mess before

in Julie's room, when she went through an "I don't want to go to school" stage. "Hibla, why is this room dirty?"

"The lady won't permit us to clean it," Hibla said. "Her father ordered it cleaned once, and we did. The lady returned it to its previous state within a week."

Just as I'd thought. I turned to Desandra. "May I come closer?"

She stared at me.

I waited.

"Sure." She shrugged.

I crossed the room, stepping on clothes—there was no choice. Something crunched under my feet. I sat next to her on the bed.

"I get what you're doing. You don't feel in control of your life, but this bedroom is your space and you can do whatever you want here. Here you're in control. Unfortunately, having food on the floor isn't healthy. It rots. Mold grows on it and gets in your lungs." And the mess made her that much harder to guard.

She sneered at me. "I'm a shapeshifter."

"Shapeshifters are resistant to disease but not immune. Rotten food also gives bugs a place to breed, and it smells bad. Broken glass isn't safe for anyone to walk on. People who bring you food may not always be shapeshifters. They could be hurt, and they're only doing their job."

"I don't care."

"Having a dirty room doesn't really help you regain control over your life. That fight is out there." I pointed at the open door. "The mess just makes you appear deranged, which signals to people that it's okay to treat you as if you're not a person."

Desandra dug her hands into her matted hair. "What do you want from me?"

"May I have your permission to clean this room?"

"Why do you care?"

"Because I take pride in my job. Right now my job is to take care of you and keep you safe. This bedroom is unsafe for you and your future children. The mess also makes it difficult to protect you."

Desandra stared at me. "And what if I rip out your throat?"

I dug through my memory to fights with Julie. "Why would you do that? I didn't do anything mean to you."

"What if I say no?"

Andrea shrugged. "If you say no, then we won't clean the room. But I do have to tell you that the room smells bad, and that smell has settled in your clothes and hair."

At least in the United States, telling a shapeshifter they smelled bad was the ultimate insult. If that didn't motivate her, nothing would.

Desandra growled in my face.

"I'm on your side," I told her. "If you want to demonstrate that you're in control of yourself, you might want to take it into consideration."

"I don't want you to clean anything."

"Very well." I rose.

I made it ten steps to the door before she said, "Fine. Clean it."

"Thank you." I turned to Hibla. "Please bring trash bins, cleaning supplies, and hampers."

Desandra growled. "Are you always such a doormat?"

"Yes."

"So you always ask permission for everything?"

"She's the alpha of the Atlanta Pack," Derek said without turning. "She killed twenty-two shapeshifters in eleven days to be one, and she has the same power as the Beast Lord. She doesn't have to ask anyone's permission to do anything."

That wasn't exactly helpful. "I'm here for one purpose only: to keep you safe. I act in your best interests. I don't care who is born first and I won't be taking any bribes. I will do my best to accommodate you, but when your safety is on the line, I'll do whatever I need to do to keep you safe. If it means I have to hog-tie you and stuff you into a bathtub, I'll do it and not worry about your feelings."

Desandra sighed.

Hibla reappeared with bags and a cart filled with cleaning supplies, including gardening gloves. I put them on and began picking up the trash. Andrea joined me. Desandra watched us for about five minutes, trying to ignore the fact that we were there, then got off the bed and started stomping around and picking up her clothes.

That was how Doolittle found us, on our hands and knees, scooping up trash.

"What's going on?"

I straightened. "This is Dr. Doolittle. He is the Pack's medmage."

"Doolittle?" Desandra peered at him. "For real?"

"It's what I choose to call myself." Doolittle peered at her, then looked around the room. "Oh my. Now then, young lady, why are you dirty?"

Desandra sat on the floor and looked at him with a helpless expression on her face. "Because I like it."

"I do realize that this is a castle," Doolittle said in that patient soothing voice that made it impossible to say no. "However, I have used the restroom and it appears that modern plumbing was successfully installed."

"You can't make me clean myself," Desandra declared.

"My lady, you are not two years old. In fact, you appear to have reached maturity, and I'm reasonably certain that nobody can make you do anything you don't want to do. Come on up to the bed, please."

I held my breath. Desandra sighed again, got up off the floor, and sat on the bed. I exhaled quietly. Doolittle put his fingers on her wrist, counting her pulse.

"Incoming," Derek said.

"Who is it?"

"Jarek Kral."

I joined him at the doorway. Andrea moved to the middle of the room, between us and Desandra, and checked her crossbow.

The man I had seen in the photograph during Barabas's briefing strode down the hallway toward us. He seemed bigger in person, taller, wider, with the type of raw strength that usually meant a nasty fight.

I turned to Desandra. "Do you want to see your father?"

"Does it matter?" she asked, defeat plain on her face.

"It does to me."

"Then no. I don't want to see him."

Jarek Kral reached the door. This close the photograph really did him justice: same wavy brown hair, same large, roughly hewn face. His features could've been more refined, if they weren't tinted with cruelty. I knew the type. He was the type of man who could explode over the smallest thing and the explosion would be violent.

The sneer was bigger in person as well.

He reached the door. "Move," he said in an accented voice.

"Your daughter doesn't want to visit now," I said.

He stared at me with dark eyes under heavy lids, as if he just now realized I was blocking his way. "Who are you?

"You may call me Kate. I'm the Consort of the Beast Lord."

"Step aside." His eyes flashed green.

"No."

Behind me someone gasped.

His voice boomed. "Who told you you can do this?"

And here we go, straight into the lake of drama without taking our clothes off first. "You did." I pulled the contract from my pocket. "This document says I must serve your daughter's best interests. She determined it's in her best interests not to speak with you right now. This is your signature. It gives me all the authority I need."

He snatched the paper from my hand and ripped it.

"I have another copy," I said.

"I'll rip out your throat!" he snarled.

Like father, like daughter. "If you try, you won't live to see your grandchildren and my job will be done. I'll get to go home early. So please do try. I miss my house already."

His eyebrows came together. His upper lip trembled.

"An assault on the Consort will be treated as an act of war," Derek said.

A guttural snarl ripped from Jarek. Clearly, he hadn't bothered to look up "personal restraint" in the dictionary.

I reached behind me and put my hand on Slayer's hilt. "This is your last warning. Do not attempt to enter."

"What's going on?" A man ran up the stairs. He was blond, tall, and muscular, with features that would make an angel proud—Desandra's first husband, Radomil, from the Volkodavi pack. A woman followed him, slightly older than me, slender, with a wealth of golden hair braided back from her face.

"Stay out of this!" Jarek snarled. "You've done enough."

Radomil shot back something in a language I didn't understand. A torrent of words spilled from Jarek.

"You're a pig!" Radomil snarled back in English. "A filthy pig. Leave Desandra alone!"

"Get out of my way!" Jarek roared.

"If Kral doesn't abide by the agreement, why should we?" the blond woman said.

I let them scream at each other. It didn't affect me unless one of them tried to enter the room.

A tall, dark-haired man closed in on us. Where Radomil's face had a healthy, sun-tanned glow, this man radiated intelligence and weary awareness. He saw Jarek and Radomil. His dark eyebrows came together. His lips narrowed into a hard line. Yellow light rolled over his irises. Uh-oh.

The man accelerated. It had to be one of the Belve Ravennati brothers, but which one I couldn't tell.

Without slowing down, the Italian raised his fist and swung at Jarek. The big man moved aside and the Italian hammered a punch into Radomil instead. Radomil snarled like an animal and lunged at the Italian.

More people flooded the hallway from the left, an older dark-haired woman in the lead.

Jarek spat something. Radomil and the Italian grappled, snarling.

"If they change shape, we bar the door," I murmured.

Derek nodded.

Radomil shoved his opponent forward, tripping the Italian. The dark-haired man dropped to the ground with a lupine growl. Any moment now they'd go furry, and then things would be infinitely worse.

An eerie hyena cackle rolled through the hallway, a high-pitched, insane laugh that made you shiver.

Suddenly everyone stopped. Aunt B stood in the hallway.

"So this is what our European brothers and sisters have been reduced to," she said, her voice carrying through the castle. "Brawling in the hallways like spoiled schoolchildren. No wonder you had to send for our help."

Go, Aunt B!

The alpha of Clan Bouda looked at the dark-haired woman. "Hello, Isabella. It's been a long time."

"Hello, Beatrice," the dark-haired woman squeezed through her teeth.

"Is that your son on the floor?"

Isabella snapped a short command. The dark-haired man rolled to his feet and strode over to her. Isabella slapped him.

The sound rang through the hallway. The Italians turned and left without another word.

I looked at Jarek Kral. He pointed his finger at me, opened his mouth, clamped it shut, turned, and walked away.

The blond woman said something to Radomil. He pulled away from her and stalked off.

"You must forgive my brother," the blond woman said. "He is a very kind man. He just doesn't understand politics." Her eyebrows came together. She pointed over my shoulder. "Who is that man?"

"He is a medic," Andrea answered.

"A medic? Is something wrong?"

"No," I said. "He is just performing a routine physical exam."

She actually looked concerned. "Is he going to draw blood? Desandra, I can hold your hand if you need me."

"It's fine," Desandra called.

I pulled my official Order voice out of the mental trunk where I'd kept it stashed for months, ever since I quit my tenure with the Knights of Merciful Aid. "I'm sorry, I have to ask you to leave."

"Fine, fine. Just . . . Don't torture her. She's been through enough." The woman turned and hurried down the stairs after Radomil. I glanced over my shoulder. Doolittle was holding a large syringe filled with pinkish liquid. Desandra petted her stomach.

"What is this for?" I asked.

"Amniocentesis," Doolittle said. "It's a routine screen of amniotic fluid. We want to make sure everything is proceeding as it's supposed to."

Aunt B approached us. "Well, that went nicely."

"You told my father no," Desandra said to me.

"Sure."

"He'll kill you for it," Desandra said.

"He may find it much harder than it appears, dear," Aunt B told her. "Dinner is coming up. Kate, you may want to change. You smell like the sea. You two go. Derek and I will watch after Desandra while you're changing."

I turned to Derek. "I will send Eduardo. When Desandra is ready to go, the two of you will follow her. Nobody comes in the room if she doesn't want to see them."

"Got it," Derek said.

"The rooms are just down the hall," Aunt B said. "Here, I'll walk partway with you then head back."

We strode down the hallway.

"I told you so," Aunt B said quietly.

"Told me what?"

"Please, Kate. The fresh young thing on the pier? She even wore white."

"And?"

"Nothing at all, dear. Just reflecting on the color. How virginal and bridal."

Yes. I'd noticed. If they were trying to influence Curran by shoving Lorelei under his nose, they weren't very subtle about it.

"Yours is the first door on the right. Andrea, you and Raphael are across from them. The rest of us are just down the hall," Aunt B said. "The sound really carries through here. You can hear practically everything, so if you call we'll come running."

Got it. Nothing said in the rooms would be private, and our hosts were likely listening really hard. "Good to know."

"I've checked and the dinner is a formal affair. Do wear a dress, Kate."

I killed a growl, and Andrea and I went down the hallway.

"We've worked worse jobs," Andrea said.

"Mm-hm. This whole place doesn't feel right to me."

"I'm with you," she said.

We reached my door. I waited until Andrea opened hers across the hall and went inside, and then I stepped into our room and shut the door behind me.

A sizable room, as far as bedrooms went, with tapestries and rugs on the stone walls. An open door offered access to the bathroom on the left. A large wooden poster canopy bed waited in the center, complete with silk pillows and gauzy purple curtains. It looked like something out of the historical romances Andrea liked to read.

Curran came out of the bathroom.

I nodded at the bed. "Someone robbed an ancient music video."

"I know. It creaks like a sonovabitch, too."

"Great. If we decide to make love, we might as well just get down to it in the hallway. Half of the castle will know about it anyway."

Curran closed the distance between us. His voice was a quiet whisper in my ear. "There are no peepholes that I can see, but someone is listening to us. I heard him breathing through the wall."

So we were trapped in this stone cage, with a pack of unstable shapeshifters, trying to protect a woman in need of urgent psychological help, and spies were listening to our every breath.

I put my arms around Curran and leaned my head against his shoulder. "Have I ever told you how much I like the Keep?"

"No."

"I love it."

He grinned. "Even the stairs?"

"Especially the stairs." The stairs separated our top floor from everybody else, and the walls were soundproof.

He kissed me. His lips sealed my mouth and the world stopped for a long moment. When we came up for air, I didn't care if anybody was listening to us. Little golden sparks danced in Curran's eyes. He didn't care either.

"Do we have time?" he asked.

I looked at the clock. Twenty before ten. "No. We'll be late."

"Tonight, then."

I grinned at him. "It's a date."

Guard Desandra, get the panacea, go home. A simple plan. All we had to do was get through it.

THE DINNER TOOK PLACE IN A COLOSSAL GREAT hall, and I walked into it with my hand on Curran's arm. The Beast Lord wore a black suit and a gray shirt. Curran always stopped me in my tracks, whether he wore jeans and a T-shirt, sweatpants, or nothing at all, but this was new. Custom-cut, the suit flattered him while allowing for freedom of movement, and if he had to change shape, the weak seams ensured that the suit would come apart with minimal effort.

In all of our time together I had seen him in a formal suit exactly twice, including today. Curran could be described in many ways: dangerous, powerful . . . insufferable. "Elegant" usually wasn't one of the adjectives used, and as he walked next to me, I wished I had a camera so I could commemorate the moment. And then blackmail him with it.

He shrugged again.

"You keep doing it, the suit will fall apart."

"I should've worn jeans."

"Then I'd look ridiculous next to you." I should've worn jeans, too.

"Baby, you never look ridiculous."

"Smart man," Aunt B volunteered behind us.

I wore a black dress. Like Curran's suit, it was custom-made for me by the Pack's tailors specifically for the trip. The elastic fabric hugged me like a glove, giving a deceiving impression that it was constraining. The artfully draped skirt fell in straight lines, hiding the fact that it opened enough to let me kick an attacker taller than me in the head, and the diagonal strap over my right shoulder ensured that the dress wouldn't fall off if I had to move fast. The dress also had to be doing wonders for my butt, because Curran had managed to run his hand down my back twice since we left our rooms.

But even the best dress offered no way to hide Slayer, so I didn't bother. The dress came with a built-in fabric sheath, lined with leather, and my sword rested securely against my back. I'd left my hair braided. Plain black shoes with a low heel fit my feet like slippers. I would've felt better in my boots, but boots didn't go with the dress. Even I had standards.

I did have to surrender my knives, but I wore a bracelet on each wrist and a long necklace, all made of braided silver. They looked like strips of chain mail and weighed as much. Curran insisted on my new fancy jewelry. Given that we were trapped in a castle filled with hostile shapeshifters I didn't fight him on it.

Behind us Desandra walked in, sandwiched between Bara-bas and Derek. Aunt B, Mahon, and George followed, then Andrea and Raphael. Raphael was a picture of urbane elegance in black, while Andrea wore a deep rust-red. It looked like blood and she was a knockout.

Doolittle declined to go to dinner and remained behind in his quarters, and I asked Eduardo and Keira to stay with him as well. This place was making me paranoid. They locked themselves in and barred the door before we left. Hopefully Keira wouldn't decide to explore her buffalo steak fantasies.

Vast, with towering walls, the great hall seemed cavernous. Four big tables, each large enough to seat at least twenty people, stood in two long lines, leaving a large space between them. Toward the opposite end of the chamber, a head table, shaped like a rectangular horseshoe, waited on a raised platform.

I scanned the room, looking for problems. Three exits: the one we just came through, one on the left, and one on the right, each manned by a pair of djigits. No matter where I sat, unless it was at the head table, my back would be to one of the doors. Ugh.

On the left a discreet stairway led to a minstrel's gallery, a high indoor balcony that spanned the length of the entire left wall. Shadows shrouded the gallery. I saw no movement, but if I wanted to kill someone, I'd put a sniper up there.

None of this was making me feel warm and fuzzy.

About fifty people milled about the hall, some talking in small groups, others by themselves. Men wore suits and tuxedos. Women wore gowns. Most eyes flashed with a shapeshifter glow. People turned and looked at us, looked at Curran, looked at the handle of my sword protruding over my shoulder. A few men looked lower at my chest. They were shapeshifters and notoriously difficult to kill, while I was a human. The fact that I carried a sharpened strip of metal on my back didn't worry them any. I was an oddity, the human mate. They appraised me like a horse at a livestock market, and my breasts were clearly making a bigger impression than my sword.

Curran locked his teeth.

"We just got here," I whispered. "It's too early for you to start killing people."

"It's never too early for me," he said.

"Double standard much?"

Hibla met us halfway across the hall and led us to our seats. Curran and I sat at the head table on the right side of an oversized wooden chair that wanted very much to be a throne and had to belong to the head of the table. Place of honor. Whoop-de-doo. At least my back was to a solid wall.

Curran took his seat, I sat next to him, Desandra sat next to me, and Andrea parked herself on the other side of Desandra and looked at the balcony. Raphael sat next to her, and Mahon and Aunt B sat next to him. George stood behind her father. Barabas stood behind me.

"You're hovering," I told him.

"I'm supposed to hover."

I settled in the large chair. The minstrel's gallery loomed above us to the right. It bothered me. I couldn't see into it. If someone shot at us, I wouldn't know until it was too late. We might as well have pinned a target to Desandra's head.

"Hibla?"

Our guide leaned toward me. "Yes, lady?"

"Could you tell me who chose these seats?"

"Lord Megobari."

Great. Changing seats would likely offend him to death, and besides, all seats at this table offered a great target from the gallery.

Curran leaned to me. "What's the matter?"

"I don't like the gallery. She isn't safe."

People turned toward an entrance directly across from us.

"Someone's coming," Barabas murmured.

Curran inhaled. "Kral."

Jarek Kral walked into the room. He wore a black suit and walked as if everyone in the room owed him allegiance. A few people glared back, while others tried to fade into the woodwork. Four men walked behind him, moving in unison, a well-honed unit. The way they scanned the room for threats telegraphed experience. Wasn't surprising. Jarek didn't strike me as the type to make friends.

Jarek made a beeline for our table and took a seat on the other side of the throne. Two of his guys sat next to him, the other two stood behind him. Barabas had given us a basic rundown on Kral's people. This was his inner circle: two brothers with the last name Guba, a middle-aged bald man who looked like he could run through solid walls, and Renok, Kral's second-in-command, a tall shapeshifter in his midthirties with a boxer's jaw contoured by a short dark beard.

Jarek looked at Curran. "I see you grew up, boy."

Did he just call Curran *boy*? Yes, he did.

"I see you grew old," Curran said. "You look smaller than I remember."

"I'm still big enough for you."

"You never were, and now you never will be. You're getting on, Jarek."

"Last time I wanted to kill you, but you had Wilson with

you. Now you're all alone. I *will* kill you this time." Jarek smiled, a controlled baring of teeth.

Curran smiled back. "I wish you'd scrape enough balls together to try. I'm already bored."

If Jarek managed to provoke Curran into physical violence, the fault would be with Curran. Even if Curran won, we'd have to go home empty-handed and Desandra likely wouldn't live long enough to give birth.

The Belve Ravennati entered the room and took their seats on the left side of the horseshoe. Aunt B waved at Isabella. Isabella studiously ignored her. Her two sons sat by her. The Italian brothers looked very similar: both dark-haired, both with intelligent, sharp eyes and a carefully shaped sprinkling of dark stubble on their jaws. The taller, leaner one had striking eyes, pale hazel and framed with dark eyelashes. They stood out in sharp contrast to his nearly black hair. The other was shorter, more compact, with dark eyes. One of them was Gerardo and the other Ignazio, but I couldn't remember which was which. I couldn't recall which had married Desandra either, but I was pretty sure the shorter of the brothers was the one who got slapped.

I leaned over to Desandra. "Which one is the father?"

"The handsome one," she said, her voice filled with mourning.

Thanks, that helps a lot. "Hazel eyes or brown?"

"Hazel. Gerardo."

So the shorter, slapped one, was Ignazio.

A moment later the Volkodavi came through the right exit and took their seats on the right side of the horseshoe. Good idea. Minimized the chances of them lunging across the table at the Belve Ravennati and trying to murder each other with their forks.

People were taking their seats. The dinner was about to start.

"You're not fit to sit at this table," Jarek said.

Round two.

"Make me move," Curran said.

"You're nothing. You will always be nothing," Jarek said. "Weak like your father."

You bastard. I reached over under the table and touched Curran's hand. He squeezed my fingers.

"My father has a son who rules the largest pack in the Southeast of the United States," Curran said. "How big is Budek's territory? Oh wait. Your son doesn't have a territory, because you murdered him."

A string of servants came in, rolling enormous barrels.

"Is that beer in the barrels?"

"They're called casks, Kate," Barabas said quietly behind me. "And I believe they're full of wine."

Lyc-V, the shapeshifter virus, treated alcohol like poison and tried to get rid of it the moment it hit the bloodstream. But if a shapeshifters drank fast enough and in large volume, they managed to hit a buzzed stage. Besides, there were some humans in the hall. This place already was a pressure cooker: one wrong word and it would explode. Why the hell would anyone want to add alcohol to this mix?

"The only reason you rule at all is because your country is filled with gutless dogs," Jarek said. "Here you're not fit to scrape shit off my boots. Come over here and I'll teach you what a real alpha is."

He just wouldn't shut the hell up.

"You've been scheming and plotting for thirty years and your territory will fit into mine ten times," Curran said, his tone slightly bored. "I could give the same amount away and not miss it."

On the left Gerardo was glaring at Radomil across the table. The wine barrels kept coming in. Could this get any worse?

"You had a chance to join me," Jarek said. "You spat on it. And you think you can come here and tell me what to do with my daughter?"

"Make way for the lord of the castle," a man called out. The djigits at the entrance directly opposite us came to attention.

"Your daughter is a grown woman," Curran said. "She can speak for herself."

"Until she belongs to another man, she is mine to do with as I please," Jarek said.

That does it. I leaned forward. "Hey, you. Either put your claws where your mouth is or shut the fuck up. Nobody wants to hear you yip."

Jarek's eyes bulged. Green flared in the depths of his irises, an insane hot flame. He opened his mouth but nothing came out.

"Yes, just like that," I told him. "Less talking, more quiet."

It dawned on me that Curran was sitting completely still, staring straight ahead with focused intensity.

"Lord Megobari," a man announced.

I turned. At the far entrance, between two djigits, Hugh d'Ambray strode into the hall.

CHAPTER 7

———◆———

THIS WASN'T HAPPENING. THIS WAS A HALLUCINA-
tion, caused by stress. Hugh d'Ambray, Roland's warlord,
wasn't here. He was back in the United States serving my biological father. This was his long-lost twin with the same
height, build, and hair, who knew nothing about me.

Hugh looked straight at me and smiled. It was the smile of
a fisherman who'd just pulled a prized catch out of the water
and into his boat.

No, it was him. All this time I'd been breaking my brain
trying to figure out what Curran or the Pack had done to be
targeted for this trap. It wasn't Curran or the Pack. It was *me*.

"Please rise for the lord of the castle," the same man
called out.

People around me stood up. I locked my teeth and forced
myself to move. Curran was squeezing my hand so hard it hurt.

Damn it all to hell. Could I not catch a break just once in
my life?

Hugh waved. His voice carried through the hall, a kind of
voice that could be quiet and intimate or cut through the
clamor of a battle. "Sit, please. No need for formality, we're
all friends here."

He was real. He was *here*. Adrenaline rushed through me, sending electric needles through my fingertips. If he thought I would roll over and give up without a fight, he would be deeply disappointed.

Everyone at our side of the table went very still. They were all watching Curran and me, and they realized something was really wrong. Andrea's face turned chalk-white. She recognized d'Ambray. Before she left the Order of Merciful Aid, she had climbed high enough in its ranks to receive briefings about Roland, who was considered the greatest danger the Order would eventually face. She watched Hugh the way one watched a rabid dog. Raphael leaned closer to her, his eyes fixed on Hugh as well. He knew, too. She must've told him.

Hugh crossed the hall, coming toward us. Tall, at least two inches over six feet, he was muscled like a Roman gladiator, and his suit failed to hide it. He moved with perfect balance, gliding as if his joints were liquid. Before my mother and Voron had run off, Hugh had been Voron's protégé. My adoptive father trained him, honing him into the perfect general to lead Roland's armies. Fighting Hugh would be like fighting my father. It would be the second-hardest fight of my life. The first would be my real father.

I scanned the doorways. No troops. Hugh hadn't called in the reinforcements. Did he think he could take me and Curran by himself?

Hugh was getting closer. Dark, almost black hair fell over his shoulders, longer than the last time I saw him. A small scar marked his left cheek—also a recent souvenir. His eyes were an intense dark blue and they laughed at me as he approached.

I stared back at him. Yep, the gig was up. Now what?

Hugh circled the table. He would have to sit next to Curran. Dear God.

Curran's face turned into an expressionless mask. He squeezed my hand and leaned forward slightly, putting himself between me and Hugh.

Don't attack him, Curran. Don't. Do. Anything.

A djigit pulled Hugh's chair out for him. Hugh smiled, a happy wolf confident in his lair, and picked up a glass. A server appeared as if by magic and poured red wine into it.

Hugh raised the glass. "We have been truly fortunate to host the mighty Obluda of the Carpathians . . ."

He turned to Jarek Kral, who raised his fist with a self-indulgent smile. Behind him the four shapeshifters howled, and others echoed their howls at the tables.

". . . the famous Volkodavi of Ukraine . . ."

Radomil and his family nodded. The members of the Volkodavi hooted and pounded their tables.

". . . and the fearless Belve Ravennati."

The Italian brothers nodded. Their pack members howled and slapped their table.

"Tonight we welcome honored guests to our humble abode." Hugh turned to us. "The Beast Lord and his Consort join us to add their wisdom and expertise to the joyous occasion of welcoming new life into this world. You honor us with your presence."

The silence was deafening. We would not be hooting or punching things.

Curran unlocked his jaws. "The honor is all ours."

Hugh turned to the gathering. "Let us eat, drink, and celebrate."

He sat, set down his glass, and turned to Curran. "I do so hate speeches."

"I can imagine," Curran said, the same calm expression on his face.

Hugh flashed him a quick smile. "I thought you might. You and I, we are men of action. At least once the speech is done, they'll bring us food."

A nod to *The Princess Bride*. It was my favorite book. Did he know or was this a coincidence? If he knew, how the hell did he know?

A string of servers came into the hall, followed by a cart pushed by another four. On the cart an enormous roasted boar lay on a huge platter lined with grape leaves.

"Ahh. Excellent." Hugh picked up his fork. "I'm bloody starving."

My heart was hammering at my chest as though I had just run a marathon. Voron's ghostly voice whispered at me, *"Run. You're not ready."*

If I ran, Hugh would kill our people one by one until I

came back. Not only had he trapped me, but he had trapped a handful of hostages with me as well. There would be no running.

The servers began distributing oversized platters heaped with meat and bread. The shapeshifters dug in. A plate was set in front of me: a thick cut of meat, cooked just enough not to be raw, bread, and a pomegranate split open, the red seeds glistening with the color of blood.

Barabas leaned over between Curran and me and cut a small piece from my meat.

Okay.

He ate it, cut a piece of the bread, scooped a couple seeds from the pomegranate, ate them and stood quietly, chewing slowly. Finally he leaned to me and said quietly. "It's not poisoned."

"A weremongoose," Hugh said. "Most prudent of you."

"We mean no offense," Barabas said.

Hugh waved at him. "Of course. Would've done the same in your place. Can never be too careful."

Apparently I had acquired my own personal poison tester. I made a note to talk with Barabas once the dinner was over.

Desandra rose. "I have to go to the bathroom."

Andrea and I stood up. My legs felt wooden. Desandra rolled her eyes and went around the table to the door on the left. We followed her. Behind me Hugh said, "So, Lennart, how was the trip? The Atlantic can be dangerous this time of year."

We crossed the hall and stepped into the corridor. I sped up and took the point. We'd run the basic two-person detail. In trouble, one of us would secure the body, the other would deal with the threats. The magic was up, and that made me better equipped for countermeasures. During tech, we'd switch.

"Turn right," Desandra said. "Will the two of you watch me pee, too?"

"Why is your English so American?" Andrea asked, her voice wooden.

"My mother took off two years after I was born," Desandra said. "A nice American woman looked after me. My father hired her so I would learn the language. He said it would be useful. He wouldn't let me take Angela with me when I got married. He threw her out of the pack. I haven't seen her since."

I didn't like Desandra. I didn't know her and she would prove difficult to guard, but I felt sorry for her.

Ahead of me an intersection waited. "Which way?"

"Left."

We turned the corner. Another long deserted hallway lit with yellow feylanterns. No danger. No guards either. Hmm.

"Finally," Desandra breathed. "Stupid pregnancy. Stupid babies. Can't sit for more than two minutes without running to the bathroom. I swear if that little bastard, whichever one he is, kicks me in the bladder one more time, I'll punch him."

And my sympathy evaporated. "If you try to punch your unborn children, we will restrain you."

"Cool your tits," Desandra said. "I'm not going to punch myself. I just want these kids to be superachievers and get out of me already. Here. This door."

Thank you, Universe.

I swung the door open. A typical bathroom: three stalls, a long stone vanity with two sinks. Solid floor, solid ceiling, a small ventilation window near the ceiling, six feet long, six inches wide. Steel bars guarded the window.

I checked the stalls one by one. Empty. I stepped out into the hallway. "Clear."

"Oh, good. Can I pee now? Sometime in this century would be nice."

Metal clanged against metal behind us. I spun around. A section of the floor to our right slid aside, and a metal grate dropped from the ceiling and sank into the floor, sealing the hallway and us inside it.

"That never happened before," Desandra said.

To the far left, something growled, a rough, ugly sound, like gravel being crushed.

The hair on the back of my neck rose.

A creature turned the corner, huge, bright amber. The roar rolled forth, pulsing, threatening.

I pulled Slayer from the sheath and stepped into the center of the hallway.

Andrea punched the bathroom door open, grabbed Desandra, shoved her into the bathroom, rushed after her, and slammed the door shut. Working with Andrea was effortless. We didn't even need to talk. First, it would have to go through

me, then through the door, then through Andrea. Desandra
would be at the very end of that very long trip.

The beast took a step toward me. *Hello, varmint. And what
mythology did you jump out of?*

In the bathroom, metal whined followed by a thud. Andrea
was ripping the doors off the stalls and barricading the door.

The beast took up most of the width of the hallway, standing at least four feet tall at the shoulder. Powerful legs, almost
feline and corded with hard ropes of muscle, supported a
sleek body with a broad chest that flowed into a thick, long,
but mobile neck. Its head was feline too, round, armed with
jaguarlike jaws, but strangely wide. Two folds rose behind its
shoulders. I couldn't get a good look at them because it faced
me straight on.

From this angle they looked like wings. Deformed, but
still wings.

What the hell are you? It wasn't a manticore. I'd seen manticores before, and they were smaller, and the outline of the
body was completely different. Manticores were built like
giant stocky boxer dogs, square, with every muscle defined
under smooth brown hide. This creature was more catlike,
built with agility and dexterity in mind.

As if hearing my words, the beast took another step forward and grinned at me, displaying a forest of eight-inch teeth.

My, my. Scary.

I zeroed in on the way it raised its paws. Living with shapeshifters had given me some pointers. In hunting, the chief difference between cats and dogs came down to the length and
shape of arm bones. Cats could turn their paws palm up, while
dog paws were fixed permanently downward, a fact that
shapeshifter instructors drilled into their students when they
trained for the warrior form. Rotating the paw gave cats
greater capacity to suppress their prey after they rushed it. It
meant the difference between an ambush predator and a pack
hunter. This beast was an ambush predator. It would claw and
swipe, and those teeth and jaws meant it could bite through
my skull. I had to treat it like a jaguar.

Luckily I had practice fighting with jaguars.

The monster took another step. As its paw touched the
ground, the orange fur suddenly turned jagged. Now what?

Another step.

It wasn't fur. The creature was covered with sharp orange scales and it'd just raised them, like a dog raised its hackles. They looked thick too, like mussel shells. So it was big, it had wings, it was catlike, and it was armored. My list of probable targets just shrunk. With my luck it would spit fire next.

Was it a dragon? Some kind of drake? Somehow it seemed too feline for that. Not that I had come across many dragons. The only one I'd seen was undead and rotting, but it was the size of a large T. rex and its head had the trademark reptilian lines. This was a mammal.

No power words. No heavy-duty magic. Not with Hugh less than two hundred yards away. He knew I could use a sword, but the extent of my magic was a mystery to him and I had to keep it that way as long as possible. There could come a time when the surprise of my magic could mean the difference between living and dying.

The creature's bright blue eyes fixed on me. A cold steady fire burned inside its irises. The beast looked hungry. Not hungry for food but hungry for violence. This thing was no scavenger. It hunted the living and it enjoyed the hell out of it.

Let's see how smart you are. "Can we speed this up? I have a dinner to get back to."

The beast tucked its deformed wings to its body and charged.

It understood me. Never a good sign.

The creature came toward me, picking up speed, fangs bared, eyes glowing, gulping the distance in short leaps.

Every animal instinct in my body screamed, *Run!* I stood my ground. It was a cat. It would pounce at the end.

Leap, leap, leap.

Pounce.

It was a glorious jump, propelled by the steel-hard muscles of the beast's legs. It came at me, claws out, paws raised for the kill.

I dove forward, turning as I fell, and slid under it. The bulk of the beast's body landed on me and I sank Slayer deep into its groin. Hot blood sprayed my face and mouth. The beast screamed.

I clamped its left leg to me, trying to keep it from disemboweling me, clung to it, and ripped Slayer through its insides. The creature yowled and raked at my side with its right hind leg, trying to rip me open. Claws shredded the dress. Pain lashed my side. Argh. It hurt like a sonovabitch. Next time they told me to wear a dress instead of leather, I'd shove it up their asses.

I stabbed again, driving Slayer deeper. More blood gushed in a sticky hot flood. The beast should be going down. It wasn't. It struck at me and I scrambled its insides again and again. *Die already.*

Magic burned my side, as if someone had grabbed a handful of ice and thrust it straight into the cut. My blood recognized an invader and reacted, purging it from me. Lyc-V. This fucking thing was a shapeshifter.

Its regeneration meant it wouldn't bleed out. I wasn't causing enough damage. I had to get to its vital organs.

I slashed the ligament on its left leg.

The beast charged forward, dragging me with it. I slashed it again trying to cripple it, let go, and rolled to my feet. For half a second its back was still to me, and I jumped on it, right between the wings, grabbed its neck, and slashed its throat. Slayer's blade slid from the scales, barely drawing blood. Shit. It would have to do. The beast braked. I yanked the necklace off my neck, looped it over its throat, and slid Slayer into the loops.

The beast reared as silver pressed against the cut. *Choke on that, why don't you?*

I turned Slayer, twisting the necklace into a makeshift garrote. My side felt like someone was trying to cook me alive.

The beast shook, gurgling as the necklace bit deeper into the gash. I hung on with everything I had. To fall was to die. It veered left. I jerked my leg up a fraction of a moment before it slammed into the wall. I turned Slayer another half a turn, praying my bloody fingers wouldn't slip.

The creature shook again. My arms shuddered from the effort.

It flipped. There was nothing I could've done. The beast's weight pinned me in place. A crushing pressure ground at my chest. It rolled on me. My bones whined and I cried out.

One more twist of the garrote. Just a quarter turn.

Don't black out, don't black out.

Just a quarter turn.

I held on. My breath was coming in shallow tortured gasps. The beast convulsed on top of me.

I couldn't feel my fingers.

The big body went rigid on top of me. A long hissing breath escaped it, and it went limp.

Get up, get up, get up. This alone wouldn't do it. It wasn't dead. It had just passed out. I could lie here all day, choking it, and Lyc-V would keep it alive.

I crawled, pushing the weight off my legs, and rolled to my knees. The necklace had bitten deep into the beast's throat. It had likely cut its windpipe. I pulled on Slayer. Stuck. I grunted, lifting the beast's head, and turned Slayer counterclockwise. Little more. Little more . . .

The chain of the necklace began to loosen.

Little more . . .

The beast's eyes snapped open, a hot infuriated blue. I yanked Slayer free and chopped down, straight into the wound. Bone crunched under magic steel. The head rolled free from the stump of the neck.

I slid against the wall, trying to catch my breath. I'd just rest here, for a second. My chest hurt with every breath. Ow.

The beast lay still.

I spat blood out of my mouth. "Clear!"

Thuds came from the bathroom. The door burst open and Andrea stepped into the hallway. "Holy shit."

I tried to wipe the blood from my face, but since my hands were bloody, I just smeared some more gore on myself. Great thinking there.

Desandra peeked over Andrea's shoulder. Her eyes widened. "What the hell is that?"

"Ever see one before?" I asked.

"No."

She sounded sincere to me. I'd seen all kinds of odd things, but I'd never seen one of these either.

The body shuddered. Andrea jerked her crossbow up. I jumped to my feet.

The golden scales boiled, viscous like molten metal, and shrank. A beheaded human torso sprawled in the hallway. I nudged the now-human head so I could see the face. A man in his forties. Brown hair, brown beard. Never saw him before.

Andrea swore.

I leaned over, trying not to wince as my chest protested, picked up the head by the hair, and showed the face to Desandra.

She shook her head.

"Maybe someone in the hall knows. Why don't we go and ask?"

Andrea nodded at the floor. "Any of the blood yours?"

"It doesn't matter now, does it?" Hugh had me here in the castle. He went through a hell of a lot of trouble to get me here. He wouldn't have done it if he weren't certain of the only thing my blood would tell him: I was his boss's daughter.

"I suppose it doesn't," Andrea said.

We went down the hallway, away from the grate.

"What are we going to do about Hugh?" Andrea asked.

"Nothing, until we know what his plan is."

"Who's Hugh?" Desandra asked.

"Someone we both know," Andrea said. We turned the corner, crossed another hallway. The noise of the hall was getting closer.

Suddenly Desandra stopped. She covered her stomach with her hands. Her expression went slack.

"What is it?" I asked.

"Somebody just tried to kill my babies." Desandra blinked and vomited on the floor.

CHAPTER 8

I WALKED INTO THE GREAT HALL, CARRYING MY sword in one hand and a severed head in another. As one, people stopped what they were doing and turned to look at me. Nostrils flared, sampling the blood stench. The conversation died.

Hugh saw me and froze. Either he was one hell of an actor or he had no idea what had happened.

Curran half rose in his seat. I knew exactly what he saw. Twenty minutes ago I'd left for the bathroom. Now torn shreds of my dress hung from my side, drenched in red. Blood stained my face and hands. Behind me Andrea supported Desandra, who was pale as a sheet.

I raised the head. "Who does this belong to?"

You could hear a pin drop.

"Who owns this man?"

No answer.

"He turns into a feline creature with wings. Someone has to know him."

A sound of slow, measured clapping broke the silence. Jarek Kral grinned at me. "Nice joke. Very funny."

I would kill that man before this was over.

"Do you know this man?"

Jarek spread his arms. "Nobody knows this man. You bring this to us and tell us this wild story and we're supposed to do what with it?"

"It was a monster," Andrea said.

"We are all monsters here. Or did you forget?" Jarek chuckled. His shapeshifters grinned.

Desandra screamed something in a language I didn't understand. Jarek barked a derisive reply.

"This could be a servant's head for all we know." Jarek leaned over and looked at Curran. "Perhaps you should tell your pet human to stop hacking heads from castle staff or we might not get any wine."

People laughed.

Gray fur dashed down Curran's arms and melted.

"What?" Jarek rose. "What, boy? Are you going to do something?"

Curran locked his hands on the table. It was an enormous table. It had to weigh over two thousand pounds.

The table creaked and left the ground.

The snickering died. People stared, slack-faced.

Curran held the table a foot off the ground for a long second. His face didn't look strained.

Someone made a choking noise.

Curran set the table down, pushing it sideways, toward Jarek's side.

"Thank you for your hospitality," he said. "I think we're done eating for the day."

He stepped down. Our people rose. He led them across the hall, then wrapped his arm around me, and we walked the hell out of there.

"WHAT DID IT LOOK LIKE?" MAHON ASKED.

We'd dropped Desandra off in her rooms. Aunt B and George decided to spend the night there. The rest of us gathered in our room. The moment Doolittle saw me, I had to submit to having my side examined. Then I was poked, my wounds were rinsed, and now he was chanting them into magical healing under his breath.

"About sixty-five inches at the shoulder, definitely feline, covered in amber scales. The scales were really thick and translucent, with sharp edges. It had wings." I shook my head. "I have no idea what it is. What he is."

Mahon looked at Andrea. "And you saw it?"

"Are you calling Kate a liar?" Barabas asked, his voice dry.

"Yes, I saw it," Andrea said. "She sawed through his neck with a silver chain. It wasn't a hallucination."

Doolittle finished chanting. A welcome, soothing coolness spread through my side. "Good as new."

"Thank you, Doc."

The edges of the wounds had stuck together. Without Doolittle, I would've needed stitches.

"Wings?" Doolittle asked.

"Wings."

"Feathered?"

"Sort of," Andrea told him. "The feathers weren't fully formed. Each was like a simple filament with a little bit of fuzz on it."

Doolittle frowned. "The scales, you see, they would add weight . . ."

"It doesn't make sense," I told him. "I know. But this is what I killed."

"Just because it has wings doesn't mean it can fly," Mahon said. "They can be vestigial."

"They definitely didn't look right," I said.

Doolittle nodded. "I'll test the head."

Mahon glanced at Curran. "I spoke to the Volkodavi and Belve Ravennati at dinner. Both are convinced Jarek wants to kill his daughter. When he originally promised the pass, it was one of the four ways through the mountains. They've had some natural disasters since then. Now it's one of two. He'll do anything to hold on to it."

"Too obvious for Jarek," Barabas countered. "I studied him and he likes to pin the blame on someone else. He would've used a lynx or a wolf, so he could finger one of the other packs. Two birds with one stone. Instead they used something nobody has ever seen before."

"The question is why?" Keira said. "Jarek is still the only one with the obvious motive. If Desandra dies, he doesn't have to give up the pass."

"If she dies, he can kiss his shot at grandkids good-bye," Barabas said.

"The other two packs hate him," Mahon said. "If Desandra gives birth, they won't let him have the children. He may value retaining the pass more."

"Enough," Curran said.

They fell silent.

"We're on full alert," he said. "Move in groups. Lock your doors. Nobody goes or stays anywhere alone. You have to use the bathroom in the middle of the night, you wake everyone up and you go together."

"We need to have a meeting in the morning," I told them. "We need to set the guard shifts and work out a schedule. Let's meet at Doolittle's room at eight."

"Nine." Curran said. "Now she needs rest."

People filed out of the room. He barred it and crouched by me. "Shower?"

"Please."

He disappeared into the bathroom. The sound of running water was like a whisper of heaven. I was suddenly so tired. I dragged myself to my feet and into the bathroom. A shower waited for me, a tiled stall, half-hidden by a purple curtain on a curved rod. Steam rose from the tile. I tugged on the zipper of my dress. Stuck.

Curran reached over. His careful hands touched my shoulders. The sound of ripping fabric screeched and the shreds of the dress fluttered down.

"Thank you."

I slid off my ruined underwear, unhooked my bra, dropped them to the floor, and stepped into the shower. The hot spray washed over me. Red water swirled by my feet. I closed my eyes and stood under the water. Inhale, exhale. The fight was over. Everyone had survived. The war was just beginning.

I checked my side. Doolittle was a miracle worker. The shallow gashes were already closing and stripes of paler skin crossed my tan. I picked up shampoo and worked it into foam in my hair. It smelled like jasmine. I took a washcloth and began scrubbing: neck, breasts, stomach, shoulders . . .

Curran reached over my shoulder. I realized he was nude, standing in the shower with me.

He took the washcloth from my fingers and scrubbed my back. The water splashed over us. He closed his arms around me and I felt his muscular body press and slide against my back. In the whole world, there was no better place than being wrapped in him.

His arms were tense. The tightness vibrated in his muscles, like an electric current under his skin.

I turned in his arms. He rested his forehead on mine. I closed my eyes. Being attacked by strange beasts I could handle. Being in the same room with Hugh . . .

"One word," he whispered, his voice taut with suppressed anger. "Say one word, and I'll rip him apart. He won't see the sunrise."

I looked into his eyes and realized he would. He would step out of the shower, shift his shape, and fight Hugh until one of them stopped breathing. If I stood next to him, he would fight Hugh so I would be free, and if I chose to run, he would fight him so I could get away. Nobody in my entire life had loved me this much.

And because of me and Hugh, and because of Jarek, now Curran was trapped with me in this castle. Fury boiled inside me.

"No," I forced myself to say. "We still need the panacea."

Curran locked his teeth.

I wanted to go home. I wanted to go back to the Keep. I'd cut off my arm to teleport all of us back there and forget we ever came here. The frustration built inside me, fueled by fear and anger. There was absolutely nothing I could do about it now. Running in there and fighting Hugh, as great as it would feel, would condemn everyone who came with us and everyone who stayed back home.

I put my head on his shoulder. My hands squeezed into fists on their own.

He held me. "I know," he said. "I know."

We stood like that for a long time, water washing over us. Gradually, I became aware that my breasts were pressed against him, that he was hard, and that we were both nude.

I leaned in and kissed Curran, licking him in the sensitive point under his jaw. My tongue tasted the raspy stubble. My body came to attention, suddenly aware and rejoicing in the fact that I was alive. I caressed his face, sliding myself against the slick, hard wall of his chest.

A low male sound came from him, frustration and need rolled into one. "Does your side hurt?" he whispered.

I wanted him so desperately. I needed to be in that place where only the two of us mattered and nothing except love existed. It felt like if I couldn't have him, I would burst. I shook my head and kissed his mouth, with my eyes open, and saw the precise moment he let himself off the chain. His lips closed on mine. His tongue slid into my mouth. The taste of him, the smoky, male taste, was intoxicating. My body shot into overdrive. Every cell focused on him, screaming, *More, more, more!* I felt his hands caressing my back, I tasted his mouth, I sensed every hard inch of him pressed against me. I slipped my hand down and stroked the hot length of him.

He made a rough noise, a growl born of pleasure.

Dear God, I had to have him now or I would cry.

"I want you so much," he whispered.

I opened my arms.

Our fury, our worry, our frustration, and our need collided. He picked me up and hoisted me on his hips, his hands under my butt. I felt so alive. I locked my legs around him. The muscles of his shoulders bulged under my fingers, strong like steel cables. He was looking at me, his gray eyes luminescent with golden sparks and filled with such raw, honest need that I felt light-headed.

He kissed my throat, stoking the fire inside me. I leaned back and let him kiss me more. He licked my breasts, sucking on my nipples. The jolt of desire pulsed through me, molten and electric, and when he thrust inside me, hot and hard, I no longer cared about anything but him. I didn't want to think. I just wanted to feel him touch me.

My back pressed against the cool tile. He slid inside me again and again, pumping in a smooth rhythm into the liquid heat. A yearning need built inside me, each thrust sending a pulse of slick pleasure through me, propelling me higher and higher. My nipples were so tight, it hurt. My legs shook. My joints turned fluid. The anticipation swelled inside me, like a tidal wave threatening to crest. He thrust again. Bliss exploded inside me. The wave crested and drowned me in pleasure, each contraction of my orgasm an ecstasy in itself. I cried out. A moment later he grunted and emptied himself inside me.

"You make me crazy," he told me.

"Look who's talking."

• • •

FIVE MINUTES LATER, REWASHED AND TIRED, WE left the shower. Curran sprawled on the bed. I forced myself to dress—we could end up jumping out of bed straight into a fight—and collapsed next to him. Above us the absurd purple canopy shifted gently in the night breeze. The cool wind felt nice on my skin.

He leaned over on his side, held me, and whispered in my ear, so quietly I thought I imagined it. "I meant it. One word and you'll never see his face again. In the morning, this castle will be a bonfire and we'll sail home."

I'd have to word this carefully. People were listening to us. I whispered back to him. "If we sail down the coast south-west, we'll pass by the ruins of Troy. Do you remember the story of Paris and Helen?"

"Yes," he said.

Troy's favorite son and badass archer, Paris, had sailed to Sparta. He came under a banner of truce. The Spartan king treated him as an honored guest, and then Paris stole the king's wife, Helen, and emptied his treasury. Nobody really knew if he kidnapped Helen or if she went with him. Her husband could've loved her or beaten her every day. But the whole of Greece united against Paris. At the end, Troy was a smoking ruin.

I kissed his jaw. "The bow and arrow was never your thing."

He locked his teeth, making his jaw muscles bulge.

We promised to be impartial. We came in peace. If we broke that peace and started a bloodbath, we'd get a bloodbath in return. Nobody would see it as an act of a man trying to save the woman he loved from her father's warlord. The European packs would spin it as an act of betrayal from a man who couldn't handle being insulted.

Attacking Hugh would be an act of war. Not to mention that I wasn't one hundred percent sure that even if both of us fought him, we'd survive that confrontation. Whatever the outcome, Roland would have an excuse to burn the Keep to the ground. He already viewed the Atlanta Pack as a threat, and this would be the tasty icing on his massacre cake. By the time we got home, people we knew and cared about would be dead.

"I'm sorry," I whispered. "I'm so sorry."

"For what?"

"It's because of me." I was the reason we were all trapped here. I didn't cause it, but I was the reason for it.

He pulled me to him and squeezed me. "You're worth the fight," he said in my ear.

He had no idea how much I loved him.

"We all volunteered," he whispered. "And without you, we wouldn't have a shot at the panacea. We need it desperately."

We fell silent. For a long moment I simply enjoyed being next to him. If only this could last . . .

"He hasn't attacked me on sight," I whispered. "That means he'll want to talk to me."

"No," Curran said. "Not alone."

"Sooner or later this conversation has to happen. If he planned on killing me, why go through all this trouble? He knew where I was. He could've just put a sniper on the roof across the street from Cutting Edge and put a bullet through my head as I unlocked the office."

Curran exhaled his frustration. "I'll do everything I can to keep you safe."

"I know," I whispered. "And I'll do the same for you."

We shouldn't have come here. I closed my eyes. I had to sleep. Tomorrow would be another day, another fight. Tomorrow Hugh would approach me and I had to be sharp. Once I figured out what his angle was, things would become a lot simpler.

CHAPTER 9

I OPENED MY EYES. THE MAGIC WAS DOWN AND Curran was gone. The clock said ten past seven. Plenty of time to get dressed and make it to Doolittle's quarters in time for the meeting.

A plate waited for me on the table, covered with a piece of paper. The paper said in Curran's rough scrawl, *Went to talk to Mahon. Packs want to meet to "discuss issues." Don't forget to eat.*

Under the paper, the plate contained two eggs and a lion-sized piece of ham. I ate a third of it, brushed my teeth, put on my jeans, and strapped on my sword. New day, new battle.

Our bags had been brought in from the ship. I dug through them and pulled out my beat-up copy of the *Almanac of Mythological Creatures*. I'd read it cover to cover so many times that I had memorized entire pages, but sometimes looking at it helped me connect the dots.

I've never heard of shapeshifters turning into winged cats, but since Lyc-V was present in the blood, most likely the mechanism of the transformation was the same: the virus infected some creature and then infected a human. The first step was to figure out what the creature was.

Winged cats weren't the most common motif in mythology, but they did occur. Freja, a Norse goddess, had a chariot that was pulled across the sky by two giant cats, Brygun and Trejgun, who probably had wings. They were blue and not orange and didn't change shape. The Sphinx was a feline with wings and a serpent's tail, but also a female face. It had the power of speech, and again, no scales. Griffins had eagle heads, so I could rule them out. I've seen a manticore, and that was not one.

I dug through the bags, looking for more books. *The Heraldic Bestiary* informed me that a winged lion was a symbol of Saint Mark and Venice. That didn't exactly help, unless Lorelei was from Venice and had brought over a posse of winged predatory cats to kill all of us and kidnap Curran.

Boy, she really managed to get under my skin.

No, most likely Saint Mark's lion was a reference to the four prophets from Ezekiel. Matthew was portrayed as a human, Mark as a lion, Luke as a bull, and John as an eagle. I could check Revelation; it was always good for all sorts of strange beasts . . .

Something nagged at me. I concentrated on it. Revelation. To really understand Revelation, one had to read the book of Daniel. At some point I must've come across something in the book of Daniel that was relevant to this, because my brain was telling me to go and look at it.

Let's see: Qur'an, *Mythology of Caucasus People* . . . I had to have packed a Bible. I know I did.

I flipped the bag upside down. Books scattered on the floor. A small green edition of the Bible flopped down. *Got you.*

I sat down on the floor and flipped the pages. I was concentrating so hard that when I finally found it, I just stared at it for a few seconds to make sure it was really there. It was in chapter seven, where Daniel described seeing magic beasts in one of his prophetic dreams.

The first was like a lion, and had eagle's wings: I beheld till the wings thereof were plucked, and it was lifted up from the earth, and made stand upon the feet as a man, and a man's heart was given to it.

The hair on the back of my neck stood up.

A shapeshifter. A feline shapeshifter with wings, who had the ability to transform into a man.

I racked my brain, trying to recall what I knew about Daniel. He was a Jewish noble who, together with three others, had been taken to Babylon around 600 BC to serve as an advisor at the court of the Babylonian king Nebuchadnezzar II, whose chief claim to historical fame was the construction of the Hanging Gardens for his main squeeze. Daniel had many prophetic and apocalyptic dreams and by all accounts lived to a ripe old age, managing to survive the toxic Babylonian politics.

What could Daniel have possibly encountered in Babylon to have this vision? The only remotely similar creatures were the Assyrian lamassu, but there were no records of them being shapeshifters. The Assyrian Empire lay in a region I knew well. The ancient Assyria, Babylon, and Nineveh all were around long before recorded history. They were the cemetery flowers that grew from the dead body of my father's once-mighty empire.

The clock said it was almost time for the meeting. I'd have to come back to it later. I stacked my books in the corner of the room, grabbed the Bible and the *Almanac*, made a beeline for Doolittle's room, and rapped my knuckles on his door.

"Come in!" Eduardo called.

I opened the door. A large room stretched before me, easily as big as Desandra's suite. Two doors stood open, one on the left leading to a bedroom, the other on the right opening into a bathroom. To the left two tables had been set in the shape of an L. Glass vials and beakers lined the surface. Doolittle sat in the corner of the L looking through a microscope. To the right, two oversized plush couches flanked a coffee table. Derek sat on the closest one, holding cards in his hand. He'd pushed them together into a single stack. Across from him Eduardo lounged, taking an entire couch by himself. He held his cards in a wide fan.

"What do you mean, come in? You don't even know who I am."

"Of course we know who you are," Derek said.

"He smelled you coming," Eduardo said.

Life with werewolves. Why me?

I dropped into a chair by Doolittle's table.

He looked at me. A pair of glasses perched on his nose.

"Why do you wear glasses? Doesn't Lyc-V give you twenty-ten vision?" I asked.

Doolittle tapped his glasses. "Yes, but these give me twenty-two."

His voice with its coastal Georgia overtones made me so homesick, I almost hugged him.

"How's the head?"

"Fragrant." Doolittle opened a cooler that sat next to him. Inside the severed head rested, wrapped in plastic and half submerged in ice.

"Anything?"

Doolittle leaned back. "It's a shapeshifter. The blood reacts to silver and shows the presence of Lyc-V."

"Aha! So I'm not crazy."

"You are most definitely crazy," Derek said. "But in a deranged, endearing way."

Eduardo snorted.

"Don't make me come over there." I looked at Doolittle.

"They are rambunctious this morning," he told me. "Unfortunately my resources here are limited. I don't have access to any of the genetic sequencing methods I have at home."

There was more to it, I could sense it. "But?"

"But there is the Bravinski-Dhoni test."

"I've never heard of it."

Doolittle nodded with a small smile. "That's because it's not very useful under ordinary circumstances. It's not precise. It is, however, very reliable."

He pushed a wooden rack of test tubes toward me. Each was half filled with blood. A small label identified each test tube: *Bear*, *Wolf*, *Bison*, *Hyena*, *Mongoose*, *Jackal*, *Lynx*, *Badger*, *Lion*, and *Rat*.

Most of these probably came from our team. "Where did you get the jackal, lynx, and rat?"

"The locals," Eduardo said.

"Hibla got upset," Derek elaborated. "When you fought, someone deployed a gate that sealed the hallway. The gate mechanism was guarded."

"Let me guess, the local guard was murdered in a horrible way."

"Probably," Derek said. "The body is missing but there was a lot of blood. Hibla wants to know what's going on."

Doolittle picked a pipette and dipped it into the Wolf test tube. "The essence of the test is based on the assimilation properties of Lyc-V. When faced with new DNA, it seeks to incorporate it."

He uncorked the Bear test tube and let two drops from the pipette fall inside. The blood turned black, swirled, and dissolved.

"Assimilated," I guessed. The Lyc-V had chomped on the foreign DNA.

"Precisely." Doolittle picked up a test tube marked Bear II. "The blood in this test tube is from Georgetta, but the blood in front of you is from her father."

He sucked a couple of drops from George's test tube and let them fall into Mahon's blood. Nothing happened.

"Same species."

"But wouldn't the difference in human DNA affect it?"

"It does, but you won't see a dramatic reaction." Doolittle leaned forward. "We've tested the blood from the man you killed against all of these. Every single one gave a reaction."

"Even the lynx and lion?"

Doolittle nodded. "Whatever it is, it may look feline, but it's not. If it is, its DNA is significantly different from that of a lynx or a lion."

"So where do we go from here?"

"We try to get more samples," Doolittle said.

That would be problematic, to say the least. I tried imagining walking over to the Volkodavi or Belve Ravennati and telling them, "Hi, we suspect that one of your people might be a terrible monster; can we have your blood?"

Yeah. They would just fall over themselves to donate a sample.

"I could pick a fight," Derek said. "Get some blood that way."

"No fights. We start nothing. We only react."

"That's exactly what I said." Doolittle fixed Derek with his stare. "Also, Kate, if you do run across another specimen, do try to keep him or her alive until I get there."

Ha-ha. "Will do, Doc. My turn." I opened the Bible and showed him the verse from Daniel.

Doolittle read it, raised his glasses onto his forehead, and read it again. "I've read the Bible hundreds of times. I don't remember reading this."

"You weren't looking for it."

Derek came over and read the verse.

I brought them up on Daniel's brief history. "The beasts in Daniel's dream are usually interpreted to mean kingdoms, in this case Babylon, that will eventually fall from glory. But if taken literally, it could mean a shapeshifter."

"Were there winged cats in Babylon?" Doolittle asked.

"The only thing close were the lamassu," I told him. "Lamassu served as the guardians of ancient Assyria. Assyria spanned four modern countries: southern Turkey, western Iran, and the north of Iraq and Syria. Assyrians liked to do war, and they fought with Babylon, Egypt, and pretty much everyone they could reasonably conquer in ancient Mesopotamia for about two thousand years. Around six hundred BC, Babylonians, Cimmerians, and Scyths, all the nations who had once paid Assyria tribute, finally banded together and sacked it. We don't have many records of the Assyrians. They left behind some ruined cities and stone reliefs depicting fun things like impaling entire villages of subjugated people and riding around in chariots hunting lions."

"Amusing people, the ancient Assyrians," Derek said. "They hunt, they sing, they dance, they impale people."

A joke. Finally. "Pretty much. They also built lamassu, massive stone statues that guarded the city gates and the entrances to Assyrian palaces."

I opened the *Almanac* and showed them the picture of the colossal statues. "Bearded human face, body of a lion or a bull, and wings."

"Why five legs?" Doolittle asked.

"It's conceptual: from the front the lamassu seem to be standing still, but from the side they appear to walk. Here is an interesting thing: Assyria wasn't that far from here, about a thousand miles southwest as the crow flies. It's a thousand miles of mountains and terrible roads, but in country terms, ancient Assyria and ancient Colchis were practically neighbors."

Derek frowned at the picture.

"But they have human faces," Eduardo said. "And no scales."

I nodded. "And that's a problem. Also there are dozens of theories as to who or what the lamassu represent, but not one of them says they were evil or that they ate people. They are viewed as benevolent guardians. People have found amulets with lamassu and protective spells on them, and modern Assyrians still have their images in their houses."

Doolittle studied the picture. "To show a creature with five legs demonstrates understanding rather than observation."

"What do you mean, understanding?"

"They didn't simply follow nature's blueprint and make exactly what they observed," Doolittle said. "They understood the difference between perception and reality, and they portrayed a concept rather than the exact copy of what they could see."

Doolittle took a piece of paper and a pen and began to draw. "When we are born, we start out with concrete thinking. We perceive only what we see and hear." He showed us the piece of paper. On it a dove soared above a crushed birdcage.

"What do you see?"

"A bird flying away from a broken cage," Derek said.

"What does it symbolize?"

"Freedom," I said.

"What else?"

"Escape," Eduardo said.

Doolittle turned to Derek.

"Leaving what is safe so you can be more," Derek said. "The cage is what the bird knows; the sky is all the things he still wants to do, even if it's a risk."

"Ah!" Doolittle raised his index finger. "All those are examples of abstract thinking. Our entire culture is based on the idea that a single concept can have many different interpretations. We actively encourage the development of this skill, because it helps us solve our problems in new ways. So did the ancient Assyrians, apparently. When looking at the lamassu, we have to consider not only what it is but what it may represent. We can't simply take it at face value."

The million-dollar question was, what could a scaled bull with a human face and wings symbolize?

A knock sounded and Andrea and Raphael came into the room. Keira stalked in behind them and winked at Eduardo.

"Stop that," Eduardo told her.

I leaned over to Doolittle. "What do you think it represents?"

"Let me think about it," he said.

Barabas was the last to arrive. We were missing Curran and Mahon, and Aunt B and George, who were guarding Desandra. It would have to do.

"Desandra doesn't do well with men," I said. "We need to have a woman with her at all times. I'm thinking three shifts, two people per shift. Midnight to eight, eight to four, and four to midnight. Volunteers?"

Raphael raised his hand. "We'll take eight to four."

"I can take four to midnight," I said. "I need a partner."

Derek raised his hand. Perfect.

"I'll take midnight to eight," Keira said. "I don't mind sleeping in the room and I talked to George last night. We'll work well together."

"What about me?" Eduardo asked.

"You and our good doctor are joined at the hip for the rest of our stay here," I said. "I have a feeling that Curran will be busy."

"He will be," Barabas confirmed. "I have several requests for meetings with him. He's an arbiter, so the packs will likely want him there any time they decide to talk."

"That leaves us with you, Mahon, and Aunt B," I said. "I'll talk to both of them and see if they would mind acting as standbys in case we need extra support: twelve hours on, twelve hours off. Same instructions as last night until further notice: we do not go anywhere alone, we do not take risks, and above all we do not permit ourselves to be provoked. One last thing: the most dangerous person in this castle isn't Jarek Kral or any of the other pack alphas. It's Megobari."

Keira raised her eyebrows.

"You've seen me fight," I said. "I can't explain to you why now, because it's complicated and we're being listened to, but I say this with every ounce of credibility I have: he is extremely dangerous. He has the means and ability to murder every person in this room and he will do it without any hesitation. Do not underestimate him."

If these creatures we fought were indeed lamassu, Roland would know about them. He could even have used them, which meant Hugh could use them as well. I had no idea to what end. But I would find out.

•   •   •

THE MEETING DONE, RAPHAEL, ANDREA, AND I walked to Desandra's room. They would start their shift and I wanted to check in on Desandra.

"I was thinking," Andrea said.

"That's a dangerous habit."

"I keep telling her that," Raphael said.

"Oh, you two are a riot. Anyway, I was thinking we should squeeze Desandra dry. She knows both clans. She has to have some idea what's going on."

"Think she can handle it?" Desandra seemed about as stable as the Hawaiian Islands to me—she looked pretty, but if you searched hard enough, you'd find a volcano. Last thing I wanted was for her to self-destruct on me.

"Sure. You saw her. She doesn't have anyone to talk to. As long as we go easy and wear kid gloves, she'll be happy to chat. We'll girl-talk her."

Girl talk, right.

"I'll stay in the hallway," Raphael told us.

A minute later Andrea and I walked into Desandra's room. George was sitting on the bed by Desandra, who looked as sullen as you could get without actually crossing your arms and sticking your bottom lip all the way out. Aunt B smiled in a benign way, while George carefully braided Desandra's hair.

Shreds of bright silver wrapping paper and pieces of cardboard littered the rug. Next to them lay a broken toilet bowl brush with a ribbon bow and a card hanging from it.

Long strands of blond hair lay on the carpet, over the wrapping paper. Their ends were bloody.

I pointed at the brush. "What is this?"

"Her father sent her a present," George said through clenched teeth. "The card says, *So you'll have something to defend yourself next time.*"

That bloody bastard.

I nodded at the hair. "And that?"

"After we received the gift, we got a little emotional and pulled some hair out," Aunt B said. "But then we decided that our hair was pretty, and we shouldn't disfigure ourselves, especially because it won't hurt our dear father. Not even a little bit."

"It will grow back," Desandra said.

"No worries," George told her. "I've hidden all of the bald spots."

"Why didn't you just leave a long time ago?" Andrea said. "Just walk out and keep walking until you ended up somewhere where nobody has heard of Jarek Kral."

Desandra shrugged her shoulders. "And do what? Be what? I am someone here. This is all I know. Besides, where could I go that he or one of those morons he married me to wouldn't find me?"

George finished the hair and got off the bed.

"She's all yours, ladies," Aunt B said. "We're off to freshen up."

Andrea parked herself in the doorway. She carried two SIG-Sauers in hip holsters, a military-issue assault shotgun on her back, and probably a few more guns in places I couldn't see.

"How are you feeling today?" I asked. Kate Daniels, master of girl talk.

"Like shit. Have you ever been pregnant?"

"No."

"Let me summarize for you: your feet hurt, your back hurts, your hips hurt. None of your clothes fit, because your *maternica* is stretched out from the size of an apple to a basketball. The small creatures inside you keep kicking you and turning. You can't eat things you normally eat—they make you sick. Instead you eat strange things like marinated cucumbers and you can't stop until they also make you sick. Worst of all, you're not a person anymore. You're a container. Everybody is looking at you waiting for you to pop your baby out."

I bit my tongue before I said something that would make her shut down. "Forget I asked."

Desandra shrugged.

"How about the guys?" Andrea called out. "Do any of them come to see you?"

"Radomil came twice. Gerardo did too, but he's . . ." Desandra moved her hands about as if she were dog-paddling.

"Awkward?" I guessed.

"Yeah. Radomil doesn't care. He just likes babies. But I offered to let Gerardo feel them kick, and he told me he wouldn't know if it was his or Radomil's son kicking." Desandra sighed. "He thinks I'm a whore because I slept with Radomil."

Andrea made big eyes at me and nodded. *Keep going.*

Okay, keep going. I could do that. "Why did you sleep with Radomil?"

Andrea put her hand over her face. I scowled at her. *You know what, hotshot, you do it and I'll stand by the door.*

Desandra sat up straighter. "I'm not a whore, if that's what you're asking."

"I didn't say you were. I'm just trying to make sense of things. I think it's clear that someone is trying to kill you. The more I know, the better I can anticipate new threats."

Desandra sighed again. "Fine. When I was seventeen, that *hajzel*, my father, married me off to Radomil. Radomil was in his twenties. I thought my life was over, but then I figured out it couldn't be worse than what I had at home."

"How was it?" Andrea asked.

"It wasn't bad, actually. They live in this place on the hill in Ukraine. There were orchards and woods everywhere. Villages. We'd go to town every Saturday and go through the market. Radomil would always buy me something. He is a nice guy." Desandra leaned forward. "Really good in bed. I mean really, really good. I didn't go out much. We were busy. You know."

Yes, yes, we got it. You had lots of nookie. "And his family?"

"They are okay. His sister, Ivanna, is nice, and she and his brother are pretty much the brains. Radomil . . . He isn't stupid. He's just . . . He thinks in simple ways. He doesn't worry himself about politics. I pretty much knew after a month that he would never be in charge."

"What's his beast?" I asked.

"He's a lynx. Their whole family is."

"What happened to their parents?" Andrea asked.

"Dead." Desandra shrugged. "Killed a few years ago when they were fighting for their territory. It's Radomil, his two brothers, and two sisters. Oh and their grandfather. He's really old. He walks with a cane and half of the time doesn't know where he is. I liked living there. They didn't really involve me much, but I was so young, I didn't care."

"So why did you break up?" I prompted.

"My father canceled my marriage. I only lived with Radomil for five months. Kral came and got me."

"Didn't Radomil fight for you?" Andrea asked. I could see

it in her face. If someone tried to take Raphael away from her, she would kill anything that stood in her way to keep him.

Desandra shook her head. "He didn't want me to leave, but his brother talked him out of it. Three years later I married Gerardo. I was with him for two years."

"Did you like him?"

Desandra was looking at her hands, her face tired. "Yes. I liked him. But it doesn't matter now."

"I know it sucks, but if you tell me, it might help me understand what's going on better."

Another sigh. "Isabella and her husband rule the Belve Ravennati. Gerardo and Ignazio have some power but not really enough to do anything major without their parents signing off on a dotted line. Isabella never liked me. With Radomil's family it was laid-back, but with the Belve Ravennati it's always very serious. Everything is important and it's all about duty and looking after the family's interests."

Desandra stuck a finger in her mouth and imitated retching. Charming.

"I was a beta's mate. I was supposed to have responsibilities. They wouldn't let me do anything. I was trying to learn some Italian and I walked in on their meeting once, and his mother told Gerardo that I was just a temporary arrangement. So Isabella, Gerardo, and I were at the trade summit in Budapest. They had their big meeting. I could've gone in but I sat outside with the betas."

"Why?" Andrea asked.

"Because they don't know how to keep their mouths shut," Desandra said. "They get bored and blab. If you listen carefully, you can find things out."

Okay. She wasn't nearly as dumb as she pretended to be.

"After the meeting, my father found me and told me to pack. I told him I wouldn't do it. I went to find Gerardo. He was mad out of his mind. Those four guys that follow my father around? They're killers. Two wolves, a rat, and a bear. They do whatever he tells them to. They have no . . . consciousness."

"Conscience?" I guessed.

"Yes. That. They'd been by and told him they would be taking me. Gerardo said the only way we could win this would be to fight my father." Desandra looked at me. "You have no idea how bad my father is. I've seen . . ." She bit her lip. "I've seen people die in ways you can't even imagine."

Her nostrils flared. She hunched over slightly, hugging herself. Green rolled over her irises, emerald against the black of dilated pupils. She seemed to unconsciously shrink away from me, putting more space around herself. I'd seen this emotion enough to recognize it. Desandra was scared. She was remembering something and the memory petrified her.

"I used to like this cute computer guy. He had glasses. He worked for our pack. He did something—I don't even know what—and my father stuck his head on a pike. I could see it from my bedroom window. I had to move my bed so the dead head of the cute guy I'd kissed wouldn't be staring at me in my sleep."

If I had a chance to kill Jarek Kral, I would take it. I didn't even need proof to know she was telling the truth. One could fake fear, but not the body's involuntary responses to it.

"I told Gerardo it was suicide. He wasn't good enough to take on my father with me or without me. He said I was weak and if I wasn't willing to fight with him, I should just go back. And then he picked up my clothes and threw them in the hallway."

Everyone this woman knew treated her like garbage. She made no effort to fight or to take off. She simply accepted it and tortured herself and others in revenge.

Desandra shrugged. "I couldn't believe it. We'd just had sex that morning. I thought he loved me, but instead he threw me out. I had to get out of there. We were staying in this huge hotel, so I hid on a balcony. I just wanted to cry. Radomil found me. I felt really alone and he was nice to me. He held me and he told me that it would all work out. I wanted to stick it to Gerardo, too, so we did it right there on that balcony. There you have it. The whole ugly story."

Raphael walked through the door.

Desandra sat up straighter and put one leg over another. "Hey there, handsome."

Every time I managed to scrape up a shred of sympathy for her, she did something to set it on fire.

Raphael glanced at her. "Not interested."

"It's the stomach, isn't it?"

"No," Andrea said. "It's me. What's up, honey?"

"We're going on a hunt."

"What?" I asked.

"A hunt," he said. "On horses."

What the hell . . . ? "Are we going to joust next? Maybe arrange our tables in a circle?"

Raphael shrugged. "If we do, I'm not wearing armor. We're all invited to the hunt and I'm pretty sure it's mandatory."

"Great!" Desandra jumped off the bed. "Anything to get out of here."

I pointed my finger at her. "Hush. The entire castle is going?"

Raphael nodded. "Everybody is going."

If we stayed behind, we could be ambushed, and with the castle empty, nobody would know or care. Hugh was up to something. "They do know that she's eight months pregnant?"

"It seems so. Apparently there is a prize if you win."

Going hunting in the middle of the mountains or staying in an abandoned castle with a hysterical Desandra and no assistance in case of an imminent attack? Choices, choices. "Hunt it is."

THE ROAD CURVED IN FRONT OF ME, FOLLOWING A shore of a sea-foam-green lake to our left. It lay placid, licking gently at the bottom of the mountain protruding into it. Tall Mediterranean cypresses lined the road, each perfectly straight, like a conical candle, and between them laurel trees spread their branches. On the right, grapevines lined the slope of the mountain in long, gently curving rows.

My horse was a bay, sturdy and wide-bodied, with short shoulders and a clean head. She stepped with calm surety, picking her way up the old paved road, untroubled by smells of shapeshifters on all sides. I had a feeling I could ride her straight into the lake and she wouldn't twitch an ear.

Shapeshifters walked and rode all around me. Desandra had her own horse. At first she wanted to walk, so I argued against her walking, and then I argued against the horse, but she dug her heels in at any suggestion of a cart. She would not be riding in a cart, and she was the daughter of an alpha, and if she didn't get her way, she would rip out some throats. I ended up going through all of the horses available to us and

picking the oldest, most docile creature I could find. Now I
had a heavily pregnant woman on a horse that kept flaring her
nostrils. Clearly the mare had a serious suspicion that the
human riding her was really a wolf and was considering bolt-
ing for her life. Werewolf wombs had to be made of steel,
because not only did Desandra not show any signs of distress,
but she looked fresh as a daisy.

Andrea had chosen to ride a horse as well. Being in a saddle
gave us a good field of vision, and in a pinch we could use the
horses to block an incoming threat. Derek had decided to walk
and some others did as well, including Curran, who was convinced that all horses secretly plotted against him. Since Andrea
and I kept Desandra between us, he ended up walking on my left
and slightly in front, and Lorelei chose to walk next to him.

I still couldn't figure out how she was involved in this
entire affair. As far as I could tell, she didn't appear to have
any ties to the three packs involved.

Lorelei wore a light blue blouse and jeans that hugged her
butt. Her hair was down, blowing in the wind. If we were back
home, someone would be nudging me by this point, because
by Pack standards they were walking too close and I would be
required to snarl, but we weren't at home, and Barabas, riding
on a white horse directly behind me, was quiet.

Lorelei chatted on, something about squishing grapes and
making candy out of wine. Curran nodded. I caught a glimpse
of his face. He was smiling. He seemed to be enjoying himself.
They were walking together and I was stuck here. On my horse.

It should've taken more than a pretty twenty-one-year-old
to unsettle me. This was a new and unwelcome development.
It had to be this place. Everyone was waiting to stab us in the
back, so I was probably making too much out of this. Lorelei
was a kid. Legally she might have been twenty-one, but when
he'd met her, he was twenty-two and she was twelve. That
alone should've guaranteed that nothing was happening.

She was the daughter of a man Curran knew, stuck out
here likely against her will, and he was being nice to her,
because few people were. He and I had been through so much
shit together. He loved me, I loved him, and I needed to stop
measuring the distance between them and pay attention to my
environment. I had a job to do.

Nobody demanded that I wear a dress for the hunt, so I

wore jeans, a T-shirt, and a green men's shirt, which I left unbuttoned and rolled up at the sleeves. I wore my belt with an array of herbs in small pouches, my leather wrist guards were full of silver needles, and I had taken both Slayer, which was on my back, and my second saber, which I wore on my hip. Anybody who had a problem with my extra hardware was welcome to make my day.

Hugh dropped back through the procession. He was riding a monster of a horse, a massive stallion, a darker bay than mine, with a white blaze on his forehead and white feathered stockings. There were shades of Shire horse there, and Clydesdale, but the lines were cleaner and the chest was more developed. It was the kind of stallion a knight would ride into war.

Hugh drew even with us. He wore a long black coat, the same as Hibla's werejackals. Belted and tapered at the sides, with bandoliers filled with bullets across the chest, the coat made his shoulders wider, his waist slimmer, and his body taller. He seemed to loom rather than ride. Since he pretended to be the lord of the castle, he'd probably decided to dress the part. No dagger, though. Instead he had a full-length sword in a scabbard. I could only see the hilt, simple functional leather with a cross-guard.

Andrea moved aside to let him ride next to Desandra.

Hugh bent forward, concern on his face. "How are you feeling today?"

Desandra sat straighter. It was like she couldn't help herself. Anything male instantly made her come to attention. And Hugh was handsome, in an aggressive masculine way: blue eyes, dark hair, and a clean-shaven square jaw so solid that thinking about punching it made me wince. He was surrounded by people who turned into nature's best equivalent of intelligent spree killers, but he was completely undisturbed by it, as if he knew with one hundred percent certainty that if all of us ganged up on him, he could handle it.

Curran had a feral edge. You sensed instinctively that he was never too far from violence. It simmered under his skin, and when he wanted to intimidate you, he looked at you like you were prey. But Hugh was steady as a rock. He would laugh, in a good-natured easy way, and lop your head off.

"I'm fine," Desandra said. "Thank you for asking."

"Let me know if the ride gets too rough. One word and I'll turn this parade around." He winked at her.

Desandra giggled.

What are you planning, Hugh? What's the deal?

"I'm very sorry about yesterday," Hugh said. "My people are investigating the matter. We will find whoever sent that sonovabitch."

"I'm sure you will." Desandra smiled.

I'm sure he won't.

"We'll do our best to guarantee your safety."

I think I just threw up a little in my mouth. "According to the pack contract, we are the ones guaranteeing her safety. You are"—*dragging*—"encouraging her to exert herself on this hunt."

"I love hunts," Desandra squeezed through her teeth, and gave me a pointed look.

"There is very little risk," Hugh said. "Nobody would try anything with all of us out here."

"She's eight months pregnant." What the hell was the rationale behind pulling her out of the castle anyway?

Hugh grinned at me, displaying even, white teeth. "You have to stop measuring a shapeshifter by human standards."

"I'm perfectly fine," Desandra said.

Oh, you idiot. "If the mare throws you . . ."

"That's why you've brought a medmage," Hugh said, nodding toward the back, where Doolittle rode on a chestnut. "He seems very capable."

Curran turned and was looking at us with that stonewall Beast Lord expression of his.

"Well, I shall leave you to the skilled hands of your guards," Hugh said. "Someone has to lead this expedition, or we may end up in some wilderness and have to steal sheep for dinner."

Desandra giggled again.

Hugh clicked his tongue, and the stallion smoothly carried him to the front of our parade.

"What's your problem?" Desandra stared at me.

I leaned to her and kept my voice quiet. "That man is dangerous." And if someone had asked me six months ago what would happen if the two of us met, I would've said that Hugh would attack me on sight. Instead we were now riding on a hunt, exchanging barbed pleasantries.

"He's a human," Desandra sneered. "I can rip out his throat with one bite."

And we were back to ripping throats. I thought of telling her that I was a human and in a throat-ripping contest between us, she'd come in dead last, but people were listening to us. Besides, threatening the body you were guarding was never a good idea. She would resent me, and without her cooperation keeping her breathing would be much harder.

"Not all humans are the same," Andrea said.

If Desandra thought she could fight off the preceptor of the Iron Dogs, she would be in for a rude awakening. Hugh would end her with one cut, carve his way through all of her relatives and husbands, and then celebrate with a nice bottle of local wine.

THE ROAD CLIMBED HIGHER AND HIGHER UNTIL we finally came to a clearing lined with huge slabs of gray stone. Tucked against the sheer cliff of a mountain, the clearing fanned out in a rough trapezoid shape, with the narrow side facing the mountain. A corral built with rough timbers was set directly against the mountain. Below us woods stretched, green and lush, climbing up and down mountain curves as far as we could see.

Three stone thrones stood at the edge of the clearing, chiseled from rock with rough strokes smoothed by centuries of rains. The middle throne towered, huge, as if made for a giant, and the other two were smaller. They felt ancient, just like the stone slabs under our feet. This was an old place, permeated with age. Centuries ago some kind of king must've sat here, on the stone throne, surveying the mountains.

Hibla's djigits dismounted and came for our horses. They led them to the enclosure by the mountain and tethered their feet.

Hugh sat on the throne. *Oh, spare me . . .*

"Ladies and gentlemen. The forests you see before you are rich with game. They're teeming with red deer, tur—the king of mountain antelopes—gazelles, mouflon or wild sheep, and wild goats."

He clearly had experience with public speaking. His voice resonated through the clearing, loud enough to be heard by everyone but still friendly and perfectly understandable. He must've given speeches to his troops. *"Tonight we rape, kill, and plunder . . ."*

"In these mountains we have a fine tradition of the summer hunt. The rules are simple: Teams of hunters depart in the morning and return by the end of the day. Their game is examined and judged. Only mature animals may be hunted. Those who kill juveniles or females with young will find themselves and their team disqualified. The team that wins the hunt wins the prize from the lord of the castle."

Oh boy, oh boy.

Two djigits brought out a rectangular frame covered with indigo fabric.

"We are standing within the boundaries of ancient Colchis," Hugh continued. "This is the cradle of Georgia itself. Long before the Common Era, a kingdom of warriors and poets flourished here. While inhabitants of Europe still struggled with crude implements of bronze, the sorcerer-smiths of Colchis mastered iron and gold. Today we pay tribute to their past glory."

Hibla stepped to the fabric and pulled it off with a flick of her hand.

Gold shone, glowing in the bright sunlight. People around me sucked in a breath. The pelt of a ram was stretched on the frame. Each individual six-inch-long hair of its dense wool shimmered with radiant yellow gold. Wow.

"I give you the Golden Fleece!" Hugh proclaimed.

Applause rippled through the clearing. Someone howled, excited.

"Like Jason's Argonauts, who came here seeking Colchis riches, all of you traveled here. But the riches you sought are of a different kind, the riches of wisdom and friendship. This is our gift to you. It is twelve o'clock now. You have three hours. Prove that you are the superior hunters. Prove your bravery and your skill. Hunt now and the pack that brings the best game for our feast tonight will earn bragging rights and the Golden Fleece."

The clearing shook as a hundred people cheered in unison. Excitement charged the air. They were a hair away from going furry. The prospect of a hunt after being cooped up in the castle pushed the shapeshifters into overdrive.

"And there is a second, more humble, but perhaps more useful prize."

Hibla raised a glass container. It held a plastic bag with a quart of the brownish paste in it. Panacea.

"It will be awarded to the shapeshifter who brings in the best kill."

Andrea's eyes lit up. She elbowed Raphael.

"Before I forget!" Hugh boomed. "Look to your left. You see that narrow pass between two mountains. Stay away from the pass. The creatures who live there do not welcome intruders. My people will go with yours as observers to ensure that you obey the rules of the hunt. Good luck to all!"

"The Golden Fleece will belong to Obluda!" Jarek Kral roared.

Desandra yanked her dress over her head.

"No!" I barked.

"I'm hunting," Desandra said.

"What will happen to the children when you change shape?"

"They will change shape as well," Lorelei told me with a small smile. "It's very common for shapeshifter women to change shape while pregnant. It relieves the stress on the spine. I'm surprised you don't know this."

I turned, looking for Doolittle. "Is this true?"

Doolittle nodded. "As long as she doesn't stay in the animal shape longer than a few hours and doesn't attempt a half-form, she shouldn't have an issue."

There was no way in hell I could keep up with a wolf. I turned to Curran.

"It will be fine," he said. "We'll take care of her."

What? "I thought you'd have my back on this."

"I do."

"The human is too scared to stay behind alone." Renok, Jarek Kral's second-in-command, grinned at me. "Do you want some company?"

Curran turned and looked at him. I had to give Renok credit. He didn't flinch. Either very brave or very stupid. Possibly both.

"Surely the Beast Lord won't stay behind," Hugh said. "The alphas of all other packs are participating."

And now if he stayed behind, it would be a giant insult. The pieces clicked together in my head. Hugh was eager to chat, and he really wanted to have me all to himself. He couldn't segregate me in the castle, so he'd taken everyone out of it.

Curran looked back at me. "I know you're concerned for Desandra. That's why we'll all go and make sure nothing will happen to her." He paused, making sure our stares connected. His gray eyes were clear and calm. "We'll be back before you know it."

I was still looking at Curran's eyes when the face around them grew and changed. Gray fur sheathed him. An enormous gray lion stood in his place.

People froze. Some stared, slack-jawed. Some blinked. Curran in lion form was shocking.

"Consort?" he said, human words coming out perfectly from a lion's maw.

I had to say something. "Good luck."

He raised his head and roared, the sound of his voice scattering through the mountain. Shapeshifters cringed.

Hugh shook his head, stuck his finger in his ear, and wiggled it.

Lorelei shed her dress and stepped forward, completely nude, shoulders back, head held high. The nakedness lasted only a moment before her body boiled and a lean gray wolf dropped on all fours, but a moment was enough. Curran had seen her.

She was going to hunt with him, while I was stuck here. Damn it all to hell.

Our group surrounded Desandra. Her body swirled, stretching, the transformation so fast it was almost instant, and she became a huge black wolf.

All around me people shifted. Mahon, a hulking dark mountain of a Kodiak, snarled next to George, who wasn't much smaller. Keira roared, a lithe dark jaguar. Wolves, lynxes, and jackals filled the clearing. Was I the only non-shapeshifter here?

Curran charged down the slope. Our people and Desandra followed. Barabas halted, still human.

"Go," I told him. Having him with me wouldn't make that much difference, and Hugh would find some pretext to send him off.

Barabas's body jerked. A Rottweiler-sized weremongoose dashed down the slope after them.

Curran was off hunting with Lorelei. The thought stung me, refusing to go away. It shouldn't have bothered me, but it did. I didn't want him to go.

A pack of gray wolves ran left—Belve Ravennati leaving. Jarek's crew—wolves, bears, and a couple of rats—headed southeast, while the Volkodavi, sand-colored lynxes, shot to the right. In a breath the clearing was empty. Discarded clothes littered the ancient stones. Horses snorted in their enclosure. Everyone was gone.

"So," Hugh said. "You never told me. Did you like the flowers I sent?"

CHAPTER 10

———

I TURNED AND LOOKED AT HUGH. HE SAT ON HIS throne, left arm bent, the elbow propped on the armrest, leaning his head on the curled fingers of his hand. *Comfortable, are we?*

I'd been anticipating this moment for most of my life. Now it was here and I had no clue what to do with it. Anxiety rushed through me in an icy flood. In my head I'd always imagined this meeting would involve bloody swords and stabbing. The lack of stabbing was deeply perplexing.

"Tell me, what do you do if there is no throne handy? Do you carry a portable model with you, or do you just commandeer whatever is handy, like lawn chairs and bar stools?"

"Your father once told me that a dog sitting on a throne is still a dog, while a king in a crumbling rocking chair is still a king."

Nice choice of words, considering his official title was preceptor of the Iron Dogs. "My father?"

Hugh sighed. "Come on. I saw the sword, I walked through what remained after Erra's destruction, and I found your flowers where you and the shapeshifters fought the Fomorians a year ago. I felt the magic coming off them. Don't insult my intelligence."

It was like that, then. "Fine. What do you want?"

Hugh spread his arms. "What do *you* want, that's the question. You came here, to my castle."

"That insulting-intelligence remark goes both ways. You set a trap, lured me across the ocean into it, and now I'm here. If you wanted small talk, we could've done that in Atlanta."

Hugh smiled. *Your teeth are too perfect,. Hugh. I can totally help you with that.*

I pretended to study the Golden Fleece. These were just opening feints. Soon he would get serious and go in for the kill, one way or the other. The fleece looked in too great a shape to be centuries old.

"Did you really kill a ram with gold wool?"

"Gods, no. It's synthetic," he said.

"How?"

"We took a ram pelt, coated it in magic to keep it from burning, and dipped it in gold. The real trick was getting the proportion of gold and silver right. I wanted to keep the flexibility of gold, but it's so heavy the individual hairs kept breaking, and too much silver made it stiff. In the end we went with a gold-copper alloy."

"Why go through all this trouble?"

"Because kingdoms are built on legends," Hugh said. "When the hunters are old and gray, they will still talk about how they went to Colchis and hunted for the Golden Fleece."

"So you want your own kingdom?" Aiming high.

He shrugged his massive shoulders. "Perhaps."

"Is my father aware of your plans? History says he doesn't like to share."

"I have no taste for the purple cloak," Hugh said. "Only for the laurel wreath."

The Roman emperors had assumed the purple cloak as the sign of their office, while victorious Roman generals would ride through Rome in triumph with laurel wreaths held over their heads. Hugh didn't want to be the emperor. He wanted to be the emperor's general.

"What are your plans, Kate? What is it you want?"

"To be left alone." For now.

"You and I both know that won't happen."

I touched the Golden Fleece. The tiny metal hairs felt soft under my fingers.

"I killed Voron," Hugh said quietly.

Cold washed over me. My mind served up a memory: the man I called my father in a bed, his stomach ripped open. A phantom odor, putrid, thick, and bitter, filled my nostrils. It had haunted me through the years in my sleep.

I turned.

The man sitting on the throne was no longer relaxed. The arrogance and the good-natured mirth had vanished. A somber remorse remained, mixed with a resignation born from old grief.

"Do you want a medal?"

"I didn't plan to do it," Hugh said. "I expected it would eventually come to that since Roland wanted him dead, but that day I didn't come to fight. I wanted to talk. I wanted to know why he'd left me. He was like a father to me. I went on an errand for a few months, and when I returned, he was gone and Roland told me to kill him. I never understood why."

I knew why. "Took you a while to track him down."

"Sixteen years. He lived in this small house in Georgia. I walked up to it. He met me on the porch, sword out." Old unresolved anger sharpened his voice. "He said, 'Let's see what you've learned.' Those were the last words he ever said to me. He'd raised me since I was seven, and then left without a word. No explanation. Nothing. I looked for him for sixteen years. He was like a father to me, and that's what I got. 'Let's see what you've learned.'"

I should've been furious, but for some reason I wasn't. Maybe because I knew he was telling the truth. Maybe because Voron left me just like that, without the much-needed explanations. Maybe because things I had learned about him since his death had made me doubt everything he'd ever said to me. Whatever the case, I felt only a hollow, crushing sadness.

How touching. I understood my adoptive father's killer. Maybe after this was over, Hugh's head and I could sing "Kumbaya" together by the fire.

He was waiting. This was an awful lot of sharing. Voron had always warned me that Hugh was smart. He planned strategies for fun. This conversation was a part of some sort of plan. He had to have an angle, but what was the angle? Was he trying to see how easily I could be provoked? Hearing him talk about Voron was like ripping an old wound open with a rusty nail, but Voron would tell me to get over it. Hugh wanted to talk. Fine. I'd use it against him.

"How did you kill him?" There. Nice and neutral.

Hugh shrugged. "He was slower than I remembered."

"Too many years away from Roland." Without frequent exposure to my father's magic, Voron's rejuvenation had slowed down.

"Probably. I caught him with a diagonal to the gut. It was an ugly wound. He should've died on the spot, but he held on."

"Voron was tough." *Come on. Show me your cards, Hugh. What's the worst that can happen?*

"I carried him into the house and laid him on the bed, and then I sat next to him and tried to heal him. It didn't take. Still, I thought I'd put him back together. He pulled a short sword from under the pillow and stabbed himself in the stomach."

That was Voron for you. Even dying, he managed to take away Hugh's victory.

"He passed in half an hour. I waited in the house for two days, and then I finally left."

"Why didn't you bury him?"

"I don't know," Hugh said. "I should've, but I wasn't sure if he had somebody, and if he did, they deserved to know how he died. It shouldn't have been like that. I didn't want it to end like that."

None of us did. Hugh felt betrayed. He must've imagined that he would find the man who'd raised him and get all his questions answered. He must've thought when they fought, it would be a life-and-death contest between equals. Instead he found a stubborn old man who refused to talk to him. It was a hollow, bitter victory and it ate at him for over a decade. He deserved every second of it.

Voron was the god of my childhood. He protected me; he taught me; he made any house a home. No matter what hellhole we found ourselves in, I never worried because he was always with me. If any trouble dared to come our way, Voron would cut us out of it. He was my father and my mother. Later I found out that he might not have loved me with that unconditional love all children need, but I decided I didn't care.

I stood there, looking at the Golden Fleece, and smelled that unforgettable, harsh odor of death I had smelled over a decade ago. It had hit me the moment I walked through the door of our house, and I knew, I right away knew that Voron was dead. I stood in that doorway, dirty and starved, my knife in my hand, while shards of my shattered world fell down around me, and for the first time in my life I was truly scared. I was alone, afraid, and helpless, too terrified to move, too terrified to breathe because every time I inhaled, I smelled Voron's death. That was when I finally understood: death is forever. The man who had taught me that lesson sat less than twenty feet away.

I carefully stomped on that thought before it pulled my sword out for me.

"Where were you?" Hugh asked.

I kept the memories out of my voice. "In the woods. He'd dropped me off in the wilderness three days before."

"Canteen and a knife?" Hugh asked.

"Mm-hm." Canteen and a knife. Voron would drive me off into the woods, hand me a canteen and a knife, and wait for me to make my way home. Sometimes it took days. Sometimes weeks, but I always survived.

"He left me in the Nevada desert once," Hugh said. "I was rationing water like it was gold, and then there was a flash flood during the night. It washed me off the side of the hill and into the ravine. I almost drowned. The canteen saved me—there was enough air in it to hold me over when I went under the water. So I crawl out of the desert, half-dead, and he looks at me and says, 'Follow.' And then the bastard gets into his truck and rides off. I had to run seven miles to town. If I could've lifted my arms, I would've strangled him."

I knew the feeling. I'd plotted Voron's death before, but I also loved him. As long as he was alive, the world had an axis and wouldn't spin out of control, and then he died and it did. I wondered if Hugh had loved him in his own way. He must have. Only love can turn into that much frustration. Still didn't explain why he was in a sharing mood.

"I found his body."

"I'm sorry," Hugh said. Either he was a spectacular actor or this was genuine regret. Probably both.

Screw it. "You should be. You ended my childhood."

"Was it a good childhood?"

"Does it matter? It was the only one I had, and he was the only father I ever knew."

Hugh rubbed his face. Voron was the only father he knew as well, and he'd left Hugh to rescue my mother and me. I suppose in a strange way that made us even.

"Did he ever tell you why?" Hugh asked.

"Why what?"

"The man I knew had a steel core. He would never have betrayed the man he'd sworn to protect. The Voron I knew wouldn't steal his master's wife and their child and run away with them. He wasn't a traitor."

"You really don't know?"

"No."

It had to be a lie. Roland would've told him. "Why don't you ask *him*?"

"Because it hurts Roland."

Let's poke a wasp's nest with a stick and see what comes out. "Afraid your commander and chief will do away with you?"

Hugh leaned forward. "No. I don't want to cause him more pain."

Was that genuine or was he playing me? Fine. *Let's play, Hugh.*

I came closer and sat sideways in the smaller throne, my back against the armrest. "How much do you know about my mother's magic?"

"Not much," Hugh said. "Roland was unpredictable when it came to Kalina. We all maintained some distance."

Funny how he kept calling my father Roland. He knew his real name, but he wasn't sure if I did, so he was being careful.

"She was a really powerful enchantress in the classic sense of the word. Power of love and suggestion. If she wanted you to love her, you did. You would do anything to make her happy. I think Roland was immune, which probably made him really special to her."

Hugh frowned. "Are you saying . . ."

"I spoke to some people who knew them both. The description was, and I quote, 'She fried him. She had time to do it, and she cooked him so hard, he left Roland for her.' "

Hugh stared at me. Right now he was likely wondering if I

had my mother's power and if I could fry him the way she'd fried Voron. Now we were both off-balance. *There you go. Two can play that game.*

"Do you believe it?"

"I don't know. I wish Voron were around so I could get his take on it, but some asshole showed up at my house and killed him."

A long, lingering howl came from the ravine. The high-pitched song of a wolf on the hunt rolled above the treetops. I stood up on the throne. I couldn't see jack shit. Only the trees.

"Leave them to it," Hugh said. "They're animals; it's what they do. They chase, hunt, and kill."

And just like that the lord of the castle was back.

"Why the hell did you even drag us on this hunt?"

"Because I wanted to talk to you, and they hover around you like bees around a patch of flowers. What do you see in Lennart? Is it power? Or is it safety in numbers? Trying to gather enough bodies to protect yourself?"

"He loves me."

Hugh leaned back and laughed.

I wondered if I was fast enough to stab him. Probably. But the stab would put me very close to him and he would retaliate.

"He is an animal," Hugh said. "Stronger, faster, more capable than most of his kind, but at the core still an animal. I work with them. I know them very well. They are tools to be used. They have emotions, sure, but their urges always over-ride their stunted feelings. Why do you think they make all these complex rules for themselves? Stand this close but not six inches closer or you'll get your throat ripped. Eat after the alpha starts eating, but don't get up when he walks into the room. We don't have these bullshit rules. We don't need them. You know what we have? We have common courtesy. The shapeshifters mimic human behavior much like students mimic a master artist, but they confuse complicated for civilized."

Blah-blah-blah. Please, tell me more about shapeshifters, Grandpa Hugh, because I just have no idea how they think. It's not like I live with five hundred of them and end up sorting through their personal problems every Wednesday at the Pack court hearings.

"For a moment I thought you might be a real human being,

but you proved me wrong. Thanks. It will make it so much easier to kill you."

Hugh leaned forward. A strange light danced in his eyes. "Want to give it a shot?"

Anytime. "Why, you want to show me what you've learned?"

"Ooo." Hugh sucked the air in, narrowing his eyes. "Mean. I like mean."

A strange low roar cascaded through the mountains, dying down to an odd note, almost like bleating if the goat making it were predatory and the size of a tiger.

"Damn it." Hugh stood up on his throne. "I told them to stay the hell out of the ravine."

I stood up. To the left the trees shook. Something galloped up the mountain slope straight for us.

"What is it?"

"Ochokochi. Big, vicious, carnivorous, long claws. They like to impale people with their chests."

"They what?"

"They grab you and impale you on their chest. The shape-shifters spooked the herd. Stupid sonsabitches. I asked one thing—one damn thing—and they couldn't do it right. The herd is heading for us. Normally I'd move out of their way."

"But we have the horses." Then I remembered—the path up to the meeting place was narrow and steep. We had seven horses, and getting them out and down the path in time to escape was impossible.

"Exactly. When the ochokochi go mad like this, they slaughter everything with a pulse."

A dull thudding came from below, the sound of many feet stomping in unison. How many of them were there?

Hugh jumped off the throne to the ground. "They're coming straight for us."

I moved left, putting myself between the woods and the corral with the horses. The sound of thudding feet grew, like the roar of a distant waterfall. The horses neighed and paced in the enclosure, testing their tethers.

The trees shuddered.

"Don't let them grab you." Hugh grinned at me. "Ready?"

"No time like the present." I unbuckled the spare saber at my waist, unsheathed it, and dropped the sheath on the grass.

The blackberry bushes at the edge of the clearing tore, and the woods spat a beast into the open. It stood about five feet tall, half-upright like a gorilla or a kangaroo, resting the full weight of its body on two massive hind legs. Long reddish fur reminiscent of chamois dripped from its flanks. Its front limbs, muscular and almost simian in shape, bore long black claws. Its head was goatlike, with a wide forehead and small eyes, but instead of the narrow muzzle, its face ended in powerful predatory jaws designed to shear rather than grind.

What the bloody hell was that thing?

The beast saw us and rocked back, opening its limbs as if for a hug. A sharp, hatchetlike ridge of bone protruded from its chest. Bits of dried crud clung to it, and they looked suspiciously like bloody shreds of someone's flesh.

Go to the Black Sea, meet new people, see beautiful places, get killed by a mutant carnivorous kangaroo goat. One item off my bucket list.

I pulled Slayer from the back sheath. Hugh raised his eyebrows at the two swords but didn't say anything. *That's right. Hold any comments and questions till the end.*

The creature opened its mouth, baring sharp teeth, and yowled. The terrible sound rolled through the clearing, neither roar nor grunt, but a deep bellow of a creature without power of speech driven by fear and bloodlust.

I swung my sabers, warming up my wrists. Hugh unsheathed his sword. It was a plain European long sword, with a thirty-five-and-a-half-inch blade, a simple cross-guard, and a leather-wrapped hilt. The hilt was long enough for one-handed or two-handed use. The beveled blade shone with a satin finish.

The bushes broke. More ochokochi burst into the open. The leader bellowed again.

Hugh laughed.

The monsters dropped to all fours and charged.

We stepped forward and swung at the same time. I moved left, dodging the charge, and sliced the beast's shoulder. The creature screamed and swiped at me with its claws. I leaned back just enough to avoid it and spun the swords in a practiced butterfly pattern. The bottom blade caught the beast's side; the top sliced at the side of its head. Blood sprayed. The ochokochi reared and crashed down, its legs jerking in violent spasms.

I spun my blades, surrounding myself with a wall of steel. One butterfly on top, one on the bottom. If they could bleed, they should feel pain. Here's hoping they had enough brain-power to keep clear of the thing that hurt them.

A second beast rushed me. I cut. It bellowed in agony, twisted aside, sliced and hurting, and ran off into the woods. Banzai! I didn't have to kill. I just had to hurt them enough to make them flee.

They came at me together, and I wove through the incoming rust-colored bodies, cutting and slashing. They bellowed and roared. I breathed in the aggression they exhaled and lost myself to slicing through muscle and ligaments. I'd done this hundreds of times in practice and in real fights, but no memory and no practice could compare to the pure exhilaration of knowing your life was on the line. One wrong move, one misstep, and they would trample me. I would die impaled or clawed to death. The fear stayed with me, a constant knowledge in the back of my mind, but it didn't paralyze me, it just made everything sharper. I saw the ochokochi with crystal clarity, every strand of hair and every panicked and rage-maddened eye.

Hugh worked next to me. He moved with a smooth, sparse economy, the kind that can't be learned in a dojo or in a mock fight. Hugh swung with an instinctual anticipation, a sixth sense of knowing where to land his strike and how to angle his blade for maximum impact, and when his sword touched flesh, the flesh tore. He cleaved bodies like they were butter, wasting no effort, moving without a pause, as if dancing to a rhythm only he heard. It was like watching my father. They called him Voron because death followed in his wake, the way it followed ravens in the old legends. If Voron was Death's raven, Hugh was its scythe.

We moved in perfect unison. He tossed a body at me, I sliced it, drove one at him, and he finished it with a precise, brutal cut.

More ochokochi splashed against us like a furry wave.

Two beasts descended on me, pounding the ground in tandem, barely two feet of space between them. I had nowhere to go and I couldn't stop both. I reversed the blades and stood.

They came at me, screaming. Twelve yards.

"Kate!" Hugh barked.

Ten. A moment too soon, and they would crush me. A moment too late and my life would be over.

Seven.

Five.

The breath from their mouths spilled over me.

Now. I dropped to my knees and slashed across their forelegs with both swords in a single cut.

Before they tumbled forward, the severed muscles and tendons failing under their weight, I pulled the swords to me and stood up. The two beasts passed on both sides of me and crashed behind my back, crippled.

"Damn, that was beautiful!" Hugh shouted, pulling his blade from a shaggy body.

An ochokochi lunged at him, too fast for the sword strike. Hugh swung his left arm. The back of his fist hammered the creature's skull. The ochokochi swayed and fell.

I had to avoid being punched by him at all costs.

There were no beasts within striking range. The wave of ochokochi had broken against us.

The remaining ochokochi fanned out, trying to flank me. I backed away until my spine touched Hugh's. I had no idea how, but I had known with one hundred percent certainty that his back would be there to brace me.

"Getting tired?" Hugh asked.

"I can do this all day."

The lead ochokochi bellowed. If they came at us all at once, we'd have a hell of a time protecting the horses.

Another roaring cry. The ochokochi turned as one and streamed in a rust-colored current to the right, through the bushes and trees away from us.

I exhaled.

"Looks like we dodged a bullet." Hugh grinned.

I surveyed the clearing and the heaps of brown fur dotting it. "Do ochokochi count for the hunt?"

"No."

"Damn it. There goes my chance for glory."

"You're out of luck," he said.

I slumped forward, catching my breath, straightened, and pulled a cloth from my pocket. I had to clean my swords.

•   •   •

AFTER THE FIGHT HUGH MADE NO EFFORT TO TALK. The sharing hour had passed, apparently, and we concentrated on getting the clearing back into shape.

At three o'clock Hugh pulled a horn out of his saddlebag and made a noise that would have made the dead sit up in their graves. Fifteen minutes later teams of shapeshifter hunters began trickling in. Curran and company were second on the scene after the Volkodavi. The brush rustled and the colossal gray lion pushed through it. The leonine lips stretched in a distinctly human grin. If lions could look smug, Curran did.

I raised my eyebrows. Carcasses of dead deer, tur, and goats were piled on Curran's back. He shook, tossing them to the ground, the gray mane flying in the wind, and looked at me. And then at the pile of shaggy red bodies behind me. Hugh and I had dragged them all into a big heap on the edge of the clearing to make space and keep the horses from freaking out.

The lion shrank, and a man straightened in his place. "What the hell is this?"

"Hi, honey." I waved at him from my perch on a rock and kept polishing Slayer with a little cloth.

Curran spun to Hugh. His voice was a snarl. "Did you do this?"

"I can only claim responsibility for half of the kills. The rest belong to your wife . . . fiancée?" Hugh turned to me. "You're not married, right? What is the term?"

Oh, you bastard.

"Consort." Barabas rose behind Curran. "The term is 'Consort.'"

"How quaint." Hugh winked at Curran. "No marriage, no division of property, and no strings attached. Well played, Lennart. Well played."

Curran's eyes went gold. "Stay out of my business."

Hugh smiled. "Heaven forbid. Although you should know that if the hunt had a prize for the most elegant kill, she would've won it." He turned away.

Curran looked at me. He'd never asked me to marry him. It didn't come up. This fact hadn't bothered me until Hugh rubbed our faces in it. Come to think of it, it still didn't bother me.

I slid Slayer into the sheath on my back. "How did the hunt go?"

"Fine," he said.

"Anybody hurt?"

"No."

A lean gray wolf padded over and stopped next to Curran. Its body stretched and contorted, and Lorelei stood next to Curran. Nude again. Imagine that.

"It was a most glorious hunt," she said. "Curran is amazing. I've never seen such power. It was . . ."

"I'm sure it was." I waited for him to tell her to move. He didn't. She was standing so close, their hands practically brushed. Neither of them wore clothes, and he didn't tell her to move. He didn't step away. A cold steady anger rose inside me and refused to dissipate. Nudity wasn't a big deal to shapeshifters, but if a naked man stood that close to me, Curran would bite his head off.

I waited for him to react. Nope. Nothing.

"I wish you could've joined us," Lorelei said.

I smiled at her.

Lorelei blinked and took a careful step back.

"I had my own fun right here." I got up and stepped between them. Lorelei shied to the side, letting me pass. Curran made no move toward me. I checked his face. Blank. He was closed off. It felt like a door slammed shut in my face.

Say something. Say you love me. Do something, Curran.

Nothing. Argh.

Behind Curran, now-human Desandra put her hand in the small of her back, pushing her stomach out, and winced. Radomil was standing by her, saying something in a language I couldn't understand. It must've been something funny, because she laughed. And then she subtly glanced to her left, where the Italians were sorting out their clothes. I glanced, too. Gerardo wasn't looking her way. Her face fell.

My voice came out cold. "Your clothes are on that rock, Your Majesty. I folded them for you."

"Thank you," he said, his voice casual.

"Is something wrong?" I asked quietly.

"No." A spark of frustration shone in his eyes and melted. There was my pissy lion. He was up to something. Somehow that didn't make me feel any better.

• • •

THE DJIGITS SORTED THE GAME AND TAGGED THE
hooves with different types of dye. We waited for the strag-
glers while the shapeshifters put on their clothes. The amount
of game they had killed was staggering. Dozens of animals
had lost their lives. I hoped they had ability to freeze the meat
because thinking of all that game going to waste made me ill.

The team winner would have to be declared after the castle
staff had a chance to weigh and sort the animals, but the prize
catch was painfully obvious: a beautiful mature tur, at least
two hundred thirty pounds, its horns like two curved moons.
Hugh picked it out of our pile and the djigits made a big show
of carrying it around.

"Will the hunter stand up and claim their prize?" Hugh
boomed.

Aunt B stepped forward. Hugh bowed and presented her
with the glass pitcher containing a plastic bag of panacea.
Everyone applauded.

Aunt B smiled and passed the panacea to Andrea. "My gift
to my grandchildren."

Relief flashed on Andrea's face. It was there for a mere
blink, but I saw it. She hugged the pitcher for the tiniest second before handing it over to Raphael.

Clothes were put back on, horses were freed, and we began
our descent to the castle. People around me seemed happier,
calmer, satiated.

Curran walked in front of my horse. Lorelei must've sensed
it wasn't a good time to test my patience, and she had moved to
talk to George behind us. Curran kept walking and I kept riding. Either something had happened on that hunt or he had
hatched some sort of demented plan and was now following it.

We didn't speak.

On my right Desandra chatted with Andrea about the hunt.

For the first time in months I felt completely alone. It was
a familiar but half-forgotten feeling. I hadn't felt this isolated
since Greg died. He'd taken care of me for almost ten years
after Voron's death. I had taken him for granted, and when he
was murdered, it felt like someone had cracked my life apart
with the blow of a hammer. The shapeshifters never treated
me like an outsider, but at this moment I knew exactly how a

third wheel felt. They were all still high on the thrill of the chase. It bonded them together, and here I was, the lone human on a horse, and Curran wasn't talking to me.

It was an unpleasant feeling and I didn't like it. I would deal with it. I didn't know what Curran's problem was, but I would find out. Curran never did anything without a reason and he was so controlled, even his one-night stands were premeditated.

Curran wouldn't lose his head over Lorelei, no matter how pretty and fresh she looked. He had cooked up some sort of plot, and now he was implementing it in his methodical Curran fashion, and the fact that he didn't tell me about his plan meant I really wouldn't like it. And that was exactly what worried me.

The road curved. I felt the weight of someone's gaze on me and looked up. Hugh. Looking at me as we rounded the bend. In front of him the castle loomed on top of the mountain. It was time to put my badass face on.

Twenty minutes later we dismounted in the courtyard. A djigit took my horse. Curran, Mahon, and Eduardo were speaking. I made a beeline for their group. I had some air I wanted to clear.

Out of the corner of my eye, I saw Hibla hurrying across the courtyard. I didn't want to talk to her. My shift with Desandra was about to start and I wanted to talk to Curran before it did. *Don't come over to me, don't come over to me . . .*

"Consort!"

Crap on a stick. "Yes?"

"Can I speak with you?"

No. "Sure."

We walked toward the wall, out of the way.

"The creature you killed. Did it have wings?"

"Did you have an attack?"

"It appears so." Hibla lowered her voice. "I do not wish to start a panic or a hunt inside the walls. Will you view it with me?"

Not alone, I won't. I searched the crowd, looking for Andrea, and saw her and Raphael at the doors ushering Desandra inside. Just as well.

"Derek!" I called.

A moment later he stepped out of the crowd like a ghost.

"Come with me, please."

CHAPTER 11

THE CASTLE SEEMED TO LAST FOREVER. WE CROSSED one hallway, turned, crossed another, climbed the stairs . . .

"It's a maze," Derek said.

"It's meant to be," I told him. "Like the one under the Casino at home. Except that one was designed to keep vampires from escaping, and this one was made to keep attackers from reaching vulnerable points."

We went up eight flights of stairs, until finally Hibla opened a heavy door. We stepped out onto the battlement and made our way along the top of the wall toward a flanking tower.

"Curran never does anything without a reason," Derek told me quietly.

Well, well, the Beast Lord's sudden breach of manners when it came to Lorelei hadn't gone unnoticed. Derek was trained by Jim to be observant, and now the kid was concerned for me. I was touched he was concerned, but irritation spiked inside me. Navigating my love life was hard enough right now without unwarranted assistance from teenage werewolves.

"Do you know something I don't?"

He shook his head.

We came to a doorway. A heavy door lay on its side next to

it. We followed Hibla through the doorway and climbed another set of stairs and emerged on top of the flanking tower. Perfectly round, the tower had been designed to permit bombardment of the northern slope. Not that anything could come up that way—the ground dropped off so abruptly, it had to be only a couple of degrees short of a completely vertical cliff.

An antipersonnel machine gun sat on a swivel mount, facing to the south. A high-speed, medium-sized scorpio sat behind the machine gun on a rotating mount. Shaped like a very large crossbow, the scorpio was the Roman equivalent of a machine gun. It fired arrows with enough speed to pierce armor, and judging by the cranks, this one was a serial-fire, self-loading siege engine. It would take two people to operate, but once they cranked it up, the scorpio would spit enough arrows to cut down a small army. Both the gun and the scorpio rested on a rotating platform, and switching between them in case of a magic wave would take mere seconds. *Smart, Hugh. Very smart.* We'd have to steal this setup for the Keep. Assuming we made it back to the Keep.

Two djigits stood by the siege engines. Both seemed pale.

Hibla nodded and they moved aside, revealing a long bloody smear on the stone. A severed arm lay against the wall. Long, thin fingers. Could be female. I crouched. Scratches marked the stone. To the right, bits of jackal fur stuck to the blocks, glued with dried blood. Next to them lay an orange scale. Hibla's jackal had gone down fighting.

I pulled a small plastic bag out and picked up the scale to take back to Doolittle. There was more than one of these things out there.

Derek inhaled, crouched low, and smelled the stones.

"There are four tower lookouts," Hibla said. "The shift changes every twelve hours, at six in the morning and six in the evening. This morning Tamara relieved the night lookout. This is all we have left of her."

"Who has access to the tower?" I asked.

"Nobody. Once the lookouts enter the tower, they bar the door behind them. The door was still barred when Karim came to relieve her. We had to take it off its hinges."

"Did the other lookouts hear anything?"

"No."

I looked at Derek. "Anything?"

"Similar scent as in the hallway," he said.

Locked door, heavy weaponry. The only access was from the air. So the wings had been functional after all. Still, the one I'd killed didn't have a wingspan wide enough for it to fly. It was a heavy bastard, too. I turned. The main building of the castle rose in front of me. Tall, blocky, with a blue roof.

"It glides," I said. "It probably took off from the main inner keep, swooped down, and rammed Tamara." The fight must've been brutal and quick, because the werejackal didn't have a chance to call for help.

"Why did it take the body?" Hibla asked.

"I don't know." Something had taken the other guard too, the one who'd stood over the mechanism guarding the hallway gate. "Have you ever heard about anything like that?"

Hibla shook her head. "It is not local. I know all of the local creatures."

"There must be miles of mountains out there." And some of them spawned mutant kangaroo goats with bone axes in their chests. "Are you sure these shapeshifters haven't crawled out of some dark ravine?"

She crossed her arms. "I told you I know all the local creatures."

I fought to keep from grinding my teeth. She'd invited me in and now she'd decided to get all defensive. "Any rumors of anything similar? Anything at all?"

"No. I need useful information. You are not being useful."

I thought of telling her to bend over so I could remove the iron stick she had jammed up her ass, but getting into a fight with the head of Hugh's security wasn't in our best interests. I needed to maintain a working relationship, because I might have to rely on Hibla later.

Derek was leaning over the wall. "Kate?"

I came over. The southern wall rose above a large square inner yard. Practice dummies sat along the walls. Past them a big metal cage hung from chains, about five or six feet off the ground. A pile of rags lay inside it.

The pile stirred. A rag was thrown back and then a grimy face stared up at me.

"Who is that?"

"A prisoner," Hibla said.

"Why is he in a cage?"

"He belongs to Lord Megobari. He's a criminal. This is his punishment."

Hugh put people in cages. Lovely. "What's his crime?"

"He stole."

"Take me to talk to him."

Hibla grimaced. "It's forbidden."

"The contract the clans signed gives me the authority to pursue and eliminate any danger threatening Desandra. A similar creature attacked her and we can now conclude there are more of them out there. That tells me Desandra is in danger. If Lord Megobari makes an issue of it, tell him I insisted. He will believe you."

Hibla's face told me she had no doubt about that part. "Follow me."

We entered the tower and descended a spiral staircase.

"Their scent is odd," Derek said. "Like someone shoved sandpaper up your nose. Must be something they give off only when transformed, because I haven't smelled it before."

"How tight is your security?" I asked.

If looks could conduct electricity, Hibla would've electrocuted me on the spot.

"I'm not questioning your competence," I told her. "I'm trying to do my job. If a stranger scales the wall, how fast would you know about it?"

"If he entered the keep, immediately," Hibla said. "We have patrols at the doors and in the hallways. They are trained to remember scents and faces."

"What if he entered one of the minor buildings?"

"We do rolling sweeps of every structure twice a day. We may not see him, but we would smell him. I would know within twelve hours."

I had to give it to Hugh, his security was good. "Any strangers since we arrived?"

"Aside from you and the three packs, no."

"How many people, besides us and you, are in the castle?"

"The Volkodavi have eighteen, the Italians have twenty, and Jarek Kral has twenty also."

That was fifty-eight, and including us would make it an even seventy. "And you are confident your people can recall seventy different scent signatures?"

Hibla looked at Derek.

"Yes," he told me. "Five hundred people come to the Keep during any week. I recognize every single scent."

I knew that shapeshifter scent memory was good, but I had no idea it was that good. Thinking about remembering five hundred scent signatures made my head hurt.

"How can you be the Consort and not know this?" Hibla said, in the way someone would say, *Of course the Earth is round; what are you, a moron?*

Derek bared his teeth. Great. If he went for Hibla's throat, I'd have a mess on my hands.

"In the U.S., shapeshifters don't volunteer information about themselves to others," I told her. "I learn as I go, and the subject of just how many scents you can recall never came up."

Hibla checked Derek's face. "We can recall thousands. Knowing this is important." Her tone made it plain she thought I was a moron unfit for duty. First Desandra, now her. I was beginning to get tired of the constant you-are-not-a-shapeshifter song.

"Learning other things was a priority."

"What other things?"

"How to effectively kill one of you with a six-inch knife. I'm a fast learner and I had a lot of practice. Turns out there is a way to jam the knife blade under the cervical vertebrae in such a way that your neck pops right out. Remind me some time, I'll show you."

Hibla blinked.

Derek laughed quietly.

"What about the head of the man I killed? Do you know his scent?"

"No," Hibla admitted.

"So he wasn't with any of the packs."

"No."

"And we don't know how he got into the castle?"

Her upper lip wrinkled. "No."

Strangers or not, the assaults had to be coming from one of the three packs. Someone had made a bargain with the devil and now these creatures were walking among us disguised.

We came to a heavy steel door barred by a metal rod as thick as my arm. It had to weigh at least fifty pounds. Hibla casually lifted it with one hand and pushed the door open. We emerged into the courtyard and I made a beeline for the cage.

The prisoner saw me. The pile of rags shifted and a dirt-smeared hand reached between the bars toward me.

"Please . . ."

Next to me Derek grimaced. A moment later I caught it too, the stench of stale urine and feces. Hugh was a fucking bastard. "Your magnanimous Lord Megobari lets him sit in his own excrement."

There was a small pause before Hibla answered. "It can't be helped."

Yes, it can. It definitely can.

We reached the cage. A man looked at me through the bars with feverish eyes. Not that old. It was hard to tell with all the dirt, but possibly twenties. Filthy dark blond hair. Scarce beard. His cheekbones stood out, sharp like blades on his gaunt face. Unless he was naturally emaciated, they were starving him.

"Please," he whispered.

English. Fantastic.

"Beautiful lady, please, water."

I pulled a canteen off my belt and passed it to him. He grabbed it and drank greedily, gulping the water.

"Easy. If you drink too much too fast, you'll vomit."

The man kept drinking. His hands shook. He barely looked human.

"How long has he been in the cage?"

"Two months," Hibla said.

Dear God. "And the last time he had water?"

"He gets a cup of water and a cup of gruel every morning."

This was torture. Hugh gave him just enough to keep him alive but not enough to end thirst and hunger. I'd done without water before. When you don't have it, that's all you can think about. I didn't care what the man had stolen; putting him in a cage and letting him rot in his own filth was inhuman. "How can you follow a man who does this?"

Hibla squared her shoulders. "My father was a dispatcher at the Gagra railroad station. When the Shift happened, he turned into a jackal in the middle of the station. Once the magic wave was over, the railroad guards cornered him and shot him, and when he wouldn't die, they threw him under the incoming train. And then they hunted down our family. Me, my mother, and my two brothers, we had to run into the mountains with nothing but the clothes on our backs. When I walk through the town now, people bow to me. You want to know why I follow Lord Megobari? I do it because I am not the one in the cage. You can be outraged all you want. It bothers me not at all."

The prisoner clutched his stomach and vomited water onto himself.

Hibla sneered. *"Abzamuk."*

The man shook his head, drank another desperate swallow, and hugged the canteen to him. "Thank you. Thank you, thank you, thank you."

"What's your name?" I asked.

"Christopher. Christopher. I am."

"Why did they put you into the cage?" Derek asked.

"I stole. Very bad, very, very bad. Wrong. It was a book. I wanted the knowledge." His gaze fixed on me. "Beautiful lady, kind lady. Thank you."

Derek glanced at me. "He isn't all there."

No, he definitely wasn't. Either he was nuts to begin with or sitting in the cage shook a few screws loose. Crazy or not, the desperation in his face was real. Hugh could let him die in this cage and it wouldn't bother him at all. It bothered the hell out of me.

"Christopher, today a guard died on top of the tower," I told him. "Did you see what happened?"

He looked at me with eyes that were luminescent with a mix of innocence and wonder. "I see everything. I see wonders."

Right. Lights were on, but nobody was home. "Could you tell me what you saw?"

"A beast." The man raised his hands, his fingers spread like claws. "Big, orange beast. Swooped down—whoosh— dead doggie."

Dead doggie was right.

"It is the hunter of heavens. A celestial protector."

Celestial protector. Chinese legends spoke of dragons that acted as celestial guardians, but none of them looked like cats with wings. "What do you mean by 'celestial protector'?"

"A guardian who no longer guards. A predator of the sky."

That didn't help me any. "In what country would I look for this predator?"

"It doesn't exist." Christopher gave a sad smile. "Rocks and memories forgotten."

"What happened after the beast killed the guard?"

"Then I died for a little while. I often die, but just for a minute or two. Death never stays. She only visits."

"Christopher, focus. What did the beast do after he attacked the woman?"

"I will tell you. I will tell you all, but water." Christopher held the canteen upside down, his face sad. "No more. All empty. Nothing left. *Sonst nichts.*"

That last bit sounded German.

"You give me more water and I will tell you. Everything." Christopher nodded.

"You'll tell her everything anyway," Hibla growled. "Or—"

Or nothing. "Derek, please give me your canteen."

Derek handed the canteen to me. I held it up. Christopher focused on the canteen.

"Tell me what you saw and it's yours."

"Water first."

"No. Information first."

Christopher licked his lips.

I moved the canteen toward Derek. I would go to hell for this.

"The beast took the woman. Off the wall. There!" Christopher pointed at the wall. "It bit her neck and carried her away."

On the other side of the wall was a sheer cliff. Made sense. Tamara was a grown woman, at a minimum an extra hundred pounds of deadweight, probably more. To carry her off, the beast would have to start a glide somewhere high. Leaping off the wall with several hundred feet of clear air under you would be perfect and nobody could follow it. Our investigation just withered at the root and died.

"Did the beast speak? Did you see anything else?"

Christopher shook his head and reached for the water. We wouldn't get anything else out of him. I gave him the canteen. He clutched it and hid it under his rags. Crazy, yes. Dumb, no.

We walked away.

"I shared with you," Hibla said. "What are your thoughts?"

I had to be diplomatic. "I'm formally advising you to double the patrols."

"We will," Hibla said. Green rolled over her eyes. She'd

asked for my advice, but she really didn't like me telling her what to do.

Diplomatic. "Did you tell Lord Megobari about this?"

She raised her chin. "We provide security. It is our problem."

Right. Someone in the castle was turning into a giant creature nobody had ever seen before and then making off with the guards, but let's not tell the person in charge about it. Why, that would be ridiculous. In fact, let's keep him in the dark as long as possible, so when he's attacked, he will be caught completely off-guard. Kick-ass strategy.

"Glorious lady!" Christopher called from the cage. "You are so kind!"

At least I had made his life easier, if only for a little while. "We need to see the top of the main tower."

Hibla raised her chin. "I will take you."

As we walked away, Christopher grabbed the bars. He didn't say anything. He just sat there and watched us walk away.

"You seem to think that I know nothing," Hibla said, as we walked through the hallway up to another set of stairs. "I am good at what I do."

You know what, screw it. "I get it. You probably worked hard to get where you are now. You run this place the way you want to run it, and usually you have no issues. Now you have a castle full of heavy hitters who are at each other's throats, a human who is stepping on your toes, and some weird creatures that are killing your people. You are trusted and you don't want to let anyone down. This is your home and your job. I don't want either."

She stared at me. I couldn't tell if I was getting through or not.

"All I want to do is to keep my people safe and go home. We are not opposed to each other. We want the same thing: you want us gone, and I want to be gone. I'm not a threat. I have experience, and together we would be much stronger. You must realize this, because you found us and brought us to your murder scene. But I can't work with you if every time I suggest something or question something, you bristle like a hysterical hedgehog. You can choose your pride and lose more people, or you can work with me. You still might lose more people, but at least you'll know you did everything you could to avoid that. Let me know what you decide."

She studied me. "What's a hedgehog?"

"A animal with needles on its back."

"How do I know it isn't you who is doing this? It started when you came."

"Good question," I said. "We didn't do it, because we have no motive. We want the panacea. Making sure Desandra safely gives birth is the only way to get it. Why would we attack her or your guards?"

Hibla clamped her jaws shut and didn't answer. We climbed the stairs, made our way through more hallways, and finally emerged onto the roof of the main keep, a square of stone.

Derek turned and sniffed. Hibla did, too.

"I smell urine," Derek said for my benefit.

They walked to the edge of the roof, and the stench hit me, a musky, ammonia-soaked odor, like someone had mixed vinegar, onions, and fresh urine, given it a good shake, and let it fly.

"Ugh." Derek grimaced.

"Cats." Hibla loaded so much scorn into the word, her voice was practically dripping with it.

A stain marked the stones by the west edge. Derek shook his head and paused by it. "Marks."

Long white scratches scoured the stone, where a cat had dragged his claws across the floor. The scratch marks were four feet long. Tall bastard.

"How did your people not hear this?" Derek asked.

"The castle is full of strange people," Hibla said. "They probably heard it but didn't note it." She bared her teeth. "He marked in our territory. In our house. When I find him, he will die."

Shapeshifters. The fact that he'd killed two of their people was less important than some scratches.

I surveyed the landscape. On the left the sea stretched to the horizon, blue and inviting. I would have to go swimming before this was over. On the other three sides mountains rose, like tall folds of green velvet.

"How many ways can you get to Gagra?"

"The port is the best way. Most of the roads have been destroyed by natural disasters, but there is a mountain pass to the northeast. And the railroad. The trains don't run, but one can walk it. Also there are small private train cars. They go slowly, but you could hire one in one of the bigger cities."

"These shapeshifters are strangers. Suppose a group of them came here. You said they're not local, so they wouldn't know the mountains and they likely have equipment and gear. They don't know the land. They could've flown partway, but gliding always lands you lower than your starting point. It doesn't seem very efficient or very fast. And they would be very noticeable, especially if they flew during the day."

Hibla nodded. "They didn't come through the port. I am notified of everyone who arrives."

"That leaves us with the railroad or the pass. Is there a way to check if anybody came through either?"

Hibla nodded. "There is a fort at the pass. I can tell you by tomorrow if anyone came through."

"What about the railroad?"

Hibla shrugged. "That will be harder, but I will ask some questions. I'm going to station additional guards on the walls and put another sentry here."

"Have them carry torches or flashlights," Derek said.

"We can see in the dark," Hibla said.

"He's right," I told her. "Even with night vision, in the dark you might not notice a guard being attacked right away, but you would notice a fallen torch. It's a pain in the ass and it's tedious, but it's better than being dead."

Hibla nodded. "Yes. You have a fair point."

"I would also interview my people," I said.

"I know every one of them. None of them did this."

"It goes to the theory of the crime," Derek said. "We don't know why these murders are happening and we need to figure out why, so we can anticipate their next move."

I nodded. "Two of your people are dead, Tamara and the guard by the gate. We need to know if there was any link between them. They could be random victims, or they could be part of a pattern. You need to reconstruct their lives. Did Tamara and the other guard have enemies, were they in debt, and so on? Right now we don't know enough."

"They could be targeting Desandra," Hibla said. "They could be targeting one of the packs. They could be targeting Lord Megobari."

"Exactly," Derek said. "We need to collect information and then we can howl in the dark."

· · ·

HIBLA LED US BACK TO THE MAIN KEEP AND LEFT
us to our own devices in the main courtyard. It was mostly
empty, except for some djigits tending to the horses. Above us
the sky was so blue and beautiful. I stared into it. Maybe I'd
see a flying monster and solve all of our problems.

"Are you waiting for a clue to fall on your head?" Derek
asked.

"Yep. Tell me if you see one coming."

"Nope."

"My super mental powers must be getting rusty."

We walked toward Doolittle's room.

"Thoughts?" I asked Derek.

"Jarek," he said. "He has the most to gain."

I had to agree with the reasoning. Desandra's father was
the only one who really won if she failed to survive. He
wouldn't want to be blamed for it, so he'd somehow hired or
allied himself with some weird shapeshifters and now they
were trying to nuke his daughter. It was a good theory. Except
again Jarek Kral the founder of the dynasty didn't fit with
Jarek Kral the daughter killer.

"Why take the bodies?" I thought out loud.

"Hiding the evidence. For kicks. Or food."

I glanced at Derek. Cannibalism was forbidden to shapeshifters. Eating human bodies triggered a catastrophic avalanche of hormones that led straight to loupism. It drove the
shapeshifters insane.

We reached my room. I opened the door and stuck my
head in. Empty.

"Curran?"

Nope. No Curran. Yep, he had a plan. Yep, I wouldn't like
it. Now he was actively avoiding me. Great.

The door ahead opened and Barabas stepped out. "A
moment of your time, Alpha."

"Sure." I nodded at Derek. "Will you take the scale to
Doolittle?"

He nodded. I passed him the bag and he walked off. We
watched until he walked into Doolittle's room.

"He's getting grimmer and grimmer," Barabas said.

"Derek?"

"Yes. Before long he will start emitting his own dark cloud."

"Maybe we can all sneak around under the cover of his darkness. Do you have some information for me?"

"Yes. But not here." Barabas started down the hallway, back to the stairs. I followed. We climbed the stairs and turned, Barabas opened a door, and we stepped out onto a wide, square balcony.

"This place is a maze," I said.

"And people listen to us in the walls."

We walked to the far end of the balcony.

"Lorelei Wilson," Barabas said. "Twenty-one, daughter of Mike Wilson and Genevieve de Vos. The de Vos family runs one of the largest wolf packs in Belgium. They are based in the Ardenne Mountains, in Walloon, which is a French-speaking region of the country. The family is very prosperous. They obtained their wealth during the nineteenth century from coal mining, and over the years they increased it, using the mineral-rich region to their advantage. Currently they produce steel, and Genevieve, and Lorelei in turn, have access to the money, so it's unlikely that her motives for being here are financial."

She really was a werewolf princess. "How did you manage to get all of this?"

Barabas gave a small predatory smile. "People love to talk and I love to listen. Being a handsome devil doesn't hurt either. I am charming."

"And so full of humility as well."

"Indeed."

"What is she doing here, Barabas? She isn't part of any pack that I can see. How did she even know about this meeting?"

"That I can't answer. Not yet. I can tell you that she definitely has an agenda. I watched her flit about yesterday and today. She starts every conversation with flattery. It's a deliberate choice on her part."

"Thanks."

The humor drained from Barabas's face. "As your nanny, I now have to bring up an uncomfortable fact."

"Shoot."

"Lorelei's standing too close to Curran. She's also monopolizing his time."

"I noticed."

"I don't know why he is doing this, but it's sending a signal to the other packs, and they also noticed."

Ugh. And there was nothing I could really do about that. Threatening Lorelei would paint me as insecure. Not threatening Lorelei would make me look either indifferent or clueless. It would be a hell of a lot easier if His Furriness got with the program and rebuffed her.

"I'm sure it's part of the plan," Barabas said. "I would just like to be clued in on the plan. Just for the benefit of the overall strategy."

That made two of us. "I'll talk to Curran," I said. "What about the creatures?"

"Nothing so far. Nobody has ever seen anything even remotely like this, or if they have, they're not talking."

Figured. "I need to meet with the three packs individually. Can you set this up for tomorrow?"

"Sure. To what purpose?"

"I'd like to howl in the dark."

Barabas frowned. "I don't follow."

"It's a wolf term. When you sense someone in the dark but you don't know if he's prey or a rival, you howl and see if he runs or answers. I'd like to howl at the packs and see if somebody snarls back."

"I see. They will talk to us to avoid offending us and to remove suspicion from themselves, but they might not answer any questions and we can't really compel them to do so."

"I'll take what I can get."

"Okay. I will let you know as soon as I find out more. And Kate?"

"Yes?"

"I have your back," he said.

"Thank you."

I left the balcony. Thinking about Lorelei pissed me off, but there was nothing to be done about it now. I would find Curran today and I would figure out what sort of demented plan he had cooked up. Until then, I had to concentrate on keeping Desandra alive.

Both Andrea and George had hunted and changed shape

twice in less than six hours. They would be tired. Between the man in the cage and Lorelei, I, on the other hand, was fresh as a daisy. Anger—a better alternative to caffeine.

A shadow peeled itself from the wall and followed me. Derek, moving silently along the hall, like some lethal shadow on soft wolf paws.

"This whole stealthy walking-behind-me thing you're doing is making me feel stalked. Why don't you catch up?"

He trotted over. "Just trying to keep you safe."

Et tu, Brute? "First, Barabas tells me he's got my back and now you're shadowing me. Do the two of you know something I don't?"

Derek shrugged his shoulder. "I don't like this place."

"Neither do I. Did Doolittle look at the scale?"

"Yes. He wants to talk to you."

I reversed my course. We stopped by Doolittle's room. Inside, Eduardo and Keira were playing cards. The good doctor was reading a book by the window.

"How did it go with the scale?" I asked.

"As can be expected, given the lack of equipment." Doolittle peered at me. "I'm not a miracle worker."

"He's stumped and it's making him cranky," Keira said.

Doolittle rolled his eyes. "The scale isn't a scale in the traditional sense. It's a scute."

"That explained nothing," I told him.

"Have you ever heard of a pangolin?" Doolittle asked.

"No."

"It's a mammal of the Pholidota family native to some parts of Africa and Asia. It's similar in appearance to an anteater covered with long horny scales."

"It looks like a walking pinecone," Eduardo offered. "Picture an anteater that an artichoke threw up on."

"The bony plates of pangolin are made of keratin," Doolittle said. "Same as our claws or fingernails. The skin has several layers. The top layer is the epidermis, which consists of dead cells. In snakes the scales are formed from the epidermis and they are connected, which permits ecdysis. In other words, snakes eject the entire outer layer of their skin during molting. In theory, a reptile shapeshifter would have scales every time he or she transformed. Scutes are formed in the dermis, the deeper layer of the skin. They are similar to hair in composition in that each one is individually rooted, and while they may be similar in appearance to scales, the two are different."

"So the scale is a scute. What does it mean for us?" I still wasn't quite sure where he was going with this.

"I believe they have a choice," Doolittle said. "When a shapeshifter changes form, he or she controls certain aspects of the change: the length of claws, the density of fur, the bone mass, and so on. That's what makes warrior form possible. If these shapeshifters are capable of both fur and scute production, they may choose which to sprout. Because scutes originate deeper in the dermis, a shapeshifter can keep them hidden until necessary. I also tested the tissue samples from the severed head," Doolittle said. "Their levels of Lyc-V and hormones are nearly double ours. The higher the levels of Lyc-V, provided they don't result in loupism, the greater the shapeshifter's control over his or her body."

"Okay. So what you're telling me is that they can choose to have scales or not to have scales?"

"Yes."

"But what about the wings?"

Doolittle spread his arms. "Bring me a wing and I'll tell you more."

I sighed and took myself to Desandra's room. Derek followed me, which was just as well since he was my partner for the shift.

I stuffed Lorelei far into the deep corner of my mind, the same place I put the realization that Hugh d'Ambray was within killing distance. If I concentrated too hard on either one, I'd do something rash. *Rash* wasn't in my vocabulary under the present circumstances. Not if I wanted to keep all of us breathing.

At least the Lorelei thing could be solved very simply. I had to find Curran and talk to him. He wouldn't lie to me. Of course, he wouldn't.

CHAPTER 12

WHEN I WALKED THROUGH THE DOOR, ANDREA'S eyes were really big and she had that pained expression that usually meant she wanted to pull her gun out and shoot somebody.

"What's up?"

"The Italians won the hunt," Raphael said. "We're supposed to have a big celebratory dinner in a couple of days in their honor."

Okay. Not really surprising. I'd stayed behind, which dropped our team's numbers to eleven. Half of them had guarded Desandra, and I had a feeling that Aunt B, Raphael, and Andrea had concentrated purely on getting the best kill for the panacea.

"I was just telling them it was Gerardo," Desandra said. "It's his long legs. He can run forever. Most men don't have sexy legs, but he does. They are very elegant."

Aha.

"And, like I was saying, he is hung."

Oh boy.

Andrea turned her back to Desandra and rolled her eyes. Raphael grimaced. They both looked scandalized. Dear God, what could she have said to scandalize a bouda . . .

"No, really!" Desandra nodded. "Okay, so most guys don't have a nice ball sack, right? It looks all hairy and wrinkled like some small animal died between their legs, but Gerardo's is like two plums in a velvet bag . . ."

Derek, who'd been lingering in the doorway, took a careful step to the left behind the wall and disappeared from my view.

Kill me, somebody. I raised my hand. "Hold that thought. I need to borrow Andrea for a minute."

I grabbed her arm and pulled her into the hallway. Behind us Raphael growled, "Don't leave me!"

Andrea leaned toward me. "Plums."

"Listen . . ."

Andrea raised her hands, imitating holding plums the size of small coconuts, and moved them up and down. Desandra had no idea, but I was about to save her life.

"I'm sorry I'm late. There's been another murder."

"Where?"

"On the tower." I brought her up to speed. "So sorry I got held up, but I'm here now to take Desandra off your hands."

"I love you. In a purely platonic way." Andrea stuck her head into the doorway. "Honey, come on."

They escaped. I came in and sat in the chair so I could see the door and Desandra. Derek parked himself just outside.

Desandra tried talking to me. I let her go on. After I listened for twenty minutes to detailed descriptions and point-by-point comparisons of Gerardo's and Radomil's private parts, complete with size demonstrations, Desandra finally wore herself out and fell asleep. She snored a little, whistling to herself, her belly propped on a small pillow.

Derek rose and walked over to sit by me. "How can you stand her?"

"She is lonely. She's pregnant and scared. Her father is probably trying to kill her, and neither of the men she married is offering her any support. Nor can they protect her from her own father. I don't mind cutting her some slack. She isn't the worst body I've guarded."

"Who was the worst?"

"One of the state senators got on the bad side of the law and took some bribes. His accountant blew the whistle on him. His wife was convinced that state protection wasn't good enough, so they called in the Guild. I was with them for seventy-two hours. The accountant and his wife fought the entire time. There were four of us guarding him, and by the end of the fourth day, Emmanuel, he was one of the mercs, big, cut Latino guy, really calm, walked away. He just got up and left. I asked him about it later and he said it was that or he would knock their heads together just so they would shut up . . ."

A familiar revulsion rolled over me, like an unclean oily residue laced with rotten fat. A vampire. Moving in from the right.

The only person who could possibly have a vampire in this castle full of shapeshifters would be Hugh. He either piloted it himself or had some Masters of the Dead stashed someplace, but somewhere a necromancer was pulling on a vampire's strings, sending it steadily toward us, like a worm on a hook.

Trying to figure out if I could sense vampires. *Nice try, Hugh.*

"A good way to piss away your fee," Derek said.

The vampire came closer, its mind a pinhead of hateful magic. The urge to reach out and crush its mind like a walnut was almost too much. It was close, too close. My hand itched. I wanted to get my sword and stab it.

I couldn't leave it just sitting here. If by some miracle it wasn't Hugh, it could get into the room and kill Desandra. She would give it a run for its money, but a vampire was nature's closest equivalent to a killing machine. It had no thought, consciousness, or doubts. Like a huge predatory cockroach, it obeyed only one basic impulse: feed.

I lowered my voice. "It was mostly about self-preservation. Do you remember when you and I went to White Street? The time you got your leg ripped open?"

Derek nodded. "I remember."

Here was hoping he remembered it was a vampire who tore his leg. "I think that's how Emmanuel felt. Like something was closing on him and he just had to get out."

Derek looked at me, his brown eyes focused.

"Another ten hours or so and he might have committed a homicide." *Come on, Derek. Vampire. Ten o'clock. In the wall.*

"So let me guess, he got no money." Derek rolled into a crouch in a fluid move. He was only half listening to me.

The vampire was almost directly to the left of me. I felt it. It was precisely eleven feet away, which put it right at the end of the room. The wall had to be hollow, because I saw nothing.

"Nope. And the Guild slapped him with an abandon-ment-in-progress fee."

The vampire shifted about ten inches to the left. Derek turned slightly. He was tracking it.

"In his place I would've left, too. When you've got to go, you've got to *go*."

Derek shot toward the wall. He sprinted for half a second, jumped, flying through the air, and hammered a kick to the wall. The stone block cracked and fell, breaking. Before the last chunks bounced off the floor, I was up and moving. Derek shoved his hand into the hole and yanked a desiccated, ropy arm out. He twisted the wrist, locking the elbow, and I stabbed into the dark opening. Slayer sank into vampiric flesh, sliding along bone. *Need to adjust the angle.* Coils of smoke rose from the blade as it bit into undead tissue and began to melt it. I freed it with a sharp tug and thrust again. The point of the saber pressed against the hard ball of heart muscle and I felt the precise moment the bloodsucker's heart ruptured. It writhed on the end of my sword. Still alive, nasty bugger.

In less than a breath Desandra was off the bed and next to us. "What . . . ?"

Derek kicked the wall directly under the opening. Cracks split the stone blocks. He kicked it again. Chunks of plaster showered the floor. Faux stone. Ahh. That explained it. Last time I checked, shapeshifters were strong but not strong enough to kick through solid stone.

Derek yanked the vampire out of the wall, slapping it on the floor and pinning it. I moved with them, keeping Slayer right where it was. A pale body writhed on the floor: hairless, nude. Its pale green-tinged skin fit too tightly over its frame, and every muscle and ligament underneath was clearly visible, as if someone had taken a world-class athlete, bleached him, and stuck him in a dehydrator for a few weeks. The vamp hissed. Its eyes bore into me: hot, bright red, and devoid of any thought except for an insatiable thirst for hot blood.

Slayer smoked. The flesh around the blade began to sag as the saber liquefied the vampire's heart, trying to digest it. The vamp struggled to rise. Derek strained. The muscles on his body bulged. I leaned into Slayer.

The vamp arched, lifting Derek off his feet for half a

second. The moment I removed the blade, it would go for my throat. Slayer was taking too long. We couldn't hold it.

"Drop it." I jerked the blade free. Derek hurled the vamp out and onto the stone floor. The pale body landed with a wet thud, and I beheaded it with one quick stroke. The vamp head rolled toward Desandra. She nudged it with her foot and wrinkled her nose. "Stinks, doesn't he?"

I wiped Slayer down.

Derek rolled to his feet and stuck his head into the opening. "I can see a ten-foot-wide passage to the side with a vertical shaft at the end." He indicated a rough rectangle of the wall. "This is plaster. Looks like the size of a small doorway. The rest is stone."

A light staccato of steps came down the hallway and four djigits ran into the room and halted.

"Tell Hibla we need maid service," I said. "We could handle trash in our room and an odd smell, but now we have a dead body. If this continues, we won't be able to give your hotel a decent rating."

"Yeah," Derek said, his voice completely deadpan. "The continental breakfast better kick ass or we'll complain to the manager."

DINNER WAS SERVED AT MIDNIGHT. I HAD EXPENDED some calories—Doolittle's healing made the body burn through food with wild abandon—and I was so ravenous, I could've eaten one of those mountain goats in the courtyard raw.

Sitting still while Desandra napped and the castle staff poured alcohol on the vampire blood, set it on fire, and then scrubbed it off the floor, diligently ignoring my questions such as "How did a vampire get into the castle?" and "What was it doing in the wall?" gave me a lot of time to think.

I started thinking about Curran and Lorelei, decided it would drive me nuts, and focused on the winged shapeshifters instead. I wished I had access to the Keep's library. I wished I could call a couple of people and ask them if they'd ever heard of something like that. But I had no resources beyond what was in my head and what few books I'd brought with me. Fixating on lamassu would do me no good; there was no indication that lamassu were shapeshifters. When an investigation first began, you simply collected facts. I was still in the collecting-facts stage. Drawing conclusions at this point would cause me to select facts that supported my theories and ignore those that didn't. That was a slippery slope at the end of which lay more dead bodies.

Magic had ways of spitting out new and bizarre things into the world, so just because I hadn't heard of them didn't mean these guys didn't have a long and bloody history somewhere. Up until now, I would've questioned the existence of were-dolphins as well, but having killed a few turned me into a believer. If a werewhale waddled into the castle, I wouldn't blink an eye. I'd look for a harpoon, but I wouldn't be surprised.

So suppose this was some odd scale-covered weirdo type of never-before-seen shapeshifters. Why wasn't Hugh turning the castle upside down looking for them? Hibla struck me as smart and capable but also a bit inexperienced. That wasn't a strike against her—it was unlikely that this castle had ever been attacked and she cared about keeping it safe, so much so that she'd swallowed her pride and come to me for help. Considering how everybody and their mother had been lamenting the fact that I was not a shapeshifter and, therefore, must be inferior, Hibla's coming to me was nothing short of a miracle.

So she didn't have the experience to deal with it, but Hugh had experience in spades. Why wasn't he taking any action?

The better question was, did he engineer this whole thing? If this was some sort of elaborate setup, I couldn't see what he had to gain by it, but I couldn't mark him off the list of potential suspects either, just like I couldn't cross out Jarek Kral, the Volkodavi, or the Belve Ravennati.

I would have loved to eliminate one suspect. Just one. It didn't even matter which one. If I could drop one faction from the list, I would do a jig right there in front of everyone and weep for joy.

The cleaning staff left. Derek raised his head and sniffed the air.

If somebody ever hired us for another bodyguarding job, I'd fight tooth and claw to bring Derek with us. He smelled people coming before I ever heard them.

"Who is it?" I asked.

"Isabella," he said.

The matriarch of Belve Ravennati was coming to pay us a visit.

"I don't want to talk to her!" Desandra jumped off the bed and took off for the bathroom.

Okay. I got up, and Derek and I blocked the doorway. Isabella Lovari strode down the stairs and toward us. A young dark-haired woman accompanied her.

They stopped before us.

"I've come to check on my grandchild."

Someone must've told her about the vampire. "Desandra is safe. The babies are fine."

"I will see for myself."

"She doesn't want to see you right now," I said.

"I will have to insist," Isabella said.

"Or you could choose to talk to her later at dinner," I said.

Isabella narrowed her eyes and looked me over slowly. "For a human in the den of beasts, you have a lot of arrogance. What makes you think you're safe?"

I'm sorry, I was a human? I had no idea. What a surprise. "What makes you think I'm not?" And what an awesome comeback that was. Wow, I showed her.

Isabella smiled, her eyes cold like two chunks of coal. "When an alpha stands in front of you, the proper response is respect and fear, you human idiot. Were you a shapeshifter, you would know this."

Name-calling, huh.

Derek bared his teeth.

"If I cringed every time an alpha of another shapeshifter pack showed his teeth, I would be you."

Isabella glared at me. The woman at her side tensed.

Did you like that? Here, have another one. "Where I come from, we don't give up our daughters-in-law just because Jarek Kral snarls. But I understand you do things differently. If Kral ever decides to take away your lunch money, let me know and we'll help you out."

Isabella blinked. The dark-haired woman said something in Italian. Isabella's stare gained a deadly edge. "This will help you not at all. You are being replaced, and you are so stupid, you don't even realize it. When a shapeshifter loves a woman, he doesn't let another woman hunt next to him, nor does he let her finish his kills. When Lennart throws you away, I will be waiting."

She turned around and marched away, her younger escort in tow. I waited thirty seconds.

"Did this happen?"

Derek paused before answering. "Yes."

"So he let Lorelei finish his kills?"

"Yes."

"Does this mean something or is she just blowing smoke in my face?"

Derek sighed. "He shouldn't have done it. It's something wolves do. It's not like offering food, but it's close."

My chest suddenly acquired a heavy rock. It rolled inside me, hurting.

"It can also be taken a different way," Derek said. "Parents let kids finish their kills. Older brothers let younger kids do it . . ."

I looked at him.

"He shouldn't have done it," Derek said. "But he never does anything without a reason."

"When I asked you if you knew something I didn't, you lied to me."

"I didn't lie. I just didn't volunteer information. I didn't want you to worry."

I wasn't worried. When Curran got here, I intended to trip him, sit on him, and shake him until he explained this thing to me. So far, he'd let her stand naked next to him, he'd let her hunt with him, he'd let her finish his kills—whatever the fuck that meant—and in the past twenty-four hours he'd spent more time listening to her than he had speaking to me.

A cold thought squirmed through me. From a purely logical point of view, Lorelei would make a better Consort. She was a shapeshifter, she had ties to the largest shapeshifter pack in the United States, and her father wasn't planning to exterminate the shapeshifters because they were becoming too powerful.

Logically it made sense, but none of that mattered, because the man who'd fallen asleep next to me last night loved me. I would bet my life on it. The way things were going, I just might have to.

Derek walked out into the hallway and stayed there.

"What are you doing?"

He nodded at the stairs. Curran jogged down, jumped, covering the last few steps, and headed straight for me, light on his toes, radiating that contained physical energy that pulled me like a magnet.

I scrutinized his face. He seemed on edge, his expression worn, the line of his mouth tired but firm. His eyes said that he was tired and annoyed, and if you got in his way now, he'd snap your neck without hesitation and keep going about his way.

I crossed my arms. "You—"

Curran gathered me to him and kissed me. It was a long, lingering kiss, made from fading exasperation, relief, and happiness. He smiled at me, those eyes so warm and welcoming. "I wanted to do this all day."

Okay. Now I was officially bewildered. I waited to see if question marks would sprout all around me, but the air stayed clear.

He noticed the hole in the wall. "What the hell happened?"

"We redecorated." I kept my voice level. "Where have you been?"

"The Belve and the Volkodavi wanted to discuss things, and I had to sit in as a witness."

"For five hours?"

"More or less. We just finished."

And Isabella must've come here right away to bug Desandra.

Curran dragged his hand over his face, as if hoping to wipe away fatigue. "They are trying to hammer out some sort of agreement to unite against Kral. I haven't eaten since the hunt. I'm starving."

"Did they succeed?"

"Hell no. Everybody was tired from the hunt and irritable as fuck. They bickered about inheriting the pass, and did their grandstanding, and accused each other of things. Radomil fell asleep. For a few minutes it looked like they might actually agree on something. Then the younger brother—Ignazio— decided it would be a grand idea to jump up and announce that when his nephew was born, at least he would be born smart like his father, so he should inherit the pass and not the other kid, who's been fathered by a *citrullo*."

"What's a *citrullo*?"

"From what I gathered, it's either a cucumber or a half-wit." Curran shook his head. "Then the Volkodavi started yelling. The Belve yelled back. Radomil woke up and someone clued him in that he had been insulted but apparently not who'd done it, because Radomil went after Gerardo and called him *parazeet* and *viridok*."

"Parasite and bastard," I translated. Voron was Russian. I spoke it well enough, better now that I had someone in Atlanta to practice with, and I'd hung out enough with Ukrainians to pick up the language. Curses were the second thing you learned, right behind *yes*, *no*, *help*, *stop*, and *where is the bathroom?*

"Ahh." Curran nodded. "That explains why Gerardo's mother went furry."

"So what happened?"

"Then I roared. Then everyone got insulted and declared that they wouldn't stand for this and the meeting was over. Good too, because I've had it with them. I wouldn't give these kids to either one of the packs. They don't give a shit about them or Desandra. As they were leaving, I could hear them yelling at each other. After Gerardo called Radomil every curse under the sun, Radomil's brother told him that smart men keep bitches in heat on a chain."

I developed a sudden strong urge to punch both of them in the face.

"He is lucky that he said that to Gerardo. If he'd said it to me about you, that would've been it. He would never say anything else."

Curran fell silent. I turned. Desandra stood in the doorway of the bathroom. Color drained from her face. "Vitaliy said that?"

Curran looked like he wanted to be anywhere but here. "Yes."

"What did Gerardo do?"

"He called him some name I didn't catch."

"But did he do anything?"

"No," Curran said.

"I see," she said quietly. "I don't think I'll be going to dinner today. My bitch chain isn't long enough."

"Desandra . . ." Curran said.

She raised her hand. "Don't." Her voice shook. She was about to snap.

I needed to talk to Curran. But Desandra was about to lose it. Abandon her or straighten this out? It would be a long conversation . . .

Desandra made a small strangled noise in her throat. Damn it. He was tired, we were both starving, and privacy was in short supply. I'd waited this long; I could wait until we were alone. I turned to Curran. "Why don't you go without me? Make an appearance, snarl, and all that. I'll be here."

Curran looked at Desandra for a long moment. "I'll be back."

"Bring us some food," I told him. "And I really need to talk to you when you come back."

"Okay." He kissed me and left the room.

Derek came inside and shut the door behind him.

Desandra sank on the bed, put her hands over her face, and began to cry.

DESANDRA WEPT.

Kill me, somebody. I never knew what to do or what to say. I got a soft towel from the bathroom and brought it to her. Desandra's shoulders shook. She sobbed quietly. At the entrance Derek was doing his best to fade into the woodwork.

I sat next to her on the bed. She cried in a thin, heart-wrenching voice, her sobs leaking complete despair, as if her world were ending. Her father was an abusive asshole who used her as a bargaining chip. The two men she had married didn't love her or her children. Right now only we truly cared about her welfare, and we did so because we would be paid with panacea at the end. I wished I could say something or do something to make her feel better.

Gradually the sobs slowed down. She pulled away from me and pressed the towel to her face.

"I feel so alone," she said quietly. "I just want one of them to care. But they don't."

"They probably don't," I told her.

Her makeup had run and dark streaks of smudged eyeliner stained her cheeks. She wiped her face with the towel. "And I won't have a choice."

"What do you mean?"

"When the babies are born, what will happen? Are they

going to force me to go with whoever's son is born first? Are they going to take my children from me and throw me back to my father, so he can tell me every day how I cost him the pass and what a worthless waste I am?"

"I don't know," I said.

She looked at me and whispered, "I'm afraid to love my own babies, because I won't get to keep them."

Oh God.

Thinking of being paid for all this misery churned my stomach. If it had been up to me, I would have said *screw it*. I'd take her out of here, away from all of them, whether I got my fee or not. But it wasn't about me. It was about Maddie lying twisted in a glass coffin while her family prayed we would make it back safe. It was about Andrea's future babies. And about mine.

"Someone's coming," Derek said.

I rose from the bed and moved to the door. Raphael and Andrea rounded the corner.

"What are you doing here?"

"We heard crying," Raphael said.

"Fuck me," Desandra said from the bed. "Can't a woman cry in peace?"

"Not with these acoustics." Andrea came into the room and showed us a plate of fruit. "I got snacks."

Derek looked at the platter with that particular longing, the way a starving dog eyes a juicy steak.

"Are you staying for a bit?" I asked Andrea.

"You bet."

I glanced at Derek. "Why don't you go and grab a bite to eat? We don't know when Curran will be back."

"Come on," Raphael told him. "I'll walk with you."

Raphael winked at me, and he and Derek took off.

Half an hour later Desandra had finished eating and was passed out, snoring up a storm. We sat on the floor on the rug, the mostly empty platter of fruit between us. I stole another apricot. I was still hungry.

"You should go to dinner," Andrea said. "I'll watch Ms. Preggers."

"It's still my shift. You had your turn already."

"Yes, but Princess Wilson isn't out there making googly eyes at Raphael." Andrea bared her teeth.

"Is Lorelei at dinner?"

"Yes. Yes, she is. She's wearing a see-through dress and she is practically melting when Curran looks at her."

There were times in my life when supreme mental powers would come in handy. Right now I wished I could telepathically reach into the dining hall and slap Lorelei out of her chair.

"I have a job to do." I leaned back against the bed and closed my eyes for a moment.

"You okay?" Andrea asked me.

No. No, I wasn't okay. People were dying. A pregnant woman was in danger. A young pretty shapeshifter girl with heavy political clout was going after Curran and there wasn't anything I could do about any of it.

"Did you know Hugh has a man in a cage in the inner yard? He's been in there for weeks. He's slowly starving to death. And I can't do anything to get him out."

"The worst change of subject ever," Andrea said. "I thought we were talking about Lorelei?"

"I don't like her," Desandra said from the bed.

Damn it. "I thought you were asleep."

"You never talk about anything interesting when I'm awake."

"That's because we don't trust you," Andrea said.

"I know that. But I've got gossip on Lorelei and you don't." Desandra scooted up, propping herself up on the pillows. "Like who invited her to the stupid meeting."

"Okay, I'll bite. Who?"

"She invited herself," Desandra said. "She wrote a letter to Lord Megobari and told him that she and Curran were childhood friends, and that she knew many people from Atlanta. This was her only chance to see him and could she please visit. She wouldn't be any trouble."

Hugh must've just loved that. The smug bastard probably laughed when he read that letter. How did Lorelei even find out about this entire affair?

"Who knew about Curran coming over to arbitrate?" I asked.

Desandra shrugged. "I didn't know until two weeks before Lorelei showed up."

"So she had insider information," Andrea said. "I wonder where she got it."

"That I don't know." Desandra grimaced. "I can tell you that when she got off the ship, she was really friendly. Really. She had the whole sweet and innocent act going." Desandra fluttered her eyelashes. *"Oh poor me, I am a sweet and honeyed flower, too delicate and . . .* What's the word when you are like, *Oh, I am so honest and I just want to help?"*

"Earnest?" Andrea suggested.

"Yes, that. But I did the same thing at her age. I could tell she was a snake. Once she realized I wasn't about to be her best friend, this whole big holier-than-thou thing came out. I had a fight with my father and she told me that I was inappropriate. Then one time . . . okay, so pregnant women get gas. Your stomach is the size of a backpack, and when you do get gas, it hurts to breathe. So I farted. I couldn't help it. She called me vulgar. I told her to mind her own business, and she said that I was shameful and no self-respecting person would associate with someone like me. I was an embarrassment to my father and my husband. I had no honor." Desandra grimaced. "She must've grown up in a fish tank or something. She has all these weird ideas about how people are supposed to interact. Like she is some kind of nobility and we're all just peasants."

Interesting. "What did you do?" I asked.

"I'd checked up on her. Her dad is some big alpha in the U.S., but her mom couldn't stand him so she took Lorelei and moved back to Belgium. There is only one major shapeshifter pack in Belgium, and Lorelei's grandparents are running it. They didn't really want her mother or her back, so they let them come back on one condition: neither of them can have anything to do with the running of the pack. There is some family money and they are not hurting, but neither of them can ever be an alpha. They didn't want them to compete with their son. So when Lorelei told me I was an embarrassment, I told her I was daughter of an alpha and wife to two future alphas, and that three packs were crossing the sea because of me. I asked her how fast did she think they would throw her into the sea if I asked them to do it."

"Ha!" Andrea grinned.

I wouldn't mind throwing Lorelei into the sea, but right now the need to punch Curran was much stronger. "What did she say?"

"She got all shocked, worked up some tears, told me I was a horrible person, and ran away. We were eating at the time, and nobody followed her, which probably spoiled her plan." Desandra leaned forward and winced. "Ow. I keep forgetting not to do that. Anyway, I grew up in a pack that was a mine-field. I like that word, by the way. Very nice. I've seen her type before. Lorelei is intelligent, meaning she has some brains, but she's also young and inexperienced. She doesn't under-stand what makes people tick and she thinks that everyone is much stupider than her. She's a classic sociopath: she's charm-ing and manipulative, she believes she's entitled, she never genuinely feels guilt, and when she offers an apology, it's superficial. She mimics happiness and she can probably mimic love. She isn't psychopathic—her temper is pretty even, she isn't necessarily predatory, and I can't see her trying suicide. Way too narcissistic."

"How the hell do you know all this?" Andrea asked.

Desandra sighed. "I've read a lot of psychology books. I started when I was a kid. I was trying to diagnose my father."

Well, that was a surprise. "What's the verdict?"

"He is a severe megalomaniac. He has intense narcissistic personality disorder, complete with occasional paranoia. He displays every one of Hotchkiss's seven deadly sins of narcis-sism. That's how I learned to manipulate him. Unfortunately, knowing that didn't help me with my mental health any, and he also knows which buttons to push."

"Why don't you . . ." Andrea struggled for words. "Act more sane?"

"Self-defense," I told her. Suddenly many things made sense.

"She's right," Desandra said. "How long do you think I would survive if they knew I had a brain? The only reason I'm not locked up is because they think I'm emotional and stupid. I *am* emotional—pregnancy hormones are no joke. But I'm not dumb. My mother was smart, and if you ask my father, he'll show you many spots where people who thought they were smarter than him are hidden six feet under the ground. If Gerardo's mother thought for a moment that I had more brains than a butterfly, she'd have kept me under lock and key the entire time I was married to him. When I told Gerardo we couldn't fight my father, I didn't do it because I was weak. I did it because I knew we couldn't win. I thought about it and

I weighed the odds, and they were not in our favor. Personally I hope Jarek pisses Curran off. That would be about the only person here who could kill him. Anyway, did you see Lorelei's book?"

"What book?" I asked.

"Some fantasy book she carries around. Something about a princess on the throne in some kind of crystal. There is this older knight who has known her since she was a child, so he goes on some sort of journey to get a magical blue rose gem to rescue her. He gets the gem, frees her, and she makes him her king." Desandra stared at me. "Lorelei wants her throne. She knows in her heart she is entitled to it. In her head Curran is the only way she can get it. Kate, she will do anything to get it. It's so close, she can taste it. If I were you, I wouldn't stand near cliffs when she's around, because she will push you over."

"At this point she would have to get in line." What Lorelei did or didn't want mattered very little. Lorelei had promised me nothing. Curran, however, had promised me everything. If he was planning on pulling the plug on us, I wanted to know why.

I would sleep on it, and tomorrow morning, I'd get my answers, whatever they would be.

The sound of steps came from behind the door, followed by a knock. If it kept going this way, we'd have to invest in some iron bars and one of those sliding windows, so I could open it and yell at people to go away.

"Who is it?"

"It's me," Hugh said.

Andrea reached for her SIG-Sauer.

What the hell was he doing here? Just what I needed. I walked up to the door. "Whatever you're selling, we're not buying."

"Open the door, Kate. I'm not going to attack you in Desandra's room."

Fine. I unbarred the door and opened it. Hugh stood on the other side in all his glory: black boots, dark pants, dark leather jacket thrown over a blue T-shirt. His dangerously square jaw was freshly shaved. Well, well. Someone had dressed up for dinner.

He glanced at my shoulder. I looked out of the corner of my eye. Black streaks from Desandra's eyeliner stained the green fabric of my T-shirt. She must've brushed against me when she was crying. Considering that it was also smudged with dried blood from the ochokochi, my shirt was beginning to look tie-dyed.

"Can I help you?"

"You weren't at dinner," Hugh said, leaning one arm on the wall. "I came to see if all was well."

That was quite a pose. "Couldn't you just send another vampire instead? I haven't gotten my evening exercise."

"I'm sorry. Next time, I'll be sure to find some lambs for your slaughter."

He showed no signs of leaving.

"Did Hibla tell you that a djigit was killed on the tower? A woman. Her name was Tamara."

"She did."

"Are you behind these attacks?"

He smiled. "And if I were, wouldn't telling you defeat the purpose?"

"I don't know what your plan is, but if you interfere with my ability to do my job, you will regret it."

"Do I look scared to you?" he asked, his voice lazy.

He was trying to goad me into a pissing contest. Been there, done that, got the T-shirt. "No, and that worries me. You're supposed to provide a safe environment for this pregnant woman. Instead your guards are dying and some creature tried to kill her two hundred yards from your dining hall. Why aren't you foaming at the mouth? Doesn't it bother you that someone's making a fool of you in your own castle?"

Hugh opened his mouth.

Curran walked up the stairs carrying a platter heaped with food with one hand. George walked next to him. Curran saw Hugh and focused on him with a single-minded intensity.

"Here comes the cavalry." Hugh winked at me.

Curran stepped between me and Hugh. His voice was cold. "One of us isn't supposed to be here."

"Let me guess, would that be me?"

"Yes. Your guests miss you."

Hugh chuckled. "We'll continue our conversation later, Kate." He walked away.

"Couldn't you have waited thirty seconds?" I growled. "I wanted to hear his answer."

"No. He has no business talking to you and anything he says is a lie."

"Is that food?" Desandra called out. "I am so hungry."

"We were just leaving," Andrea said.

"Yes, we were," George confirmed. "I came to walk you to your room."

They took off. I sighed and passed the platter to Desandra.

Later, after we ate, Desandra fell asleep, exhausted, for real this time. Derek came back from dinner, saw Curran, and excused himself to the bathroom. Curran and I barred the door and checked the balcony door and the windows. I put a spare blanket on the floor. He stretched out on it and I lay next to him. Around us soothing darkness filled Desandra's cavernous bedroom.

Derek was still in the bathroom. The boy wonder was giving us an illusion of privacy.

"Are we being listened to?" I asked.

"If we are, I can't hear them."

Figured. Once we nuked the vampire, the hiding place was exposed.

"I saw Doolittle at dinner," Curran said. "He said he has something important to tell you."

"Is it urgent?"

"He said it would wait till the morning. We couldn't really talk. Too many people around. What did you want to talk about?"

This would have to be done carefully, with some finesse. I opened my mouth, trying to find the right words. Think subtle . . .

He raised his eyebrows. "What's the holdup?"

"Trying to find the right words."

"Why don't you just say it?"

"What the hell is wrong with you? You're letting Lorelei stand next to you naked, kill your crap, and do your hunting? Are you out of your mind or do I need to pack up and leave?"

Damn it. Subtle, really subtle.

He smiled at me. "I love you. You don't need to worry about Lorelei. She's happy she's grown up, so she flaunts it. It's harmless."

"What about the hunt?"

"Who else would she hunt with?" Curran shrugged and pulled me closer. "I have no interest in Lorelei. She's a kid."

"So this is not part of some plan you thought up?"

"No."

This should've been the end of it, but the suspicion remained, nagging me. I crushed it. He said he wasn't interested. End of story.

"What did you and Hugh talk about while we hunted?"

"He said he killed Voron." I tried to keep the hurt out of my voice and couldn't.

Curran paused. "Is he lying?"

"I don't think so. Voron raised him the way he raised me, then abandoned him. I took him away from Hugh and then Hugh took him away from me. I suppose that makes us even. I still want to murder him."

"Maybe we'll get that chance," he said.

"Maybe."

"Did he say anything else?"

"Nothing important. He feels shapeshifters are ruled by their urges."

"If I were ruled by my urges, he'd be dead."

Or you. "Curran . . ."

"Yes?"

"I saw him fight. You remember my aunt? Hugh is better."

"It doesn't matter," Curran said. "I will end him."

But it did matter to me. If Curran killed Hugh but died fighting him, it wouldn't be worth it. I just had to kill Hugh first. Piece of cake.

"It's this place," I told him. "It's driving all of us out of our skin."

"We'll go home soon." He closed his eyes.

A deafening crash shattered the silence. I jumped to my feet. Derek burst out of the bathroom.

The familiar grating roar, like gravel being crushed, rolled down the hallway, followed by an enraged deep bellow, pure fury expelled in a single mindless torrent. I'd heard that sound before and it was impossible to forget. It was the war cry of a werebuffalo.

CHAPTER 13

———◆———

CURRAN FLUNG THE DOOR OPEN AND CHARGED into the hallway. I slammed the door shut behind him, just as Derek tried to run after Curran. The boy wonder spun on his foot at the last moment, avoiding the collision. Desandra was our first priority. If she died, Maddie and our chance at the panacea died with her.

"What's going on?" Desandra rolled off the bed.

I barred the door and pulled Slayer free. Derek yanked off his clothes. Fur dashed up his frame.

In the hallway a chorus of vicious snarls broke into yelps of pain and deep growls. Something howled. The hair on the back of my neck rose. I flipped the light switch. Bright yellow light flooded the bedroom.

"What's going on?" Desandra yelled.

"I don't know. Get behind me."

Something smashed into the door with a loud thud. The boards creaked.

Another thud hammered the door.

I backed away, Slayer ready. Next to me Derek bared his monster teeth.

The door boards snapped with a sharp crack, the sound of

splintering wood like a gunshot. Two bodies tumbled into the room, one gray, one gold. Curran landed on his back, a scaled yellow beast on top of him. The beast raised its feline head and snarled at me, stretching two enormous wings. Two green eyes stared at me with a hot, terrible hatred.

Curran's mouth gaped. He jerked the beast down and bit into its shoulder. The giant lion fangs cut into the flesh like scissors. Thick red blood wet the scales.

The beast howled in pain and raked Curran's side with its hind claws, trying to rip his stomach open. Blood drenched the gray fur. The two cats rolled, clawing and snarling.

The balcony door exploded in a glittering cascade of shards. A second amber beast shot into the dark room.

"Down!" Andrea barked from the doorway.

I shoved Desandra into the corner. Andrea's gun barked, spitting thunder and bullets. *Boom! Boom!*

The beast jerked, each shot knocking it back.

Boom! Boom!

She kept firing. The bullet tore through the creature's flesh.

The magic wave crashed into us in an invisible flood. Tech vanished from the world in an instant. Lights went out, the sudden darkness pitch-black and blinding. Andrea's gun choked on the bullets.

The lavender feylanterns flared into life, spilling eerie purple-tinted light into the room.

Andrea spun to the side, and a spotted bouda shot past her and leaped onto the creature, tearing into it with a yowl. Raphael.

The beast shook, an amber blur, and batted Raphael aside with a clawed paw. The bouda landed in a roll and ran back at the beast.

I lunged at the orange monster. Claws raked my thigh, ripping my jeans and skin in a hot flash of agony. I ignored it, thrust, sinking Slayer deep between its ribs, and withdrew. Derek jumped, clearing the wings, and clung to the beast's back, clawing into its spine. The creature howled and spun, its wings straight out. I ducked under the wing and the massive tail took me off my feet. My back hit the wall. Ow. The world swam.

No. No, you sonovabitch, you won't kill a pregnant woman today. Not on my fucking watch.

I bounced onto my feet and slashed across the creature's

flank. The beast shook, trying to throw Derek off its back. Derek hung on. On the other side Raphael snarled, biting and clawing.

Desandra lunged at the beast, grabbed a wing, and wrenched it to the side. Bone snapped.

The beast spun again. I dropped, ducked under, and sliced a deep cut along the beast's gut. Innards spilled out in a hot bloody mess. I stabbed the scaled flank again and again, trying to cause damage. *Die. Die already.*

A massive shaggy shape shot into the room and a thousand pounds of furious Kodiak crashed into the beast like a runaway train. The impact drove the creature back into the bed. The heavy piece of furniture flew, knocked aside by their bodies. The beast crashed against the wall. The Kodiak's enormous paw rose like a hammer. The thick bones of the beast's skull crunched, an egg dropped on the pavement. Wet mush splattered the wall.

The Kodiak moved, and I saw Curran rise at the opposite wall, his arms locked on the winged creature. Covered in blood, his eyes glowing, he looked demonic. The Beast Lord strained. A rough growl ripped out of his mouth. The left arm and a part of the orange creature's chest moved away from the right side and its head, the bones wrenched apart. Blood gushed from the gap studded with broken bones.

The beast flailed, screaming. Curran bit into its exposed throat, grabbed its head, and ripped it off the body, hurling it to the floor.

The Kodiak melted into a human shape. My brain took a second to process that it was female and not Mahon. George's wide eyes stared at me. She grabbed my hand. "Doolittle is hurt!"

"GO," ANDREA YELLED AT ME. "GO, WE GOT THIS!"

I ran after George into the hallway. My right side and thigh screamed. Blood soaked my jeans, most of it my own.

Chunks of orange corpses littered the floor: a wing, a scaled leg. I never understood why a dead shapeshifter turned human, but chunks of him torn in a fight stayed in the animal shape. "What happened?"

"Aunt B and Dad," George yelled over her shoulder. "Faster, Kate."

I chased her, slid on gore, and half stumbled, half ran into

Doolittle's room. A werejaguar blocked my way and snarled in my face, big teeth snapping.

"It's me!" I yelled into her open maw.

Keira shook her furry head and half stepped, half swayed aside. Blood soaked her left side.

The furniture lay in shambles. Broken glass littered the floor. In the corner Eduardo slumped, breathing in shallow gasps, his human body slick with blood. Jagged gashes crossed his chest and stomach. Red muscle crawled in the wounds—the Lyc-V was scrambling to repair the damage. I crouched by him. Good strong pulse.

George grabbed my arm and pulled me to the corner. A huge honey badger the size of a pony lay on the floor, his head twisted at an odd angle. Oh no.

I dropped by the body and searched for a pulse on his neck. A vein fluttered under my fingertips, weak, so weak. My hand came away red. He was bleeding and with all the damn fur, I didn't even know where.

I began to chant, pulling the magic to me. Whatever little healing I could do was better than nothing. *Come on. Come on!*

Doolittle lay unmoving. He hadn't turned, which meant he was still alive. It also meant Lyc-V didn't have enough juice to change his shape. He was dying.

No, no, God damn it. I chanted, putting all of my magic into the healing. Without knowing what the injury was, all I could do was hold on to him. I wasn't a medmage, but I had raw power.

George stood next to me, tears running down her face. "Save him. You have to save him."

I chanted, focused on the body and the fragile weak shiver of life inside it. It pulled me in, drawing me deeper and deeper, until it was just me and the weak fragile spark of Doolittle's life. I cradled it with my magic, trying to anchor it.

Magic boiled inside me, sucked into Doolittle's body in a painful whirlpool. It felt like my flesh was ripping off my bones.

"How is he?" Aunt B asked, far away.

A shadow loomed over us. I caught a glimpse of dark fur—Mahon towered by me.

Doolittle's body shuddered. A tremor shook his limbs. Slowly the fur melted. The medmage drew a hoarse breath. Blood slipped from his bruised lips.

Doolittle's kind eyes stared at me, bloodshot and glassy. "Broken spine." His breath came out whistling. His voice was weak and hoarse, barely a whisper.

Shit. Shapeshifters healed broken limbs, but a broken spine was a different story. "Don't talk. Did you bring any tank powder with you, Doctor?" It was the same powder used for the solution in which Maddie rested back home.

Doolittle smiled, a weak sad smile. My heart broke.

"Yes."

"Get the tank."

"What?" George bent over me.

"Find the powder for the healing solution and get the tank ready."

"We don't have a tank!"

"Use whatever you can find." It wasn't the tank that mattered, but the solution inside it.

I heard her tear through the room, throwing debris out of the way.

"It won't help. C2 and C3 are fractured."

Cervical vertebrae. The higher the number, the closer to the skull and the worse the injury. "Don't talk."

"C4 is crushed," the medmage whispered. "Spinal cord damaged. It hurts to breathe."

I resumed chanting, pulling the magic to me in a desperate rush. His neck wasn't just broken. Broken would be okay. The fight had flattened Doolittle's neck. The crucial upper vertebrae had shattered, cutting the link between his brain and his body. He was shutting down.

"Nonsense, Darrien." Aunt B crouched by him. "Of course you can. Kate will heal you."

No, I can't.

"I'm bleeding internally. I can't stop it." His voice dissolved into a hoarse groan.

Heat rolled down my cheeks.

"Don't cry." Doolittle smiled. "Please don't. I had a long life . . . A long useful life." His voice broke into a horrible noise. He sounded like he was choking. "I'm . . . ready."

"We're not!" George cried out.

My lips moved. I willed him to live with each whispered

word, but he was fading, slipping through my fingers. Doolittle had saved me more times than I could count. I would
keep him alive. Whatever magic I had, it was his. It would
have to be enough.

Live, I willed. *Please, please live. Please don't go.*

He slipped further away from me. I was losing him, just
like I had lost Bran.

I chanted, concentrating all my will on that little spark.

The world faded. The noises receded.

My lips moved, whispering the words on, and on, and on . . .
It was a very simple chant that most people in my line of work
learned. It was designed to boost the body's regeneration, and I
poured all of myself into it. Only the next word and the tiny bit
of magic it invoked mattered. If only I could claw myself open
to get at the magic to keep him alive, I'd do it in a heartbeat.

My lips were numb. I couldn't feel my legs. The bottom
half of me turned into a hole filled with pain. Too much magic
drained too quickly.

Doolittle's eyes rolled back in his skull.

"Kate!" George yelled.

"Let me through!" Hugh roared in the back. "Let me
through, damn it!"

Half a dozen snarls answered.

The chant had consumed me. I'd sunk every iota of my
magic into it and now I struggled to break free. My voice was
a mere whisper. "Let."

Curran crouched by me.

"Let him." *Let him in.*

Curran rose. "Let him through."

A moment later Hugh knelt by Doolittle. "Broken neck."

"Yes."

Hugh looked at me, his blue eyes studying me.

"Do you want him to live?"

"Yes."

Hugh rocked back, raised his head, and closed his eyes.
Magic pulsed from him, like the toll of a colossal bell. It
touched the bloody floor. Blue vapor rose from the blood,
streaking upward.

The air around Hugh began to glow. I felt the magic move,
a massive heavy current of it. So much power. Holy shit.

I held on to Doolittle with my magic, afraid to let go. I

chanted, keeping him tethered to life. The ache in the pit of my stomach grew into a steady burn. A cold painful fire spread from my stomach into my chest and neck.

Hugh's body shook from the strain of the magic vibrating around him, fighting to break free.

Hugh opened his eyes. They glowed, filled with a supernatural, electric, luminescent blue. He spread his arms, palms up . . .

The magic tore from Hugh and spilled onto Doolittle in a deluge. Bones crunched.

Hugh blinked and his eyes looked normal again.

"Done," he said. "He'll live. You can let go."

I fell silent. The magic snapped, shorn. The fire inside me splashed through my head and I had an absurd notion it spilled out of my eyes.

Raphael ran into the room. "We spotted another one. He's injured and heading for the mountains."

Hugh jumped to his feet. Curran spun, half rising, and looked at me.

"Go!" I told him.

He took off, nearly colliding with Hugh as they ran out of the room.

Doolittle's chest fell and rose in a steady, smooth rhythm. He was breathing.

I slumped back and realized my jeans were soaked through. I was sitting in a puddle of my blood.

I LAY BACK ON A PILE OF BLANKETS, WATCHING shapeshifters through the doorway as they moved around the bigger room, sorting through the wreckage of Doolittle's lab. They'd carried me and Doolittle into the bedroom so we would be out of their way. I lay on the blankets on the floor, while Doolittle was submerged in a healing solution in a tub the shapeshifters had wrenched out of the bathroom. The bedroom door lay in pieces on the floor, and from my lovely perch on the blanket, I could see the entire suite.

Keira, now back in human form, was trying to clear the debris. She said she was still dizzy. I told her to lie down. Instead she tied a wet towel on her head. It must've been one hell of a hit, because normally shapeshifters shrugged concussions off and kept on rolling.

Next to Keira, Derek fished plastic jars with various medicines out of what used to be a cabinet. Eduardo was still out like a light. Desandra walked around in a bloody, shredded dress and heroically tried to pick things up, despite her stomach. I'd expected her to curl into a ball, but instead she rushed around all hyper. Mahon had ushered her into the room shortly after Curran had taken off. From my blanket, I could see Mahon looming by the front door.

Normally the sight of a twelve-hundred-pound bear didn't fill me with confidence, but right now knowing he was blocking the doorway made me downright warm and fuzzy. Especially since keeping Doolittle alive had taken every drop of strength I had. My arms had turned to wet cotton and lifting my head was an effort. Right now if a butterfly landed on me, I wouldn't wake up till the next morning.

No word from Curran. He, Hugh, Aunt B, Raphael, and Andrea had gone off over an hour ago.

Doolittle rested next to me in the makeshift tank. The green healing solution soaked his body. He hadn't said anything or opened his eyes, but his breathing was even.

I wanted him to wake up. I wanted him to open his eyes and chide me about something, anything. I would drink whatever medicine he demanded, I'd promise to stay in bed, I'd do anything just to have him wake up.

Hugh had said he would live. Being in a coma did technically count as living.

I pushed that thought away from me. That way lay dragons.

Barabas strode through the door, wearing a pair of sweatpants and nothing else. A wide gash streaked across his neck and his pale chest. He saw me and came into the bedroom. George followed him, carrying scissors, and pointed at my bloody jeans. "I'm sorry. I have to cut them off."

"I don't suppose I can get some privacy?" I asked.

"No," Derek said.

"Absolutely not," Keira said. "You can be modest later, when we're not under attack."

"This is probably a shock to you." Barabas crouched by me. "But we have all seen naked women before. The sight of your legs isn't going to traumatize anyone."

"Thanks."

George took the scissors, stretched my jeans, and cut. The

fabric tugged on the wound. I inhaled sharply. Argh. George cut the other side and pulled the blood-soaked denim rag away. "Okay. There are wounds. I'm not sure how severe this is for a nonshapeshifter."

"Mirror?"

Derek got up and passed George a handheld mirror. She held it. The left corner of it was gone, but enough remained to give me a view of my side. Three long jagged gashes cut the lower right side of my stomach, stretching all the way across my hip down over my thigh.

"Tilt it toward me?"

She did.

The wounds looked shallow. They bled and hurt like all get-out, but none of them would impair my ability to swing my sword. I tried moving my leg. Still worked. Little creaky. Little agonizing. But it still worked.

My face hurt, too. My lip felt swollen. "How's my face?"

George picked up the mirror. "Ready?"

"Hit me."

She raised the mirror. A big bruise blossomed in all of its blue glory on the left corner of my jaw. My mouth was puffy and swollen, and a long cut snaked its way from my hairline down to my right ear. The swelling and the bruise came courtesy of being hit with a shapeshifter's tail. The cut, I had no idea.

"I'm a sexy fiend, aren't I?"

She winced. "It's not that bad."

"It's good that Curran is gone. He might not be able to contain himself. If he decides to ravish me in public when he comes back, I expect all of you to look the other way."

Mahon cleared his throat at the door.

"You've got a status report for me?"

"The attack involved five creatures," Barabas said. "It started here. They busted through the door. One smashed Doolittle's equipment and attacked Eduardo and Keira. They crippled her and then the doctor latched onto her throat. That's her." Barabas pointed at the woman's corpse outside the window, on top of a short tower.

"He never let go," George said quietly. "When I got here, she'd smashed everything, rolled, flailed, rammed the walls with him. Eduardo got knocked out, and Keira would jump out of the way, but Doolittle never let go. I had to rip him away, and then she tried to fly away."

"She was dying," Keira said. "Doolittle had clamped onto her neck and severed the jugular. His teeth kept her wounds open and bled her dry. Thirty seconds more and she wouldn't have been able to fly." She put her hands over her face. "We should've fought harder."

"We're all still here," Mahon told her from the door. "You did your job."

"While Doolittle was fighting, the second and third attackers blocked access to this room," Barabas said. "Aunt B and Mahon took down one in the hallway, and Curran met the third in the hallway and fought it into Desandra's room. The fourth busted in through the balcony into Desandra's room after the fight began. The fifth, we are not sure."

"Injuries?" I asked.

"Doolittle is the worst of it," Barabas said. "Derek has a broken arm. There are some cuts and wounds, but everyone is still alive and moving around."

They hit here first. "Doolittle was the primary target."

"It appears that way."

Curran had said Doolittle wanted to talk to us. He must've found something, something that made him a target.

Barabas sat on the floor next to me, his face serious.

"Whenever you have that face, it means something nasty is coming."

"Do you remember that you asked me to set up meetings with you and the three packs tomorrow morning? Do you want to cancel?"

"Hell no. I want to go and look them in the eye when they tell me they didn't attack our medmage in the middle of the night." Anger flared inside me. I would find the assholes responsible and they would pay. Nobody hurt Doolittle and lived. "He was a noncombatant. We will find whoever went after him and I will personally make them regret the day they were born."

"What she said," Keira said. "Nobody touches the medic and lives."

George swung into my view. She held a bottle of brown liquid in her hand.

"What is that?"

"Whiskey." She handed me a wadded-up rag. "Here, I need you to bite down on this."

What the hell? "Why?"

"I'm going to clean your wounds."

"The hell you are." Not with alcohol. It didn't disinfect the wound unless one drenched it, it killed the living cells, and it generally did more harm than good. Not to mention the wound would take forever to heal after being treated with alcohol, and pouring whiskey on an open gash guaranteed scars.

"Kate," George said, her voice suddenly very patient. "You don't have a shapeshifter's immune system. Your wounds need to be sterilized."

"You're not sterilizing them with whiskey. Are you nuts?"

"They always do it in movies and in books. So many people can't be wrong."

I channeled every iota of menace I had into my voice. "George, if you come near me with that bottle, I'll hurt you."

"Right." George looked at Barabas. "We may need to hold the Consort down."

Barabas looked at Derek. Derek shrugged, as if to say, *I don't know.* Barabas clamped my arms to the floor.

"Do you need me to help hold her?" Desandra called out. "Because I can totally do that."

"George!" I snarled.

She uncorked the bottle. "I'm sorry it's going to hurt. I don't want you to get sepsis."

"Barabas, let go of me. This is an order." I strained, but I had no strength left. I might as well have tried to lift a car.

"It's for your own good," Barabas said.

George stepped toward me with the bottle.

"Let me go, you idiots!"

"I'll make it quick." George leaned over me.

"Stop!" Doolittle said.

Everybody froze.

"Georgetta, put down that bottle."

George sat the bottle on the floor and stepped away from it.

Doolittle had raised himself in the tub and was looking at us. "I don't have the strength to tell you all of the things that are wrong with what you doing. Release the Consort this instant."

Barabas raised his hands. I slumped on my blanket. Thank God. He was conscious. *Thank you, thank you, Universe.*

"Derek, find a large blue bottle marked STERILE SALINE SOLUTION. Georgetta, look for a green wooden box with clean gauze. Keira, did you hit your head?"

Keira's eyes got really big. "Yes. Among other things."

"Is that rag on your head cold?"

"Ummm . . ."

"It should be cold. Preferably iced. Blurred vision?"

"No."

"Did you vomit?"

"A little. I'm fine now."

"You need to ice that rag. Why is Eduardo naked? Did none of you think about the man's dignity? Find him a clean sheet. Has anybody checked his vital signs? There is a pregnant woman here covered in blood and none of you are alarmed by this. Nobody is helping her to get clean." Doolittle surveyed us. "I leave you for a few brief minutes, and you're courting disaster."

Suddenly everyone became terribly busy.

"I'm glad you're okay, Doc," I told him.

"I shouldn't be alive." He looked at me. "It seems it was my turn to be the patient."

"Let's not do that again," I told him. "You're so much better at being the doctor."

Doolittle hesitated. "What kind of healing . . ."

I read the question in his eyes. He had seen me heal Julie. He'd watched my blood sear hers, cleaning it of the virus and binding her to me, and now he wanted to know if I had done something with my magic that compromised his free will. I looked into his eyes and I didn't see gratitude or joy at being alive. I saw suspicion and fear. He was terrified that I had turned him into an abomination. In that moment I knew with complete certainty that Doolittle would rather die than be brought back to life by me.

An invisible wall slammed into place around me, cutting me off. I was still in the room. I still heard people I viewed as my friends move around, talking, but they seemed impossibly far away. I sat there, disconnected and alone.

No matter how much time I spent being a part of the Pack, no matter how much I sacrificed or how dedicated I was, Doolittle's eyes told me that the divide between me and them would always remain. The man who'd brought me back from death time and time again now looked at me with dread, afraid of being tainted.

I forced the words out. "Just strong medmagic. The usual kind. It wasn't me. You were healed by a medmage." Or at least I was pretty sure Hugh would be rated as one had he bothered to apply for certification. "You're still you, Doc." *I didn't turn you into anything you're not.*

The tension melted from his face.

The desire to get away swelled in me, so strong that if I could've stood up, I would've walked out. I didn't want to be in the same room with anyone. I wanted to be by myself.

George appeared, holding the saline solution and a green box. "I have the gauze."

"Desandra first," I told her.

George turned to Desandra. "Come with me. Time to get cleaned up."

"But I like my war clothes."

"If you need me to hold her down," I growled, "I totally can do that."

"Fine, fine." Desandra sighed and followed George into the bathroom. They shut the door.

Doolittle looked at me. "Do *you* need to be restrained?"

"I'm fine."

"Lie back, Kate." Keira walked into the room and picked up the spare bottle of saline solution and gauze.

I hadn't realized I was sitting. I forced myself to lie flat.

"Very well. Saturate the wounds, rinsing them with gentle pressure. Make sure no debris remains," Doolittle said.

"Got it." Keira poured some saline on the gauze and began to gently blot my leg.

"Curran mentioned you wanted to tell me something."

"I kept thinking about that verse from Daniel," Doolittle said. "One part, in particular, stood out to me. It says, *I beheld till the wings thereof were plucked, and it was lifted up from the earth, and made stand upon the feet as a man, and a man's heart was given to it.* Note it doesn't mention that the lion's fur or his claws were gone. Only that the wings had been plucked and they were the difference between the beast and man."

"I don't follow," I said.

"Do you recall how I told you that these things may be able to hide their scales?"

"Yes."

"I've wondered if, since the verse mentioned the wings specifically, they might be the final stage of their transformation. Most common shapeshifters have two complete forms, human and animal."

"And the warrior form," Keira said.

"That's a hybrid form that one has to concentrate to maintain," Doolittle said. "I'm talking about final-stage form that a shapeshifter can maintain indefinitely. I think our orange friends have three: human, animal, and winged beast. I believe that in their animal stage they may look very similar to naturally occurring animal species."

I didn't like the sound of that. "Why?"

Doolittle lowered his voice to a whisper. "Do you recall how I tested the blood from the severed head against all the other blood samples?"

"Yes."

"I had taken fluid samples from Desandra. Blood, urine, and amniotic fluid. I completed my diagnostic run, and since I had exposed every other fluid sample to the creature's blood, I tested Desandra's blood and amniotic fluid just to be on the thorough side. Her blood reacted. Her amniotic fluid did not. One of her children is not what he seems."

Oh dear God.

Keira froze with the gauze in her hand. If we told Desandra that one of her children was a monster, there was no telling what she would do.

"This can't leave this room," I said.

"Agreed," Doolittle said.

I glanced at the main room.

"I didn't hear anything," Derek said.

"Me neither," Barabas told me.

There could be only two possibilities. One, Desandra had had sex with a third man, besides Gerardo and Radomil. That was extremely unlikely. For all of her flirting and outrageous declarations, she never actually came on to anyone, and her distress when she told us about Gerardo throwing her out was genuine. She wouldn't have taken a chance on having sex with some random stranger. She'd slept with Radomil because she knew he would be kind, and she had needed that kindness. That left door number two: either Gerardo or Radomil sprouted wings in his spare time and amused himself by swiping guards off the towers.

If Doolittle was right, the winged shapeshifters could assume human and animal shapes that let them mimic normal shapeshifters. It explained why the winged freaks suddenly started showing up at the castle—they were members of either Belve Ravennati or the Volkodavi, and if they had to fight, they assumed their final form. The million-dollar question was, which one was it? The creatures looked more feline to me, but that didn't mean anything.

"What about the other child?"

"It's a wolf," Doolittle said.

That told us nothing. A child of two shapeshifters rolled genetic dice: he could inherit a beast from his father or his mother. Desandra transformed into a wolf. If she had a child with Gerardo, he would be a wolf. If she had a child with Radomil, he could be a wolf or a lynx. We still knew nothing except that she was growing a monster inside her. Eventually I would have to tell her this. Could this get more fucked up?

At the door Mahon crossed his arms. "Who are you?"

A woman answered quietly. The big werebear stepped aside and a tall woman in her late forties stepped through the door. Dark-skinned and graceful, she looked Arabic. An adolescent boy and a younger girl followed her.

"My name is Demet," the woman said slowly. "Lord Megobari sent for me. To heal." She put her hand over her heart. "Healer."

"That's very fortunate," Doolittle said. "Because I can't move my legs."

CHAPTER 14

EDUARDO PACED UP AND DOWN THE COMMON area, stomping as if he had hooves and glaring at the bathroom door. Demet asked for privacy, and the bathroom was the only place that still had a functional door. Derek went in there with them. His face alone was enough of a deterrent even if she had decided to try something.

Eduardo exhaled and turned back for another pass. Red streaks stained his white T-shirt—his wounds were deep and he wasn't doing them any favors.

Keira paced too, to the wall and back, turning just a hair before her body touched the stone. Barabas sat in the middle of the room, his face grim. At the door, Mahon loomed, a somber shadow.

It never occurred to me that something was wrong. When Doolittle sat up in his tub, I felt an overwhelming avalanche of relief. I never thought to ask if he was okay . . .

Curran walked through the door. Blood drenched his right side. On the left, deep cuts where monster claws had gouged his flesh crossed his muscles. Being hugged by a flying eight-foot long leopard left its mark.

He walked over to me and crouched.

"Are you okay?"

Define "okay." "Yes. Did you get him?"

"It was a woman. She threw herself from the cliff. Her brains are splattered on the bottom of the ravine."

Damn it.

"What's going on?" he asked.

"Doolittle woke up. He can't move his legs."

The door of the bathroom room swung open and Demet stepped out. Her teenage son followed her.

Curran rose. "How is he?"

Demet said something. Her son turned, presenting us with his back. "First injury." Demet pointed with her fingers at the top of his neck, drawing an invisible line. "Cervical. Healed. No problem. Second injury."

She swept her hand lower, indicating the small of the back and lower.

"Lumbar. L1 and L2."

Demet held up one, then two fingers and tapped the boy on the shoulder. He turned.

"Full feeling here." Demet drew her hand from his head down to his stomach. She struggled for a word. "Not full . . . ?"

"Some," Barabas offered.

"Some feeling here." Her hand moved from the stomach down through the pelvis. "Legs, no."

Doolittle was paralyzed from his hips down. My mind ran against that thought and splattered.

"Will he ever walk again?" Curran asked.

Demet spread her arms. "Possible. I did everything I could for him." She paused. "Time. Time, magic, and rest."

She turned to me. "You have wounds."

"I don't care."

She shook. "You not like them. No time. Must heal right away."

"It's my fault," Eduardo said. "I couldn't hold her."

"She flew," Keira told him. "And she was strong. All three of us couldn't hold her."

Eduardo's eyes bulged. He turned in place, looking like he would break into a charge any second. He was going into a tailspin, fast.

"It's my fault. I was supposed to watch him. I let him get hurt."

He turned, stomping toward the door. Curran stepped into his way. "Stop."

Eduardo skidded to a halt.

"Look at me."

The big man focused on Curran's face.

"Man up," Curran said, his voice saturated with force. "We're still in danger. I still need you. Don't fold on me."

Eduardo exhaled through his nose.

"That goes for all of you," Curran said. "Later we can sit around and wonder what if and cry about what we should've done different. Right now, we work. We've been attacked. They're still out there. We will hunt them down and take them apart."

Barabas sat a little straighter. Keira pushed herself from the wall.

Curran looked back at Eduardo. "Okay?"

"Okay," the big man said.

"Good." Curran turned to Demet. "Heal Kate."

I WOKE UP WITH CURRAN SITTING NEXT TO ME. HE didn't say anything. He just sat next to me and looked at me.

"Were you watching me sleep? Because I thought we agreed that's creepy."

He didn't answer.

We were alone in the room. Doolittle and his tub, Keira, and everyone else were gone. On second thought the covers under me looked familiar. I was on our bed. He must've carried me to our room. I usually woke up if someone moved outside my room behind a closed door. How did I sleep through him carrying me? Doolittle had a habit of slipping sedatives into my drink, because I ignored his instructions to lie down and rest, but the last I saw him he was in the bathtub. Demet and her children had chanted my wounds into regeneration. I recalled a rush of soothing coolness foaming over my wounds. And then George handed me a glass of water.

"George sedated me. Okay, the drugging thing has to stop. Also, if one of them ever attempts to hold me down and pour booze on my wound, I will kill somebody. That's not an idle threat either."

Curran didn't say anything.

"Are you okay?" I asked.

He nodded at the wall.

I concentrated. The magic was still up, and as I quested forward, I felt something stir behind the stone. Not a vampire, but something odd. Something I hadn't felt before. We were being listened to.

Curran's mouth was a hard slash across his face. He was angry. Monumentally, terribly angry.

I reached over and touched his face, looking for that intimate connection. *Hey. Are we still okay?*

He took my hand, his strong fingers hot and dry, and squeezed it. Okay. We were still okay. He didn't have to say anything else.

"Did Doolittle talk to you?" I asked.

He shook his head.

I reached over to the night table, took a small notepad, and a pen, and wrote on it, *He tested Desandra's amniotic fluid. One of the babies could grow wings.*

Curran's eyes widened. He took the pen. *Did she sleep with one of those things?*

Most likely Radomil or Gerardo is one of those things.

How is that possible?

You have two forms, human and animal. Doolittle thinks that these guys have a third one: human, animal, and monster with wings.

Curran shook his head. "Which one is it?"

No way to tell. The amniotic fluid indicates that one baby is a wolf and the other is something else. The Lyc-V with wolf genes could come from Desandra. They must've known or suspected Doolittle found something out. That's why they wrecked his lab.

Who knew that Doolittle had taken the amniotic fluid? Curran wrote.

Ivanna for sure, I wrote. Radomil's sister had offered to hold Desandra's hand in case she was scared. At the time I thought she was a decent human being. *Anybody could've seen it. Radomil and Ignazio were all brawling in the hallway while Doolittle worked.*

A familiar careful knock sounded through the door. Barabas.

"Just a minute." I flipped the piece of paper over. *I'm going to ruffle the packs to see if I can get a reaction.*

Anybody who isn't watching Desandra will be watching Doolittle, he wrote.

Perfect. "I have to go meet with the packs this morning," I said aloud. "Anything you may want me to pass along?"

"Yes." Curran took the note folded it and methodically tore it into confetti. "Tell them that there is no escape from me."

THE BELVE RAVENNATI WERE MY FIRST STOP. WE met by a giant bay window in one of the public rooms where soft tan furniture sat arranged around a coffee table. The wolves from Ravenna didn't want me in their quarters.

I sat in a love seat across from Isabella Lovari. Gerardo sat on her left. His brother was nowhere to be found. Three other people joined us, all with a similar bearing: clean-cut, the two men clean-shaven, the woman's hair pulled back into a ponytail. They gave off an almost military air, and they watched me with a single-minded attention. This was a wolf pack, and I was clearly the enemy.

Barabas stood behind me, taking notes on a legal pad.

"Thank you for agreeing to meet me," I said. The swelling hadn't gone down as much as I would've liked, and talking hurt.

Isabella looked me over. "I'm surprised you're still here."

"I'm hard to kill."

"Like a cockroach."

"Not sure that's a good comparison. I never had trouble killing small insects," I said.

Barabas quietly cleared his throat.

Isabella raised her eyebrows. In her early fifties, she had a kind of sharp precision about her. Over my time with the Pack I had watched alphas work. Some struggled, like Jennifer. Some, like the Lonescos of Clan Rat, had a natural ease about interacting with people in their charge. Isabella had neither. She radiated the air of command. It was obedience or else.

"As you know, we're attempting to discover the nature of the attacks on Desandra's life," I said. "Her well-being and the well-being of her children is our first priority."

"Are you trying to imply that we're under suspicion?" Isabella asked.

"I'm not implying; I'm saying it. I'd like nothing better than to strike you from my list."

Barabas passed me a small note card with a single word: *diplomatic*.

Isabella leaned back. "I'm insulted."

"I don't give a fuck," I said. "Last night your daughter-in-law was attacked. Our people were hurt. I've got ten shapeshifters howling for blood. I'm looking for someone to hunt. It can be you or it can be Kral or the Volkodavi. I don't really care. So go ahead. Give me a reason to paint a target on your chest."

The Belve Ravennati stared at me in stunned silence.

Isabella laughed quietly. "Ask your questions."

"Where were you last night around midnight?"

"In our quarters. My sons were with my husband and me."

"Can the guards account for your whereabouts?"

"No."

Isabella's wolves turned their heads toward the hallway. Someone large was coming toward us. I leaned forward to get a better look. Mahon. Now what?

The bear of Atlanta approached us, slowly, clearly in no hurry, and came to stand next to Barabas behind me. "Sorry I'm late."

Backup. Wow. Knock me over with a feather.

The Belve Ravennati were looking at me. Right. Where were we?

I concentrated on Isabella's face. This was the reason I had come here in the first place. "We have reason to believe we can identify the creatures who attacked Desandra through a blood test. Would you be willing to provide us with a blood sample?"

"Absolutely not."

Unfazed. She wouldn't give us the blood, but the fact that we could test it didn't bother her any. Gerardo's face showed no anxiety either. "Why?"

"Because blood is a precious commodity. I won't give you access to it only to have it used against my family by magical means."

Well, it was worth a shot. I looked at Gerardo. "When did you find out that Desandra had been attacked?"

"A guard told us after it happened," he said.

"Did you make any efforts to assist us in making sure Desandra was safe?"

Gerardo unlocked his jaw. "No."

"Did you make any efforts to visit the future mother of your child and make sure she is alright?"

"No."

"Why?"

"I forbade it," Isabella said. "My son is overly fond of that woman. Since she's now a target, being near her puts him in danger."

I looked at Gerardo. "Don't you think you owe some loyalty—"

"To a slut who slept with another man?" Isabella raised her eyebrows. "I can understand why you might feel sympathy for her. You are not married either."

Behind me the pen creaked in Barabas's fingers. He must've squeezed it too hard.

I regarded Isabella. Straight for the jugular, huh? The strange thing was, it hurt. It stabbed me right in some deep female part of my psyche that I had no idea existed. "Loyalty to the woman who was your wife for two years and who is now carrying your child."

"You don't understand what it's like," Gerardo said. "To never know if your wife loves you or if she's just waiting for the right moment to stab you in the back because her father told her so."

Isabella's eyebrows came together. "My son deserves a woman who is honorable and strong, who will be a partner and an alpha, instead of a weak half-wit who is only a liability. This is a pointless conversation." Isabella looked past me at Mahon. "We all know that the human is being replaced. Last night's dinner was definitive proof of that."

What happened last night?

Mahon leaned forward, his hands on the back of my chair. The wood groaned under the pressure of his fingers. "She's earned my loyalty. Do not insult her again."

The world stood on its ear.

"Fine," Isabella said. "You may play this game of pretend, but I'm done. Your human knows it, too. One only has to see the look on her face when Lorelei Wilson walks into the room." She looked at me. "You are an open book, and you know you are being set aside. Take your pets and leave us."

I rose.

Mahon looked at Gerardo. "You can't hold on to your mother's skirt forever."

The werewolf bared his teeth.

"Enough." Isabella rose and walked away. Her wolves followed. A moment and we were alone.

"What happened at dinner?" I asked once they were out of earshot.

"Lorelei sat next to Curran," Barabas said.

"In my chair?"

"Yes."

Curran had lied to me. The realization hit me like a punch to the stomach.

He came into Desandra's room, lay next to me, held me, and told me I didn't have to worry about Lorelei, all after she sat in my chair at dinner. He had to know exactly what kind of signal it would send to everyone else. She had literally taken my place and he allowed it.

The Universe spun out of control. I struggled to hold on to it. I had to finish this. I couldn't drop everything and search Curran out so I could punch him in the face. No matter how much I wanted to do it. No matter how much it hurt.

I managed to make some words happen. "And you didn't think to mention it?"

Barabas sighed. "I didn't want to upset you. I didn't expect them to be so blunt. They don't want to answer the questions, so they're trying to exploit any weaknesses."

Curran lied to me. I tried to wrap my mind around it and couldn't. All my life, first Voron, then Greg had taught me to trust no one. Trust, intimacy, complete honesty with another human being wasn't for me. It was a luxury someone with my blood couldn't afford. I ignored it all and trusted him. I trusted him so completely, that even now, faced with evidence of his betrayal, I was looking for possible explanations. Maybe it was part of some plan he lied about having. Maybe . . .

I stomped on that thought and crushed it into pieces. I had a job to do. I would deal with this later. I stuffed those sharp shards into the same dark place where I stuffed everything. They scoured me on their way down. My storage capacity for the problems I couldn't handle was getting full. Not much more would fit.

"What's next?" I asked.

"The Volkodavi," Barabas said.

"Lead on."

The Volkodavi met me in their rooms, in a large common area. Vitaliy, the head of the clan and Radomil's brother, shook my hand. Like Radomil, he was tall and blond. He was handsome but lacked the near perfection of his brother.

I sat in a chair. Radomil sat across from me.

"Where is Ivanna?" I asked.

"She'll be here," Vitaliy said.

I asked them the same set of questions and got much the same responses. Yes, they were in their quarters; no, they couldn't account for their whereabouts; and they didn't do anything to help or check on Desandra. Radomil wanted to go but Vitaliy stopped him, because Desandra was a nice girl but she wasn't worth getting hurt over.

"Look," Radomil told me in broken English. "We don't mind talking to you, but it's not going to help. You and the Wilson girl, it's made things complicated. You not married."

Like dragging a cheese grater across my soul. *Yes, I know, I'm not married. Yes, Lorelei sat next to Curran at dinner. I'm irrelevant, I'm human, I'm being replaced* . . . "Can I see Ivanna, please?"

Vitaliy sighed and called, "Ivanna!"

A moment later Ivanna walked into the room. She looked exactly how I remembered her—a slender blond woman—except for the left side of her face. Scaly dark patches of damaged skin covered her left temple, disappearing under her hair.

"What happened to your face?" I asked.

Ivanna waved her arm. As she moved, her hair shifted, and I caught a better glimpse: the scaly blotches covered the entire left side of her face, from the temple down over her cheek and neck, barely missing her eyes and lips. Her cheekbone had lost some of its sharpness too, its lines smoothed. I'd seen this before—her bones had been crushed by blunt trauma and Lyc-V was in the process of rebuilding it layer by layer.

"It's stupid," Ivanna said. "We have a fireplace in the room. I was really tired after the hunt and Radomil and Vitaliy came into my room and decided to argue with each other. Vitaliy was waving his arms."

"I got excited," Vitaliy said.

"He knocked my jewelry stand into the fireplace. I yelled at them, went to fish my necklace out, and accidentally pressed the ignition. A fire flared and burned me. At least I had put my hair up for the night or I would be bald."

Bullshit. That was a chemical burn, complete with a spray pattern. She was lying through her teeth. Either she was stupid, or she thought I was really stupid, or she just didn't care. I was betting on the latter. She and everyone else in the room knew that without a clear, indisputable smoking gun I couldn't force her to do anything.

"That's terrible," I said.

"It will heal in a couple of days. Is there anything else you wanted?"

"Yes. We have reason to believe that the creatures who attacked Desandra are hiding here in the castle. We've developed a blood test that lets us identify these creatures."

Vitaliy, Radomil, and Ivanna stared at me, their faces so carefully neutral that it had to be a controlled exertion of will.

"Would you be willing to provide us with a blood sample?"

"No," Vitaliy said slowly. "Blood has too much power."

"We don't want to be cursed." Radomil shook his head.

"Thank you for coming," Ivanna said. "You're not a bad person. We're sorry your man is being so unfair."

We left. As we walked away, Mahon rested his hand on my shoulder. It was a quiet, almost fatherly gesture.

"Did you see their faces?" I asked.

"We got a reaction," Barabas said. "I don't know what it means, but we got one."

Jarek Kral was my last stop. The Obluda pack occupied the northern side of the castle. I knew exactly what was coming.

"He'll try to provoke you," Barabas said.

"I know." If I gave Jarek any pretext to attack me, he would be overjoyed.

"Don't react, Kate," Barabas murmured.

"I know."

"If he touches you, you can touch back," Mahon said.

Oh yes. I will. You can be sure I will.

We turned the corner. A long hallway unrolled before us, the light from the windows painting light rectangles on the floor. Men milled about in the hallway. One, two . . . twelve. Jarek had pulled most of his pack out of their beds to give me a proper welcome.

Jarek's shapeshifters stared at me. Some openly leered. A dark-haired, older shapeshifter on the left stuck his tongue out and wiggled it. Wasn't he a charmer.

Your tongue's too long. Come closer, I'll fix it for you.

I kept walking, Barabas and Mahon behind me. The anger and hurt inside me crystallized into an icy cage. I hid inside it, using it as my armor. Whatever punches Jarek Kral threw at me, they wouldn't breach it. The ice was too thick.

As we moved through the hallway, the shapeshifters fell in behind us. Someone whistled. Someone catcalled. I kept walking.

Ahead an arch offered a view of a large room. A familiar grouping of cushioned seats and coffee tables waited—Hugh clearly believed that if a furniture set did its job, there was no reason to get creative. Jarek Kral sprawled on the love seat, watching me walk toward him. His inner circle flanked the seat. A tall blond—one of the two brothers who followed Jarek around—an older man with a shaved head and muscles like a heavyweight prizefighter, and Renok, my buddy, dark-haired, with a short beard, and a deep inborn viciousness in his eyes.

This would be interesting.

"Curran's whore comes to visit us," Jarek said in accented English.

The three men laughed as if on cue. I glanced at Mahon. "You really shouldn't let him talk to you like that."

Mahon's bushy eyebrows came together.

I sat in the chair. "Your daughter was attacked last night."

"And?"

"Looking for some fatherly reactions here: is she okay, was she hurt?" I leaned forward. "You know, things men ask when their children are attacked."

Jarek shrugged. "Why should I worry? That's why we hired you. To keep my precious daughter safe."

"Where were you last night at midnight?"

"Here. Wasn't I?" Jarek spread his arms.

"Yes," the older bald man said.

"Here," Renok said and winked.

Jarek Kral leaned toward me. *Oh boy. Here we go.* "What does he see in you?" His tone was light, almost conversational. "You're not a shapeshifter, you're not powerful, and you're not beautiful. No body. No face."

Behind me Barabas took a sharp breath.

"Do you give good sex?" Jarek Kral propped his elbow on the table and rested his chin on his fist. "Do you suck his cock?"

Oh look, someone looked up a couple of dirty words in the English dictionary. Cute.

Jarek leaned a little forward, happy with himself. "Does he like his cock sucked? Or did you not do a good job? Is that why your face looks like this?"

Amateur. "Why are you so curious about Curran's cock? Are you looking for something new to suck? You're welcome to ask him, but I'm pretty sure he doesn't like you like that."

The three men drew back. Jarek blinked. Barabas laughed under his breath.

"Try to pay attention," I told him. "I will speak slowly, so you can understand. Your daughter was attacked. There are strange creatures in this castle. We have a blood test that can identify them. Will you let us test your blood?"

Jarek laughed.

He didn't seem nervous, but he was so animated, I couldn't tell if he was reacting at all.

"Maybe we should test your blood." Renok grabbed my left arm. He was fast, but I saw him move and I let him do it. His fingers closed on my wrist. He pulled my arm, bending it at the elbow to expose the inside of the forearm. I waited half a second to make sure everyone saw it and drove the flat palm of my right hand against his wrist. He was strong, but he didn't expect me to be. His hold slipped. I grabbed his wrist with my right hand and twisted it, wrenching his arm. He bent forward, trying to keep his shoulder in its socket. I yanked a throwing knife out of my sheath and drove it through his trapezius muscle at the top of his shoulder, nailing him to the coffee table with a knife.

The whole thing took half a breath.

"So I take it, that's a no on the blood?" I asked.

Jarek Kral stared at me.

A rough, jagged growl tore from Renok, part fury, part pain. He strained.

Barabas leaned forward and put his hand on Renok's neck. The shapeshifter went still.

I rose. "I see no women in your party. That's a mistake. Desandra is her father's daughter. She fought last night and she enjoyed it. She will kill you one day, and then she'll go on to have children who'll never know your name. Your pathetic attempt at a dynasty will die with you."

The blond and the prizefighter jumped to their feet. Mahon shook his head. "Think about what you're doing," he said quietly, his voice deep with menace.

Jarek said something. The wolves backed away.

I rose and walked out. Mahon and Barabas followed me.

I marched down the hallway heading toward the stairs at a near run. Outside the windows the day was bright: golden sunshine, blue sky, pleasant wind . . . I wanted to punch the happy day in the face, grab it by the hair, and beat it until it told me what the hell it was so happy about. I was keyed up too high and I was sick of this place. Sick of shapeshifters, sick of their politics, and sick of holding myself back. Thinking about Curran just poured more gasoline on the fire. I had to fix myself and I had to do it now, before I exploded.

We came to a padded bench set in the shallow nook.

"Let's sit here a minute," Mahon said.

I didn't want to sit. I wanted to punch something.

"Please," Mahon said.

Fine. I sat. He sat on the other end. Barabas leaned against the wall next to me.

"I was born before the Shift," Mahon said. "For me, magic changed everything. Martha is my second wife. I buried my first and I buried our children. I have no love for 'normal' people. To me, I'm normal. I'm a shapeshifter, but I'm human. Things that I endured were done to me by 'normal' humans, and they did them because they never tried to understand me and mine, and even if they did, they couldn't. I didn't belong with them and they sure as hell didn't belong with me or my family. There was no common ground between us."

Why was he telling me this? I already felt like I'd been through a gauntlet. I didn't need extra punches.

"You'll never be a shapeshifter," Mahon said. "If you live

with us for a hundred years, a newborn werebear will be more of a shapeshifter than you are."

Barabas looked at him. "Enough. That back there was plenty. She doesn't need any more shit today."

"Let me finish," Mahon said, his voice calm. "You'll never fully understand what it's like and we'll never fully understand you. But it doesn't matter. You're Pack."

I blinked. I must've misheard.

"Why take their abuse?" Mahon asked. "I know it goes against your nature."

"Because it's not about me. It's about the panacea, our people, and a pregnant woman. I can make them eat their words, but it will derail everything. They're counting on me blowing my gasket, and playing to their expectations helps them and hurts us. I would rather win big at the end than win small right now."

"And that's why no matter what happens, you will always be Pack. Because you have that loyalty and restraint." Mahon raised his hands, as if holding an invisible ball. "The Pack is bigger than all of us. It's an institution. A thing built on self-sacrifice. We're a violent breed. To exist in peace, we have to sacrifice that violence. We have to praise control and discipline, and it starts at the top. Having an alpha who is a loose cannon is worse than having no alpha at all. The world is falling around us in pieces and will be for some time. It's all about stability now, about giving people a safe place, a reassuring routine, so they don't feel frightened and so they don't feel the need to resort to violence, because if we go down that road, we'll either self-destruct or be exterminated. That's why we build so many safeguards. In time, I'd like to see things change. I'd like the challenges to go away. We lose too many good people to those. But it will come with time, a long time, perhaps years, perhaps generations, and it will start at the top. We lead by example."

I never knew that about him.

Mahon faced me. "You and us, we have things in common. You know what it's like to not be 'normal,' except in this case you're the odd one out. You may respect our ways, but you don't have to try to be something you are not. Some people will take longer to adjust, but in time, you will be accepted just as you are. Not 'human,' not whatever, but Kate. Unique and different, but not separate. Kate is just Kate and you belong with us. That's all that matters."

I was the badass Consort and he was the grim Pack's executioner. Hugging him in the hallways would be entirely inappropriate.

"Thank you for your help," I said.

"Anytime," Mahon said.

Barabas spun toward the stairs. Lorelei circled the landing and kept going up the stairs, her dark green dress with a diaphanous skirt flaring as she walked.

Barabas inhaled. "Is that . . . ?"

"Now isn't the time," Mahon said.

Oh no, now was the perfect time. She was walking upstairs, and unless Curran waited for her in her room, he would be alone and available for a little chat.

"Where would Curran be now?" I asked.

"It's lunch," Barabas said. "In the great hall."

Good. It was about time I talked to him.

BY THE TIME WE REACHED THE GREAT HALL, COMmon sense had kicked in. Marching in there and punching Curran, as satisfying as it might be, wouldn't accomplish much except make me look like a jealous idiot who couldn't control herself. I wouldn't give him and the other packs the satisfaction.

I halted at the door. "Why don't the two of you go in. I'll be right behind you."

Mahon went on. Barabas lingered for a long moment.

"I just need a minute to myself."

"Kate . . . I'm the last person to give love advice. I find calm, grounded guys, because I know I'm high-strung and I need someone to steady me, and then I get bored and act out until they leave me. I know I'm doing it, but I keep repeating the same mistake over and over, like a moron, because I keep hoping it will be different with this guy, because he is different. But it's always the same, because I don't change. People don't suddenly change, Kate. You understand?" He leaned forward and looked into my face. "Just . . . take longer than a minute. So there are no regrets later."

He went into the great hall.

People sat at the tables, eating, drinking, talking. Tension vibrated in me. I was a hair away from violence. I imagined walking in there and stabbing Curran with a fork. Barabas was right. I needed more than a minute. I needed to splash some water on my face.

Across from me a short hallway led to the side. If I took it, it should lead me to one of the two bathrooms. I stepped into the hallway. A door stood ajar on my right side, leading into a small room where a set of dark wooden stairs climbed up.

Maybe it was the way to the minstrel's gallery.

I climbed the stairs. If there were any snipers up there, I wanted to meet them for a friendly conversation. If not, I could look at the dining hall unnoticed.

The stairs ended. I passed through a doorway in the stone wall and found myself in the minstrel's gallery in the great hall. Score. Something went right today.

The great hall had no windows, the only illumination coming from the electric lights or, right now, with magic up, from the feylanterns shaped like faux torches. It could've been mid-morning or midnight—the outside light made no difference. The gallery lay soaked in gloom, the dark wooden beams almost black. I walked the length of it. Two doors, one at the far wall and the other at a midway point, interrupted the stone wall. Aside from that, nothing. Empty.

I leaned down on the wooden rail. Below me the great hall stretched, brightly lit and loud with people. The windows in the castle hallways must've been opened to vent the air heated with human breath and still-warm food, and a draft flowed from below, bringing with it a hint of spices and stirring the long blue-and-silver banners on the wall to the left of me. From this point I was probably nearly invisible to those beneath me.

I hadn't realized how high the gallery was. Leaping over the rail was out of the question. My bones would snap from the impact.

Curran strode through the door into the hall. He walked to the head table, where Barabas sat on the side next to Mahon, and asked Barabas something. Barabas spread his arms in response. Curran's face snapped into a familiar unreadable mask. He sat back in his place in the middle.

A moment later Lorelei floated up. She wore tight jeans

and an off-the-shoulder, nearly sheer blue peasant blouse. Her hair streamed over her shoulders. Her face looked flawless. How the hell did she have time to change and get here so fast?

Curran turned to her and said something. She sat next to him. Her smile was nothing short of radiant.

It felt like someone had dropped a brick into my stomach.

She asked him something. He reached for a plate of carved meat.

If he offered her food, I'd jump right off this gallery and kick him in the face with my broken legs.

Curran moved the dish toward her.

Don't.

He set the platter down.

Lorelei smiled at him, speared a slice off the platter with her fork, and leaned in to tell him something, a little sly light in her eyes.

They were sitting too close. I stared at Curran, wishing I could see through his skull into his head. *Why are you doing this? Why?*

"Perhaps because she is younger and fresher," Hugh said behind me.

I hadn't realized I'd spoken out loud. I didn't hear him walk up to me either. Shit. This situation needed to unscrew itself up really fast, because it was distracting me.

Hugh came to lean next to me, a hulking shadow. He wore jeans and a gray T-shirt. The thin fabric lay across his broad back, following the contours of his trapezius and latissimus dorsi muscles. I knew this build: a meld of strength and high endurance, flexible, mobile, but capable of crushing power. Hugh would be very difficult to kill.

He turned, watching Curran down below. "Perhaps he wants her because she is a shapeshifter and his people would accept her. She'll birth him a litter of cubs and everyone will cheer. Perhaps because she would bring a political alliance. Perhaps because she won't argue with him. Some men enjoy obedience."

"Thank you for your analysis, Doctor. Measuring others by your own standard?"

He tilted his head, presenting me with a view of his square jaw. Punching it would be a bitch. I'd bruise my hand for sure. Voron had chosen well. Usually I didn't have any issues with my body, but right now I wished for another six inches of height and an extra thirty pounds of muscle. It wouldn't make us even, but it would tighten the gap.

"Interested in my standards?" Hugh asked.

Danger, icy lake ahead. "No."

"If we're talking a one-night stand, I'm looking for enthusiasm. Perhaps for someone fearless. Blind obedience is boring. I want to have a good time, I want her to have a good time, and I want to make a memory I'll enjoy remembering."

"Too much information." Hugh's one-night stands were the last thing on my need-to-know list.

"You asked. But you're not his one-night stand, Kate. Or are you?"

I gave him my hard look.

He grinned, a wolfish sharp grin. "You know what I'm looking for in a partner? A challenge."

"Good luck."

He laughed quietly, a raspy sound. "Perhaps we're overthinking it. Maybe your Beast Lord is leaning toward her because he needs a wife and her father isn't planning to destroy everything he stands for."

Ouch. "Is that what Roland wants to do?"

Hugh sighed and surveyed the people below. "Look at them. They think this gathering is about them, their petty territorial clashes, their problems, their lusts, wants, and needs. They gorge themselves, squabble, and flash their fangs, and all the while they have no idea that it is all about you."

Thin ice. Proceed with extreme caution.

He turned toward me, blue eyes luminescent. "There are thousands of shapeshifters. Kill a hundred and there are always more. But there hasn't been another one like you for five thousand years. I would slaughter everyone in that room below for a shot at a single conversation with you."

The imaginary ice was cracking under my feet. He was taking this someplace very strange. "Laying it on kind of thick, don't you think?"

"I'm only stating facts." Hugh leaned back on the rail. "Spar with me. You know you want to."

I leaned forward and pointed to my forehead. "Tell me if you see *IDIOT* written on there."

"Scared?"

I shrugged. "Scared of what will happen after I ruin your face and Hibla starts a massacre."

"You have my word I won't let you anywhere near my face."

"Let?"

Hugh grinned.

In another minute, I'd need a rag to mop up all of the smugness dripping off him. "Big talk for someone with a scar on his face."

"If you win, I'll tell you how I got it."

I waved my hand at him. "That's okay. I don't want to know that badly."

"What *do* you want to know?"

"Does it matter? So far you've ducked every question I asked."

"I didn't think I had a fighting style," Hugh said. "If it comes within range, I can kill it, but I thought what I did was a hodgepodge of techniques that worked. It's not something one ponders: what is my special brand of violence? And then I saw you. Admit it, you felt it."

I did. I'd never before seen anyone who fought like me. We had been completely in sync, so perfectly that the memory of it was disturbing.

He looked at me. "I want to experience it again. Spar with me."

"Sorry, but I'm done playing."

"Kate, come on."

"I mean it. No."

Hugh chuckled. "Mean *and* a tease."

Below us Curran stood up. Lorelei stood up, too. Now what? Curran walked across the hall and out through the door under the gallery. Lorelei followed him.

"Would you like to spy on the lovebirds?" Hugh asked.

"No." I didn't need any favors from him.

"Having the right intelligence is the key to winning a war."

"I'm not at war."

"Of course you are, Kate. You're at war with yourself. A part of you knows that there is more to life than being the Consort. A part of you is wondering if he is betraying you. They are going to talk, whether you listen in or not, and hearing them won't change what they have to say." He nodded to the left. "I'm going. Feel free to join me."

Something inside me snapped. I had to know. I didn't trust the man I loved enough not to listen in. That said volumes about me and right then I didn't care. "Fine."

Hugh walked to the nearest door and held it open. I walked through it into a long curving hallway. I could see a balcony at the end. A light breeze, cold and spiced with the salty dampness of the sea, swirled around me. The sky was a brilliant blue, and against this happy, sunlit turquoise, the pale rail of the balcony seemed to almost glow.

A long rug stretched across the stone, swallowing our footsteps. Voices drifted up from below. I stopped just short of walking onto the balcony and propped myself against the wall.

Hugh leaned against the opposite wall, watching me.

"You don't take good care of yourself," Lorelei said.

And she was ready and willing to help him with that.

"You make so many sacrifices."

He couldn't possibly be buying this crock of bullshit. The man who manipulated seven different sets of alpha personalities on a daily basis couldn't possibly be this stupid.

"It must be lonely sometimes."

"It is," Curran said.

He was lonely. We had been together almost 24/7 for the past two months, yet he was lonely. When in the bloody hell did he have a chance to be lonely, exactly?

"It gets to be too much sometimes for one person. I understand," Lorelei continued. "After my mother left my father, I had to go with her, and I didn't really have a choice. I miss my father. I miss being somebody. In Belgium, because of my uncle, my mother and I aren't permitted to actually do anything in the pack. You can't imagine what it's like to be aware every minute that you are a guest and you must think over every word that comes out of your mouth. I would give anything for a place where I belong. Sometimes I wish I could sprout wings and just fly away. Just be gone to someplace better. Some place where I matter."

She fell silent.

"I'm sorry it happened to you," Curran said. "Sounds like you feel trapped and alone."

"I do. I'm sorry, I didn't mean to heap my problems on you."

"It's alright."

"No, it's not." Lorelei sighed. "Sometimes I just feel like I have nobody to talk to. At least no one who understands me. I'm sure you know how that feels. Your mate is human. There are some things that she simply can't understand."

I fought to keep from grinding my teeth.

"We are different," Curran said.

Yeah, those differences didn't bother you until now, jackass.

"I'm sorry she couldn't be with you and share in the thrill of bringing down the prey after a long hunt. It is such a rush to hunt next to your mate. You are so selfless to give up that joy. I don't know if I could do that."

Oh, give me a break.

"We all must make sacrifices. Hunting with my mate is just one of the things I can't do."

The way he said it, with deep profound regret, stabbed me straight in the chest.

"Perhaps she could become a shapeshifter?"

"She is immune," Curran said.

Lorelei inhaled sharply. "So you gave up half of your life for her? I'm so sorry. What if her children are born human?"

You bitch.

"Then I will deal with it." He sounded cold like a glacier.

My chest hurt. The world gained a slight red tint. I concentrated on breathing. Inhale. Exhale. Inhale.

"I shouldn't have mentioned it. It's just that she's so much more fragile than we are. Humans die of disease. They're weaker and easily hurt. If her children are born human, they would inherit her weakness . . . You shouldn't have to give up your . . . I'm sorry. Forget I said anything."

Exhale. Inhale.

"I appreciate your kindness. It's about time for us to go back," Curran said. "I will be missed."

Exhale.

"Of course."

A door thumped closed. Hugh shook his head. "I wasn't sure before, but now I know—the man is an idiot."

The pain sat in my chest, hot and solid. "Don't say it."

"He's a man of limited vision, Kate. All he cares about is the immediate: she's telling him that you can't hunt with him, you don't grow fur, and he isn't defending you. Sweet gods, your children might be human. The horror. He hasn't even considered what it means to have you on his side long-term. You handed him a priceless red diamond and he's reaching for glass beads because they are bigger and flashier."

"It's none of your business." This was it. This was his angle. Separate me from Curran and present himself as a better alternative. Hugh was playing me. I was walking along the edge of a cliff and needed to be sharp or I'd plunge down, but the red mist in my head was making it hard to concentrate.

"There are dozens of girls like Lorelei. They think they are special because they were born shapeshifters and they are cute and spoiled. They expect the world to bend for them." Hugh pointed toward the hall. "I can go in there right now, ask for one, and by morning I'll have ten just like her. You are special, Kate. You were born special, and then you passed through Voron's crucible, and you've excelled. Curran can't see it. There is an old word for it: unworthy."

"Will you be quiet?" I ground out.

He kept talking, never raising his voice, his tone reasonable but insistent. "I work with shapeshifters. I know them. I have them in my order. They don't think like us. They like to pretend they do, but their physiology is simply too different. They don't experience complex emotions, they experience urges. It's a cold, hard fact. Shapeshifters are ruled by instincts and needs: the urge to survive, to eat, and to produce offspring. Everything they do is dictated by animalistic thinking: they feel fear and it drives them into forming packs; they're driven to procreate and so they become aggressive toward their competition in an effort to pass on their genes; they make children—"

Maddie's mother flashed before me. "They love their children! They defend them to the end."

"So do cheetahs and wolf spiders. But expecting compassion or complex emotions from them would be foolish. It's a survival instinct, Kate. When a human mother loses a child, it's a life-breaking tragedy. When a shapeshifter child turns loup, they grieve and weep for a month or so, and then they get to work on a replacement."

Hugh raised his hands in front of him about a foot apart, palms facing each other. "They have tunnel vision and they live in the moment. Right now Curran's instincts are telling him you are a problem. Being with you is too complicated.

You don't fit neatly into the structure of his world, and others are questioning his choice. You are a source of friction and now he's found a more suitable alternative."

I didn't want to hear any more. I pushed from the wall, but he blocked my way.

"Move."

"Ask yourself if you will be content living your life in his shadow. You know you were meant for greater things. Deep down he knows this, too. He knows he can't hold you or he would've begged you to marry him. When a man wants to share his life with a woman, he offers her everything."

"Move." If he didn't, I would move him.

"You need to blow off some steam. I have an exercise yard full of swords. Spar with me."

"No."

"If you're too scared to try, just say you're scared, and we'll come back to it when you grow a backbone."

Voron. That was what Voron used to say to me. He would critique my fights, he would batter me in practice, and when I came up short, he'd reprimand me. "Do better" was bad. "Sloppy" was worse. But nothing compared to "Say you're scared." There was no worse sin than to not try because you couldn't scrape together enough courage.

The anger that had simmered boiled over. The ice cage cracked. I was so done. He wanted a fight, I would give him a fucking fight. "Fine. Lead the way."

CHAPTER 15

I FOLLOWED HUGH DOWN THE STAIRS. WE EMERGED into the hallway and I nearly walked into George. She saw Hugh. Her smart eyes narrowed. "Hey, Kate."

"Hey."

"Where you going?"

"Out for a little exercise."

George turned. "I'll come with you."

"Suit yourself."

We walked through the hallways to a door. Hugh pushed it open and we emerged into the inner yard. Six large racks of weapons greeted me, spaced in a crescent along the nearest wall. Swords, axes, spears. He must've taken time to prepare. It wouldn't help him.

I strolled along the racks. I recognized a few Japanese blades, but most were European, bastard swords, rapiers, sabers. An ancient falcata waited by the Greek kopis, a Roman gladius rested next to a hand-and-a-half, and a German messer next to its descendant, the saber. Falchions, claymores, tactical blades, every single one of them not only functional but beautiful, a kind of weapon that was a tool of war and a piece of art. Voron would've loved this. It had to be Hugh's personal collection. It was beautiful, as long as one ignored the man in the cage slowly dying of thirst in the corner.

I glanced up. Christopher was watching us through the bars with haunted eyes. I had meant to bring him water this morning.

Hugh stalked on the other side, watching me.

"Kate," George said. "What are you planning to do?"

"We're planning to spar," Hugh told her. "Just a friendly competition."

"This is a really bad idea," George said.

"What do I get if I win?" I asked.

Hugh nodded at his priceless swords. "You can have anything here."

I surveyed the blades. I would be insane to turn one down. "Anything?"

"Anything in this courtyard. But if I win—"

"You won't."

"If I win," Hugh said, "you'll tell me how you killed Erra. What magic you did, what moves you used. You will re-create that fight for me, down to the last little detail."

George shook her head. "Kate . . ."

"Deal."

George sighed.

I shrugged off my sheath and set Slayer down by the closest rack. I needed a similar blade, something with the same reach, weight, and balance.

Hugh stalked along the racks, thinking.

Falchion . . . No. A saber would give me an advantage, but this had to be an even contest. He was stronger; I had no doubt of that. He was six inches taller, muscled like a gladiator, and outweighed me by sixty-five pounds at the very least. His shirt molded to him, and the muscle on his torso looked hard like body armor. But all that muscle mass came with a price. It would cost him in endurance and speed, and I had endurance coming out of my ears.

We stopped at the same rack. Two nearly identical swords waited before us, each thirty-two inches long. A deep bevel ran down the length of the double-edged blades. People called it the blood groove, because they imagined blood dramatically running down the bevel. In reality the groove wasn't made to channel blood, but to lighten the weight of the sword without compromising its resilience. Despite its size, one of these twin swords would likely weigh only about two and a half pounds. Let's see, a classic type six cross-guard, with widened flat-tened ends bent slightly toward the blade. A four-inch grip, wrapped with a leather cord. A plain round pommel. Not a work of art, but a brutally efficient tool, designed to take lives.

"Fate," Hugh said.

I took one sword; he took the other. I swung my blade. Hmm. Lighter than two and a half pounds. More like two pounds, six ounces. No, five. Point of balance about five inches. Good sword. Fast, strong, lively.

We walked away from the racks, giving ourselves some space to dance.

"Why don't you use your own sword?" George asked.

"He might break it."

"I wouldn't." Hugh put his hand on his heart.

"He would," I told George. "He's a sonovabitch."

Hugh laughed. "We just met and she knows me so well."

I shrugged my shoulders, moving them forward, stretching my back. "Rules?"

"Full contact," Hugh said. "Yield."

I had expected first blood. "Full contact, yield" meant nei-ther of us would hold back and we wouldn't stop until one of us was backed into a corner or in real danger of losing a limb or our life. One of us had to say uncle for the fight to end.

"You sure about that?" I had a lot of aggression to work out.

"Are you afraid?" Hugh asked.

"Nope. Your funeral. Ready?"

Hugh spread his arms. "Introduce me to the afterlife."

I thought you'd never ask.

I walked toward him. He would expect a European open-ing with a European sword. He wouldn't get one.

If I killed him now, he would never tell Roland about me. It could be just a sparring accident. *My sword slipped and cut through his aorta. Oopsies. Dreadfully sorry.*

I was closing the distance. Hugh still had his hands out. He had no idea how pissed off I was.

I could make it look like an accident. I could make him pay for everything that hurt inside me.

I picked up speed, spun, and let myself off the chain, flying into movement like a pebble shot from a slingshot. The world slowed; each second stretched as if underwater.

I slashed diagonally, right to left over his chest. He stepped back to dodge.

I sliced right to left. Another step, hands up.

A low lunge, cutting left to right across his lower stomach. Hugh still dodged, but now with a purpose. He'd identified the cuts—I was hitting along eskrima's cardinal angles. About time. I reversed the slice, cutting in the opposite direction across the stomach. Hugh moved to parry, point of his blade down, body turning, planning to catch me with his left elbow.

Our swords touched.

I hammered my left fist into his jaw. The jawbone crunched and popped out of its socket. Hugh's mouth hung open, his lower jaw out of place. I've had my jaw dislocated before. Right now the pain was exploding in his skull and it had to be excruciating.

Hugh stumbled back. I drove him across the yard, striking as fast as I could. Hit. Hit. Hit. He staggered. My blade caught his biceps. Blood swelled, bright and red. The magic vibrated in it like a live electric current. First blood to me.

Hugh punched himself. The jaw slid into place. He reversed the grip and brought the sword down, cutting at me with powerful strikes. Dodge, dodge, parry. Ow. I batted his blade aside with the flat of mine, but if it had landed, the sheer power of it would have taken my arm off. Good that I wasn't planning on standing still.

"Temper, temper."

He opened his mouth and growled. *Ha-ha, hurts to talk, doesn't it?*

"You look in pain. Do you want a time-out to pull yourself together?"

He parried. His sword came over his head, slicing forward. I dodged and too late realized he had expected me to, because as I moved, he continued the swing, drawing his blade back. For a moment he looked almost like a batter, his body angled, his hips turned, as he put all of his momentum into the underhand swing. I barely had time to thrust my blade before his.

The blow knocked me back. I staggered. He kept coming, pounding on me with methodical heavy strikes. The precision of a scalpel, the power of a sledgehammer. I shied left, right, turning, trying to keep movement to a minimum to keep from getting tired out.

He thrust.

I blocked, half an instant too slow. The sword grazed my right shoulder. Pain lashed my muscle. Argh.

"Dance faster, Kate!"

His jaw started working again. That was some regeneration. I ducked out of the way. Hugh rammed me with his shoulder. I flew and crashed into the wall. My back crunched from the impact. *You sonovabitch.* He sliced at me. I ducked under the cut and twisted away. His blade struck stone. It cost him a third of a second and I landed a mule kick to the back of his knee. The knee bent, Hugh pitched forward, and I smashed the heel of my left hand into the back of his head. *Face, meet rock.*

Hugh grunted, a savage sound, one part pain, three parts pure fury.

I could cut through him. I could bury my sword in his back right now. But it wouldn't look like an accident.

I launched a kick.

Hugh dropped down and swept my leg from under me. I dropped. I was still in the air when Hugh's enormous fist flashed, coming toward me. I hit the ground, flexing my stomach, as I fell.

Hugh hammered a punch into my solar plexus.

Aaahhh. Aaahh, that hurt. Pain drowned me, hot, intense, and blinding. My stomach melted into agony, the air turned to fire in my lungs, and every nerve in my body screamed.

Hugh rolled to his feet fast like a dervish and flung blood from his face.

I squeezed the sword grip in my hand, fighting through the pain. I had to get up. He could've killed me. He hadn't, but I could not let him win. No. Not happening.

He would expect me to roll to my feet and catch me on the way up.

I could swear I heard people screaming somewhere far away. "Get up, Kate."

Hugh's right foot swung back, aiming for my side. "No time to rest."

I rolled into the kick, my knees bent. His foot connected with my shins. I grabbed his boot and kicked straight out at his other leg.

Hugh crashed down. I rolled backward and to my feet, sword up.

Hugh flexed and hopped off the ground. He bared his teeth at me, his eyes alight with madness. He looked insane.

You know what, fuck it. Accident or not, I no longer cared. I would end him here.

I grinned back, my own deranged psychotic smile.

Hugh bellowed like an animal. It was a happy roar.

I charged. His defense was too good for the inside strike, so I went for the arms. Big body, big heart. Let's see how much blood you've got in you, Preceptor.

We clashed and danced across the clearing. I sank into the flurry of strikes, melting into the rhythm, fluid, quick, the sword so natural in my hand that wielding it was like breathing. He was fast, but I was faster.

"You want to know how I killed Erra? Like this." I sliced his left bicep. "And like this." Another cut, across the chest. "Hang around. I'll tell you the whole story."

He scored a cut across my side. I opened two gashes across his arms. Two to one. I liked those odds.

Hugh shook his head, trying to fling blood out of his eyes. I kept coming. He took a step back. Another.

Twenty-six years. Twenty-six years of looking over my shoulder, of living in constant paranoia. Twenty-six years of worrying about being found, of pretending to be weaker, of denying myself basic human contact. I let them fuel me. My sword became a whip, lashing, cutting, slicing, turning, drawing hot red blood again and again. He tried to match it, but I was too fast. I thrust and laughed when the sword found resistance.

Pain hummed inside me, but it had receded into a far place. He cut me, but I didn't care. The real world faded. Only anger remained. I was so tired of losing everyone I loved. He was everything that caused me pain and I had to destroy it.

He fought like Voron: skilled, smart, and deadly. Fighting him was magic. It was like sparring with my father. But I had beaten Voron when I was fourteen. I would beat Hugh as well. I was too angry to stop.

I walked him backward across the courtyard. It was him and me and two swords. I could go on forever. I would go on forever. He would slow down first.

Die, Hugh. Die for me.

Die.

"Kate!"

Curran.

I pulled back, just enough to glance in the direction of his voice. He was in the window on the right. Lorelei stood next to him, her face slack with shock. Bloody hell.

Every window had someone in it. People had piled out onto the balconies. Above us on the parapet, Hibla's djigits leveled crossbows at me. At the far tower, two more of Hibla's werejackals primed the scorpio.

Reality crashed into me like a runaway train. If I killed Hugh, they would fill the courtyard with arrows. I would die.

I didn't care. It would be worth it.

I turned and glimpsed George as she moved away from us.

George would die with me. They'd hit her with enough arrows that even her shapeshifter regeneration wouldn't be able to cope, and even if she survived, the Pack would retaliate. There would be a bloodbath.

I had to disengage. I wanted to keep fighting so bad, it hurt.

I thrust to Hugh's chest, dropping the angle sharply. He parried, but we both knew it was a quarter of an inch too low. My blade slid along his and I felt it sink into his right oblique muscle. Anger faded from his features. The wall was right behind him. Hugh took a slow, deliberate step back. I followed, my sword an inch into his upper stomach. If I pressed, he'd suffer a lacerated liver.

He leaned against the wall. A slow smile stretched his bloodstained lips.

"I'd like to hear it."

Hugh leaned forward, forcing the sword to bite deeper into his muscle. A strange expression claimed his face, a kind of focused but slightly amused look, possessive, no, *inviting* . . .

Hugh opened his mouth. "Uncle."

It wasn't a surrender. It was a dare. A year ago I might've mistaken it for something else or convinced myself I was reading too much into it, but a year of being in love and being wanted gave me enough of a basis to identify that look. Hugh was turned on.

It wasn't an act. This was real.

Damn it all to hell.

Do not react.

I freed the sword, wiped it on my shirt, and offered it to him hilt first. "Excellent sword. Thank you for the workout."

"No, thank you." Hugh pushed from the wall. Blood soaked his T-shirt. His face swelled on the left side. He must've turned when I rammed his face into the wall. Probably tried to save the nose. A broken nose made your eyes tear. I would've finished him much faster.

All the aches and pains screamed at me at once. My stomach hurt. My left side was likely cut. My right side felt slightly off, with a familiar throbbing pain. Cracked rib. Hopefully not broken. My arms ached in ten different places. My T-shirt hadn't turned completely red, like his, but bright stains blossomed on it here and there.

I turned, stretching slightly. Ow. I felt like someone had beaten me with a bag of razor-studded potatoes.

A small noise made me pivot. Curran marched toward us, his face dark, his eyes almost completely gold. He must've jumped out the window. Imagine that. Whatever would Lorelei do all by her lonesome?

"You owe me a rematch," Hugh said.

"Maybe. One day." *When you aren't surrounded by two dozen bodyguards.*

"That's a promise."

Curran moved toward me. "Are you okay, baby?"

"He calls you baby." Hugh laughed. "I love it."

"Shut up," Curran said.

I raised my voice, so the audience could hear. "About my prize?"

Hugh smiled. "Of course," he said, his voice carrying. "You are welcome to anything in the courtyard."

I turned and pointed at Christopher in the cage. "I want him."

Hugh blinked and locked his jaw.

Yes, yes, you've been had. Put your big-boy pants on and pay up.

Hugh's face looked grim. He really didn't want to give up his torture toy.

"Is there a problem?" Curran asked.

"No problem." Hugh raised his voice and barked an order in another language.

Hibla strode out, pulling a large keychain from her pocket. Two djigits followed. We watched as they unlocked the doors.

Hugh pulled off his shirt, displaying an award-winning

torso. He was built like an anatomy model—every muscle honed to precision and just the right size: strong, powerful, but flexible. And bloody. I must've cut him over twenty times. Most of the wounds amounted to little more than nicks and shallow gashes. He was really good. Had I been less angry, he might've won. That thought worried me.

Hugh turned his left arm, showing off three precision cuts across the bulging triceps. Had I managed to cut deeper, I would've disabled the arm with each one. "Look at this." Hugh indicated the cuts to Curran. "Like a fucking artist."

I started toward the cage.

"Touch her again and I'll kill you," Curran said quietly behind my back.

"She doesn't need your help," Hugh said. "But any time you want to play, let me know."

I kept walking. My hip hurt, too. Red seeped through my jeans. Another cut. Deeper than others. Hell would freeze over before I limped.

The djigits swung the door open and backed away from me, hands in the air. Christopher stared at me with owl eyes.

"Come on," I told him.

He blinked. "My lady."

"You're free. Come with me. We have food and water." I reached for him.

He grabbed my arm with both hands and kissed it. "My mistress. My beautiful mistress. Thank you, thank you, thank you."

He had a death grip on my wrist.

"My kind mistress, my sweet mistress, thank you, thank you . . ."

"Barabas!" I called. I was ninety percent sure I'd heard him during the fight.

A movement and he appeared by my side as if by magic. "Alpha."

"Deadly mistress," Christopher whispered. His fingers brushed my blood. He stared at me, his face all shining eyes. "My lady! Will serve forever . . ."

"Shhh." I put my left index finger to my lips. "Hush now."

Barabas reached over me and gently disengaged Christopher's fingers. "That fight was amazing," he said quietly.

Good to know I still gave good show, because I sure as hell

wasn't good for much else. "Please make sure he gets a shower, a fresh change of clothes, and some food and water. Don't give him too much, because he'll gorge himself. He isn't all there."

Barabas pulled Christopher out of the cage. The man stared up at him. "I died, didn't I? Are you an angel?"

"Sure," Barabas said. "Follow me to the Heavenly Shower."

Christopher walked a couple of steps on wobbling legs and spun back, looking at me with an expression of complete desperation on his face.

"Go with the angel, Christopher," I said. "We'll talk later."

Barabas turned him around and guided him into the building.

I turned to follow them. Curran stood in my way. "What the hell were you thinking?" he asked quietly.

"Move," I told him, keeping my voice down. The audience was dispersing but not fast enough for my taste.

Lorelei chose that precise moment to rush out the door. She saw my face and stopped. *That's right. Keep your distance, delicate flower. The weak human is still very angry.* In my mind, I dashed at her and swung. She had a thin neck. Wouldn't be too hard.

I crushed that thought. I wouldn't lose it.

Curran clenched his teeth. His face had that relaxed icy quality that usually meant a storm was about to erupt. "I need to talk to you."

"Not right now." I'd had it with him.

"Yes, now."

"But how will Princess Wilson survive without your manly protection while you and I talk?"

Gold rolled over his eyes.

"I tell you what. She is over there and I'm here. Pick."

"It's not that simple."

"Then I'll pick for you." *Watch me walk away.*

"Is that a threat?"

"No, that was a test and you failed it. Don't follow me."

He grabbed my arm. I jerked back. "Do not follow me," I snarled through my teeth. "Or I swear to God, I'll get my sword and fucking stab you in the heart with it."

He let go. I marched across the yard, picked up Slayer, and kept walking all the way into our room, where I barred the door.

CHAPTER 16

SOMETIMES THE SIMPLE PLEASURES IN LIFE ARE best. Like a hot shower after a sweaty, bloody fight. A dull, heavy numbness crept into my arms. Hugh hit like a battering ram. I would really pay for blocking him in the morning, but the pain had already started. I felt tender all over. With luck, I'd still be able to move tomorrow.

I stood under the water, trying not to think, and concentrated purely on shampooing my hair and then dragging a soapy sponge against my cuts. It hurt and I welcomed it.

Andrea once told me that I had a problem processing emotional pain. I couldn't handle it, so I replaced it with physical pain instead: either I inflicted it on others or I suffered through it myself. Well, I had physical pain aplenty. If she was right, I should be floating on a cloud of bliss right about now.

Finally the water ran clear. I stepped out and looked at myself in the mirror. The gashes on my thigh and stomach had come open. Demet was really, really good at medmagic, but I was still human and now I was all cut up to hell. In the past, Doolittle had spent so much effort on healing me that some of my old scars had faded. Clearly, this created an imbalance and the Universe had decided to compensate.

Half a dozen shallow cuts crossed my arms and torso. Hugh's handiwork. I shouldn't have let him goad me. Voron always told me that he'd trained Hugh to fight, but also to command and plan. But he had trained me to kill. Hugh would be directing an army, leading it into battle, while I was a lonely assassin on the sidelines, cutting my way through the mass of people to my target. In a simple one-on-one sword fight, I had an edge.

Neither of us had used magic. I still didn't know the full extent of his, and he still didn't know much about mine. At least I hadn't given myself away completely.

Someone had left bandages on the night table. Probably a gift from Doolittle. I bandaged the worst of it, sat on the chair very carefully—my thighs hurt—and slumped forward. My body hurt all over. I closed my eyes. It was just pain. It would pass. I just needed a minute. I still had three hours before my shift with Desandra started.

Someone knocked. I stared at the door, hoping to burn through it with my gaze and explode whoever was on the other side.

Knock-knock.

"Yes?"

"Can I please talk to you?"

I didn't recognize the voice. Okay. I pulled on a clean T-shirt and a new pair of jeans, picked up Slayer, and opened the door. A young man stood in the hallway, dressed in a djigit outfit. Young, barely eighteen. Dark blond hair, brown eyes. He stood, rocking forward on his toes, as if expecting to be jumped any second.

"What is it?"

"You're looking for the orange creatures," he whispered in a heavily accented English.

"Yes."

"I will take you where they nest. If you pay me. But we have to go fast and be very quiet."

Aha. "What's your name?"

"Volodja."

A Russian name, short for Vladimir. "How far is it?"

"Two hours. On the mountain. I want three." He held up three fingers. "Three thousand dollars."

"Sounds like a good deal to me."

"I'll wait in town by the statue." He took off down the stairs.

My howling in the dark had paid off. Someone got upset over the blood test and now they had decided to make me disappear. The only other party interested in getting rid of me would be Lorelei, and she had no reason to fight with me. She was winning.

They really thought I was stupid. At least he didn't offer to sell me a nice beachfront property in Nebraska.

I pulled off my T-shirt—it hurt—and strapped myself into a bra. It also hurt. I put the T-shirt back on, found my boots, and headed to Doolittle's room. I'd finally found the end of a thread in this messy knot. If I pulled on it the right way, it would lead me to the guilty party. But I'd need backup.

The door stood wide open and I heard Aunt B's voice from down the hall. "And then I told him that beads were just fine, but a woman had to have certain standards . . . Come on in, dear."

How did she know? I was pretty quiet. I stepped through the door. The debris was gone. A clean, tidy room greeted me, furnished with new bedding, chairs, and desks. Doolittle sat in a wheelchair. I did my best not to wince. Eduardo stretched out on the bed to the right. George sat on the other bed. Keira sat on the windowsill, while Aunt B occupied a chair. Derek lay on the floor, reading a book.

Everybody, except Doolittle and Aunt B, studiously pretended not to look at me. We'd been attacked, we were still under siege, and the shapeshifters had turned grim. My fight with Hugh must've made things worse somehow. Either that, or all of them also knew that Curran had found himself a new main squeeze. Awkward.

"A young djigit stopped by my room," I said. "His name is Volodja and for three thousand dollars he will walk me deep into the mountains and show me where the bad shapeshifters live."

"How fortunate." Aunt B's eyes lit up. "Would you like some company for this wonderful trap, I mean, adventure?"

"I would."

"I'll come," Derek said.

"No. I get you into enough trouble as is." Derek and I were close. If Curran did decide to pull the plug on our relationship, I didn't want to divide the boy wonder's loyalty. That was how the packs split, and both Derek and Barabas were just idealistic enough to dramatically exit with me. It was best to start distancing myself now.

"I'll come, too," Eduardo said.

"Why don't you let me go instead," Keira said. "You can barely stand."

"I don't know, all he has to do is come with us and loom," Aunt B said.

Eduardo crossed his arms on his chest, making his giant biceps bulge. "What do you mean, loom?"

"We need you to stand there with your arms crossed and scowl," I translated.

Eduardo scowled. "I don't do that."

"Just like that," Derek said.

Eduardo realized his arms were crossed and dropped them. "Screw you guys."

"That settles it. I'm going." Keira hopped off the windowsill. "Besides, I owe you, bison boy."

"For what?" I asked.

"He got hurt trying to save me," Keira said. "When the thing pinned me down, he picked it up and slammed it on the floor. It was very heroic."

Eduardo shook his head.

Perfect. Between Jim's sister and Aunt B, my back would be covered. "I'll need to check on Christopher and we're good to go."

Three minutes later I was knocking on Barabas's door, with Aunt B and Keira looking over my shoulder. Barabas opened the door.

"How is he?"

Barabas's face took on a pained expression. "So far he threw up and tried to dive in the bathtub."

"At the same time?"

"Thankfully, no. He's soaking. The dirt is embedded in his skin. Are you going somewhere?"

I explained what was going on. "If we play along, we can get to the bottom of who hired him. Unless it's a one-in-a-million chance that he actually is telling the truth."

"Be careful," Barabas said.

We left the castle and took the winding road down the mountain. The sea sparkled like an enormous sapphire. The sun shone bright and the air smelled of salt water and the light scent of apricots. The beauty of it was so startling, I stopped and looked.

"We should go swimming," Keira said.

We all knew that a relaxing day at the beach wouldn't be happening, but it was nice to dream. "There are no frogs in the sea."

"Why would I be interested in frogs?"

"Jim told me one time that he didn't swim unless there were frogs involved. I assumed he ate them."

"That's disgusting," Keira said. "You really should stop listening to my brother. And he swims like a fish, by the way. The Cat House has an Olympic-sized pool and he swims a couple of miles every time he stays over. Frogs. That man has never eaten a frog in his entire life."

Aunt B laughed.

We started down the winding road. The gravel path smelled of rock dust. Dense blackberry bushes formed a solid wall of green on the sides. I suddenly realized I was starving. I pulled a handful of berries off the bush and stuffed them in my mouth. Mmmm. Sweet.

"Berries are always best off the branch," Aunt B said. She wore a bright yellow dress with a white paisley design on it, sunglasses, and a straw hat. Keira wore a sundress with a light brown bodice and a wide skirt made of strips of light turquoise, white, and brown fabric. It came up to her knees and made her look five years younger. The two of them appeared to be on vacation, while I, with my sexy bruised face, big boots, jeans, and a sword, looked like I had a camp of bandits to destroy.

"What's the connection between you and our handsome host?" Aunt B asked.

Blackberries taste much worse when they try to come back up your throat. "Uhhhh . . ."

"*Uhhh* is not an answer," Keira informed me.

Andrea must not have told her about Hugh, and I had no desire to explain who my dad was. "We never met but we were trained by the same person. Now he works for a very powerful man who will kill me if he finds me."

"Why?" Keira asked.

"It's a family thing."

"That explains the attraction," Aunt B said.

"Attraction?"

"You're that thing he can't have. It's called forbidden fruit."

"I'm not his fruit!"

"He thinks you are. The word you're looking for is 'smitten,' my dear." Aunt B smiled. "I'm sure the way Megobari looked at you made Curran positively giddy."

Hearing his name was like being burned. "Will you stop meddling in my love life?" I growled.

"I'm not meddling. I'm offering commentary."

Ugh. "I just want to go home."

"Not until we get all of the panacea we've been promised." Aunt B adjusted her hat. "You have no idea what it's like to lose a child to loupism. True, you've endured Julie's tragedy, but I had given birth to my babies. I nursed them, I nurtured them from the time they were tiny and helpless, I fanned the tiny flames of their potential. I had so many dreams for them. Children think you are a god. You are the center of their universe, you can fix anything, you can shield them and protect them, and then one day they find out you can't. I remember the look in my sons' eyes before I killed them. They thought they were abandoned. That I had betrayed them. Raphael will not go through this. Not if I can help it."

Her voice told me that the wound was still there. It had formed a scab over the years, but Aunt B still mourned her dead children. When she told me that she came on this trip to keep an eye on me, it was a white lie. She had come here for panacea and she would do anything to get it. The one bag she'd earned wouldn't be enough. I thought of Maddie in the glass coffin. I couldn't blame Aunt B. I would do anything to spare my child this kind of pain.

If I didn't have children with Curran, I wouldn't have to worry about it.

Wow. I wasn't even sure where that came from.

"I'm glad this Volodja came to you," Aunt B said.

"Why?" My fight must've made a bigger impression than I thought.

"Because some Abkhazians speak Russian. They're neighbors. You're the only one in our group who can translate in a pinch."

And here I thought she was awed by my incredible martial skills. One deflated ego? Check.

We went through the streets. Abandoned houses stared at us with empty windows, shells of their former selves. On the wall of an empty apartment building, little more than a gutted carcass of concrete and steel, someone had drawn a pair of angel wings. Hope for a better future, or a memory of someone who died. We would never know.

"That must be the statue." Keira pointed to a bronze djigit on a horse. It rose in the middle of a small plaza. Behind it sat a small café.

Aunt B inhaled. "We should go this way." She made a bee-line for the café. "He is a werejackal. He'll find our scent."

The café sat in the shade of a huge walnut tree, a turquoise-blue building that had seen better days.

"Bakery," Keira announced.

You don't say. I grinned. Back home Aunt B preferred to conduct her business over a platter of cupcakes or a slice of pie.

"Is something funny?" Aunt B asked.

"We crossed half the planet and you found a bakery."

"I don't see the humor in that."

Keira laughed under her breath.

"You're supposed to look menacing," Aunt B told her. "You're Eduardo's stand-in."

"Yes," I agreed. "Less laughing, more looming."

Keira crossed her arms and pretended to scowl.

"We should've brought the werebuffalo," Aunt B said.

We walked into the café. An older woman with gray hair smiled at us from behind the long counter and called out in a lilting language. Aunt B pointed to some things, money was exchanged, and suddenly we were sitting at a table with some pastries filled with apricots. We had been sitting still for about fifteen minutes when the kid walked through the door. He carried a rifle. A backpack hung off his shoulder. He saw Aunt B and Keira and halted.

"You have friends."

"Yes."

"It's okay. Did you bring the money?"

"We did," Aunt B assured him.

"Are you ready?" Volodja asked.

"Ready if you are," Aunt B said.

THE STEEP TRAIL CURVED SOUTH, AWAY FROM THE castle. Blackberry bushes flanked the path, stretching thorny branches across the gravel and dirt. Our guide hadn't said a word since we left the city behind about an hour ago. I did my best to turn my brain off and concentrate on memorizing the way back. Thinking about anything inevitably led back to Curran. I wanted to stab something. Failing that, I wanted to pace around. None of that would be helpful. Emotional raging just tired you out.

"How do you know where the orange shapeshifters nest?" I asked. Any distraction in a pinch . . .

"I've seen them." Volodja shrugged, adjusting the rifle on his shoulder. "It's not far now."

I couldn't wait to find out who pulled his strings.

"Come on, dear," Aunt B said. "Where is your spirit of adventure?"

Midway up the trail, the magic wave drowned us. We paused, adjusting, and moved on.

One hour later the trail brought us up onto the crest of the mountain. Straight ahead the sea sparkled. Behind us, low in the valley, lay the city. A tall cliff rose to the left and within it gaped a dark hole.

"Cave," Volodja explained. "We go in."

"You first."

Volodja took a step forward. The bushes on our right rustled. A dark-haired man stepped in the open. Around thirty, with a short beard, he carried a rifle and a dagger and wore a beat-up version of a djigit outfit. A bundle lay across his shoulder with mountain goat legs sticking out of it. A big gray-and-white dog trotted out and sat next to him. Broad and muscular, she had a dense shaggy coat. She might have been some type of Molosser—she looked like someone took a Saint Bernard and gave it a German shepherd's muzzle and coat.

The hunter squinted at Volodja and said something. The kid answered.

The hunter waved his free arm. I wished I had a universal translator.

"What is he saying?" I asked.

"He is . . . crazy." Volodja put his index finger to his temple and turned his hand back and forth.

The hunter barked something. The dog at his feet woofed quietly. I missed Grendel. I wished I could've brought him. Maybe he'd bite Hugh and Curran for me.

Volodja waved at him, like you would at a mosquito, and started to the cave. "We go."

"Plokhoe mesto," the hunter yelled.

Accented Russian. That I understood. "He says this is a bad place."

Volodja pivoted on his foot, his gaze sharp. "You speak Russian?"

"I do. I also get very angry when people try to trick me."

He raised his hands. "No trick. You want orange things or not?"

"We do," Aunt B said. "Lead the way."

"Agulshap," the hunter said. *"Don't go into the cave."*

Agulshap didn't sound like a Russian word. "What does *agulshap* mean?"

"I don't know," Volodja said. "I talked to you: he is crazy."

Keira shook her head. "I don't like it."

I didn't like it either.

"Come along," Aunt B said. Her face still had that pleasant, sweet-as-sugar smile, but her eyes were hard. Suddenly I felt sorry for Volodja.

He pulled a torch out of his pack and lit it.

The mouth of the cave grew closer with every step. A few more seconds and it swallowed us whole.

THE CAVE STRETCHED ON AND ON, TALL, GIANT, vast. Stone steps carved into the living rock of the mountain led down below, and my steps sent tiny echoes bouncing up and down from the smooth walls.

"Little far," Volodja explained over his shoulder.

"Clear as mud," Keira muttered.

The stone steps ended. The only light came from the torch in our guide's hand. We crossed the cavern floor to a rough arch chiseled in the rock. Volodja stepped through. Aunt B followed, and then I did, with Keira bringing up the rear. We stood in a round chamber, about thirty feet wide. Another exit, a dark hole, yawned to the right.

"We wait," Volodja said.

We stood in darkness. This wasn't filling me with oodles of confidence.

Keira touched my shoulder. Something was coming.

The kid dove forward, through the second opening. I lunged after him and ran into a metal grate that slammed shut in my face. The second clang announced another grate slamming into place over our only exit.

I pressed against the wall, between the two exits.

"I thought so," Keira said.

Aunt B sighed.

We just had to figure out if this was a straight robbery or if someone had hired them to do it.

Someone shone a light through the grate. "I have crossbow," a deep male voice said. "Silver bolts. Give money."

"I don't understand," Aunt B said. "Where are the orange shapeshifters? Volodja?"

"No shapeshifters." Volodja laughed, a little nervous giggle. "You give money and you can go. Human girl stays."

"Don't I feel special."

"You trapped with us. Give money!"

"You have it wrong, dear," Aunt B said. "We are not trapped here with you." Her eyes sparked into a hot ruby glow. "You are trapped in here with us."

The happy dress burst. Her body erupted, as if someone had triggered the detonator, but the explosion of flesh swirled, controlled, snapping into a new form. A monster rose in Aunt B's place. She stood on powerful legs, her flanks and back sheathed in reddish fur spotted with blotches of black. Her back curved slightly, hunched over. She raised her arms, her four-inch claws held erect, like talons ready to rend, and great muscles rolled under her dark skin, promising devastating power. The monster snapped her hyena muzzle, the distorted, grotesquely large jaws opening and closing, like a bear trap.

Keira's dress flew. A werejaguar rammed the grate. The crossbow twanged; the shot went wide. The metal screeched and the grate flew past me and crashed into the wall. Men screamed. A body flew, like a rag doll hurled by an angry child.

I kept my place, staying clear. There was room for only one of them in the passage and I would only get in the way.

Aunt B dashed after Keira, yanked a struggling man, and slammed him against the wall next to me. Volodja's glassy eyes stared at me in sheer panic. He hadn't turned, which meant he likely couldn't hold the warrior form.

Aunt B's hand with fork-sized claws squeezed his throat. She snapped her teeth half an inch from his carotid. A deep ragged growl spilled from her throat. "Who hired you?"

"Nobody," he squeezed out.

"Who hired you?" Aunt B pulled him from the wall and slammed his head back against the stone.

"Kral! Jarek Kral!"

Aunt B squeezed. Her claws drew a bright red line on the kid's chin. "What were you supposed to do?"

"He wants human killed," Volodja struggled in her grip.

"Why?"

"I don't know! I didn't ask!"

Aunt B hurled him across the room and ducked into the opening. I moved to follow. Something clanged. The floor dropped from under my feet and I fell into the darkness below.

A SECOND DOESN'T SEEM LIKE MUCH TIME, BUT THE human mind is an amazing thing. It can pack not one but two short thoughts into the space of a second, thoughts like *Oh shit* and *I'm about to die.*

Rock flashed before me and I plunged into vast empty darkness, crouching in midair, trying to brace for impact.

The air whistled past me.

My ears caught a hum. My instincts screamed, *Water!*

I hit the sea. Like smashing at full speed into concrete. The impact slapped me and all went dark.

NO AIR.

My eyes snapped open. I was suspended in salty water.

My lungs burned. I jerked upward. My head broke the surface and I gulped the air with a hoarse moan. It tasted sweet and for a few moments I could do nothing except breathe.

I survived. The impact must've knocked me out for a few seconds. My cuts hurt. Kate Daniels, extra-salt-in-the-wounds edition.

I tried kicking. Legs still okay. Arms moving. Body check complete, all systems go. I turned around. Weak green luminescence came from the moss growing in the rougher spots on the walls, doing little to combat the darkness. Still, it was good enough to see. During tech, this place would've been pitch-black. *Thank you, Universe, for small favors.*

I floated on my back, trying to look around. A huge cavern rose around me, its floor flooded with seawater. You could fit half a football field into it.

I turned and swam along the wall. I had a pretty good breaststroke but my boots weren't doing me any favors. They sat on my feet like two bricks.

No way up. The nearly sheer walls rose straight up. A small stone ledge protruded on one side, barely four inches wide. Even if I could somehow climb onto it, I couldn't stay on. Far above, a black hole punctured the ceiling. I must've fallen through it. A few feet to the left and I would've splattered against the stone wall on the way down.

When I got out of this, I'd have to track down Volodja and his friends and thank them for this fun excursion. Assuming there was anything left after Aunt B and Keira were done with them.

How the hell was I going to get out of here?

Something bobbed in the water in front of me, a dark bundle. I sped up. A canvas sack, watertight. Hmm.

The sack moved.

I put six feet of water between me and the sack with a single kick. Clearly I'd had too much excitement for one day.

The sack twisted. A bulge stretched the fabric on one side.

Maybe someone had stuffed a cat into a bag and thrown it down here. Of course, if my experience was anything to go by, the sack would contain a giant brain-sucking leech that would immediately try to devour me. Then again, considering the current mess, the leech might not view me as a tasty treat. Nope, no brains here.

The sack twisted.

No guts, no glory. I swam to the bag, pulled my throwing knife out, and sliced at the cord wrapped around its top. *Here goes nothing.* I pulled the sack open and looked into it.

A human face peered at me with bright eyes. It belonged to a man in his forties or fifties, with a short gray beard, a hawkish nose, and bushy eyebrows. There was nothing exceptionally extraordinary about it except for the fact that it was about the size of a cat's head.

I'd seen some freaky shit, but this took the cake. For a second my brain stalled, trying to process what my eyes saw.

The owner of the face lunged out of the bag into the water and sank like a stone.

He sank. Crap.

I dove down and grasped the flailing body. He couldn't have been more than eighteen inches tall. Deadweight hit my hands. At least thirty pounds. I almost dropped him. I kicked, dragging him up.

We broke the surface.

I gasped for breath. A small fist rocketed toward me. Pain exploded in my jaw. Good punch. I shook my head, dragged the struggling man to the stone ledge, and heaved him onto it. He scrambled up.

We glared at each other. He wore a bronze-colored tunic with an embroidered collar, dark brown pants, and small, perfectly made leather riding boots.

What in the world would he be riding? A Pomeranian?

The man blinked, studying me.

I'd managed to find a hobbit in the Caucasus Mountains. I wondered what he would do if I asked him about second breakfast.

The man opened his mouth. A string of words spilled out.

"I don't understand," I said in English.

He shook his head.

"Ne ponimayu."

Another shake. Russian didn't work either.

The man pointed to his left, waving his arms, frantic. I turned.

Something slid through the water at the far wall. Something long and sinuous that left ripples in its wake.

I flipped the knife in my hand and pressed against the wall, as close to the stone as I could.

The creature slid downward, into the water. The surface smoothed out.

Another ripple, closer. Smooth water again.

The opening bars of the theme from *Jaws* rolled through my head. *Thanks. Just what I needed.*

If I were something long and serpentine with big teeth and I was hunting for some lunch, I'd swim up from underneath my victim.

I took a deep breath and dove.

A silvery-green beast sped toward me through the clear

water. Fourteen feet long, as thick as my thigh, with the body of an eel armed with a crest of long spikes, it swam straight for me, its eyes big and empty, like two yellow coins against the silver scales.

The serpent opened its mouth, a big deep hole studded with a forest of needle-thin teeth.

I pressed against the wall, my feet against the rock.

The serpent reared and struck. I launched myself from the wall, grabbed its neck, hugged it to me with every drop of strength I had, and jammed my knife into its gills. The sharp spikes sliced my fingers. The serpent coiled around me, its body a single, powerful muscle. I dragged the blade down, ripping through the fragile membranes of its gills.

The serpent contorted, churning the water. I clung to it. To let go was to die.

My lungs begged for air. I stabbed it again and again, trying to cause enough damage.

The serpent writhed, impossibly strong.

Black dots swam before my eyes. *Air. Now.*

I let go and kicked myself up.

The serpent lunged at my feet. The teeth clamped my boot but didn't penetrate the thick sole. I jerked, trying to kick myself free. I could see the shiny ceiling where the air met water right above me. *Another foot. Come on.* I rammed my other foot into the serpent's head.

The teeth let go. I shot up and gulped air.

The tiny man on the ledge screamed.

The silver spine broke the surface next to me. I slashed at it, trying to cut it in half. The serpent clenched my foot again. Teeth bit my ankle and yanked me down.

I kicked as hard as I could, trying to swim back up. If it dragged me down, it would be over. Magic was my only chance. I pulled it to me. Not much there—a weak magic wave.

The serpent pulled, drawing me deeper and deeper under the water. I kicked its head. One. Two . . .

The serpent let go, turned, and swept at me. I swam up like I'd never swum before in my life. My muscles threatened to tear off my bones.

I broke the water. I needed a power word. I could command it to die, but *Ud*, the killing word, usually failed, and when it didn't work, the backlash crippled me with pain. The stronger the magic, the less pain, but this magic wave was weaker than most. The killing word would hurt like a sonovabitch.

I couldn't afford to be crippled right this second or I'd end the day as fish food. The only other attack word I had was *kneel*. The serpent had no legs.

The serpent reared, rising from the sea, its mouth gaping. A moment and it would slam into me, like a battering ram.

The small man spat a single harsh word. *"Aarh!"*

A torrent of magic smashed into the serpent. It froze, completely still.

I lunged at it and thrust the knife into its spine. The serpent shuddered. I sawed through its flesh, nearly cutting it in two.

The serpent jerked and crashed backward. I kicked free.

The creature convulsed, whipping the sea into froth. I swam away from it, to the ledge, gasping for breath. The small man slumped against the stone. A small dribble of bloody spit slid from his mouth.

He'd used a power word and it worked. *Thank you. Thank you, whoever you are upstairs.*

I held on to the ledge. The small man leaned over and held my hand, helping me hold on.

The serpent flailed and thrashed, until finally a full minute later, it hung motionless in the water.

The man petted my hand, wiped the blood from his lips, and pointed up. Above us, about seven feet above the stone shelf, a narrow hole split the wall, a little less than a foot across. Not nearly wide enough for both of us.

The man held his hands together, as if praying, and looked at me.

"Okay," I told him. No reason for both of us to be trapped.

I moved along the ledge to its widest point. A whole six inches of space to work with. Oh boy. It took me four tries to crawl up onto it—my feet kept slipping—but I finally managed and hugged the wall.

The man grabbed my shirt and pulled himself up. Feet stomped on my shoulders. Forget thirty pounds, he was more like fifty. He should've weighed one third of that at his size. Maybe he was made of rocks.

The man stood on my shoulders. I locked my hands and raised my arms flat against the wall. He stepped on my palms and kicked off.

I slipped and fell backward into the water. I broke the surface just in time to see him scramble into the hole and vanish.

I was all alone. Just me and fourteen feet of fresh sushi bopping on the waves. I was so tired. My arms felt like wet cotton.

Maybe I'd hallucinated the whole hobbit episode. I'd hit the water hard, ended up with a concussion, and started seeing small magic men in riding boots.

I forced myself to swim. Hanging in the water didn't accomplish anything, and I was too exhausted to keep it up for long. Another trip around the cavern confirmed what I already knew—no escape. Sitting here waiting to be rescued was a losing proposition. Even if Aunt B and Keira did somehow manage to find me, I'd spend hours waiting for them to get a rope long enough get me out. The chances of the small man returning with a detachment of Pomeranian cavalry to liberate me were even slimmer.

The serpent had to have come from somewhere. There simply weren't enough fish in this small cavern to keep it alive, and unless they fed it a steady diet of Abkhazian hobbits, it had to move freely between the cavern and the sea.

I swam to the wall where I'd first seen it and dove deep down through the crystal-clear water. Fifteen feet down, the mountain ended and a ten-foot-wide tunnel stretched before me, leading out. I had no idea how long it was.

To dive into an underwater tunnel of unknown length, possibly drowning, or to stay in the cavern until I wore myself out, possibly drowning? Sometimes life just didn't offer good choices.

I breathed deep, trying to saturate my lungs with oxygen, and dove under. The tunnel rolled out in front of me, narrowing until it was barely four feet wide. I kept going, kicking off the walls. I once heard it was a good idea to not think about holding my breath while holding it. Yeah. That's like not looking down while crossing over a cliff. Once someone says, "Don't look down," you're going to look.

The walls were closing in on me.

What if I swam out into the nest of sea serpents?

My heart hammered in my chest. I'd run out of air. I swam, frantic, desperate, fighting the water for my life.

The ocean was turning dark. I was drowning.

The tunnel's walls opened abruptly, and above me translucent blue spread. I flailed, heading straight up.

My face broke the surface. A bright beautiful sky stretched overhead. I gulped in the air. Oh wow. I lay on my back for a long second, breathing. I wasn't ready to kick the bucket. Not just yet.

Hanging in the water was lovely and all, but if more sea serpents were floating about, I had to get the hell out of the water. I straightened up. I was in the open sea. The shore—a solid vertical cliff—towered before me. The mountain was nearly sheer. Climbing it right now was beyond me.

I turned in the water. A vast indigo sea stretched around me, a constant field of blue except for a tiny island about twenty-five yards away. Only twenty feet across, it was more like a rock than an island, but right now even the runt of the island litter would do.

I swam to it. The warm water, crystal clear, slid against my skin, caressing me gently. I was so happy to be alive.

I reached the rock, climbed up its mussel-studded side, and landed on my ass. Solid ground. *Beautiful, wonderful, immobile solid ground. I love you.*

I lay on my back. I could probably find my way to the city once I'd rested. I'd just have to move along the shore until I reached civilization, but right now moving wasn't an option. Hanging out on this rock sounded like a really good idea. I could sit right here on this little island and think about the choices that resulted in my ending up in this place, half-drowned, exhausted, with my ankle bleeding, and a possible concussion causing hobbit hallucinations.

The warm sun heated my skin. I flipped over on my stomach, rested my forehead on my arm to keep my face from being cooked, and closed my eyes. My imagination painted a scaled monster crawling out of the sea to chew on me. I shoved the thought aside. I was safe enough here, and I was too tired to move.

"AAAAY!"

I sat straight up. In the west, the sun was rolling toward the sea, the sky gaining a pale orange tint. I'd slept until evening. All my fingers and toes seemed to be still there. No monsters had come out of the sea and nibbled away any digits. My face didn't hurt either. My skin looked tan even in winter and didn't burn easily, but I had managed it a couple of times in my life and I didn't care for the experience.

"Aaay!" a man called.

I turned. A boat drifted toward me. The hunter I'd met earlier sat at the oars, his shaggy dog waiting next to him. At the nose of the boat, the small man waved his arms at me.

"We have come to save you," the hunter called out in accented Russian.

"Thank you!"

"It looks like you have saved yourself." The hunter slowed the boat and it bumped gently against the rock. I climbed aboard.

The small man smiled at me.

"Hello," the hunter said.

"Hello."

"We have an important decision to make," the hunter said. "The city is that way." He pointed north. "Two and a half hours. My house and dinner, that way." He pointed northeast. "One hour. I will take you either way, but I'll be honest: night is coming. Not good to travel in the dark while magic is in charge. Mountains are not safe."

Two and a half hours to the castle meant he would have to make a return trip in the dark by himself or stay somewhere in the city. His tone of voice told me he didn't care much for cities. If some strange mountain beast ate him on the way back, I wouldn't be able to live with myself. The castle and everyone inside would just have to survive without me for another twelve hours.

"Your house and dinner, please."

"Good choice."

THE HUNTER'S NAME WAS ASTAMUR. HIS DOG, which turned out to be a Caucasian shepherd, was named Gunda, after a mythical princess with many magical hero brothers. According to Astamur, the small man wouldn't give us his name because he was afraid it would grant us power over him, but his kind was called atsany, and he didn't mind being called that.

"They live in the mountains," Astamur explained, as the boat glided along the shore. "They don't like to be seen, but I rescued one of their young once. They don't mind me as much. They are very old people. Been here thousands of years. Left their houses all over the place. Now they are coming back."

"How did they survive?" I offered my hand to Gunda. She sniffed my fingers, regarded me with a very serious expression, and nudged my hand with her nose for a stroke. I obliged. I really missed my attack poodle.

Astamur shrugged. "The atsany slept. Some say they turned into rocks and came back to life when magic returned. They won't say."

"How did he end up in the sack?"

Astamur asked Atsany in his language. The small man crossed his arms on his chest and mumbled something.

"He says gyzmals caught him."

"Gyzmals?"

Astamur bared his teeth at me. "Men-jackals. It's bad luck to kill an atsany, so they put him in a bag and threw him into the water."

Volodja and his fellow shapeshifters. "Not the brightest lot. They tried to rob us."

"When magic first came, some people turned into gyzmals. Stories said they were evil. People were scared. When people get scared, bad things happen. Many gyzmals were killed. Then Megobari came. Now the gyzmals run the town, do whatever they want. Nobody can say anything. But robbing people, that's going too far. The boy that led you into the cave has a mother in town. I'll tell her about it. She'll take care of him." Astamur shook his head at me. "I tried to tell you: bad place. That's where Agulshap lives. The water dragon."

A lot of their words started with *A*. "Not anymore."

Astamur's eyebrows crept together. He said something to Atsany. The small man nodded.

Astamur laughed, his deep chuckle carrying above the water. "I thought I was saving a pretty girl. I was saving a warrior! We should have a feast. We'll celebrate."

He landed the boat and I helped him drag it ashore. We climbed up the mountain for about an hour, until the trail brought us to a valley. Mountains rolled into the distance and between them lay an emerald-green pasture. A small sturdy stone house crouched on the grass, and a few yards away, a flock of sheep with gray curly wool baaed in the wide enclosure.

"I thought you were a hunter."

"Me? No. I'm just a shepherd. There is a bathroom inside. You are welcome to it. My house is your house."

I stepped through the door. Inside the cottage was open and neat, with beautiful stone walls and a wood floor. Colorful Turkish rugs hung on the walls. A small kitchen sat to the right with an old electric range. There must be a generator somewhere. I walked through the living room, past a comfortable sofa covered by a soft white blanket, to the back, where I found a small bathroom with a toilet, shower, and sink. I tried the faucet. Water splashed into the metal basin. Running water all the way out here. Astamur was doing well for himself.

I used the bathroom inside and washed my face and my hands. When I came out, Astamur built a fire in a big stone pit behind the house.

"We're going to cook over fire," Astamur announced. "Traditional mountain dinner."

Atsany ducked into the house and returned with a stack of blankets. I helped spread them on the ground.

Astamur brought out a large pan filled with chunks of onion, meat, and pomegranate seeds in some sauce and started threading them onto big skewers.

I caught the aroma of the sauce, a touch of vinegar and heat. My mouth watered. Suddenly I realized I was starving.

Astamur set the skewers above the fire and went to wash up. The aroma of smoking wood mixed with the smell of meat sizzling over the fire. The sky slowly turned orange and deeper red in the west, while in the east, above the mountains, it was almost crystalline purple, the color of an amethyst.

Astamur offered me a skewer. I bit into the meat. The tender meat practically melted in my mouth. This was heaven.

"Good?" Astamur asked with concern.

"Mm-hm," I told him, trying to chew and talk at the same time. "Delicioush. Besht shting I ever ate."

Atsany leaned back and laughed.

The shepherd smiled into his mustache and handed me a bottle of wine. "Homemade."

I took a swallow. The wine was sweet, refreshing, and surprisingly delicate.

"So you live here all alone?" I asked.

Astamur nodded. "I like it here. I have my flock. I have my dog. I have a fire pit, a clear mountain stream, and the mountains. I live like a king."

Atsany said something. Astamur shrugged. "Castles are for rulers. Kings come and go. Someone has to be the shepherd."

"Do you miss being with other people down in town? Must get lonely up here." I wouldn't miss them. I would totally hitch up a house in the mountain and live all by myself. No shape-shifters. No brokenhearted mothers. No, "Yes, Consort," "Please, Consort," "Help us, Consort." Right now that sounded like pure happiness.

Astamur smiled. "Down in the cities people fight. I fought too for a while until I got tired of it." Astamur pulled up his pant leg. An ugly scar punctured his calf. Looked like a knife or a sword thrust. "Russians."

He wagged his eyebrows at me and pulled his shirt off his shoulder, exposing an old bullet wound in his chest. "Georgians." He laughed.

Atsany rolled his eyes.

"Does he understand what you say?" I asked.

"He does. It's his own kind of magic," Astamur answered. "If it weren't for supplies, I'd never go back down to town. But a man has to do what a man has to do. Hard to live like a king without toilet paper."

We finished eating. Atsany pulled out a pipe and said something with a solemn expression.

"He says he owes you a debt. He wants to know what you want."

"Tell him no debt. He doesn't owe me anything."

Atsany's bushy eyebrows came together. He took out his pipe and lectured me in a serious voice, punctuating his words by pointing the pipe at me. I was clearly on the receiving end of a very serious talking-to. Unfortunately for him, he was barely a foot and a half tall. I bit my bottom lip trying not to laugh.

"Do you want a short version or a long one?" Astamur said.

"Short one."

"You saved his life, he owes you, and you should let him pay it back. That last part is advice from me. It will make him very unhappy to know that he owes someone. So what do you want? Do you want him to show you where there are riches? Do you want a man to fall in love with you?"

If only love were that easy. I sighed. "No, I don't want riches and I have a man, thank you. He isn't exactly a man. And I don't exactly have him anymore, but that's neither here nor there."

Astamur translated. "Then what do you want?"

"Nothing."

"There has to be something."

Fine. "Ask him if he would share the magic word with me."

Astamur translated.

Atsany froze and said something, the words coming fast like rocks falling down the mountain.

"He says it might kill you."

"Tell him I already have some magic words, so I probably won't die."

"Probably?" Astamur raised his eyebrows.

"A very small chance."

Atsany sighed.

"He says he will, but I can't look. I'll check on the sheep." Astamur got up and went toward the pasture. "Try not to die."

"I'll do my best."

Atsany leaned forward, picked up a skewer, and wrote something in the dirt. I looked.

An avalanche of agony drowned me, exploding into a twisting maelstrom of glowing lines. I rolled inside, each turn hurting more and more, as if my mind were being picked apart, shaved off with some phantom razor blade one tiny, excruciating layer at a time. I turned inside the cascade of pain, faster and faster, trying desperately to hold on to my mind.

A word surfaced from the glow. I had to make it mine, or it would kill me.

"Aarh." Stop.

The pain vanished. Slowly, the world returned bit by bit: the green grass, the smell of smoke, the distant noises of sheep, and Atsany wiping the dirt with his foot. I'd made it. Once again, I'd made it.

"You didn't die," Astamur said, coming closer. "We are both very glad."

Atsany smiled and said something.

"He wants me to tell you that you are kind. He is glad that you have the word. It will help you in the castle with all those

lamassu. He doesn't know why you have them up there anyway. Don't you know they eat people?"

MY BRAIN SCREECHED TO A HALT.

"He thinks we have lamassu at the castle?"

"He says you do. He says he saw one of them carry off a
body and then eat it."

"Something is killing people at the castle," I said. "But I've
seen pictures of the lamassu statues. They have fur and human
faces."

Atsany waved his pipe around.

"He says it's a, what's the word . . . allegory. There are no
animals with human heads, that's ridiculous."

*Look who's talking. An eighteen-inch-tall magic man in
riding boots, werejackals, and sea dragons are all fine, but
animals with human faces are ridiculous. Okay, then. Glad
we cleared that up.*

Atsany stood up, walked a few feet out into the grass, and
started walking, putting one foot in front of the other, as if he
were walking a tightrope. He turned sharply, walked five steps,
turned again, drawing a complex pattern with his steps.

"The atsany have long memories. Watch," Astamur said.
"This is a rare gift. Not many people will ever see it in their
lifetime."

The small man kept going. A shiver ran through the grass
as if it were fanned by invisible wings. The grass blades stood
straight up in Atsany's wake. A faint image formed above the
grass, semitranslucent, shifting like a mirage. A vast city
stood, encircled by tall textured walls. Two enormous lamassu
statues stretched along the city wall, facing an arched gate,
and two others, smaller, guarded its sides. Just inside the gates
a tall narrow tower rose, so high I had to raise my head to see
the top. It was early morning. The sun hadn't risen yet, but the
heat had already begun its advance. I smelled a hint of tur-
meric, smoke, and moisture in the air—there must've been a
river nearby. Somewhere a dog barked. It was like a window
through time had been opened just a crack.

This was my father's world.

A column of smoke rose from one of the towers. A man in
a long orange robe walked out of the gates, followed by two

others. All three had long textured beards and conical hats, and each carried a gold ewer with a wide spout.

A distant howl rolled through the morning. The image turned and I saw a pack of wolves running hard across the plain. Light gray, with long legs and large ears, they were too large to be natural.

The pack closed in on the gates and stopped. The wolves shook, their bodies twisted, and men rose in their place. The leader, an older bald man, stepped forward. The bearded man said something and handed him the ewer. The werewolf drank straight from the spout and passed it on. The ewers made the rounds until every shapeshifter had drunk, and the pack returned the ewers to the bearded men.

The robed men stepped aside and two soldiers emerged from the gate, wearing lamellar armor shirts over kilts. They dragged a man bound by his hands and ankles, dropped him on the ground, and stepped back.

The man curled into a ball, babbling in sheer terror.

The shapeshifters went furry. Lupine lips bared fangs and the pack ripped into the man. He screamed, howling, and they tore him to pieces, snarling and flinging blood into the dirt. Acid rose in my stomach. I looked away. I could kill a man or a woman in a fight. This made me sick.

Finally he stopped screaming. I looked up and saw Astamur watching me. He nodded at the mirage. "You'll miss it."

I looked. The bloody shredded ruin of the man's body lay by the gates. The wolves sat, as if waiting for something.

A minute passed. Another.

The alpha's body split open. He grew, the flesh and bone spiraling up. Wings thrust from his shoulders. Scarlet scales sheathed his body. The bones of his skull shifted, supporting massive leonine jaws. The alpha roared.

Holy shit. Doolittle was right.

One by one the werewolves turned. The leader dashed through the gates and into the tower. The rest followed single file. A moment and the alpha leaped from the top of the tower, spreading his massive wings. He swooped down and soared and his pack glided behind him.

Atsany stopped. The mirage faded.

The small man began to speak, pausing for Astamur's translation. "Long ago there was a kingdom of Assur past the mountains to the south. The kingdom had many wizards and their armies were often gone to conquer, so the wizards made lamassu. They used tribes of gyzmals and changed them with magic. That's why there are many different kinds of lamassu: some have bull bodies, some have lion, some have wolf. They chose bulls and lions for their statues, because they were the largest.

"When not needed, the lamassu were just like normal gyzmals, but when a city was in danger, the wizards would feed lamassu human meat, and then they would grow strong and vicious. They would gain wings and terrible teeth, and then they would fall on the enemy from above and devour them."

I'd never heard or read anything remotely like this, but just because I'd never heard of it didn't make it impossible.

"The statues are a warning. They mean 'This is a city protected by lamassu.' The human heads to show that they are both human and beast, and the five legs to show that they are not always what they appear. We have known of lamassu for a long time and we stay clear of them. Not all lamassu are evil, but those who choose to eat human flesh are."

If he was right, then any of the packs in the castle could be lamassu. "So how can you tell if a shapeshifter is a lamassu?"

Atsany shrugged. "Feed it human meat," the shepherd translated.

Duh. Ask a dumb question . . . "Is there any other way?"

"No."

"Do they have any kind of weakness? Anything special?"

Astamur sighed. "He says they don't like silver."

I must've looked desperate, because Atsany came over and petted my hand. *It will be alright.*

I sighed. "Can I have more wine?"

THE SKY TURNED DARK. I LAY ON THE BLANKET watching the stars sparkling like diamonds. The moon shone bright, spilling veils of ethereal light onto the mountains. Maybe it was my imagination, but the night seemed brighter here. Perhaps the mountains brought us closer to the moon.

A soothing calm came over me. The castle and the strain of being there had worn me down, and right now I couldn't care less about Curran, Hugh, or Roland. The pressurized walls that had ground on me while I was there fell away. I just wanted to stay here, lie on my blanket, and be free.

Maybe if I was extra lucky, Hugh and Curran would elope together and take Lorelei with them while I was gone.

I would probably go back in the morning. But right now I just didn't want to, and the thought of running away tasted so sweet, I was afraid to turn it over in my mind. I could disappear into these mountains and live a simple life: hunt, fish, grow fruit trees, and not have to worry about anything.

Atsany told us great stories of his people, of fighting giants and dragons, of great heroes—*narty*—and winged horses. Astamur translated quietly, sitting propped against a pillow.

". . . the great Giant-adau saw the strange herd of horses in his pasture. He crossed his huge arms and bellowed. 'Whose horses are these? They look like the *narty's* horses, but the *narty* wouldn't dare—'"

Astamur fell silent. Atsany blinked and poked the shepherd's boot with his pipe. I leaned over. Astamur was staring at the mountain, his jaw slack.

I turned.

A massive beast dashed along the mountain apex. Huge, at least six hundred pounds, the creature covered the distance in great leaps. The moonlight traced his gray mane and slid off the thick cords of his muscles. He was neither beast nor man, but a strange four-legged meld of the two, built to run despite his bulk.

How the hell did he even find me?

Atsany jumped up and down, waving his pipe. Without taking his gaze from the beast, Astamur reached for his rifle. "A demon?"

"No, not a demon." I might have preferred one. "That's my boyfriend."

Atsany and the shepherd turned to look at me.

"Boyfriend?" Astamur said.

Curran saw us. He paused on a stone crag and roared. The raw declaration of strength cracked through the mountains, rolling down the cliffs like a rockslide.

"Yep. Don't worry. He's harmless."

Curran charged down the mountain. Most nonlamassu shapeshifters had two forms, human and animal. The more skilled of them could hold a third one, a warrior form, an upright, monstrous hybrid of the two designed for inflicting maximum damage. Curran had a fourth, a hybrid closer to the lion than to a human. I'd seen it only once before, when Saiman pissed him off out of his mind and Curran chased him and me through the city. It was the night we made love for the first time.

If he thought this would win him any favors, he would be seriously disappointed.

The giant leonine beast galloped down the mountain and across the grass, heading straight for us. The moonlight spilling from the sky set his back aglow, highlighting the dark stripes crossing the gray fur.

Twenty yards. Fifteen. Ten.

Atsany and Astamur froze, rigid.

Five.

The colossal lion jumped and landed a foot away from me, the dark mane streaming. The impact of his leap sent sparks flying from the fire. His eyes burned with molten gold. The powerful feline maw gaped open, showing terrifying fangs as big as my hand. Curran snarled.

I swatted him on the nose. "Stop it! You're scaring the people who rescued me."

The gray lion snapped into a human form. Curran jerked his hands up as if crushing an invisible boulder. "Aaaaaa!"

Okay.

He grabbed the edge of a big rock sticking out of the grass. Muscles flexed on his naked frame. He wrenched the boulder out of the ground. The four-foot-long rock had to weigh several thousand pounds—his feet sank into the grass. Curran snarled and hurled the rock against the mountain. The boulder flew, hit like a cannon ball, and rolled back down. Curran chased it, pulled another smaller rock out of the dirt, and smashed it against the first one.

Wow. He was really pissed.

Astamur's eyes were as big as plates.

"I can get him to put those back after he's done," I told him.

"No," Astamur said slowly. "It's fine."

Curran picked up the smaller rock with both hands and threw it onto the larger boulder. The boulder cracked and fell apart. Oops.

"Sorry we broke your rock."

Atsany took the pipe out of his mouth and said something.

"Mrrrhhhm," Astamur said.

"What did he say?"

"He said that the man must be your husband, because only someone we love very much can make us this crazy."

Curran kicked the remains of the boulder, spun, and marched toward me.

I crossed my arms.

"I thought you were dead! And you're here, sitting around the fire, eating and . . ."

"Listening to fairy tales." *Helpful, that's me.* "We're about to have s'mores and you're not invited."

Curran opened his mouth. His gaze paused on Atsany. He blinked. "What the fuck?"

"Don't stare. You'll hurt his feelings."

Atsany nodded at Curran in a solemn way.

Curran shook his head and pivoted toward me. "I almost killed B. The only reason she's alive right now is because she had to show me where you fell."

"Oh, so Princess Wilson let you out of the castle? Did she have to sign your permission slip? You got a hall pass, woo-hoo!"

"So this is what it's about? This is your mature response— to go off into the mountains rather than talking about it and have s'mores with a gnome and a mountain man."

"Yep."

"What's your plan for tomorrow? Brunch with a unicorn?"

"As long as it doesn't involve you, it's fine with me."

"So really? That's it, just like that." Curran turned around. "Wait a minute. Where is Hugh? Shouldn't he be flexing for you?"

"I'm surprised you noticed."

He squeezed his hands into fists. I picked up a grapefruit-sized rock and handed it to him. It went flying. Home run, Beast Lord style.

"I noticed. I just can't do anything about it."

"You know what the difference is? Hugh can stand there and flex all he wants. I can't control what he does. I can control what I do and I don't encourage him. You let her parade in front of you naked. You told me you had no interest in her and then you invited her to sit at the table in my chair. You went on a little rendezvous with her where you explained how you were lonely and cried about all the sacrifices you made by being with me."

His eyes sparked with gold. "You. That was you on the balcony."

"You spend every waking moment with her, while I get told endlessly that nobody has to answer any of my questions, because I'm clearly on my way out and she's on her way in and since we're not married, I'm easy to replace."

"You want to get married? I'll marry you right now. Is the gnome a preacher, because I'll do it."

"That's a hell of a proposal."

"What did he say?" Astamur asked.

"He wants me to marry him."

Astamur relayed it. Atsany waved his pipe and Astamur translated back. Ha!

"What?" Curran snarled.

"Atsany says you're not ready for marriage. You don't have the right temperament for it."

Curran struggled with that for a second.

"Let me know if your head's going to explode, so I can duck."

"We're not married because every time I bring up marriage or children, you freak the hell out."

"I don't!"

"Three weeks ago I asked you if you wanted to have kids. You looked like you were ready to bolt."

"I had just come from watching a child go loup for hours while trying to comfort her mother." I waved my arms. "You know what, you're right. Let's have kids. Let's have a brood of them. And when my asshole father comes through Atlanta burning it to the ground, we'll both cry together as they die. Or worse, maybe our kids will be human." I put my hand on my chest. "Heaven forbid."

"Really? Human? What am I?" he snarled.

Ouch. "You're a special snowflake, that's what you are." I mimicked Lorelei. "But they can never join you on a hunt. What torture . . ."

He stepped forward. "We've been together a year. How many times have you seen me hunt?"

Umm.

"How many times, Kate?"

"None."

"That's because I don't hunt. I'm a male lion. I weigh six hundred pounds. Do you really expect me to scamper through the brush after deer? When I want a steak, I want a damn steak. I don't want to chase it around the woods for two hours and then eat it raw. I have food brought to me, and the only time I get off my ass is when something threatens the Pack. I've been on exactly one hunt in the last three years. I went because I had to go, and once they ran off, I found a nice warm rock and had myself a nap in the sun. Do you know when the last time I really had to hunt to survive was? After my parents died. Until Mahon found me half-starved."

I stared at him.

"Hunting together is something young werewolves do when they're trying to learn how to work in a team. Most shapeshifters don't cavort around in the woods, unless the urge to kill something strikes them. Do you have any idea how hard it is to actually catch a deer on foot? There is a reason why humans are the most successful predators on the damn planet. Lorelei doesn't know this, because she's young and naive and she has never been outside her uncle's wolf pack. She never had to survive weeks in the forest, eating worms, mice, grasshoppers, and whatever other shit she could catch because she's starving and desperate. She thinks every pack in the world follows the same pattern, but you know me. You know better. Or you should."

I opened my mouth.

"I'm not done. Hugh understands this. He made that farce of a hunt because he gets off on making us run through the woods, fetching meat for him like we're subhuman, like we're his dogs, and then when we bring it back, he gives the one who debases himself the most a treat. If I didn't have to keep Desandra breathing, I wouldn't have gone. I just want to know, is that what you think of me? Am I a fucking dog to you?"

"No, you're the man I love and who is supposed to love me back. Instead, you spend all your time with another woman. Apparently you pulled the plug on us and forgot to forward me the memo."

"Am I with her now?"

"Where were you this morning when I went to speak with the packs?"

His eyes told me I'd hit home. It hurt. "Don't bother to answer. I always thought that if you decided we weren't working out, at the very least you would have the decency to tell me up front."

"I'm thirty-two years old," he said. "Women have thrown themselves at me since I was fifteen. Do you honestly think that Lorelei has anything I haven't seen before?"

"She has the Wilson name."

"And she can stick it up her ass for all the good it will do her. I don't need to ally myself with Ice Fury. They're four thousand miles away. What the hell would I do with them?"

He did have a point, but I was too mad to admit it. "Whatever."

"Not only that, but if I wanted that pack, I would go to Alaska and take it from Wilson, and I would take everything in between me and him. I don't need Lorelei. And even if I did, what does she have, Kate? She isn't an alpha; she has no concept of leadership or obligations. She isn't her father, and she doesn't get to claim his accomplishments as her own because he happens to be her dad."

I was suddenly so tired. "So let's review: she didn't impress you with her personality and brain, she has no strategic value, and you don't really want to get into her pants."

"Yes."

"So why are you spending all of your time with her? What you are doing looks like a betrayal. A public, obvious betrayal. I know you understand all of this."

He looked at me, his jaw set.

I sat on a rock. "Anytime."

Curran sighed. "There is a contract on your life."

I slumped forward, resting my face on my hands. No, he wouldn't . . .

"The pirate attack was targeted—someone hired them specifically to kill you. They had your description: dark hair, sword, and so on. The pirate described a man who looks a lot like that asshole who hangs out with Kral, Renok. He said the man had a Romanian accent. They were paid in euros. Thirty thousand, which is a lot of money. Jarek isn't about to drop thirty grand on getting you killed. He likes to do that sort of work himself."

Why me . . . ?

"The euro notes are numbered. The first letter of the serial number on the money denotes the country. After we disembarked, Saiman took the pirate back to his people in exchange for looking at the money. It was printed in Belgium. That meant that Lorelei and Jarek Kral made some sort of deal."

I just looked at him.

"Lorelei arrived here with three of her uncle's people for an escort. I bribed one of them—they don't like her all that much—and she said that Lorelei and Jarek Kral had signed a contract. She didn't know the exact terms, but it involves Lorelei becoming alpha of the Pack and spells out your death. Lorelei did this because she's a naive child and she actually thinks things in the real world work like that. Jarek Kral did it because he's likely planning to either blackmail her with it or use it to his advantage in some other way. Either case, if I can get my hands on the contract, it will bite him in the ass, because it will give me proof that he plotted to murder my wife. I can legitimately kill him."

You've got to be kidding me. "I'm not your wife."

"I couldn't fight the war on two fronts," Curran said. "Something was attacking Desandra, and with everything concentrated on keeping her safe, I couldn't gamble with your life. I didn't want someone to shoot you or a giant rock to fall on your head. I couldn't be there with you because they kept me busy. I was locked into choosing between getting panacea for the Pack or keeping you alive. So I became interested in Lorelei, because if they thought I was nibbling their bait, there was no reason to kill you and risk turning you into a martyr. I've been taking her on long walks where nobody would see us, while Saiman's been walking around the castle pretending to be her, trying to find the contract and find someone who knows something about it."

"Saiman's in the castle?"

"He's been in castle the entire time except for the first night. I walked him in as Mahon the morning after the first dinner."

I knew the answer, but I asked anyway. "Why didn't you tell me?"

"Because you can't lie, Kate. Everything you think is right there on your face. I've met kindergarteners who are better actors than you. I needed you to look jealous and worried, and I needed it to be genuine, so they would dismiss you as a possible target. The entire plan hinged on it."

Aha. "That's some plan."

"It was a good plan. I thought of it and I executed it, and it was going along fine until you decided to go off into the mountains."

I hid my face in my hands.

"Kate?" he asked.

I should have been angry and screaming, but I just felt tired and hollow.

"Kate?" he repeated. "Are you okay?"

I looked at him. "No."

He waited.

"You put me through hell because you think I'm a bad liar." My voice was completely flat. I couldn't scrape together enough feelings for anything else.

"That's not what it is."

"Yes, it is," I said quietly. "Curran, think about it for a minute. My life is in danger and you don't trust me enough to tell me about it. You have no idea how bad you made me feel."

"I was trying to keep you alive. Even if it meant we couldn't be together. Even if it meant watching Hugh making circles around you like a fucking shark. You don't trust me either, Kate. All the shit we've been through should've bought me some time, but you believed I lost my head over some girl after three days."

I didn't even hurt anymore. I just felt this empty dry sadness. "And that's exactly the problem."

"Kate?" He crouched by me, one knee on the ground, and leaned forward to look at my face. "Baby? Punch me or something."

I struggled to sort everything into words. It didn't work. I just shut down like an overloaded circuit.

"Talk to me."

Some sort of words finally came out. "Where can we even go from here . . ."

"I don't want to go anywhere. I love you. You love me. We're together. We're a team."

Suddenly my emotions sorted themselves out and anger finally ran to the front of the pack. "No, we're not a team. You made me a patsy in your scheme. You treated me like I'm an idiot. I thought about hurting her. I thought about hurting you."

"You wouldn't hurt her. She's weaker than you."

"You're an arrogant bastard."

"Fair enough," he said. "You got more?"

"Yes. You're a smug asshole."

"Yes, I am." He motioned at me. "Don't hold back. Tell me how you really feel."

I punched him in the jaw. It was a good solid hook.

Curran shook his head. "I deserved that. Are we okay?"

"No."

"Why?"

"You still don't get it. Hugh is playing me. He thinks I'm gullible and naive, and he thinks he can run circles around me. And you, you did the exact same thing. I trusted you and you used it against me. You led me around like I was blind. We're not okay."

"What are you saying?" He was looking up at me. I saw something odd in his gray eyes and realized it was desperation.

"I'm really mad at you, Curran. This isn't one of those fights where we both lose our temper, spar, talk, and we're okay. This is my line in the sand. I don't know if I can roll with this punch."

"So this is it?"

"I'm trying to decide."

I trusted him and he broke that trust, and while I could think around it, I couldn't feel my way past it. It felt like he came up to give me a hug and slid a knife between my ribs.

Curran unlocked his teeth. "I did the only thing I could do. Everything I've done and everything I've said was to keep you alive. I'm sorry I made you go through it, but if I had to do it over, I would do it again. Even if that means you'll leave with Hugh tomorrow. You being safe is more important to me than having you. I love you."

I loved him, too. Inside me a small voice told me that in his place I would've done the same thing, no matter the fallout I had to endure at the end. Having him alive and mad at me was infinitely better than having him dead. But loving someone and being with him were two different things.

"If your father walked out of the darkness right now and said, 'Come with me, or everyone here will die,' you would go with him," Curran said. "Knowing that I would fight for you with everything I've got, you would walk away. You would leave me a note that said I shouldn't look for you, because you would want to protect me."

There was no point in lying. "Yes."

"That's my line in the sand," he said. "Would you still walk away?"

"Yes." If his life were on the line, I'd do it in a heartbeat.

"Even if I leave you because of it?"

"Yes."

He spread his arms.

"I can't change who I am," I told him. "Neither can you. I get it."

"I love you and you love me, and we're both too fucked up for anyone else. Who else would have us?"

I sighed. "Well, clearly we're both crazy and this relationship is doomed."

"I love you so much," he said. "Please don't leave me."

He leaned forward. I knew he would kiss me a moment before he did, and I realized I wanted it. I remembered him holding me. I remembered him risking himself against impossible odds for me. I made him laugh, I told him things that would make most normal men run screaming, things I spent all my life keeping secret, and I drove him to the point of near-blinding rage. In my darkest moments, when everything was crashing down around me, he told me everything would be okay. The taste of him, the feel of his lips as his mouth covered mine, the way he made the world fade, as if kissing me were the only thing that existed in his life, pulled me right back through time, before the castle, before Hugh, and before Lorelei. Curran was mine. If my life were on the line, he would do it again, and I would be mad at him again. And if the reverse ever happened, he would rage and roar, and I would tell him that I loved him and that I would fight to the death to keep him breathing.

He was right. We loved each other and nobody else would put up with us.

"I'm still mad at you," I whispered, and put my arms around him.

"I'm an ass," he told me, pulling me closer. "I'm sorry. You should make my life hell for the next hundred years."

"Do we need to give you some privacy for the makeup sex?" Astamur asked.

CHAPTER 17

———◆———

AN HOUR OR SO BEFORE SUNRISE, CURRAN AND I decided that we did need some privacy. We borrowed a couple of blankets and climbed the mountainside to a small ledge. We made love on the blankets and now we were lying quietly.

"Still mad at me?" Curran asked.

"Yes."

"Are you going to stay?"

I shifted my head on his biceps and looked at his face. "Yes. I'm stuck."

"How?"

"I love you too much to walk away."

He kissed my hair.

"I'm used to watching for people with swords," I told him. "I never saw the knife. You were too close."

"Kate, I didn't stab you."

"Are you sure? Because it still hurts."

"I'm sorry," he said.

"I'm sorry, too. Did you really think I would leave you?"

"I thought I would lose you either way. I've known you long enough."

He deliberately put this whole scheme into action all the

while thinking I would walk away. It must've sucked being trapped, his back against the wall, desperately trying to juggle me, Lorelei, and the three packs. And in his place, I might have done the same thing. Life was complicated.

"I almost pulled the plug on it," he said. "But then I realized that any conversation with you, no matter how bad, is better than talking to a hole in the ground."

"I don't know. A hole wouldn't argue with you."

I wanted him to laugh. Instead he pulled me closer. "There is nothing I wouldn't do to keep you safe," he said.

"I know."

We lay together, touching.

"I can't believe I let Hugh goad me into a fight. If you hadn't called me, I would've run him through, and then all of us would be dead."

A hint of a snarl raised his upper lip. His body tensed next to me, the violent urge traveling through it like fire down the detonation cord. "Every time he looks at you, I want to kill him," Curran said. "I've been picturing snapping his neck."

"I've imagined killing Lorelei. I guess your plan must've worked, because Isabella told me I have a look on my face when I see her."

"You do."

I turned to him. "What kind of look?"

"Murderous." He kissed me. "Barabas tried to attack me yesterday."

"What?"

"When Aunt B and Keira came back. I saw it in his face. He was walking to me, and George tackled him and called me a cold bastard."

"Did you hurt him?"

"No."

"You're not winning any popularity contests lately. Maybe you should work on that."

"I know. Maybe I'll be lucky and get voted out of office. If I did, would you go away with me?"

"In a heartbeat."

He finally grinned. "Good."

"By the way, why use Saiman?"

He grimaced. "I had no choice."

"He wants to stab you in the back."

"As a person, Saiman is completely amoral. But as a businessman, he's above reproach. Remember when he signed the contract?"

"Mm-hm."

"There is a provision in it that stipulates he will do everything he can to maintain our safety as a group and as individuals."

"Nice." Saiman was incredibly scrupulous when it came to business. He prided himself on it. We signed the contract and became his clients. Now the same ego that had nearly cost him his life made him work for us, because for him nothing short of a hundred percent effort would do. I just hoped his professional ethics would hold up.

The sky had grown pale. A golden glow spread from behind the mountain. The sun was about to rise. Soon we would have to go back to the castle and Hugh.

I loved Curran, and most of the time being with him was so easy. But when it was difficult, it nearly broke me. I wondered if it was like that for him, too. Being alone was simpler, but I couldn't give him up. He made me happy. So happy that I kept looking over my shoulder, as if I had stolen something and any minute someone would demand I give it back.

"This wasn't supposed to happen," I said.

"What?"

"You and me. This wasn't in the plan. The plan was to be alone, to hide, and to kill Roland. Being happy was never one of the bullet points. Some part of me is still convinced it's a fluke and eventually it will be ripped away from me. Deep down I expect it. Any hint of it and I roll down the cliff. You're mine, you know that, right? If you ever try to leave me, it won't go well."

"I don't deserve you," Curran said. The same desperate thing I saw last night flickered in his eyes. "But I got you and I'm an entitled selfish bastard. You're all mine. Don't leave me."

"I won't. Don't leave me."

"I won't. If you ever disappeared, I would leave the Pack and I would look for you until I found you. However long it took."

I knew he wasn't lying. I could feel it. He would find me.

"I'll try not to disappear."

"Thank you," he said.

• • •

WHEN THE SUNRISE SPLASHED OVER THE MOUN-
tains, Astamur guided us to town, where we said our good-
byes. I asked if there was anything we could do for him. He just
shook his head. "Next time someone comes to you for help,
help them for me. I help you, you help them, we keep it going."

We climbed the road, me and the enormous lion. It was
decided that fur was preferable to no clothes, and although
Astamur had offered some, they wouldn't fit Curran and we
both had a feeling the shepherd didn't have that many clothes
anyway. The castle loomed before us.

I sighed.

"I know," Curran said, human words emerging perfectly
from the leonine mouth. "We're almost done."

"I'll remind you of that the next time you see Hugh."

A low growl reverberated in Curran's throat.

"Temper, Your Majesty."

We both knew that picking a fight with Hugh was still out
of the question. I still had no idea what his plan was. He'd gotten me into this castle. He wasn't trying to actively murder
me. He flattered me and called me special. If things kept
going this way . . . I shuddered.

Curran looked at me.

"Just pondering what Hugh's version of flowers and candy
will look like."

"Like bloody mush," Curran said. "Because I will crush
his head and his brain will ooze out of his ears."

I just wanted to know what the final plan was.

We walked through the gates. The cage had been moved
from the inner courtyard. It now hung from a beam affixed to
a guard tower, front and center in the courtyard. Hibla sat in
it. I stopped. She stared at me with haunted feverish eyes, her
desperation so obvious, I had to stop myself from walking
over there and pulling her out.

"There you are," Hugh strode out of the opened doors of
the main keep. "Safe and sound."

"Why is she in a cage?"

"Cages need occupants. This one was empty and she
seemed like the best candidate."

Hibla had failed one too many times. She'd let me out of

the castle and lost me, and now he'd stuck her into the cage for everyone to see. "Please let her out."

Hugh sighed. "What is it about the cage? Is there anyone I could put in there you wouldn't want to get out?"

"You."

He shrugged his massive shoulder. "It wouldn't hold me."

"Talk is cheap. Try it on, d'Ambray," Curran said.

"I'd love to, but as I've said, it's occupied." Hugh turned to me. "So where did you go?"

I looked at the cage.

Hugh shrugged. "Oh, fine. Someone get Hibla out!"

A djigit left his post by the gate and ran down to the cage.

"I went to some caves, fell in, swam around, and was rescued by an atsany and a local shepherd."

"Sounds eventful."

"I'm tired and hungry," I said.

Hugh smiled. "I'll see you later, then."

And why did that sound ominous?

Curran moved between him and me and we went into the castle.

Ten minutes later, I was sitting on our bed eating food George brought for me from the kitchen. Curran changed shape and put on clothes.

Mahon appeared at the doorway. "I'm glad you're okay," he told me.

A moment later Barabas walked through the door. A man followed him into the room. A cloud of silky hair, completely white, framed his narrow face. His skin must've been naturally olive, but now it had a slightly ashen tint. He looked to be in his midthirties, not just lean, but so slight that clothes hung on him the way they would on a coatrack. The man saw me and smiled. His entire face lit up, suddenly young and blissful, his blue eyes luminescent, at once beautiful and impossibly distant.

"Mistress," he said.

Whoa. "Hi, Christopher."

He came over and sat on the floor by my feet and sighed happily. "Beautiful mistress."

"How are you, Christopher?"

He looked at me with a blank smile and stared at my shoes.

"How is he?" I asked Barabas.

"What you see is what you get. He's here one minute, and then he isn't. I think we finally settled on the fact that he isn't dead. He insists that he used to know how to fly, but he forgot. He occasionally tries, so I have to watch him closely in high places."

Oh boy. "Christopher?"

He looked up at me.

"You're free."

"I am." He nodded. "I'll serve you forever. To the end of time."

"No, you're free. You don't have to serve me. You're welcome to stay, but you can go if you want."

He leaned over and touched my hand with long fingers. "Nobody is free in this world. Neither princes, nor wizards, nor beggars. I will serve you forever, my mistress."

Aha. "Let's come back to that later, when you feel more like yourself."

"Great," Curran said. "Another fine addition to your collection of uncanny misfits."

"I take offense to that," Barabas said.

"Don't worry, I count myself in, too," Curran told him.

"What did you do for Hugh?" I asked.

"I took care of his books." Christopher's fingers twitched as if stroking invisible pages. "He has the most interesting books. Do you have books, lady?"

Great. I rescued Hugh's librarian. "Some. Probably not as nice as Hugh's."

"That's alright." Christopher offered me a smile. "I will help you get more and then I will take care of them for you."

"Christopher, about the orange beast," I said. "The one who killed a guard, you remember?"

"The lamassu," Christopher said helpfully.

"You know what they are?"

"Yes." He nodded with that same faraway smile.

"Why didn't you tell me when I talked to you?"

"You didn't ask."

I turned and bumped my forehead against the wooden post of the bed.

"Okay, mistress needs a moment," Barabas said. "Come on."

"Does that help?" Christopher asked with interest.

Barabas took him by the arm and gently lifted him to his feet. "We should go eat."

"Real food?"

"Real food. Come with me."

They left the room.

"You know he's crazy, right?" Curran asked.

"Yep. He won't survive on his own."

"As you wish," Curran said.

I SPENT THE DAY IN BED, SLEEPING, EATING, AND then sleeping again. Curran stood guard over me, and any suggestion that I should go and guard Desandra was met with a stone Beast Lord face. He had a point. I was tired and my whole body hurt, as if I'd been through a meat grinder.

Ten minutes before six I woke up because someone knocked on our door. Curran blocked it. Beast Lord in hover mode.

". . . information," Hibla said.

I rolled out of bed.

Curran stepped aside. She walked into the room, holding herself very straight, her chin raised, her spine rigid. She couldn't have looked more fragile if she were on the verge of crying. I'd warned her. *Be careful who you serve.*

"What do you have for me?"

"A large group of strangers came to the mountains. They didn't use the pass or the sea. They came on the railroad tracks on foot. They passed a small village not too far from here." Hibla passed me a photograph. The body of a young man lying on his back stared at me with empty eyes. A bright red hole gaped where his stomach used to be, his flesh gouged out by claws and teeth. They'd fed on him. The second picture showed a close-up of his face. Purple blisters marked his features. I'd seen them before on Ivanna's face.

I held up the photograph and showed it to Hibla.

"The villagers said the bigger ones spit acid."

"What do you mean?"

Hibla shrugged. "We don't know. There were only six survivors. They had killed forty people and eaten most of them. I saw these marks on Ivanna."

"I saw them, too," I said.

"If she was attacked, why didn't she say anything?"

"Unless she was attacked by her own kind," Curran said.

I pulled a piece of paper out and began writing. "The first time I saw Ivanna was before dinner, when Radomil and Gerardo had a fight in the hallway. She saw Doolittle examining Desandra and she was upset."

I wrote it down and drew an arrow down. "Desandra was attacked." I drew another arrow.

"Meeting between the packs," Curran said.

I added it and drew another arrow. "Doolittle is attacked. Next morning Ivanna has purple blisters."

"If I were a lamassu, and assuming that one of Desandra's babies is a lamassu," Curran said, "knowing that a medic is examining her would make me nervous."

"One of Desandra's children is one of those things?" Hibla's eyes narrowed.

"Probably," Curran told her.

"Suppose Ivanna is a lamassu," I said. "She sees Doolittle take the blood. She knows that there is a chance he will discover that a child is a lamassu, and that will blow their pack's cover. She panics and tries to have her killed. Except someone in her pack, either Radomil or more likely Vitaliy, takes exception to that. The attack failed, they're down a shapeshifter, and they still want the child to be born, because they want the mountain pass."

"Of course they want the pass," Curran said. "They glide. Mountains give them a huge advantage. Vitaliy spits on her as a punishment and then decides to destroy the evidence Doolittle had collected instead."

"Doolittle said they smashed his equipment." It wasn't bad reasoning: no need to kill Desandra when you can just destroy the blood. "They also were the only pack that reacted when I asked for the blood test. The Italians and Kral wouldn't give me the time of day either, but the Volkodavi looked worried."

"But why do they eat people?" Hibla asked.

"It lets them grow bigger and sprout wings," Curran told her. I had brought him up to speed on the whole lamassu story. "There are likely a large number of them hiding out nearby. If the birth doesn't work out in their favor, everyone can storm the castle. That's how I would do it."

"I can arrest them," Hibla said.

"We don't have any evidence," I told her. "Besides, Desandra is still pregnant. Once a baby is born, it will be undeniable. We don't know it's them; we suspect. We have to watch them. Tonight at dinner, for example."

Hibla's face turned solemn. "This is why I came. Lord Megobari asked me to find out about the medmage's health and to ask if you would join him for dinner tonight outside the castle. Alone."

"No." Curran said.

Hibla took a step back.

"Yes."

"No."

"Tell Lord Megobari I'll be there."

Curran crossed his arms.

"I will pass on your message." Hibla turned and fled out of the room.

"No," Curran said. "You're not going."

"Are you ordering me not to go?"

"I can't order you to do anything. Nor would I try. You want to go alone to have dinner with a guy who killed your stepfather, who serves your father, and who gets a hard-on when you beat the shit out of him. How is this a good idea?"

That's my psycho. Blunt but fair. "He brought us here. You and me and all of us. I want to know why. I think he will tell me, because he wants me to know how big, bad, and smart he is. We need to know what we're up against."

"He puts people in cages and keeps undead in his walls."

"What is he going to do that he hasn't had an opportunity to do already? Before you went to talk to Lorelei on the balcony, he told me that it was all for me. He made this entire meeting happen. Don't you want to know how he managed to get all these packs together and orchestrate this? Aren't you curious?"

The muscles on his jaw stood out. I won.

"Take Derek. Hugh will bring someone with him."

He took a step forward. I could take one, too. "No problem. I can even bring another person if you want."

"Derek is fine," Curran said.

"I'll be back tonight," I told him. "It will be okay. Don't worry."

• • •

AT SEVEN, HIBLA CAME TO GET US. WE FOLLOWED her down the road to a narrow mountain path that led north, to a low mountain thrusting up like a dragon fang north of the castle. The western half of it had been blasted to make room for the railroad, and layers of rock thrust out of the sheer cliff. The path reached the mountain and turned into a paved sidewalk that dived into the mountain's forested side.

Trees rose on both sides of us, not wild growth but carefully cultivated greenery, cut back to please the eye. Every few feet there would be a stone step. Short feylantern torches glowed on both side of the path, with bright sparks of deluded fireflies dancing around them. Unlike the lavender feylanterns in the castle, these were yellow, a color mages in Atlanta fought for but couldn't achieve. Magic wrapped around us. Hugh went all out.

The path climbed up, turned, climbed up again, and turned again . . . We kept zigzagging up the mountain until finally we came to a small sitting area: a wooden bench with a table and some meat and bread under a wire hood.

"You and I will wait here," Hibla told Derek.

"If anything happens to her, you'll die first," Derek told her.

Well, that settled that.

I climbed farther up the path. The greenery parted and I saw a large table set under the trees. The trees on the west side had been sheared and an evening sea stretched before me, azure and beautiful, as the sun slowly set into its cool waters.

Hugh sat at the table. He wore jeans and a black T-shirt. Lord Death at his most casual.

He rose and smiled at me. I sat across from him on the north side, while he sat on the south. My back was to the path. Argh.

"Nobody will be coming up," he said and raised a bottle. "Wine?"

"Water."

"You don't drink much," he said.

"I drank too much for a while."

"I did, too," he said, and poured two glasses of water, one for himself, one for me.

The table held three platters: fruit, meat, and cheese. Everything a growing warlord needs.

"Please," Hugh invited.

I put some cheese and meat on my plate.

"Beautiful, isn't it?" He nodded at the sea.

It was. There was something ancient about it, something impossibly alluring. Thousands of years ago, people gazed at the sea just like we did now, mesmerized by the pattern of evening light on the waves. They had their own dreams and ambitions, but at the core they must've been just like us: they loved and hated, worried about their problems and celebrated their triumphs. Long after we were gone, the sea would still remain, and other people would watch it and be bewitched.

"The Volkodavi are lamassu," I said.

"I know," he said.

"When did you find out?"

"When I saw one fly out of your medmage's room. The Volkodavi have a good reputation back in Ukraine, but I've heard some stories. People disappearing. Monsters eating human bodies. I put two and two together. They came out of nowhere a few years ago, took over the local pack, and then the strange shit started." Hugh cut a piece of meat. "Your father hates the breed. He says they were badly made. I think they could be useful under the right circumstances, but they have very little discipline. Hammering them into usable soldiers would be difficult. You'd have to get them from childhood, and even then there is no guarantee."

"You're talking about them like they are pit bull puppies."

"Not a bad analogy, actually. It would take a few generations to breed the crazy out of the lamassu. Why bother? A properly trained German shepherd can kill as well as an undisciplined pit bull, and it's a lot easier to handle."

This conversation was getting under my skin. I drank my water.

"I like it here," Hugh said.

"It is beautiful."

"You should stay," he said. "After Desandra gives birth and the Beast Lord takes his pack home. Have a vacation. Live a little, swim in the sea, eat delicious food that's bad for you."

"I'm sure it would be a glorious vacation right up to the point where you serve my head on a silver platter to Roland."

"For you, I'd spring for gold," he said.

"Somehow that doesn't make me feel any better."

"Are you actually planning to fight him?" Hugh leaned forward.

"If it comes to it."

Hugh put down his fork and walked to the edge. "See that rock down there?"

I got up and stood at my edge of the table. He was pointing at a jagged boulder jutting from the side of the mountain.

Hugh opened his mouth. Magic snapped like a striking whip. An invisible torrent of power crashed into the rock. The boulder broke into shards.

A power word. Nice. When I used mine, it ripped me up with pain. Hugh didn't seem any worse for wear.

"I only have a tiny fraction of his power. You have no idea what it's like to stand behind him when he lets it go. It's like walking in the footsteps of a god."

I sat back in my spot. I'd heard that before.

Hugh studied the boulder below. "You've been alive for twenty-six years. He's been alive for over five thousand. He doesn't just play with magic; he knows it, intimately. He can craft impossible things. If I were to stand against him, he would crush me like a gnat. Hell, he might not even notice I'm there at all. I serve him because there is no one stronger."

Hugh turned to me. "I've seen you fight. I'm a fan. But if you plan to fight the Builder of Towers, you will lose."

I realized he wasn't bluffing. It hit home. If Roland came for me now, I would lose. Looking at it now seemed kind of absurd. I wasn't even thirty. I didn't know how to use my magic. What few tricks I had up my sleeve barely scratched the surface. In my head I always suspected that I wouldn't be able to hold him off, but the way Hugh said it made me pause.

"What makes you think he wants to kill you?" Hugh sat down.

"He tried to murder me in the womb, he killed my mother, and he sent you to find and kill the man I called my father. What makes you think he doesn't?"

"He's lonely," Hugh said. "It eats at him. He can age himself. It takes a lot of effort, and usually he stays around forty. He says it's a good age, mature enough to inspire confidence, young enough to not suggest frailty. He stayed at it for years, but now he is actively aging. Last time I saw him, four months ago, he looked closer to fifty. I asked him why. He said it made him appear more fatherly."

How sweet. "I'm not buying it."

"Think about it, Kate. You are deadly, smart, beautiful, and you are capable. Why wouldn't he want a daughter like that? Don't you think he would at least try to get to know you?"

"You're missing the point. I don't want to know him. He killed my mother, Hugh. He robbed me of the one person every child counts on for unconditional love. Do you remember your mother?"

"Yes," Hugh said. "I was four when she died. Three years later Voron took me off the street."

"I don't remember mine. Not a murmur, not a trace of a scent, no smudged image, nothing. Voron was my father and my mother. The Death's Raven was an undisputed authority in my life. The only authority. You knew him. Think about what that really means."

"So it's vengeance and a pity party at the same time," Hugh said.

"No. It's not vengeance. It's prevention. I want to kill Roland so there will never be another me."

"That would be a tragedy," Hugh said.

"That would be a blessing," I said.

"Let the shapeshifter sail off," Hugh said. "Stay with me for a while. No strings attached. No obligations or expectations. See if I can change your mind."

"I thought we already covered that ground. It wouldn't be a good idea."

"What's holding you to him? The man does care about you in his own stunted way, but you will never fit in with them, Kate. Deep down you know this. They'll always look on you as if you're a dangerous freak. People fear what they can't understand, but they can work with it. Animals can't. They shun the strange or try to destroy it. You can bleed for them for a hundred years and you won't change their minds. Make one small misstep and they will turn on you."

I turned and looked at the sea. Curran would fight to his last breath to protect me. If I asked Derek to walk into fire, he would do it. But then again there was Doolittle looking at me with horror in his eyes . . .

"It's slipping," he said.

I arched my eyebrow at him.

"Your cloak," he said. "Some of your power is showing. Just how much are you hiding?"

"I guess you'll never know," I told him.

Hugh rested his elbows on a table. "Where do you see yourself in five years?"

"If Roland doesn't find me?"

"Yes."

"In the Keep, doing what I'm doing now."

"How long will that last, Kate?"

"Hopefully for a long, long time."

"You're lying to yourself. Voron made us into serial killers. We can be okay without violence for a few weeks, but after a couple of months, the hand starts itching for the sword. You start looking for that rush. You get irritable, life turns stale, and then one day some fool crosses your path, attacks, and as you cut him down, you feel that short moment of struggle when he leverages his life against yours. If you're lucky, he's very good and the fight lasts a few seconds. But even if it doesn't, that short moment of triumph is like getting an adrenaline shot. Suddenly color comes back into life, food tastes better, sleep is deeper, and sex is rapture."

I knew exactly what he was talking about. I lived it and I felt it.

"You don't have to say anything," he said. "I know I'm right. You and I are birds of a feather. We weren't just born, we were forged, ground, and sharpened to be exactly what we are. You felt it when we sparred. I sure did. I don't know what you've got going with the werelion, but whatever it is, it will go flat and soon. I bet you already see signs of it. Some part of him enjoyed Lorelei's attention. It's flattering. A young, attractive girl, hanging on your every word, putting out all the signs that she's available to you alone. It makes you feel like you've still got it. He didn't do anything, but as another man, I can tell you he thought about it. Sex is a funny thing: it's always kind of the same, but you always want more of it and with different people."

I leaned on my hand and sighed. "Please continue, Doctor. Let me know when our time is up so I can write a check."

He chuckled. "The man is an egomaniac. You know this. He doesn't fully understand what you are, and he doesn't appreciate it. Give him a few years, and the next time a Lorelei swings into his orbit, he might bang her. He will tell himself it's not a big thing. It wouldn't mean anything. He won't leave you for her. The next time will be easier. The next easier still. Before you know it, it will become a regular thing. Why the hell would you want to put up with that?"

"Speaking from personal experience?"

"Yes. When I realized I'd stopped aging, I went for it. Let me tell you, no matter how creative you get—and I got creative—the mechanics of sex are always the same. The difference is passion. Passion makes it special. Having sex with an attractive woman is fun, but add passion, make her that one woman that you love or hate, and the whole experience changes. You feel something for me, Kate. Whether you want to admit it or not, something is there. I can guarantee we would never grow tired of it."

Wow. He'd put his best game face on and hit me with everything he had. "No."

His eyebrows came together. "No? That's it?"

"That's it."

"Why?"

"Because you put people in cages, Hugh. Even if I were alone and Curran weren't in the picture, I still wouldn't. You came here and did just as much as necessary to earn enough goodwill to build this castle twenty years ago. The people down in town live in poverty. Your werejackal castle guards are robbing strangers on the roads, and nobody comes to you and complains, because they don't expect you to do anything about it. You want to know the difference between you and Curran? If you gave this castle to him, within a month there would be a court, due process, and a working police force accountable to its citizens. Curran sees himself as serving the people he leads; you see yourself as being served. You brought stability to this place, but it's the stability of a scared slave who knows he will be pummeled with a stick if he holds his head up too high. You're content with things as they are, and when someone fails you, you stick them in a cage and slowly starve them to death."

Hugh leaned back and smiled, amusement curving his mouth. "You are his daughter," he said.

I wasn't sure how to take that. I leaned back and crossed my arms.

"You know what your father's best talent is? He can look at

you and determine exactly where your best place is. That's why he wasn't thrilled when your aunt woke up. There was no place for her in this world."

"So he looked at you and said, 'You will make an excellent wrecking ball.'"

Hugh nodded. "Before there can be civilization, I come and I subdue. I crush resistance, I break their will, and then your father arrives and reins me in. He brings order, justice, and fairness. He is their salvation."

"Be careful, your charming mask is crumbling."

"There isn't much point in it now."

"Oh, so sitting through your sales pitch finally earned me the right to the no-bullshit version?"

He grinned, baring his teeth. "Here it is: I can't let you get on that boat."

Figured.

"It will be a lot harder to pry you out of their fort. You force my hand."

"I didn't know you were so easy to push around."

"Before you left, I had my people load panacea onto your ship," he said. "Your boy got a note telling him about it and explaining that my welcome is withdrawn."

"I thought you promised no bullshit. Where did you even get that much panacea, Hugh? The packs guard it like gold. They would never sell that much of it to you."

"I have no need to buy it from them. My people make it."

"Bullshit."

"Your father was taught how to make it when he was young. It's a complex process, with a lot of magic done in correct order, so it was his equivalent of a graduation project." Hugh's eyes turned steel-hard. "I control the entire supply on this part of the continent. The only way for the Pack to get their paws on an ounce of it is to sail now, without you."

Curran wouldn't leave me.

"If he chooses to stay, the gloves come off." Hugh said. "I warned him. He knows if he stays, it's war."

"He will stay."

"God, I hope he does. I've been looking forward to killing him for three years. I will enjoy the hell out of it."

Hugh hadn't just taken advantage of Desandra's pregnancy. He'd engineered this whole thing. He'd pulled the strings and the shapeshifters had obeyed, because he held panacea over their heads. He'd manipulated everyone just to get me here.

"If you hurt him, I will kill you," I said.

"You'll try, and I will enjoy that, too. I meant what I said, Kate. You make me feel that interesting something. That's rare for me. And I like having you around. You're funny."

"Funny. Does your jaw hurt when you laugh?"

" 'My hand won't shake,' " he quoted. " 'My aim won't falter. My face will be the last thing you'll see before you die.' You're hilarious."

Those were the words I'd said to the Pack Council when Curran was in the coma and they'd tried to separate me from him. My skin crawled. Hugh had a mole on the Pack Council.

"I think we're done here." I rose.

"I always get what I want, Kate," he said. "That's how I'm wired."

I walked down the path and kept walking. Derek saw me, rose, and followed.

"The ship might not be there," I told him quietly.

"I heard," he said. "They will be there. Don't worry."

We kept going.

"Are you really Roland's daughter?" he asked.

"Yes."

"I don't care," he said. "Some people might, but they don't matter."

I didn't say anything, but the night grew a little brighter.

CHAPTER 18

———◆———

THE CASTLE HUMMED WITH ACTIVITY. SERVANTS strung garlands of feylantern lights in the hallways. People moved back and forth. The air smelled of roasting meat and spices.

I walked through it, strangely disconnected, the quiet sounds of my footsteps lost in the celebratory chaos.

Derek raised his head, listening. "It's the hunt dinner. They finally got all the game sorted and cooked. We are supposed to celebrate the winners at midnight."

Great. Everyone stuffed back into the single dining hall. That would go well.

I made it up the stairs. My heart beat a little faster. I picked up speed. He wouldn't leave without me. Not even with the panacea on the line.

I walked into our room.

Empty. A stack of my books had disappeared. Curran's clothes, thrown on the chair, had vanished. The bed was made.

No way.

The sound of running water came from the bathroom and Curran emerged, wiping his hands with a towel. He wore trademark Pack sweats. Gray and thin, they fell apart when a shapeshifter shifted form.

Behind me Derek stepped into the hallway and shut the door.

"You're here," I said.

"Where else would I be?"

"Hugh owns the panacea." *He's also a complete fucking bastard.*

"He sent a note." Curran crossed the floor and hugged me to him. My bones groaned.

I put my face into the bend of his neck. The world suddenly calmed. The fractured pieces snapped into place.

"Did you think I'd leave?" Curran whispered into my ear.

"No." I hugged him back. "What happened to all our stuff?"

"Anything nonessential is packed and loaded. I kept your belt with all your stuff out. Got any messages for me?"

"If we go to that dinner, we'll have a fight. Also, he hopes you will be a challenge."

Curran smiled. It wasn't a nice smile.

We looked at each other. We both knew Hugh would make his move tonight, and after that, everything would be over. We could try to fight our way to the ship now, except we had promised to guard Desandra. Abandoning her wasn't an option. We had given our word.

"Are you hungry, baby?" Curran asked.

"Starving."

"I think we should go to dinner."

"Great idea."

"What are you going to wear?"

"My badass face."

"Good choice," he said.

"Let me just get my knives and powdered silver."

WE WALKED INTO THE GREAT HALL TO FIND A NEW seating arrangement indicated by small name cards: The Italians were sitting at the head table on the right side of Hugh, all the way around the right side of the horseshoe table. The rest of us were seated on the left of Hugh: I was first, then Curran, then Desandra, then the rest of our party. Without saying a word, Curran and I switched seats. If Hugh wanted me to sit next to him, I would sit as far away as possible.

I surveyed the hall. Everyone on our side of the table was dressed to impress: loose sweatpants and T-shirts. Andrea saw me looking and grinned. Raphael winked at me. Mahon was right. I was Pack. At least everyone in gray sweatpants thought so. If I had to fight, I wouldn't fight alone.

The walls of the great hall had gained new decorations: swords and axes hung in hooks within reach. The door to the side exit on the left was shut. That left us with the right exit and the front entrance.

Jarek Kral stared at the hall from a side table to the right, a sour grimace distorting his features into an ugly mask. On the other side, to the left, Vitaliy and Ivanna sat, stone-faced. I scanned the rest of the faces and my gaze slammed right into Lorelei. She stared at me with obvious hatred. I winked at her. She glared back, outraged.

Someone moved into position behind me. I turned. Barabas grinned at me.

"Where is Christopher?" I asked.

He pointed at the side table. Christopher sat next to Keira, his eyes clear as a summer sky without a single thought clouding the blue. He saw me and rose. His lips moved. *Mistress*.

The belt around Christopher's waist looked familiar, especially the pouches hanging from it. I was pretty sure they were filled with my herbs. "Is he wearing my spare belt?"

"Yes," Barabas said. "He somehow got his hands on it when we loaded supplies onto the ship. I tried taking it off him, but it really upset him and I didn't want to injure him."

"That's fine. Let him have it."

I smiled at Christopher.

He sighed happily and sat down.

Desandra strode into the hall, escorted by Aunt B and George. Doolittle followed her in an ancient wheelchair.

Desandra landed in the chair on my left. "You survived."

"I did."

"Nobody told me." She sighed. "Nobody ever tells me anything."

I shrugged, feeling Slayer's comforting weight on my back. The tension in the air was so thick, it made me itch.

The fey torches in the great hall flickered. The conversation died.

Through the wide-open doors of the front entrance, I could

see the main hallway. Along the wall feylanterns blinked in their sconces. The steady glow flickered. A moment and I felt it too, a swell of magic approaching fast. Someone was coming. Next to me, Curran tensed.

A foul magic washed over me as if someone had thrust my mind into a rotting liquefied carcass. Vampires. A lot of them.

People turned to look at the hallway. Some rose and leaned over their tables to get a better view.

Horns blared in a chorus, an ancient alarming sound taut with a warning. The banners on the walls stirred.

People marched down the hallway, coming toward us. They wore black and gray and they moved in unison, two by two. I focused on the leading pair. Hibla walked on the left. Her hair was pulled back from her face and she stared straight at me with a cold predatory glare. Gone was the woman who'd asked me for help and pleaded silently from behind the cage bars. This was a killer, disciplined, icy, and lethal. A familiar insignia marked her chest: a small five-rayed star with a half circle above it and a tall triangle on the right: the ancient hieroglyph of Sirius, the Dog Star. Voron's voice came from my childhood memories: *If you ever see this, run.*

"We've been had," I said. "These are the Iron Dogs."

"What are they?" Aunt B asked.

"Roland's elite unit," Curran said.

"How bad?" Mahon asked.

"Bad," Curran said.

Bad was an understatement. Each Dog was a highly trained ruthless killer. They used weapons, they used magic, and a lot of them weren't human and hid more surprises than a Swiss Army knife. A single Iron Dog could slaughter a dozen normal soldiers. They served as my father's commando force. Hugh d'Ambray was the preceptor of their order.

I stared at Hibla's face. I'd felt bad for her. I'd tried to help her. I'd bought her clueless local bumpkin act hook, line, and sinker. How could I have been so stupid? No matter. Next time I'd know better.

The first pair of Iron Dogs stepped into the great hall and split, standing on each side of the door, locked into an at-ease pose.

Two men and two women followed, wearing impeccable business suits. As the first woman stepped through the door, her high heels clicking quietly on the stone, an emaciated arm hooked the top edge of the doorway. A vampire crawled into the great hall over the top edge of the doorway, muscles flexing like steel cables rubbing against each other under its pallid hide. Another undead followed. They scuttled up the wall like some grotesque predatory geckos, driven by the navigators' will.

Hugh had brought his Masters of the Dead. This was just getting better and better.

The Masters of the Dead took positions behind the twin lines of the Iron Dogs. The hallway stood empty for a long breath.

You could hear a pin drop. The shapeshifters froze, silent and wary.

Hugh turned the corner. He wore leather armor. Supple, but reinforced with metal plates, it molded to him as if it had been melted, poured over his body, and allowed to harden. Loose but thick leather pants shielded his legs. Wrist guards of hardened leather and metal plates protected his wrists. A strip of leather, likely hiding a thin flexible length of metal, guarded his neck. He had come to fight shapeshifters. Raking him with claws would do no good.

He marched down the hallway, wearing black and cloaked in magic. He looked unstoppable. He would soon learn that looks could be deceiving.

"Hail to Hugh d'Ambray," the Iron Dogs intoned in unison, their voice one loud chorus.

Hugh strode through the door and walked to our table, straight to Desandra's chair on my left.

"You're in the wrong seat." He held out his hand.

Desandra blinked, stood up, and put her hand into his. Hugh led her to his chair on Curran's right and held it out for her. She sat. He turned and sat in her place, next to me.

Great.

"You didn't bring enough," Curran said quietly.

"It will suffice," Hugh said. His voice boomed. "In honor of the hunt, I bring you entertainment."

The Iron Dogs took three steps backward, turning, moving in unison until they formed a line along the wall to our right, behind Jarek's werewolves. People entered the minstrel's gallery, carrying small round drums, accordions, and other instruments. A line of men walked into the great hall, dressed in identical jet-black djigit coats. The musicians plucked at their instruments, adjusting and settling down.

A wild melody started, fast and limber, the rhythm of the drums like a racing heart. The men spun across the floor, dancing like a flock of graceful ravens, pivoting and leaping. The lead dancer dropped down and spun across the stage on his knees. I winced.

Hugh pretended to be absorbed in the dance. *What are you planning, you bastard?*

Something tugged on my jeans. I glanced down carefully. Atsany stood by my chair.

You've got to be kidding me.

The small man patted my leg with his pipe, winked, and pointed to the side. I glanced up. Astamur stood by the door, leaning against the wall. He wore a long wide coat of black fleece that covered him from head to toe. A rifle rested in his hands. He looked straight at me and his eyes were grim. The nearest Iron Dog was feet away and oblivious to the man behind him. Nobody paid him any attention, as if they couldn't see him.

I glanced down. Atsany was gone. I leaned to Curran. "Do you see him?"

"Who?"

"Astamur. By the door."

Curran frowned. I looked back. Astamur was gone.

Okay, I did just see that. That wasn't a hallucination.

The dancers snapped into their final poses. The music died. Hugh clapped. Reluctant applause followed from the side tables.

"Is there going to be a play next?" Curran asked. "I never took you for the dinner theater type."

"I promise it will be a show you never forget," Hugh said.

A man and a woman walked in. The man, lean and graceful, wore the black djigit outfit, his profile hawkish, his dark hair slicked back. The woman wore a silver-white gown that covered her head to toe. Fitted in the bust and the waist, the gown flared at the skirt. She looked like a swan. Her black hair fell in four braids, two over her chest, two down her back, all the way past her narrow waist. A small hat perched on her glossy hair, with a white veil trailing from it to hide her back.

The woman turned, standing side by side with the man. Her face was beautiful. I felt a brush of magic. It felt ancient.

"Thousands of years ago Suliko's family entertained the

ancient kings of Georgia," Hugh said. "Today she honors us with her presence. She will dance the *kartuli* for us. Count yourself fortunate. You will not see another dance like that."

A song started with a solo of some sort of reed pipe, so old it rolled through me, familiar and new at the same time, like an echo of some racial memory buried deep inside me, in the places mind and reason couldn't reach. The man held his hand out. The woman placed her fingers on his. He led her forward. They bowed.

Magic shifted. The shapeshifters sat, oblivious. This wouldn't be a normal dance.

"What are you up to?" I squeezed through my teeth.

"You've been sleepwalking for so long, you forgot who you are," he said "This is your wakeup call."

"What's going on?" Curran asked.

"Magic," I told him.

"Yours isn't the only ancient family," Hugh said.

Drums joined the reed pipes in a quick rhythm. Suliko and her partner backed up—he moving on his toes in tall leather boots, she gliding as if she had wheels—and split, moving to the far ends of the room. The woman stood, her arms raised, so graceful it was almost painful to watch. The man approached her, drawing a big circle with his feet, one arm bent at the elbow and pressed to the top of his chest, the other extended straight to the side. He stopped, dignified, waiting for the woman to accept the invitation. She did and they glided across the floor, their arms raised, in sync but never touching, a black raven and a white swan.

Magic wound about them in invisible currents. It tugged on me. It was impossible not to watch them.

The dancers split again.

The music quieted, the wild quick notes of the pipes slowing, careful rather than fast. The woman moved with breathtaking grace, gliding backward, turning . . . So beautiful. I couldn't look away. The magic held me spellbound.

Desandra began crying quietly. At the side tables, closest to the dancers, the people wept.

The music was now a mere breath of sound, delicate and intricate, pulling me in. Suliko turned . . .

Hugh picked up a knife and cut across my hand. Magic tore from my blood straight into the complex twisting currents surrounding the woman, like a lit match thrown into a room filled with gasoline fumes. The magic exploded.

Curran moved. I grabbed his arm before he could lunge at Hugh in full view of a dozen vampires and the Iron Dogs. "No!"

The currents spun, sparking with gold and purple, and a transparent scene unfolded, stretching the entire length of the room, hanging feet above the floor. A bloody battle raged on a vast field. Fire and lightning streaked. A machine gun spat glowing green bullets. Fighters tore at each other, shapeshifters disemboweled their opponents, vampires ripped into bodies in tactical armor. Carnage reigned, the roar, bellows, and moans of the dying blending into a terrible din.

A body fell aside, cleaved in two, and my aunt swung onto the scene. She wore the crimson blood armor and carried two swords. Blood stained her face, her hair flaring, loose. Fighters locked their ranks. She opened her mouth and screamed. The word of power burst from her. The magic cleaved through the fighters, mangling the bodies, straight as an arrow. My aunt tore into the gap, cutting like a dervish in a familiar lightning-fast pattern, severing limbs and spraying blood, unstoppable, without mercy.

"That's my girl." Hugh grinned.

She carved a shaggy ursine shapeshifter in half, disemboweling him with a precise stroke, and I saw her sword.

She carried Slayer.

The hair on the back of my neck rose. It wasn't my aunt. My aunt was dead.

I watched myself slaughter, reaping a harvest of lives, spitting magic and bringing death. On the left a clump of bodies exploded, and Hugh roared, covered in blood, a bloody axe in his hand. They connected, the blood armor–wearing Kate and Hugh, back to back. For a brief moment they stood alone in the carnage, and then they broke apart and charged back into battle.

The vision vanished. Suliko stood, her face shocked.

"What the hell is this?" Jarek Kral snarled.

"The future," Hugh said.

Hell no. No, this wouldn't be my future. Not if I had anything to say about it.

"No!" Suliko waved her arms. "A future!" Her accented

voice vibrated with urgency. "Do not always to be this way. One possibility!"

She yelled something at Hugh in a language I didn't understand. The man moved between her and Hugh, shielding her.

"You lied!" Suliko screamed.

Her partner ushered her out. The musicians fled.

"No matter how much you fight, you are what you are," Hugh said to me. "Your boy knows it too, don't you, Lennart?"

"Enough." Curran growled. "Enough bullshit, d'Ambray. Let's go. You and me."

Lorelei got up and walked over to our table.

"Big talk," Hugh said. "Can you back it up?"

I stood up and held my arms out. "Ladies, you're both pretty. We still have a job to do. Last I checked, we were still guaranteeing Desandra's safety."

The two men glared at each other. They obviously didn't give a rat's ass about Desandra.

"I challenge you." Lorelei pointed at me.

I put my hand over my eyes.

"Sit the fuck down," Hugh told her.

"She'll kill you," Curran said. "Go sit down."

Lorelei opened her mouth.

"Sit down!" Curran roared.

Lorelei's face turned red. She shrank away. She must've rehearsed this, and being ordered back to her seat wasn't part of the fantasy.

A second Lorelei walked through the entrance.

Hugh swore. The first Lorelei gasped.

The second Lorelei winked at Curran and walked toward us. Her body flowed like molten wax, reshaping itself, and twisted into a new body, male, lean, and bald. Saiman held up a document and placed it in front of Curran.

"As requested. What did I miss?"

Curran took the document and scanned it. "George?"

George stepped toward him and examined the document. "Yes. Signed and notarized. It's legally binding."

"Show it to him."

George walked over and placed the paper in front of Jarek Kral. His eyes bulged. "What is this?"

"This is a contract between you and Lorelei Wilson, in which you promise her you will kill the Consort so Lorelei can take her place," Curran said. "In exchange she's supposed to provide you with one of our future children."

Everyone spoke at once.

"You bastard!" Desandra jumped to her feet. A mix of foreign words and English spilled out of her. "You sonovabitch. You would take his child over mine?"

"He's a First," Jarek roared. "It will be a child fit to rule. Not dirt like you."

Desandra's dress tore. Shreds of fabric fluttered to the ground and a huge werewolf in a warrior form dashed over the table toward Jarek. Damn it.

"No!" Doolittle yelled. "Not the half-form!"

Desandra leaped forward, landing in a crouch on the table. Jarek stood up, his face disgusted. His body expanded, fur sheathing his limbs. "You wouldn't dare—"

She swiped, huge claws like scythes. A chunk of Jarek's throat went airborne. I caught a glimpse of his spine, bloody and torn. Blood gushed. The enormous werewolf that was Jarek Kral leaped over the table at his daughter.

George's voice rang out. "Challenge accepted!"

Renok and the bald-headed guy jumped to their feet. I leaped onto the table and pulled Slayer out. *Oh no, you don't.*

"Interfere and die," Curran said.

Jarek's people halted.

The two werewolves rolled across the floor, snarling and biting. Jarek bit Desandra's left arm. She hammered a vicious punch into his face and rolled on top of him. Jarek tried to rear. Desandra raised her hand and smashed it into his chest. Ribs snapped like toothpicks. Desandra thrust her hand into her father's chest, tore out his heart, and threw it on the floor.

Everyone stopped.

"Rot in hell, you bastard." Desandra straightened, her monstrous clawed hands bloody. "Anybody else want to take my children? Anybody? Come on!"

She spun, pointing her hand at the Belve Ravennati, Volkodavi, and Jarek's people. "I'm waiting!"

Nobody moved.

Desandra's monstrous face jerked. She fell back, changing in midair, and landed on her back. Bulges slid across her stomach. "The babies!"

"She's going into labor," Doolittle said in a clipped voice. "I need access."

Renok jerked a sword off the wall and jumped, aiming for Desandra. As I cleared the table, I knew I was too far.

Andrea's bolt sprouted from Renok's neck. He ignored it, swinging at Desandra.

I sprinted, trying to squeeze speed out of every fraction of a second.

The sword rose in a gleaming metal arc and came down like an executioner's axe. George thrust herself between Renok and Desandra. I saw it in slow motion, as if time froze: the glint of the metal blade as it traveled down, the angle of the strike, and the precise moment the razor edge cut into George's right shoulder. Crimson blood washed the blade. It cleaved through the shoulder joint, passing through muscle and bone with ridiculous ease.

George's arm slid off her body and fell down.

I stabbed Slayer into Renok's chest and cut a hole in his heart.

George grabbed Renok's neck with her left hand, squeezed, and pushed him back. He flew and crashed into the table. George slid on her own blood and fell next to me.

Mahon roared. His face twisted, his eyes mad, and the massive Kodiak charged the fallen werewolf, almost mowing me down.

Curran landed next to me, picked up Desandra, and jumped over the table, putting distance between us and the raging Kodiak. Derek swiped George and her arm off the floor and followed him. We ran to the back of the great hall.

Mahon crushed Renok and ripped into another werewolf. Jarek's people went furry in a flash of teeth and claws.

"Damn it all to hell," Hugh growled. "Do not engage."

The Iron Dogs backed away.

"Form a perimeter!" I barked, and pulled my sword out. Andrea stood next to me on the right, Raphael next to her, Eduardo and Keira on my left. We became a semicircle, shielding Desandra. She screamed.

Aunt B ripped a banner down and dropped it on the floor. Curran lowered Desandra onto it, turned, and jumped, changing in midleap. A moment and he tore into the werewolves next to Mahon. The remaining two packs moved away, hugging the wall to avoid being caught in the carnage.

George moaned in Derek's arms.

"Hold on," he told her.

"I'm okay, I'm okay," George said.

"I need clean water," Doolittle called out. "Beatrice . . ."

"It's under control," Aunt B said. "Not my first time reattaching a limb."

"Can I be of assistance?" Saiman asked.

"Have you ever delivered a child?" Doolittle asked.

"Yes, I have."

"Good. We have to perform a C-section. One of her unborn is trying to kill the other."

"Fascinating," Saiman said.

A werewolf dashed our way. I sliced his legs, Raphael slit his throat, and Andrea shot him through the heart.

Isabella marched to us, her sons in tow. "I will see—"

"Don't," I warned.

She opened her mouth. Eduardo shifted, gaining a foot in height and another across the shoulders, and bellowed at her. Isabella took a step back.

Desandra howled, a sharp cry of pure pain.

At the other wall Curran and Mahon raged, tearing werewolves apart. The last of the shaggy bodies stopped moving. Curran and the giant bear were the only two left standing. Mahon swung and hit Curran, huge claws raking a bloody trail along his gray side. Curran roared. Mahon rose on his hind legs. Curran lunged forward, locking his arms on the bear, and took him to the floor.

"It's me," he said.

Mahon snarled.

"It's me," Curran repeated. "George is safe. It will be fine."

I held my breath. Sometimes werebears snapped and went berserk. That was how Curran had become the Beast Lord— he had killed a mad werebear. But Mahon was always calm. He was always in control—

Mahon reared, tossing Curran aside like he weighed nothing. Curran landed on his side and rolled to his feet. The bear bellowed and ran straight into the door, taking it off its hinges. A moment and he vanished down the hallway.

"Fucking animals," Hugh said, disgust on his face.

A deep voice rolled through the castle. "I've seen enough." Everything stopped. Astamur stood in the doorway.

Hugh turned. "Who are you?"

Astamur opened his mouth. No sound came, but I heard him in my head, clear as if he stood right next to me.

"I am the shepherd."

The rifle in his hands flowed, as if liquid, turning into a tall staff. Astamur looked at Hugh. "For twenty years I watched you. You're bad for this land. You're bad for my people. Tell your master he wasn't welcome in the mountains when he was young. He is not welcome still."

"Cute," Hugh said. "Kill him."

The nearest Iron Dog moved toward the shepherd.

Astamur raised his staff. I felt a spark, a tiny hint of magic, like a glimpse of a titanic storm cloud in a flash of lightning. The butt of the staff hit the floor. A brilliant white light drowned us, as if a star had split open and swallowed us whole.

THE FLOOR SHOOK. THUNDER CRASHED, SLAPPING my eardrums with an air fist. Next to me the shapeshifters clutched at their ears, screaming. The floor shuddered under my feet. I blinked, trying to clear my vision. Things swung into focus slowly: an empty space where Astamur used to be and a widening crack crawling upward through the wall. A gap sliced the floor to the right of me, fifteen feet wide and running all the way across the great hall and into the hallway. Bright blue flames shot out of the gap, cutting the great hall in two. We, the Volkodavi, and the vampires were on one side. Curran, Hugh, the Iron Dogs, and the Belve Ravennati were on the other.

Astamur had split the castle in two. Holy shit.

I turned to Curran. The flames burned between us.

Curran took a running start.

A vampire fell off the ceiling into the fire, bursting into flames. The fire seared undead flesh. He blazed bright like a sparkler and vanished into a cloud of ash.

"No!"

Curran veered, avoiding the flames at the last second. *Oh good.* I exhaled.

Desandra shrieked, and then a child cried, a weak mewling sound. I glanced back. Saiman lifted a newborn boy, wet and bloody. A moment later Doolittle handed a second infant over to Aunt B. She turned. The thing in her arms wasn't a human baby.

It wasn't a wolf, it wasn't a cat, it was a strange creature covered in soft scales, the beginnings of rudimentary wings thrusting from its back. The creature screeched and tried to bite Aunt B.

"Your firstborn is a wolf," Doolittle said.

The bewildered expression peeled off Radomil's face, leaving a hard ruthless intelligence in its place. "That does it," Radomil said. "Kill them all."

The Volkodavi snarled in unison. Their human skins ruptured. Flesh and bone boiled out, scales covered the new bodies, and a dozen lamassu took flight.

The flames exploded with bright orange. Heat bathed me. The castle rumbled again. Another peal of thunder rolled, dazing the shapeshifters. The crack split sideways, cutting half of the lamassu from us.

"The castle is breaking apart," Aunt B said. "We need to go."

"Not without Curran." I pulled the magic to me. Maybe a power word would work.

On the opposite side Hugh said something and staggered back, as if someone had thrust a sword through his gut. Ten to one that was a power word that backfired. I felt nothing. The flames remained unimpressed. Okay, scratch that idea.

"Kate?" Keira asked. "What do we do?"

We had to get the hell out of here, before the castle fell apart and plunged off the cliff. In the hallways, the lamassu couldn't swarm us. We'd have the advantage.

I spun to the flames.

"Go!" Curran yelled at me through the fire. "I'll find you."

There was nothing I could do to help him. I had to get our people out of there and then I'd go around and I would find him.

"I'm coming back!"

"I know!" He waved at me. "Go!"

I turned to the shapeshifters. "Grab Doolittle, George, and Desandra. We're getting the hell out of here."

"Don't lose her," Hugh bellowed at the Masters of the Dead. "Go around! Take her alive!"

"You won't touch her," Curran snarled, and charged Hugh.

I WANTED TO STAND AND WATCH. I WANTED TO know he would be okay. Instead I ran for the door. The sooner I found a way around, the sooner I could help him.

Barabas grabbed the wolf newborn, thrust him into Desandra's hands, and picked her up off the floor. Derek grabbed Doolittle out of his chair, Aunt B picked up George, and Christopher somehow ended up with the baby lamassu. They followed me.

A lamassu swooped down on us. Andrea fired. The bolt bit into the beast's eye. The lamassu spun, careened, and flew into the fire. Her body burst into white flame. The fire grew, widening the gap.

A door blocked our way. I drove my shoulder into the wood and bounced off.

"Eduardo!" I yelled.

The werebuffalo rammed the door. Splinters flew.

Another lamassu dove at us. Keira jumped, turning in midleap. A sable-black panther in a warrior form slapped the lamassu out of the air. He crashed. We swarmed it. I stabbed into the orange flesh. Keira bit into its throat, gouging huge chunks of flesh out.

The lamassu convulsed, beating one wing against the floor.

"Go!" I barked.

The shapeshifters fled past me into the hallway.

"Keira!"

She tore herself away from the lamassu, reached the door in two great leaps, and ran. I followed her.

"Kill him," Hugh bellowed in the hall. Curran's roar answered. He was saving me again. I had to find him. I'd get our people out and then I would find him.

We were on the south side, facing a sheer cliff. Flames blocked the hallway to the right. Running left, east, and then north was our only option.

A lamassu crashed into the doorway, skidding into the wall, and chased us. No room to maneuver for him or us.

Keira tried to push past me. I held out my hand. Hugh or not, I had to get my people out of the castle.

I spat a power word. *"Aarh."* Stop.

Magic ripped from me. It hurt so much, the world blinked.

The lamassu froze, its limbs locked. Keira dashed past me. A huge spotted bouda leaped over my head and tore into the lamassu, savaging its neck with a flurry of strikes. "Run," Aunt B yelled. "We'll catch up."

I ran and turned the corner. Four different hallways branched from the main one. *Damn it, Hugh.* If I survived this, I would find him and I would beat his head with a brick for building this damn labyrinth. I spun and saw Barabas's white shirt as he disappeared behind a corner to the right. I ran after him.

Keira and Aunt B caught up with me, both bloody. We galloped down the hallway. Almost to the corner.

Barabas whipped about the corner, carrying Desandra, running full speed. I threw myself against the wall. They dashed past me.

"Vampires!" Andrea yelled as she passed me.

Undead magic lashed me, swelling like a tidal wave around the corner. Damn it all to hell.

I did a one-eighty and followed them. Next to me Christopher was smiling, running with a now-human baby in his hands. "This is so fun!"

This had to be some kind of twisted nightmare.

We made a sharp left, then another, and burst into another hallway, parallel to the first one. The revolting undead magic washed over me. The bloodsuckers were coming from behind us and from the right, trying to box us in. One, two . . . Fourteen. Fourteen undead minds.

We had Desandra, who was barely conscious; two infants; Doolittle, who couldn't walk; and George, who was out like a light. There was no way we would win that fight.

I stopped and turned.

"Mistress?" Christopher called.

"Kate?" Andrea crashed to a halt next to me. "What are you doing?"

"The vampires are chasing me, not you," I said. "Go. I'll lead them off."

"Don't even think about it," Andrea said. "I'll carry you if I have to."

"I'm your alpha."

"The hell you are."

I drew Slayer across my left forearm. Blood swelled, its magic sharp. "Take our people and Desandra out of this castle. Secure the panacea. That's an order."

She hesitated.

"I know what I'm doing. Go."

"I'm coming back for you."

"Good. Go!"

She ran. Who said I wasn't a good liar?

The undead were drawing closer. I turned and walked into the side hallway, moving slowly, shaking my left arm once in a while. *Come on, sharks. There's blood in the water.*

THE SHORT PASSAGE ENDED IN A STAIRWAY. MIGHT as well. The more time I bought the guys, the better.

I reached the next floor. A round room lay before me, the top floor of a low tower under a simple roof. Arched windows turned its wall into a latticework of stone and night sky. As good a place as any.

The air smelled of thick smoke. To the left and to the right, the castle burned. Flames shot out of the fissures fracturing the stone walls.

The vampires were almost at my heels.

I stopped in the center of the room and raised my sword. I could probably grab a few of the undead with my mind, but any trained Master of the Dead would be fighting for control, and Hugh's guys were unlikely to be weak amateurs.

The first vampire scuttled out of the opening and moved to the right of me. It moved on all fours, as if it had never walked upright. A thick pallid hide shielded its body, the network of lean muscle running over its back and limbs. I could count every rib. A spiky ridge thrust along its back. Its head stretched forward as if someone had taken the bones of its skull and pulled them to support the oversized jaws. A pre-Shift vampire.

The older the vampire, the more the Immortuus pathogen transformed the original human body. This one was really far gone. No traces of a person remained.

The bloodsucker stared at me with glowing red eyes, like two coals in an old fire. I'd encountered pre-Shift vampires before and always in connection with my father. They shouldn't have existed. Before the Shift we had no magic, but there it was, a lethal, undead abomination.

Another bloodsucker joined the first. They stared at me with starved eyes, filled with mindless, endless hunger. Given free rein, they would slaughter me and keep going until they ran out of things to kill. Only the steel cage of the Masters of the Dead would keep them in check.

The undead horde spilled into the room.

The first bloodsucker unhinged its jaws and a clear cold male voice issued forth. "Lay down your sword. Put your hands on the back of your head."

I simply looked at him. I could feel the undead mind, a hateful penlight in the nearly empty skull.

"Lay down your sword or we will be forced to subdue you."

Subdue me, huh. "Why don't you try?"

A vampire lunged for my legs. I cut across his neck. My blade barely grazed it. The bloodsucker withdrew. Undead blood dripped on the floor. It called to me, the magic in it shivering and twisting, alive on its own.

"There is no need for violence."

I laughed. The glowing sparks of the vamp's mind taunted me. I'd always wanted to crush one. Just squeeze it with my magic until it snapped like a flea caught between two fingernails. I'd never tried it. I always had to hide my power.

The undead shifted in place, moving into position. They would rush me in a minute.

"When a vampire dies while the navigator is controlling its mind, the navigator's brain thinks he died instead of the vampire. Two outcomes are possible," I said, gathering my magic. "One, the navigator goes catatonic. Two, he goes mad."

The vampires stared at me.

"Which one do you think you will be?"

"Apprehend her," the male said.

I reached with my magic, grabbed the nearest undead minds, and squeezed. The heads of the three vampires right in front of me exploded. Bloody mist splattered onto the stones and neighboring bloodsuckers. Undead blood spilled onto the stone floor. Two vampires in the back screamed in a high-pitched female voice, a mindless gibberish howl.

A vamp leaped at me. I sliced it with Slayer, grabbed more minds, and squeezed again. More heads exploded, the undead blood spray blossoming like crimson carnations. Its magic begged me to touch it.

Another bloodsucker leaped, while the third raked its claws down my back. I crushed their minds one by one, until only one remained, the one whose navigator had ordered me to surrender.

Hot crimson painted the stones of the tower around me. Its scent enveloped me. Its magic called to me, pulling me, pleading, waiting and eager, like a cat arching its back for a stroke. What did I have to lose anyway?

I reached out and answered the blood's call.

The undead crimson streamed to me, pouring out of the headless corpses, merging together into currents like capillaries flowed into veins. The thick, viscous liquid pooled around my legs. I pumped my left arm and let the blood from the cut drip into the puddle of red below.

The first drop landed and the reaction it set off sparked through me, like a rush of adrenaline. The blood twisted about me, suddenly malleable. It coated my feet, my legs, wound about my waist, and climbed higher, covering my body. It wasn't well-formed, not an armor yet but a flexible coat that felt like an extra layer of skin, that wrapped around me like crimson silk. It felt like I was dreaming.

The lone vampire knelt on one knee and bowed his head. "My lady," the navigator said.

I raised my hand. The blood silk ran down my forearm, hardening into a three-foot spike. I shoved it forward. The bloodsucker's eyes flared bright red—the Master of the Dead had fled its mind—and I rammed the spike into its skull, scrambling its pitiful excuse for a brain.

The spike crumbled into dust. The bloodsucker toppled over. I moved and the blood moved with me, pliant and light. So that was how one made blood armor.

A roar tore through the night. A giant lamassu swept through the sky toward me. The scales on its stomach glowed with orange, reflecting the flames below. Beautiful . . . So large, like a dragon come to life. It swooped closer and rammed the tower's roof. Stones rained down around me. A chunk hit my shoulder and bounced off the armor. The wind from the lamassu's wings buffeted my face.

It flipped around, diving for me.

Reality smashed into my magic-addled brain, shattering the dreamlike haze. *Oh shit.*

I DUCKED, BUT TOO LATE. THE CLAWS HOOKED MY shoulders, piercing the thin layer of blood armor. My legs left the ground. I gritted my teeth and stabbed straight up with Slayer, right into the beast's gut, not enough for serious damage but enough to make him pay attention. Fire flashed below me, the sections of the castle like stone islands in the sea of flames. The lamassu careened, swinging above a tall square tower. The top of the main keep. Now was my chance.

I strained and stabbed straight up, again and again, mincing muscles with Slayer. Blood ran down the pale blade. *Drop me. Drop me, you sonovabitch.*

With a thunderous roar, the beast let go. I plunged through the air, bending my knees. The impact punched my feet. I landed on the balls of my feet, rolled forward, trying to spread the collision force, and scrambled up.

We were on the top of the keep, a square of stone. The lamassu landed at the end, its distinctive green eyes furious and familiar. Radomil.

The lamassu walked paw over paw, his cavernous mouth open wide.

I flexed my left wrist, popping a silver spike out of the wrist guard into my palm. I used to have needles, but I could afford more silver now.

Radomil bent his head low, his muscles tensing.

"Bring it." I pulled magic to me. I'd timed it last time. I'd have a second and a half.

He charged.

I sprinted. *"Aarh!"* Stop.

The pain of a power word exploded in the back of my skull. Blackness mugged me. My momentum carried me through it. I tore through the haze.

Time slowed to a crawl.

Radomil stood frozen in midstep. I punched the spike into his throat, stabbed Slayer into his gut, and dragged the blade, wrenching it with all my strength, ripping a gap in his stomach from foreleg to hindquarters.

Radomil's legs trembled. I yanked a bag of powdered silver granules from my belt, ripped it, and emptied it into the wound.

Radomil whipped about. Claws scoured my back. It felt like someone had dripped molten metal down my spine.

I ran.

Right now silver was burning his insides. The longer it melted his innards, the less work I'd have to do. The sound of huge feet thumping behind me chased me, blocking out the roar of the fire. I lunged to the side. He hurtled past me and whirled, snarling. Gray blood wet the cut. Singed with silver, the laceration refused to close, and his body sped up the bleeding, trying to purge the poisonous metal from his system.

Radomil swayed and charged me. A big feline paw raked at me. I sliced with my sword. He swiped at me again, like a housecat trying to shred a toy, except Radomil was forty times the size of a housecat. I cut across his paw.

Radomil rammed me. I clutched onto his scales and stabbed into his chest with my sword. He leaped up, the wings beating, roaring in pain. I hung from his neck fifty feet above the fire raging below. To let go was to die. Radomil bent in midair. The claws of his hind feet ripped into my armor, down my side, and deep into my right leg. My whole body hurt so much, I no longer cared.

Radomil careened back toward the keep, screaming. The gap in his stomach hung open. Now or never. I stabbed my sword straight into the wound. Radomil plunged down. My hand slipped off the scales. For one desperate half-second I held on, and then I fell. There was no time to right myself. The orange body thudded onto the stone with a wet thud. I fell next to it.

THE WORLD SWAM. THE AIR VANISHED, SUCKED out of the Universe. I gulped like a fish on dry land, trying to inhale and failing. *Don't pass out. Just don't pass out.*

My lungs opened. I inhaled smoke-ruined air, coughed, and rolled upright. My left arm hung limp. It hurt so much, I couldn't tell if it was broken. Hot wetness ran down my back. I was bleeding.

The orange body shivered and melted back into human form. Radomil's beautiful face looked at the sky.

Everything hurt. It hurt so much, I could no longer tell what hurt the worst. But I was still breathing. Without the armor, I would've been dead. His claws would've finished me.

I staggered to my feet and dragged myself to the door leading down. A wall of fire greeted me. The heat pushed me back. Out of the question. The flames would cook me two steps in.

I limped to the eastern side of the keep and looked down. The wall was sheer, the stones fitted together so closely they might as well have been a single smooth block of concrete. No way. With a rope, maybe, and even that was risky. Bleeding, ropeless, and with one bum arm, no.

Flames filled the courtyard. The roofs of the side towers had crashed down and the blackened beams popped like logs in the fireplace. Cracks filled with orange-and-blue flames fractured the huge building. The castle was breaking apart. It looked like hell on Earth.

The doors of a side tower burst. Furry shapes ran out—shapeshifters in half-form making a break for the gates. I saw Christopher's blue shirt. The familiar gray werelion was missing. Curran wasn't with them. He hadn't made it out. *Where are you?*

I inhaled a lungful of sooty air. "Hey! Andrea! Look up!"

They didn't hear me. They were running too fast, the way one ran when chased.

People in black and gray poured out of the doors. The Iron Dogs, at least fifteen, probably more.

The shapeshifters ran through the fire. Derek's shaggy back flared, the fur igniting in a flash. He kept running, carrying Doolittle forward. The Iron Dogs followed as if the fire weren't even there.

Go, I willed, *go.*

A lean, darker bouda stopped and turned around. Raphael. Andrea skidded to a stop, a smaller slender creature.

The first Iron Dog fell on them, a tall lean man, swinging an axe. Magic sparked and bit Andrea in the chest. She snarled and clawed the Iron Dog's side. Raphael tore his stomach. The man swung, oblivious to his guts hanging out. The axe grazed Raphael. He batted it aside and sliced the man's throat.

Raphael and Andrea backed away, toward the gates.

A huge woman, six and a half feet tall and wearing armor, ran at them. Eduardo wheeled about and charged, back toward the fight. Andrea and Raphael stepped to the side and he rammed into the woman. They struggled, locked in a deadly grappling match. Eduardo clamped her, and Raphael and Andrea ripped at her from both sides. She shuddered.

At the gates, Aunt B handed George to Keira, spun around, and headed back.

The three shapeshifters dragged the Iron Dog down, ripping her apart. An arm flew, tossed aside.

The rest of the Iron Dogs were almost on them. I squeezed my fists. *What are you doing? Go! Run.*

Aunt B grabbed Raphael and Andrea by their shoulders and hurled them back. Eduardo reared. She screamed at him. He hesitated a moment and ran toward the gates. Aunt B followed.

The Iron Dogs were closing in, Hibla in the lead.

Raphael and Andrea cleared the gates. The werebuffalo charged through with Aunt B at his heels.

It wouldn't help. The Dogs would chase them all the way to the ship. That ship couldn't pull out fast enough.

Aunt B stopped before the gates.

No. No!

She hit the winch on the side of the gate. The metal portcullis crashed down, cutting her off from the rest of the shapeshifters.

Andrea screamed. I heard her even through the roar of the fire. Raphael grabbed the steel grate.

Aunt B planted herself in front of the winch. She could scale the wall, but she stayed where she was. She was buying her son and Andrea time.

Someone pulled Raphael away from the portcullis from the other side.

The Iron Dogs were almost there.

I had one more power word left in me. One more. I wasn't getting off this tower anyway. I pulled together what weak magic I had left and spat it out. *"Osanda."* Kneel, you bastards.

The world turned red. The pain bent me in half. I slumped over the parapet. Magic burned my lips—blood streamed from my nose over my face.

Three Iron Dogs directly by the keep plunged down. The rest closed on Aunt B. My magic didn't reach far enough. It didn't reach all of them.

The first Iron Dog leaped, unnaturally high. He sailed over the flames, his human face turning into something monstrous, inhuman, and covered in needles. Aunt B jerked him out of the air, tore open his stomach, and threw him into the fire. He flailed, burning.

Run! Go, climb the wall, get out of here. Go!

A towering man charged at her from the left, swinging a huge blade, while another, smaller and faster one, lunged at her from the right. Aunt B grabbed the giant's sword and tore it out of his hands. The smaller man sliced her side, and she backhanded him into the fire.

The giant grabbed at her. The bouda thrust her claws into his gut and wrenched his intestines out. He howled, his mouth gaping open, and she pushed him aside.

The Iron Dogs circled her, wary. Maybe she would get out of this. She had to get out of it.

Hibla raised her hand. A man behind her bowed his head and began to chant. A mage.

Aunt B shifted from foot to foot, watching them with red eyes.

Get out of there, I willed. *Go!*

The mage jerked his arms up and out. Three silver blades shot out of him, dragging silver chains behind them. Aunt B shied to the side, but the blades turned and pierced her chest and stomach, biting into the ground, their ends fusing at the last moment into a silver knot. For a second she stood frozen, the silver chains stretching behind her, wet with her blood.

Oh God.

The mage brought his arms together. The chains snapped taut, anchoring Aunt B in place. She strained, roaring—the silver was burning her. But the chains held. She could barely take a step.

Hibla waved her arm. Two Iron Dogs stepped forward with crossbows.

No, damn it, at least fight her. Fight her, you bastards.

The first two bolts tore into Aunt B, the impact shaking her. She snarled, straining.

Hibla nodded. I would find that bitch if I had to turn the entire fucking planet upside down. I would find her and I would kill her slowly.

The crossbowmen reloaded. Two more bolts tore through her. I jerked as if I'd been shot.

Another two.

There would be no more sundresses.

Two more bolts.

She would never see her grandchildren. I wanted to cry. I wanted to cry so badly, but my face was dry.

Two more bolts.

She screamed and screamed and they shot her. And I was stuck here on top of the tower. I couldn't even help her.

Aunt B sagged. Her knees trembled. She lunged forward, her body bristling with arrows. She howled to the sky. The silver knot ripped through her stomach. Hibla shot forward, swinging a wide sword. The blade cut through Aunt B's thick furry neck. Her head rolled to the ground.

She died. She was really dead.

They tossed her body aside like garbage and strained to raise the grate with the broken winch.

A dark beast charged out of the fire. The massive bear scattered the remaining Iron Dogs like bowling pins. *Too late, Mahon. Too late.*

I saw him rip into them, but staying upright was no longer an option. I sagged to the ground. My heartbeat was so loud in my ears. The bear would kill them all.

I wanted to see Curran again. I wanted to close my eyes and imagine us back at the Keep in our rooms making love on top of the ridiculous bed . . .

I had to get up. I had to get up and find him.

I would get up. I just needed a minute. Just one minute.

A lion's roar rocked the night. It came from the right.

I rolled onto my knees. My arm hurt. The gashes on my right leg were bleeding like there was no tomorrow. Something vital was cut, because the leg didn't want to hold my weight.

Crawling wasn't an option. I struggled to get up. *Easy does it. Come on, piece-of-shit legs.* I could do this. I leaned on the wall and hauled myself upright. My right leg was going numb. *If it's not one leg, it's the other. Just my luck.*

On the tower forty feet below me, Hugh and Curran fought, silhouetted among the flames. Three Iron Dogs stalked across the roof, keeping their distance from Curran, trying to flank him. Five bodies of Iron Dogs and two vampires sprawled, motionless. Curran had killed them. He'd fought his way out of that room, and he'd killed them all, because whatever Hugh had left would be right there with him on this roof. Hugh never played fair.

Only Curran could've done this and survived.

Hugh limped, favoring his left side. Curran watched him. Hugh was a big man, but Curran in a warrior form towered over Hugh. His blood-soaked hide, usually gray, now was black and red against the flames.

Curran stayed still. My throat constricted. Usually Curran moved through the fight, unstoppable, using all of his momentum and speed. He wasn't moving now, which meant he was near his limit. He had to fight all of them, while Hugh only had to fight him, and now Hugh had more stamina left. He was slowly cutting Curran down, piece by piece. It was what I would've done.

Hugh struck, his sword shining with reflected flames. He moved forward with innate grace, fast and sure. Curran batted aside one strike. The second cut across his chest but fell too short. Curran lunged forward, but Hugh danced back.

When I fought him, he'd muscled me, because it was his best chance. This was pure skill.

Curran's legs jerked. He snarled, shaking.

Hugh charged him, bringing the sword up, and moved on his toes, looking for an opening. Crusader's strike. He would reverse the blade at the end. *Dodge left, honey. Left.*

Oh God.

The blade sliced through Curran's side and Hugh withdrew in the same flawless move, but not before Curran's claws scoured his arm. The Iron Dog behind Curran, a short woman, lunged at Curran, trying to slice across his back. The Beast Lord spun and smashed his fist into her. She flew across the tower, rolled, and clumsily rose to her feet.

"It's over, Lennart," Hugh called.

Curran didn't answer.

The Iron Dogs resumed their circling, trying to get behind Curran.

Hugh raised his sword.

Not again. I'd just watched Aunt B die. I wouldn't sit here and watch him die, too.

I limped back, turned, gritted my teeth, and ran. The edge of the roof rushed at me. I jumped.

The air whistled past me. I saw the roof below and both Hugh and Curran staring up, their faces shocked.

The blood armor peeled off my body, expanding into a bubble in midair. I bounced against the stones. The blood bubble burst and shattered into dry dust. I hit the stone hard and stayed there. I had survived. Now I had to keep surviving.

My left arm was shot. My right leg was probably shot, too. My vision blurred.

"Hey, baby," Hugh said. "Nice of you to drop in. Take her."

My right arm was under me. I let go of Slayer and pulled the throwing knife out, hiding it with my body.

The Iron Dogs moved toward me. The shorter woman was at the front of the pack. I let her get close.

Hugh struck at Curran, swinging the sword in a wide arc. Curran moved forward. Hugh tossed the sword to his left hand, so fast it was as if he had two swords and one had disappeared, and slashed at Curran's side. Curran lunged forward, but Hugh danced away. *Damn it.*

The short woman grabbed my hair. I stabbed her in the foot, sliced the bend of her knee, waited half a second for her to crash down, and slit her throat.

The two remaining Iron Dogs stopped. I crouched by the body, keeping my weight on my left knee.

"What the fuck," Hugh snarled. "Look at her, she's half-dead. She isn't even on her last leg. She can't fucking stand and she's cutting you down like you're children. Bring her to me alive. Now, or I'll kill you myself."

The two Iron Dogs advanced: a dark-skinned man, lean and hard, and a bigger, stockier blond in his early thirties.

Hugh struck forward, thrusting to the upper chest. Curran dodged left. Hugh flipped his sword and slashed at Curran's neck. Curran thrust forward, fast, aiming for Hugh's left side with his huge claws. Hugh clamped his arm and stabbed Curran in the stomach. The blade sank in almost to the hilt. Hugh let go and leaped out of range.

The blond was close enough. I shot up from my half-crouch. I couldn't feel my leg, but it obeyed. I slashed across the blond's chest, knocked aside his desperate thrust, and smashed my forehead into his face. He stumbled. I elbowed the other Iron Dog in the throat, stabbed him in the neck, spun about, and made a hole in the blond's liver.

Curran was on his knees. His head sagged. Hugh was walking toward him.

I ran. My leg folded under me and I crashed.

"Wait your turn." Hugh raised his sword.

Curran surged from his knees and grabbed Hugh, jerking him off his feet and pinning his arms to his body. Hugh smashed his head into Curran's muzzle. Curran snarled, flipped Hugh into the air as if he weighed nothing, and slammed him over the stone parapet, back down. Hugh's spine popped like a firecracker. He screamed. Curran heaved him up and hurled him into the flames.

Magic punched me, a bright blue explosion shooting into the night from the spot where Hugh plunged down. Curran looked down, rocked back on his feet, and fell.

I dragged myself to him and cradled his head in my arms.

The werelion shuddered and turned human. Gray eyes looked at me. "Hey there, ass kicker."

"Hello, Your Furriness."

I kissed his bloody lips. He kissed me back.

"The bastard teleported," Curran grimaced. "Can you believe that?"

"Screw him. He's weak."

"I broke his back."

"I heard."

"He'll feel it in the morning."

I laughed. It came out a little bloody.

"Did our people get out?" Curran asked.

"Most of them."

"You have to go now," he said.

"No."

"Yes. Both of my legs are broken and you can't carry me."

I brushed the soot from his face. "How the hell did you manage that?"

"He used magic. The bones fused wrong. It hurts a bit."

It probably hurt like hell.

"Kate," he said. "You'll burn to death. Leave me and try to make it down into the yard before this place collapses."

"In a minute I'm going to get up and drag you to the edge of the tower. Then we're going to jump over the wall."

"It's fifty feet down," he said. "That's called suicide."

"Or death on our terms."

"Leave me, God damn it."

"No. It's my turn to save us. We're going to jump." I coughed. The smoke was eating my lungs. I was so tired. "I'm just going to rest half a minute. My arm hurts a little."

I lay next to him.

"Will you marry me?" Curran asked.

"You're asking me now?"

"Seems like a good time," he said.

He deserved an honest answer. "If I marry you, then you'll be my husband."

"Yes, that's how it works."

Smartass. "I would be dragging you down with me."

"I thought we covered that."

"When the time comes, I can't say, 'Don't fight him. He's just someone who doesn't matter.' We would be married."

"Do you expect that I would hide behind that?" he asked. "Is that how little you think of me?"

"No. I know you wouldn't. I know it doesn't matter to you, because you love me. It's just something I tell myself when I wake up in the middle of the night and can't fall asleep."

The heat was closer. We really had to get off this tower.

"Is the offer still open?" I asked.

He nodded.

"It's a yes. I would love to be your wife."

I reached over. He took my hand and squeezed it.

Magic cracked. The stone floor under me dropped. A smooth stone slid open under me. We rolled down it, all the way to the road, coming to a gentle stop. I blinked and saw Astamur standing next to a cart drawn by a donkey. The donkey and the shepherd regarded us.

"Well?" Astamur asked. "Are you two going to lie there all night?"

It wasn't English, but I understood him all the same. I stared at him, openmouthed.

"I would've rescued you sooner, but you were having an important relationship conversation."

"What the hell . . . ?" Curran struggled to get up.

Now wasn't the time to look the gift donkey in the mouth. I propped him up and half dragged, half carried him into the cart. He fell onto the boards. I fell next to him. The donkey moved, and the cart took us away from the castle.

Fire shot out above the stone. Slowly, as if hesitating, the castle walls came apart and crashed down off the cliff, breaking into thousands of blocks as they fell.

"Who are you?" I asked.

"I told you, I'm the shepherd. I watch over these mountains."

"Are you immortal?"

"No. Nobody is truly immortal. But I was born a very long time ago, when the magic was still strong. Then the magic waned and for a while I had to sleep. Now my power is back, and I am one with the mountains again."

"Why did you save us?" I asked.

"Your father is cooked," Astamur said. "I've known him for a long time. We met when the sea and the mountains were younger. No matter what time and the world do to him, he won't change. He is what he is. You're not so bad. You try too hard and you lust for blood, but your heart is good."

I didn't know what to say.

"One day you will have to decide where you stand," he said. "I have hope for you, so I tell you the same thing I told your father. If you come to these mountains with open hands, I will welcome you, but if you come holding a sword, you will die by it."

"What did her father decide?" Curran asked.

"He chose not to come at all, which is an answer in itself. There are ancients in the world, like him and me. They are waking up. Your father, he will want to use you. Soon you might have to make a stand."

"Do you think I can win?" I asked.

"Against your father? No, not now." Astamur said. "Perhaps in time. A smart warrior chooses the time of battle."

"I will remember that."

The donkey clopped, his hoofbeats really loud. Salty wind bathed my face. I realized we were on the pier.

"The ship has pulled away but there is a boat coming back. They are planning on rescuing you from the castle," Astamur said. "It's nice to have friends."

I raised my head and saw Andrea and Raphael in the boat.

Ten minutes later we were hauled onto the deck of the *Rush*. Andrea sat me down gently by the cabin. I leaned against the wall. Curran lay down next to me. His legs didn't look right. They would have to be rebroken. My bones hurt just thinking about it.

Derek rested on his stomach, his back covered with burns. Keira was bloody. Eduardo's whole body was covered with soot and burns. Mahon cradled George, tears in his eyes. Her arm was missing. Shit.

"It will be fine, Dad," she told him.

"What will I tell your mother . . ."

"You will tell her that I saved a woman during childbirth." George glanced to the length of sailing canvas where Desandra curled with two naked babies.

Barabas asked me quietly, "What about Desandra?"

"What about her? Unless she wants us to drop her off somewhere, we're taking her with us. Where else is she going to go?"

Everyone was bloody, beat up, and grieving.

"Finally," Saiman said. "We can be under way."

Christopher came to stand by me and smiled.

The *Rush* turned, picked up speed, and slid out of the harbor. The mountains receded.

I looked at the gathering of metal drums that sat near the nose of the ship, secured by ropes. At least we had done it. At least we got the panacea. Maddie wouldn't have to die. Aunt B would never see her grandchildren, but at least, if Raphael and Andrea had any babies, they wouldn't—

"Look!" Raphael called, pointing north.

A fleet of ships anchored behind the curve of the harbor. Six large vessels, the biggest longer than the *Rush*. They flew the Iron Dog banner.

"Hold your breath," Saiman murmured next to me.

The *Rush* glided across the sea.

A minute passed. Another. The air grew thick with tension.

We turned again and sped across the blue waves. Hugh's fleet disappeared from view. They'd let us go. They must not have known what happened.

Doolittle rolled into view. He sat in an old wheelchair. Did Saiman actually get it for him? How unlike him.

Doolittle cleared his throat. "Someone tampered with the drums."

Curran sat up. "What?"

"Someone tampered with the panacea drums," Doolittle said. "The seals are broken."

Barabas jerked the lid off the nearest drum, thrust his hand in, and recoiled. "Powdered silver."

"And arsenic," Doolittle said.

"All of it?" Curran asked.

Doolittle's eyes were ashen. "Every barrel."

God damn it, Hugh.

"How?" Andrea asked. "How did they get on board? I thought you had checked the barrels after they were loaded."

"I did," Doolittle said. "And I had personally sealed each one. Saiman had posted guards."

Saiman. Of course.

Curran surged to his feet, grabbed Saiman by the throat, and jerked him up. Saiman's feet left the deck.

"You!" Curran snarled. "You let d'Ambray poison it."

Saiman made no move to resist.

Curran hurled him across the deck. Saiman hit the cabin with his back and stood up. "Rage all you want," he said. "I didn't have a choice. The contract we signed obligates me to do everything in my power to maintain your safety. It was made abundantly clear to me that sacrificing the panacea was the only way to ensure your survival. Those ships would've never let us go. I did what I had to do so we could all go home."

Curran swayed on his feet, his eyes pure gold.

"Let it go," I said. "Let it go, honey. It's over."

Curran closed his eyes and lay back down. He didn't bother with threats and promises. They would do no good now.

"So it's all for nothing?" Andrea said, her voice too high. "Aunt B died for nothing?"

Raphael smashed his fist into the drum, denting it. Eduardo swore. Keira screamed, a sound of pure frustration.

I couldn't take it. I covered my face.

All for nothing. Aunt B would never see her grandchildren for nothing. Doolittle's paralysis, George's arm, Curran's legs, all for nothing.

Tears wet my fingers. I realized I finally was crying.

"Mistress?" Cold fingers touched my hands, gently. "Mistress?"

I forced my hands from my face. I couldn't even talk.

Christopher was looking at me, his face concerned. "Please don't cry. Please."

I couldn't help it. The tears just kept rolling.

"Please don't cry. Here." He pulled the chalk from my spare belt hugging his waist and began drawing a complicated glyph on the deck. "I will make more. I will make more panacea right now." He started pulling herbs out of the pouches. "I will make as much as you want. Just please don't cry."

Two hours later we had our first batch of panacea. Doolittle tested it and said it was the strongest he had ever seen.

EPILOGUE

———◆———

THE OCTOBER NIGHT WAS WARM, BUT THE BAL-
cony from our living room at the top floor of the Keep was
high enough for a nice cool breeze. I hid on the balcony. It'd
been a long day. The new greenhouse was finally finished,
and I'd spent the day digging in the dirt and planting the herbs
required for panacea. It was cheaper than trying to buy them
in large quantities. Learning to make it had proved to be a lot
harder than expected. I had finally managed some passable
results, but the two medmages Christopher was training had a
hard time. We would get it. It just took time and practice.

We still didn't know exactly what Christopher had done for
Hugh or how he'd ended up there. He maintained that he took
care of Hugh's books, but I'd seen him in a lab, and the way he
handled herbs and equipment telegraphed years of practice. If
he wasn't in the lab, he was somewhere outside, usually high
up. We finally persuaded him that he couldn't fly, but he loved
sitting on the walls in some sunny, hidden spot, reading a
book.

Below me in the Keep's courtyard, music played and the
teenage members of the Pack were doing their best to follow the
beat. Somewhere in the crowd Maddie and Julie danced. Or

rather Maddie danced and Julie played along, waiting to catch her friend if she fell down. The forced coma had wreaked havoc on Maddie's musculature. It took two weeks after we administered the panacea before she could move. She still used a wheelchair on occasion. The other day I caught her and Doolittle holding brooms and ramming each other with their wheelchairs in the hallways. Apparently they too were having a joust.

Doolittle was probably down there too, listening to the music and complaining about the noise. Being in a chair didn't seem to slow him down. George had fared worse. Her arm reattachment didn't take. For whatever reason, her body rejected the limb, even after Doolittle reattached it for the second time aboard the *Rush*. The arm was gone now. George had to learn how to use her left hand for everything, and it drove her up the wall. Desandra was helping her. She had adapted well. Eventually the fact that one of her children was a lamassu would have to be dealt with, but for now everyone was ignoring it. There was some friction in the Wolf Clan as to where she would fit into the Clan hierarchy, and when Jennifer attempted to chastise Desandra in her very formal way, Desandra told her to cool her tits. Every time I thought about it, I laughed.

We buried Aunt B on a sunny hill behind the Bouda House. There was no body in the grave, just the things she had taken with her on the trip. I came to visit her every other week. The left tower of the Keep was named after her. That was where the kids stayed when they had to be treated with panacea. I never thought I would miss her, but I did.

Curran stepped out on the balcony and sat next to me. I leaned against him, and he put his arm around me.

"Are you okay?" he asked me.

"Yes. Sometimes it doesn't seem real that we made it." I leaned closer against him.

"Kate?" he asked.

"Mm-hm."

"I am an ass. And an arrogant egomaniac. And a selfish bastard."

"The first two, yes. But you're not selfish." I stroked his arm, feeling the muscle underneath the skin. "You are the way you are, Curran. You have your valid reasons. I am the way I am and I have my reasons, too."

He kissed my hand. "I love you," he said. "I'm glad you're with me."

"I love you, too." I looked into his face. "What's wrong?"

He took out a small wooden box and handed it to me. What the hell could be so important about a wooden box for that kind of speech?

"What's in here?"

"Just open it," he growled.

"I'm not going to open it after you said all that. It might blow up."

"Kate. Open the box," he said quietly.

I opened it. A ring looked back at me from black velvet, a pale band with a large brilliant stone with a pale yellow tint. I knew that tint. He'd given me a ring set with a piece of the Wolf Diamond.

"Are you going to say *psych*?"

"No," Curran said.

Oh boy.

AUTHORS' NOTE

Readers often ask why we cut what seem to be perfectly good scenes. The bigger the book, the better, right? It doesn't always turn out that way. A novel is more than just a collection of scenes. It's a story, a cohesive whole, and when we edit, we try to make sure that every scene included fits into the narrative and serves some sort of purpose. We really wanted to show Saiman's rescue, but there just wasn't a way to include it in the novel. No matter where we put it, it stuck out. So instead we're offering it to you here as a bonus. Because these are deleted scenes, you will see some identical phrasing and things that tie back to the original manuscript. We hope you'll like it.

AN ILL-ADVISED RESCUE

———◦●◦———

ILONA ANDREWS

KNOCK-KNOCK.

My eyes snapped open. Darkness filled the bedroom. I reached over and touched the covers next to me. Empty. Curran must've gotten out of bed. Usually I woke up when anything in the vicinity moved, but Curran could be very quiet when he wanted to be, and he had taken it as a personal challenge to sneak in and out of our bed without disturbing me.

Knock-knock.

I dragged myself out of bed, slipped on a pair of sweatpants, and swung the door open. A tall, lean man stood on the other side. Barabas, a weremongoose and lawyer extraordinaire. Since I'd joined the Beast Lord and his fifteen hundred shapeshifter nutcases in the Keep, Barabas had helped me navigate the rough waters of Pack politics. Pack papers said he was my advisor. He ignored them and called himself my nanny.

Barabas never did anything halfway, including his hair. Bright red in sharp contrast to his pale skin, it usually stood straight up on his head like a jagged flame. Today he must've done something special to it, because his hair didn't just look spiky. It was shiny, almost fluorescent, and stiff. He looked electrocuted.

I searched his eyes. No alarm. Whatever it was, it wasn't urgent. I made some sniffing sounds.

"What are you doing?" he asked.

"Checking the air for smoke."

"Why?"

"Because you know I dragged myself to bed less than two hours ago. You wouldn't wake me up unless it was an emergency. I'm guessing you must've set the guard room on fire with your hair and now you want me to evacuate." Kate one.

"Ha-ha. You have a phone call, Alpha."

I hated to be called Alpha. Kate one, Barabas one. A draw. "Who is it?"

Barabas looked disgusted, as if someone had just offered him some moldy bread. "The Clerk from the Guild. He says it's about the pervert."

"Saiman?"

"Yes. The Clerk says it's an emergency."

Okay. "Lead on."

Saiman was an information broker who happened to also be an expert on all things magic. He'd also made a small fortune in shipping and other ventures. He charged exorbitant prices for his services, but because I had amused him, he had offered me a discount in the past. I had consulted him a few times, but he kept trying to entice me into his bed to prove a philosophical point. I'd put up with it until he'd had the stupidity to parade our connection in front of Curran. The Beast Lord and I had been in a rough spot in our relationship, and Curran didn't take that exhibition well, a fact that he expressed by turning a warehouse full of luxury cars Saiman had slipped past customs into crushed Coke cans. Since then, Saiman lived in mortal fear of Curran. He avoided me and all things shapeshifter like we were a plague.

Saiman feared physical pain, so he maintained a VIP account at the Mercenary Guild for times when he needed to use brute force. Unfortunately for him, the Pack now owned twenty percent of the Guild and I was in charge of it. I'd flagged his account, making sure I was notified about his activities. Saiman wasn't exactly vindictive, but he had a long memory, and I wanted to make sure he didn't spring any surprises on us.

Anything involving Saiman would make Curran lose his temper. A pissy werelion was rather difficult to live with. He wasn't in a great mood today anyway. We'd had some trouble with a small pack in Florida. With the Pack's headquarters located in Atlanta, they must've felt far enough away and safe, so they'd made excursions into our territory and raided a Pack business. We could quash them, but it would be bloody.

"Do you know where Curran is?"

"He went out to talk to the Lonescos."

Figured. The Lonescos ran the rat clan within the Pack. The rival Florida pack consisted mostly of rats, and Curran must've still hoped for a peaceful resolution. Peaceful in post-Shift Atlanta was a rare luxury. "Did he seem optimistic?"

Barabas shook his head. "No."

We arrived at the guardroom and Janice offered me the phone. A seasoned guard, Janice was a werejackal, about ten years older than me, with blond hair and a big smile. She looked like a soccer mom on steroids.

I took the phone and pressed the speaker button. "Yes?"

"Kate?" the Clerk's familiar voice asked. The Clerk had a name, but nobody among the mercs used it. He was simply the Clerk and he didn't seem to mind the name.

"Yep. What can I do for you?"

"Saiman's been kidnapped."

"Aha." *Aha* was an excellent word. Neither a question nor a statement.

Janice scribbled on a piece of paper, transcribing the conversation.

"They're holding him for ransom. They dropped the note off at his accountant, who called us."

"How much do they want?"

"A big one."

"A million?"

"That's right."

Barabas's eyes went wide. Janice clamped her hand over her mouth for a second. The Guild charged ten percent of ransom for rescuing kidnapped victims. That was quite a chunk of change.

"Where do they want the money delivered?" I asked.

"Mole Hole, in the crater. You know the place."

Everybody in Atlanta knew the place, but I knew it really well. That was where my insane aunt nearly killed the lot of us and almost burned the city to the ground. That was where I had killed her and almost lost Curran.

"Any details?" I asked.

"I've got the note. It says, 'I've been kidnapped. I'm under heavy guard. Please draw one million dollars and deliver it to the Mole Hole before sunrise or my attackers will see red.'"

"Odd note."

"I wouldn't know," the Clerk said. "We got one the other night that said if we didn't come and get this guy, the kidnappers would feed him to a giant tortoise. Do you want me to do anything about this?"

"I'll take it," I said.

"Just so you know, you're on record for that."

"That's fine. Thank you for calling."

"Anytime."

I looked at Janice. "Did you get all that?"

She passed me the paper. *Under guard, seeing red.* Interesting choice of words, atypical of Saiman. He spoke like a college intellectual. His philosophy was that if he couldn't pack at least three syllables into a word, it wasn't worth his attention.

Saiman was a self-admitted sexual deviant and egomaniac. The last time he put me into a life-threatening situation, he'd jumped into his car and taken off so fast, the snow from his tires pelted my face. But if I saved him, he would owe me a favor. A very large million-dollar favor.

"We're not going to pay that ransom, are we?" Janice asked.

"Hell no." I looked at the paper again. "Is Jim still up?"

"He's in his spy rooms," Janice said.

Most shapeshifters were seminocturnal. Late to bed, late to rise. The Pack's chief of security and my onetime Guild partner was no exception.

"Oh good. If Curran comes through here, this whole thing never happened."

"Are you asking me to lie to the Beast Lord?" Janice's eyes narrowed into slits. A subtle grin hid in the corners of her mouth.

"No, I'm telling you not to volunteer information." If Curran got involved, it would be all over. "What the Beast Lord doesn't know can't hurt him. Or me."

I went through the security checkpoint and down the wide staircase that ran the height of the Keep's main tower. Luckily I didn't have to go too far. Jim's spy operation occupied rooms two floors below.

I found Jim in the small kitchenette getting a cup of coffee. Tall, with muscle definition that made you wince, Jim prided himself on the ability to intimidate by simply being there. He was in his early thirties, with skin that matched the coffee in his cup and short hair, cut close to the scalp. Normally he didn't stand, he loomed like a menacing shadow, but right now he was on his home turf, and the air of threat had dropped off to tolerable levels. He leaned against the wall with one arm, drinking coffee, looking relaxed, and when he saw me, he smiled without showing his teeth. Jim Shrapshire, a sweet and welcoming jaguar. Aha. Not buying it, buster.

"Is there any coffee left?"

Jim hefted the metal pot. "There is."

I grabbed a mug and watched him pour the nearly black liquid out. Back when we both worked for the Mercenary Guild, Jim preferred to take night jobs. The giant vat of coffee was made once, in the morning. By the end of the night, no sane soul would touch it. Jim drank it like water.

Jim filled my mug. I sniffed it. So far, so good. I took a brave sip. The bitter scalding liquid slid a third of the way down my throat and got stuck. "Dear God."

He grinned.

"Jim, if I turn the cup upside down, it will roll out slowly like molasses."

"That's how you know it's good. Drink it, it will put hair on your chest."

"My chest is fine as is, thanks. You're in a good mood."

"I'm always in a good mood, Kate. What brings you to my lair?"

"Saiman called."

Jim skewed his face. He hated Saiman the way cats hated water. "What does he want?"

"He's been kidnapped and he wants someone to bring his kidnappers a million dollars."

Jim blinked. For a second his face froze, slapped by surprise, and then the Pack chief of security leaned back and laughed.

I sipped the horrible coffee. I'd known him for years and I could count on one hand the number of times I'd heard him laugh.

Jim chortled.

"Keep it coming." I waved at him. "Get it out of your system."

I managed two more swallows of coffee by the time he finally got himself under control enough to talk.

"Do you have a million dollars, Kate? You must've done a lot better at the Guild than I did."

Laugh it up, why don't you. "Have you heard anything about Red Guard going rogue?"

The Red Guard was a premier bodyguard outfit in the city. If you wanted private cops, there were none better. I'd worked with them a few times.

"Why?"

I passed him the paper with Saiman's plea for help. Jim read it and raised his eyebrows. "Under heavy guard, seeing red, huh. You remember Rene Benoit?"

I nodded. I first met Rene when she ran security for an illegal gladiatorial tournament. Since then she'd hired me for a job, and her glowing endorsement of my fledgling investigative firm was driving business my way.

"After the whole Lighthouse Keepers mess, she was promoted," Jim said. "She'd come up through the ranks and knew who was pulling their weight and who wasn't, so when she got to the top, she cleaned house. Two weeks ago twelve people got let go. A couple of them showed up at the Guild looking to enroll and bitching about how unfair it was."

"Which one of the twelve would be more likely to hammer together a gang and stoop to kidnapping?"

Jim frowned. "Leon Tremblay. He'd been in the Guard for over a decade, so he's got seniority and people would follow him. The word is, if you've got enemies with deep pockets, you don't want him to guard you."

"He sold his 'bodies'?" I hated bodyguard detail. I'd done my fair share during my time with the Mercenary Guild, and some of my clients had done everything in their power to get themselves killed, while I put myself between them and danger. Selling the life of the person you guarded went against the very spirit of the job. It made you the lowest of the low.

Jim nodded. "He wasn't obvious about it, but once every six to eight months one of his clients would manage to croak under entirely plausible but very convenient circumstances. When Rene made major, she booted his ass out on the street.

He must've been trouble, because when Rene fired him, she had six people in the room with her." Jim finished his coffee. "You're going after Tremblay?"

"Don't have anything better to do," I told him. "Thanks for the coffee."

"Kate, you know you don't have to save that asshole. He isn't worth it and he won't appreciate it."

"I know." I went to the door. "There is a method to my madness. Trust me."

"Take backup," Jim called after me. "At least take that dog with you."

Backup wasn't a bad idea, and I knew just the right person to bring with me. I climbed the stairs up one floor and knocked on Derek's room. A raspy voice called, "Come in."

I stepped into the room. Derek was doing a one-armed handstand against the wall. When I met him over a year ago, Derek had a face that made young girls turn and stare. Things had happened, and that face was gone now. The young cocky kid who owned it was gone, too. A man remained, calm, quiet, and thoughtful, with a face beaten up by life and big brown eyes that worried you if you looked into them too long. Derek watched people, preferring not to draw attention to himself, but when he acted, he attacked fast and he usually won.

As I watched, muscles flexed on his chest under a torn-up T-shirt. His biceps bulged. Derek lowered himself down and pushed up. One-arm-upside-down push-up. Young werewolves. Full of energy.

"Show-off. Shouldn't you be in bed?"

Derek kept moving, lowering and raising his body in a smooth, measured rhythm, like a machine. "I was about to turn in. Just a little end-of-the-day workout before the shower."

It's good to be a werewolf. "I need backup."

"Who are we killing?" He switched to the other arm and kept pushing.

"Some ex–Red Guards, and we're not necessarily going to kill them. We're just going to visit them and explain that kidnapping Saiman for ransom is a bad idea."

Derek stopped moving. "They kidnapped the pervert?"

I nodded.

He hopped to his feet. "This I've got to see."

• • •

THE MOLE HOLE HAD BEEN A TALL GLASS TOWER housing the offices of Molen Enterprises, until its owners obtained a phoenix egg and coaxed it into hatching. I'd seen a newborn phoenix rise once, and it looked like the old documentaries of space shuttle launches. When the fire subsided, the tower was no more. A crater, one hundred forty feet wide and fifty feet deep, gouged the ground in its place, and the fiery afterburn of the phoenix left it filled with molten glass. A few days later, the glass cooled, forming a foot-thick shell on the bottom and walls of the crater, and the Mole Hole was born.

We approached from the northeast, the shortest route from the Keep. The area had gone downhill a long time ago. Charred wrecks of houses flanked empty streets, and the hoofbeats of my horse sent echoes skipping through the ruins. Strange creatures with glowing hungry eyes watched us from their hidey-holes within the skeletal remains of the buildings. The magic flowed thick.

Slayer felt nice between my shoulder blades. Comforting, like an old friend. Ahead of us Grendel trotted like an extension of night shadows, a giant monstrosity of a dog. People more knowledgeable than me in things canine swore that he was a full-blooded standard poodle that somehow had grown to Great Dane size and was born with the trademark Doberman color scheme. His hobbies included urinating, vomiting, and farting, preferably in my general direction and at the same time, but he was loyal and fought for me, which made him a good dog in my book.

The horse flicked her ears. Jumpy. I missed Marigold. You could have ridden that mule through a battlefield of raging vampires, and she would've snorted in derision and kept going. My aunt killed Marigold in one of her futile attempts to wipe me off the face of the planet.

Ahead Grendel did a one-eighty and strutted toward us, prancing, head held high. Something was in his mouth.

"What does he have?"

Derek focused. "I don't know. Something dead and ripe."

A moment later I smelled it too, the stench of carrion. Grendel pranced closer. A dead raccoon, half-decomposed and dripping maggots. Why me?

"Drop it. Trash, Grendel."

"Trash?" Derek asked.

"That and *sit* are just about the only two commands he knows." I sank an order into my voice. "Trash."

Grendel spat out the raccoon and stared at me in disgust.

"It's bad for you. Come on."

He gave the raccoon one long forlorn look and followed us down the street.

We turned the corner. Ahead through the gap in the buildings, I could see the weak glint of the Mole Hole's glass. I dismounted and tied the horse to a twisted metal rib of half-crumbled building. Derek joined me. We ducked into the scorched structure to the left, Grendel at our heels, climbed two sets of stairs, and stopped by a hole of a window.

The Mole Hole stretched in front of us, a colossal glass dish sunken into the ground. To the far right people stood around a fire built in a bronze brazier. Above them a thick steel beam protruded from the husk of a building, supporting a large metal cage that hung from it, secured by several chains. A lone figure slumped inside the cage, too big to be human. I pulled binoculars from my pack and focused. The creature in the cage hugged his knees, his arms and legs disproportionately long and pale. His flesh had a weak blue tint, the muscle tough and knobby across his back. The wind stirred a mane of pale blue hair. Saiman. In his natural form, too. That didn't normally happen.

Saiman was a polymorph. He could reshape himself into a facsimile of any human body, any gender, any color, any age. Seeing his true form was exceedingly rare. I didn't know if he was ashamed of it, but he went to great lengths to hide it.

I passed the binoculars to Derek. He eyed the cage. His raspy voice was a quiet whisper. "Oh, the irony."

Given that Saiman had once caught him in a cage much like this one, I couldn't disagree.

He passed the binoculars back. I looked at the people by the fire. Six. If I were Tremblay, I'd put a couple of shooters in the surrounding buildings. The magic was up, so they'd have to rely on bows, and bows had a limited range. There were only two buildings close enough, this one and the one across the Mole and to the left.

A faint scratching sound came from above us, metal sliding

against the concrete. Derek looked up and held utterly still. A faint green fire rolled over his eyes. There was a wolf under the human skin, alert and cunning, and he was listening.

On the ground Grendel panted, oblivious.

A long minute passed. Another scrape. Either whoever it was on the floor above us couldn't sit still or he was setting up a mount for his crossbow.

We moved at the same time. I headed toward the staircase. Derek crossed the room and paused by a large hole in the ceiling. I climbed the stairs, pulling Slayer out of its sheath with a practiced smooth movement. Around me the dark building lay silent, the light from the pale sliver of a new moon coming through the holes in the walls. The dog followed me.

I reached the landing. My heart sped up a bit. I missed this, sneaking through the night-drenched city not knowing what waited for me around the corner. I padded across the landing and glanced into the room. A man crouched by the window, an arbalest on a stand next to him. Good-quality crossbow, solid, precise, with a steel prong, but heavy, hence the swivel mount. With a weapon like that, an archer could skewer a human at seventy-five yards. Being skewered wasn't on my list of things to do. It would take the archer at least two seconds to grab the arbalest and spin it around to target me, but if I was close enough, he didn't have to be precise with his targeting. Twelve yards between him and me. I had to get to him before he squeezed the trigger.

I ran.

Ten yards.

The man pivoted in the chair.

Five.

He yanked the arbalest off its stand.

Three.

He swung the arbalest to face me.

I knocked the crossbow aside with my left arm, forcing the man to my left, and swung my right in a wide arc. The inside of my forearm smashed into the back of the man's head. A classic karate move, more powerful than a hook punch—like being hit in the base of the neck with a baseball bat. The man dropped his crossbow and staggered back. Derek leaped through the hole, coming out of the floor as if by magic, grabbed the man from behind, clamping his hand over his mouth, and forced him to the floor, folding him in half like a piece of paper. Grendel danced around us, overjoyed at the entire affair. He didn't even try to help. My attack poodle had gotten rusty.

I pulled a knife from my sheath, knelt by the crossbowman, and showed him the blade.

"How many of you are there?"

The crossbowman tried to rise, but I'd seen Derek tear a metal coffee can with his bare hands. It took the shooter less than five seconds to figure out he wasn't going anywhere.

Derek took his hand off the man's mouth.

"Eight," he said.

"Where is the other shooter?"

"Across the Hole. The three-story building."

"How did you get Saiman?"

"Tremblay said he had money. He knew him from way back. Saiman was at a nightclub and was driving home late. We grabbed him in the parking lot. Tremblay shot him full of horse tranquilizers and then we threw nets on him. He turned into that blue thing and beat the shit out of Miles and Zhu. Broke Zhu's legs. But then the tranquilizers must've worked, because he passed out. We put him in a cage and drove him up here."

A simple plan, but sometimes simple plans were best. I surveyed the man. He folded fast and made no effort to resist. Either his heart wasn't in this or he was a coward. Killing him seemed too extreme, and tying him up would mean I'd have to send someone up here to rescue his butt.

"What's your name?"

"Mick," the man said.

"Mick, we're going to take your crossbow, go out there, and have some words with your buddies. You're going to stay right here in this building, because once we're done, somebody will need to take those still breathing to the emergency room. You will be that somebody. If you make a noise or do anything to draw attention to yourself or warn your friends, Derek here will hunt you for fun."

Derek smiled, baring sharp white teeth. Mick flinched. I'd bet right. A coward.

"He has your scent now and he's guaranteed to have lots of fun you won't like before he gets tired of playing with you. Am I clear?"

"Crystal."

"Let him go."

Derek opened his arms. Mick got up and slowly sat in his chair. Derek picked up his crossbow and we went out of the building.

"You suck," I told Grendel outside. "You didn't even help." He wagged his tail.

"Think he's going to stay up there?" Derek murmured.

I nodded. "He's too scared to move and I gave him an out—if he does as he's told, he can help his pals in the end. He can tell himself he had a moral obligation to hide and not interfere. Can you take care of the other shooter?"

"Sure."

"I'll see you later, then."

He trotted into the darkness, melting into the gloom as if he had been born from it. I counted to six hundred in my head to give him a nice head start and strode to the Mole Hole.

Years ago someone had carved steps in the crater's sides, turning it into a kind of amphitheater. I stepped over the rim and took the steps down to the bottom.

The six people watched me with unfriendly eyes. Four men and two women. The shorter woman and three of the men had the familiar Red Guard bearing: their clothes were neat, the men were clean-shaven, the woman's pale brown hair was pulled back. The taller woman and a guy standing next to her looked like street thugs: dirty, mismatched clothes and a hungry, desperate look in their eyes. Probably brought in for numbers and muscle.

I walked toward them, Grendel trotting next to me. I was in no hurry. Two Red Guard veterans would be a lot to handle. They were in shape and had the proper training. Four Guards and two street thugs would be difficult. My best bet was to avoid a fight altogether. Sometimes if you demonstrate enough willingness to hurt someone, they decide it's not worth it.

In the cage Saiman stirred.

About twenty yards from them an older, lean man barked, "Far enough."

I looked up. Saiman's eyes, cold like frosted ice, looked back at me. *Hello, Ice Giant. Atlanta hasn't been treating you so well, I see.*

"Nice cage," I said. "Must've set you back quite a bit."

"Where is the money?" the older man asked.

The male thug swore. It sounded familiar. I racked my memory and ran across a petition I'd handled about a year ago, during my time with the Order. I'd met this lowlife before. He liked breaking into older people's houses and beating them until they gave him their money.

"Hi, Frankie. Long time, no see. They let you out already?"

Frankie blinked.

"Your legs healed nicely," I told him. "Can hardly tell they were broken. Move around for me. I want to see if you walk funny."

Frankie stuck his arms up in the air. "I'm out."

The older guy scowled at him. "You walk out, you lose the money, Frankie."

"Don't be a moron," the dark-haired man behind him added.

Frankie pointed a grimy finger in his direction. "No. Fuck you and you." He raised his hands. "I'm out. Come on, SG."

The taller woman shrugged and followed him.

I smiled and watched the light from the fire play on my saber. "If anybody else would like to be excused, now is the time."

The older man gave me his hard-core stare. He carried a tactical gladius in his hand, already out of the sheath, a simple, vicious weapon. Dark gray like a Teflon pan, it had a double-edged blade about sixteen inches long with a wide fuller running down its length and a plain wooden handle polished from extended use.

He surveyed me, then looked at Grendel. "What the hell is this?"

He had to be Tremblay. I matched his glare. "This is my attack poodle."

"For real?" A short blond man behind him asked.

"Shut up, Darren," Tremblay scowled at me. "You must think you're some hot shit or something? I have scars older than you."

It's like that, huh. "So you must be easy to hit. Lucky for me."

"You listen to me." Tremblay pointed to Saiman in the cage. "One word from me and you'll be picking up your friend's brains from the bottom of that cage."

I leaned forward slightly and pulled the lower lid of my left eye down.

"What the fuck?" the stocky, muscular woman behind Tremblay murmured. Not a melee fighter. She stood flat on her feet, planted like a tree, and carried no weapons.

"She's asking you if you can see the care in her eye," Saiman said helpfully.

"Cute," Tremblay said. "You've just signed his death warrant and your own."

I peered at him. "You sure you should be mouthing off, Tremblay? Because I'm not scared and your service record's kind of spotty."

"Do you have the money?" the tall dark-haired man asked, exasperation vibrating in his voice. A long slender sword hung from his waist. A katana user.

"Do you see the money? Do I look like somebody who would have that much money and be dumb enough to give it to you?"

The dark-haired man looked at Saiman. "What are you trying to pull?" He sounded indignant, like his feelings were hurt.

"I'm not trying to pull anything," Saiman said. "In case your powers of observation failed you, I've spent the last few hours in this cage."

I glanced up at Saiman. "Are you going to pay me to kill them?"

"I'm thinking."

"I think they should pay me to go away."

Tremblay stared at me, eyes bulging.

"If they pay you, are you going to take me with you?" Saiman asked.

"Depends on how much they'll give me."

The four ex-Guardsmen stared at me.

"Wait a minute," the shorter blond man said. "She wants us to give her money to take him with her?"

"Darren, keep your mouth shut," Tremblay growled.

"Yes, that's it." I nodded at Darren. "You give me money, I take him with me, and everybody's happy."

"This isn't what you said would happen," Darren looked at Tremblay.

"Shut the hell up!" Tremblay was actually shaking. There was no way he could salvage this.

"Losing your job is hard," I said. "But you guys need to

find a different line of work, because holding people for ransom isn't your forte. You're not very good at it. Why don't you take off before your fearless leader gives himself a coronary?"

The dark-haired man was thinking about it; I saw it in his eyes. Darren looked confused.

I pushed a little more. "Cut your losses. It's time to go."

"Fuck it, fire the flare!" Tremblay snarled.

The stocky woman looked at him.

"Fire the fucking flare!"

She clapped her hands. Magic pulsed and a bright yellow spark shot from between her clasped fingers into the sky, blossoming into a fiery dandelion. The four ex-Guardsmen tensed, anticipating a shot.

Nothing happened.

"Go home," I repeated.

Tremblay snarled. "Kill the stupid bitch!"

I backed away, giving myself room to work.

Darren turned light, electric purple. His skin sprouted hard bony bumps. He stumbled back, clutching at his head. Tremblay and the mage backed away.

The dark-haired man marched at me, drawing the katana as he struck. Good fast draw. I parried, letting the flat of his blade slide off Slayer, and punched him in the jaw with my left hand. He staggered back. Blood swelled along my forearm. He'd nicked me. I'd surprised him and he still nicked me. Fast bastard.

Derek dropped out of darkness into the Mole Hole, raised the crossbow, and fired. An arrow whistled past me, missing the thing that used to be Darren by an inch. Derek looked at the crossbow in disgust, raised it . . .

He wouldn't throw away a perfectly good crossbow . . .

Derek hurled the crossbow at Darren. It broke over the man's armored head.

Derek's clothes exploded, and a monster spilled forth. His limbs grew, bones thrusting out, forming new long legs and powerful arms. Muscle coated the new skeleton, clinging to bones. Skin sheathed it, dark fur grew, claws cut through the flesh, and a new creature landed on the glass. Neither man nor wolf, but a lethal hybrid of both, a human predatory intellect locked in a savage body. Derek grinned, displaying a mouth of nightmarish teeth, and crashed into the purple armored creature that used to be Darren.

The dark-haired man recovered, approaching. The right stance, responsive but firm, good balance, katana pointing at my eyes. Step, another step, smooth, sliding his foot along the ground so every move ended in a proper stance. He would lunge, and when he did it, he would commit completely. He was classically trained, and it would be all or nothing.

The sixty-four-thousand-dollar question was, would I be fast enough to parry it?

Another step.

Our stares crossed. It would be over for one of us in a second.

Time stretched into infinity.

I focused on him, absorbing every single detail: the angle of his leading foot, the dark eyes fixed on me, the minute tensing of muscles in his right arm, the rise of his chest . . .

He lunged, striking at my midsection in a horizontal stab, driving the blade with both hands.

I saw it a fraction of a second before it began and stepped back with my right foot, dodging, turning. Even as the blade came toward me, I knew I wasn't fast enough. He saw it too and twisted the blade, the edge sideways toward me.

The katana's edge grazed my ribs, slicing skin along my side.

For a fraction of a second, his arms stretched rigid, parallel to the ground, as he drove the blade forward. I cut across his wrists, carving flesh and tendon with my saber. Blood swelled on his skin. His fingers opened as the severed flexor tendons refused to obey. The sword fell. He caught the katana with his left hand and backed away, hot scarlet dripping on the ground.

The swordsman looked at me, a question in his eyes. He was done. We both knew it. I could cut him down right there and he wouldn't be able to do much about it.

I nodded and took a step back.

He straightened, turned, and walked away.

"Where the hell do you think you're going?" Tremblay yelled. "Get back here! You fight for half a second and you're done?"

"He can't hold his sword," I told him. "Saving his sword hand is more important to him than you are."

Tremblay swore. The woman behind him was chanting, eyes closed. Magic moved toward her in a slow flood. I didn't want to taste what she was cooking.

I started toward Tremblay.

Magic pulsed, its impact slapping my skin like a blast wave from an invisible cannon. A naked Tremblay lunged at me. What the hell?

I hammered the pommel of my sword in his face. He crumpled to the ground. I backed away. A second Tremblay, also bare-assed, grabbed at my forearm. His fingers crushed my arm like steel pincers. My bones groaned. I yanked my arm to the side, exposing Tremblay's armpit, thrust, and withdrew. He dropped to his knees, his mouth oddly slack. A guttural groan echoed from the right. Tremblay's body crumbled into pale red dust and swirled into the wind.

The real Tremblay, still fully clothed, stood by the magic user, his face shaking with effort. As I watched, an outline of his body peeled off, forming another naked clone, who staggered toward me. He was a one-man army. Awesome. Was there a finite number of them, because I was bleeding all over the place, and if he made enough of them at once, they would overwhelm me.

"Hey, Tremblay, ever think of starting your own boy band?"

His face jerked. Another clone peeled off. Another. A third.

The woman behind Tremblay was chanting, pulling the magic to her and winding it like thread on a spindle. Not good.

The three clones advanced toward me. I backed away. Tremblay could've been one hell of a bodyguard—he was a whole detachment all by his lonesome. Too bad he'd chosen to sell his clients' lives instead.

A fourth clone joined the line, followed by its twin. Five now.

The Tremblays took a step forward, moving in unison. Controlling clones took concentration. I'd piloted vampires before, and sending them in the same direction was much easier than trying elaborate tactics. The Tremblays didn't need elaborate tactics. Between the five of them, they had a thousand pounds of muscle. If all of them were as strong as the one who'd grabbed me, I couldn't let them get hold of me. They could just pile on me and that would be the end. Throwing knives at them wouldn't do enough damage. I could use a power word, but doing that announced my power and ancestry to anyone with a bit of knowledge. The less I showed in front of Saiman, the better. Given a half a chance, he would sell me to my biological father faster than I could blink.

I ran. I dashed along the Mole Hole's wall, Slayer in hand. The clones followed me in a line. I picked up a bit more speed. Clones or not, geometry still worked the same, and the outside perimeter of the circle was longer than the inside one. To the left of me the real Tremblay flashed by, the magic-user woman still chanting with her head bowed. Derek and Darren grappled with each other. I smelled blood. Darren might have the armored skin, but my money was on Derek anyway.

I flew along the wall, my legs pumping. Two thirds of the way around the crater, I glanced back. The clones had started in a line running at the same speed and now that line was nicely staggered, about six feet between them. Not as much as I would've liked, but it would have to do. Any closer and I'd be too close to the real Tremblay.

I spun around and charged the first clone. Tremblay had no time to react. I swung Slayer in a classic diagonal stroke, putting all of the strength of my arm into it. The saber cut across the first clone's throat and chest, right to left, slicing flesh and cartilage like butter. The clone went down. Before he fell, I reversed the stroke, drawing a flat eight, and sliced the second clone left to right. He dropped like a cut weed.

Tremblay screamed.

The third clone jerked his arms up, trying to shield his chest and throat. Tremblay had finally reacted, but a body in motion tends to stay in motion. The clones had been running full out trying to catch me, and like a horse in a gallop, they couldn't come to a dead stop. I stabbed my sword into the clone's exposed gut, jerked the blade to the right, scrambling the organs, if he had any, and kicked him off my blade.

The fourth clone with the road rash on its face bent down, aiming to ram me with his shoulder. I dodged and ran straight into the fifth clone's punch. I saw it, I just couldn't do anything but turn into it. Given a choice of ribs or shoulder, I took it on the left shoulder. Pain erupted in my arm. I staggered back. Ow.

The fifth clone's fist was speeding toward my face. I leaned out of the way. Arms clamped my legs in a death grip—the road-rash clone anchored me in place. My legs screamed in pain. They had me.

The fifth clone lunged at me, fingers like talons reaching for my neck. The road-rash clone twisted, trying to turn my back to the attack. I reversed my sword blade up and thrust sideways, parallel to the ground. The fifth clone impaled himself on my blade. I let go of my sword, pulling a throwing knife, and rammed the short blade into the base of the fourth clone's neck. He broke into red dust.

The fifth clone collapsed on me, his forearm across my throat like a bar. The world dimmed. Suddenly there wasn't enough air. I wrapped my freed legs around his and stabbed him in the side, one, two, three, my hand slick and wet with red. The metallic scent of blood filled my nostrils. Four, five, six, seven . . . Red dust rained on my face. I coughed and rolled to my feet just in time to see Derek hurl Darren across the crater. The armored man landed on his back, clutching at his leg. It was bent the wrong way and the white stub protruding from it had to be his shinbone.

Only Tremblay and the mage were left. I picked up my sword and marched to them. I had to get to the real thing, or this could go on forever.

Tremblay bent over, breathing like a runner after a marathon. "What the fuck are you?"

He was done. Across from us, Derek made a beeline for Tremblay.

"It's over," I said.

"Not quite." The female mage clapped her hands. The magic she'd gathered sparked. A high-pitched chime, like the toll of a large crystal bell, sounded through the night, coming from a point above the woman's head. A pale glow unfurled, like an incandescent fog billowing from one small point into a yellow cloud, illuminated from within. Something long and sinuous stirred within its depths.

I accelerated. Whatever the thing in the cloud was, it wouldn't be good, and I wanted the mage out of commission before it emerged. I was twenty yards from the woman when the cloud tore. A glowing creature slipped into existence, hovering above the mage's head. About two feet long, it resembled a wood louse, wide and flattened. A shell of translucent overlapping segments radiating pale yellow luminescence shielded its flattened body. Seven pairs of thick, segmented crab legs hung from underneath the shell, moving in a flowing rhythm, as if the creature were swimming. Glowing eyes, like two orbs sheathed in metallic foil, looked at me.

"Stop," the female mage said.

My body stopped. Logically I knew I had to keep moving, but something deep in the core of my brain refused to obey. I couldn't look away. I couldn't close my eyes. I could only stare at the glowing bug-crustacean apparition.

"Don't look at it," I barked.

"Too late," Derek called out, his voice shredded by his oversized teeth.

Shit.

"Drop your sword," the woman said.

The command pulled on me. I clenched Slayer. *No.*

"Drop your sword," the woman repeated.

A low, steady ache drained down my arm in a viscous wave, all the way into my fingers. The grip of my saber burned my skin like fire. It would be so easy to just let go. So easy.

I clenched my teeth and took a small step forward. Magic anchored me. It felt like I was dragging a semi behind me. Another step.

"Her will is too strong," the woman said. "You'll have to go and finish her."

"No problem," Tremblay said.

I couldn't look away from the glowing bug, but I heard the sound of his steps. I had to lift my sword. My arm refused to obey.

Derek snarled.

"Settle down, you're next," Tremblay said.

The glowing creature stared at me, its eyes empty and endless at the same time. My whole body shook with effort. I could use a power word, but doing that in front of Saiman was extremely unwise. He'd already seen me use one. If I demonstrated any more power, he would dig deeper into my background. If he put two and two together, he'd sell me out to my real father faster than I could blink.

I could do this. I just had to lift my sword.

Tremblay's steps were closer.

I would lift it, damn it.

My arm obeyed. It felt like the muscles and ligaments in my arms were ripping apart, but I could feel the balance of the sword shift in my hand. The point of my saber was slowly creeping up. Not fast enough. Tremblay would cut me down.

Well, wasn't that a lovely predicament. Kate Daniels, rescuer of kidnapped sexual deviants, chopped down by some has-been bodyguard. If Tremblay didn't finish me, I'd die of sheer embarrassment.

Tremblay got close enough that he swung into my field of vision. His face was grim, his mouth a hard flat line. He hefted the gladius as he walked.

I took a deep breath. Saiman or not, the power word was my only option.

Tremblay raised his sword.

Something snarled, too sharp to be Derek. The crustacean creature dimmed. Its legs flailed helplessly. The hypnotic glow blinked and vanished. The hold on my body broke.

I lunged forward, breaking into a sprint. Tremblay swung the gladius to parry. I batted his sword aside, buried Slayer in his left lung, sliding it between his ribs, and withdrew. Tremblay's mouth gaped in a shocked O.

A werewolf leaped into view, sailing through the air as if he had wings. His claws scoured the creature. Magic boomed, nearly punching me off my feet, hurling the werewolf and the dying creature to the ground.

Tremblay coughed, dropped his sword, and clamped his hand to the wound. The veins on his neck began to bulge. Probably a collapsed lung. I shoved him aside.

Ahead the female mage lay on her stomach, her hands in the air. An enormous black hound stood over her, his teeth on the back of her neck. A ghostly light rippled over his sable-black fur.

Ha! About time.

To the right, Derek's prone form sprawled on the glass. The magic creature lay next to him in two glistening wet piles. He must've torn it in half. That was where the blast I just felt had come from. *Don't be dead. Don't be dead, Derek.*

"I give up," the woman croaked. "I give up, don't hurt me."

"Derek!" I called out. *Please be okay, boy wonder.* "Derek!"

He sat up slowly and shook his shaggy head.

"Are you okay?"

"Yeah. Head hurrrrts."

I exhaled and walked up to the woman. Grendel looked at me and growled low.

"Drop it."

He didn't move.

"Trash, Grendel. Drop it."

Grendel opened his jaws and sat.

"Good boy."

I pulled a plastic tie out of the pocket on my belt and wrapped the mage up. "I feel a shiver of magic from you and I'll cut your head off. Do we understand each other?"

She nodded frantically. "No, I'm done. I wasn't wild about this kidnapping plan anyway."

But she'd gone along with it. And when Tremblay told her to give the signal that would've exploded Saiman's head with a charged arrow if Derek hadn't taken out the shooter, she gave that signal without the slightest pause. If she was looking for sympathy, I was fresh out.

"Your dog transforms," Saiman said.

"Brilliant deduction, Mr. Holmes." I petted Grendel's huge head. He was a black dog, a mystic hound. Trouble was, he transformed only when he felt like it.

"I can't help but point out that I'm still confined," Saiman said.

I glanced at Derek. "Will you let him out, please? He'll just keep whining."

He scrambled up the slope of the Mole Hole, up the building, and along the beam, running on his oversized feet, his shaggy body silhouetted against the moon and the ruined city.

I checked my side. The katana's blade had left a shallow gash. It bled quite a bit, but my shirt had absorbed most of it. I pulled gauze from my pocket, pressed it against the wound, and pulled my shirt over it. I took a flask with kerosene from my belt and backtracked, pouring it on anything resembling blood. Once blood was separated from my body, I could no longer hide its magic.

Derek reached the end of the beam and crouched, untangling the chains.

I struck a match. The trail of kerosene caught fire.

"Do hurry," Saiman said.

Derek raised his clawed hands. The cage plummeted

twenty-five feet to the ground and bounced, chipping the glass. The metal door popped open.

"Ow." Saiman shouldered his way out of the cage. He towered over me, a full eight feet tall. "I don't suppose you've brought anything nutritious with you?"

You've got to be kidding me. "Slipped my mind." Being a polymorph, Saiman needed a huge amount of calories for his metamorphosis. The fight with his kidnappers must've drained him dry.

Saiman sighed. "Regrettable."

"You owe me."

"I'm well aware of that, thank you. Although in light of recent events, I believe the dog should get the lion's share of the reward."

"The dog is my employee. I mean it, Saiman. You owe me a big favor. One day I will call to collect."

"Suddenly I feel less secure than when I was confined," Saiman said.

I grinned at him and walked away, leaving his kidnappers to Saiman's tender mercy. Some men might have killed them in revenge. I was pretty sure Saiman would contact the cops and then sue the lot.

Derek caught up with me. I held out my hand and he low-fived me. Let's see, some would-be kidnappers diverted from their life of crime, an otherworldly monster killed, and one sexual deviant rescued. All in all, not a bad night.

"A hundred grand is a lot of money," Derek said.

"A favor from Saiman is worth more." Eventually it would prove useful. I was counting on it.

ILONA
ANDREWS

"Ilona Andrews's books are
guaranteed good reads."

–Patricia Briggs,
#1 *New York Times* bestselling author

For more information on Ilona Andrews,
please go to prh.com/ilonaandrews